A NOVEL

Coincidentally KISMET

Exes trying to be friends...
It's a bad idea, right?

KELLI COOKE

Copyright © 2025 by Between Pages Press, LLC

All rights reserved.

ISBN 979-8-9918321-0-6 (paperback)

ISBN 979-8-9918321-1-3 (ebook)

No part of this book may be reproduced in any form or by any electronic or mechanical means, including information storage and retrieval systems, without written permission of the copyright owner except for the use of brief quotations in a book review.

This is a work of fiction. Names, characters, places, and incidents either are the product of the author's imagination or are used fictitiously. Any resemblance to actual persons, living or dead, events, or locales is entirely coincidental and not intended by the author.

First Edition January 2025
Developmental Edit: Annie Meagle (Spare Words Novel Editing)
Copy Edit: Briana Ozor (Ozor Edits)
Cover Design: Books and Moods

www.kellicooke.com

To those who have known love and lost it.
A great love story is coming your way, I promise.

Author's Note

Dear Reader,

First and foremost, THANK YOU. Each and every person who buys this book is single-handedly supporting my dreams. I hope that these words touch your heart the way that you all have forever changed mine.

When setting out to write this novel, I had a few goals in mind. I wanted to tell a story that conveyed what love looks like in real life. Something profoundly beautiful but also at times wrought with challenges, missteps, and a hearty dose of humor. As an avid romance reader myself, it was important to me that you feel the realistic ups and downs we all experience in our own love lives. While this book is not solely focused around the military, I set out to share the deeply personal and often hidden worldview that our service members carry throughout their journey. To those that have served or are currently serving, I hope that I have done justice to the invisible scars that you conceal when returning home from war. To the families and spouses of those same service members, I see you and I stand with you in the battle to protect their hearts from the trauma they likely endure.

Because this book touches on sensitive topics, I feel compelled to call those out here. Your mental health is of the utmost importance, and while this is a work of fiction, I would never aim to harm you with my writing. Please proceed with caution if the following topics could be potentially triggering to you and opt out if necessary:

> on-page sexually explicit material
>
> post-traumatic stress disorder/anxiety
>
> discussion or mention of suicide
>
> body image/negative self-talk
>
> descriptive scenes of violence in a war setting

I will say it again, no form of entertainment, whether a book, movie, art, or any other category, is worth sacrificing your mental health. I love you and appreciate your support, even if you opt out.

Thank you again from the very bottom of my heart!

Kelli

Playlist

Music has always had a special place in my heart. While writing this novel, these are the songs that brought me joy, peace, and generally reflect the vibe of each chapter. Enjoy!

Prologue. Tin Man – Miranda Lambert
The Art of Starting Over – Demi Lovato
Platinum – Miranda Lambert
M.I.A. – Graham Barham
Miss Me More – Kelsea Ballerini
I Remember You – Skid Row
Fake Names – Priscilla Block
Lonely Boy – The Black Keys
Brave – Sara Bareilles
Poker Face – Lady Gaga
Ever Since You Left – Priscilla Block
Red Bowling Ball Ruth – The White Stripes
I Can't Explain – The Who
Boyfriend – Ariana Grande & Social House
Closer – The Chainsmokers & Halsey
Under Pressure – Queen & David Bowie
Free Fallin – The Cadillac Three & Breland
Pretty – Lauren Alaina
Whether You Love Me or Not – Meghan Patrick
Love You Again – Chase Matthew
Bad Idea Right? – Olivia Rodrigo
See You Again – Wiz Khalifa & Charlie Puth
This Feeling – The Chainsmokers & Kelsea Ballerini
9 to 5 – Dolly Parton
Call Me – Blondie
Sucker – The Jonas Brothers

You Look Like You Love Me – Ella Langley & Riley Green
Miles On It – Marshmello & Kane Brown
Two Things – Kelsea Ballerini
High Road – Koe Wetzel & Jessie Murph
Woman's World – Katy Perry
Without Me – Halsey
Set You Free – The Black Keys
I Can Do It With A Broken Heart – Taylor Swift
Thickfreakness – The Black Keys
Heartbroken – Diplo & Jessie Murph

Ex-lovers are reunited through shared friendships in this heartwarming story about second chances, forgiveness, and learning it's never too late to start over.

Cameron Wright has had her life planned out since before she was tall enough to see over the steering wheel on her dad's tractor. Find a man, marry him, and pop out half a dozen babies. Never one to miss a step, her plan was foolproof, that is until her one true love decided to ditch their college plans to become what she would refer to as the next real-life Rambo. Setting off on a new adventure across the country, working for world-renowned hairstylist Daveed Jones, she's attempting to shake off the memories and finally let go of the past. You might as well start over when everything else has blown up in your face, right?

Committing fully to seizing the reins, Cam is hitting the dating scene, forcing herself to trade french fries for salads, and making memories concocting alter egos while spinning around the dance floor at the local country bar and soaking up the sunshine with her lovable roommate. There's only one problem. After each new date, she finds herself waking up overheated, fantasizing about her ex.

Will Davenport is determined not to feel feelings. He walked away from love to avoid repeating the mistakes of his father, swearing it off altogether. When his sister makes a sudden appearance on his doorstep, the more-than-content bachelor joins his friends for a night on the town. Little does he know, the shock of his life is coming in the form of the one girl who he's always claimed as his own. Will's no stranger to navigating sticky situations, he does it daily as a special operations soldier. But the road to winning her back is paved with obstacles, two-stepping, and enough peonies to bankrupt the wealthiest of suitors.

Can Cameron resist his attempts at winning her over in favor of staying safely tucked into the friend zone? Or should she give in to fate, finally acknowledging they are coincidentally kismet?

PROLOGUE

5 years ago

Cam

"Tin Man" - Miranda Lambert

"Mom, hurry up. He's going to be here any minute. I need tissue paper." My mom is moving at a perfectly acceptable pace for a snail when what I need her to be is an energizer bunny.

"Relax, Cameron. That boy would wait forever for you, ya know." Mom clatters around, opening and closing doors in what I hope is an attempt to find the paper I desperately need to wrap this gift.

I'm bursting with excitement to give it to Will. It's not long until we head out to Iowa State, and obviously we need matching hoodies to cement the occasion. Just three short weeks to go, weeks that are seeming to drag on while I finish up my duties on the farm. I can already hear the faint whispers of freedom ringing in my ears. Freedom from the dreaded five in the morning wake-up calls, courtesy of my

dad, and from the passive-aggressive way my mother's hand carefully places a quarter on the table beside my plate when she's noticed I've had more than what a "lady" should eat. She thinks it's a silent reminder, but everyone knows it's her way of shaming me. I can't fucking wait to be free from all of it.

My parents are great, but they're also *a lot*. They have opinions on their opinions, and it's best not to challenge them. Hence why I silently set my fork down and rub the quarter between my thumb and forefinger each time it's placed gingerly beside me. I know it's a reminder born out of love for me and my well-being, but it's hurtful nonetheless. The first thing I plan to do at college is wolf down a cheeseburger without a quarter in sight.

A knock rattles the rickety front screen door as I yell once more, "Moooom!" She shuffles into the room before I can get any more words out, carefully stuffing white tissue paper into the bag and shooing me down the steps in her motherly way. There may be a hint of an eye roll tossed my direction, but I'm moving too quickly to care.

Will waits patiently at the bottom of the stairs in the entryway, soaking in every inch of me as I make my way down. His cerulean-blue eyes like beautiful pools just waiting to drag me in, that curly mop of hair a bit messy as it pokes out from under his usual baseball cap. My heart thumps a little harder each time I see him. It's not smart, by all standards, to be this gone for someone at age eighteen, but I can't help it. He's everything to me—my heart walking around outside of my body. He's the only person besides my brother who I've ever felt truly gets me.

"Hey, ready to go?" A tremble to his voice that's a touch out of place gives me pause.

"Yep, everything okay?" I ask, running my hand up and down his exposed arm, nudging my fingertips under the edge of his short sleeve as I search his eyes for an answer.

"Yeah. Let's get going." Short, a bit curt, but not completely out of the ordinary for him. Maybe something happened with his dad again. *That has to be it*, I think. Everything was perfect when we talked a few hours ago.

We make our way to his busted-up brown Chevy; I climb in when he opens the door. Scooting to my designated spot in the middle, I position one leg on either side of the gear shift and sling his gift onto the seat beside me.

Will jumps in, throws the truck in drive after turning the ignition, and barrels down my long gravel drive. There's no chatting, no sneaking hello kisses now that we are out of parental-viewing range; he doesn't even graze my leg as he reaches over to shift. Something is absolutely wrong, there isn't an eighteen-year-old boy alive who isn't ready and willing to palm their girlfriend or boyfriend's thigh while driving down the road.

"Hey, can you pull over?" The words tumble out before I can slow myself down and take a second to not overthink. I hate fighting with him, or really anyone, but I need to know right this second what's going on.

"Cam, really? You can't wait until we get to the lake?" Will's tone is terse, annoyance dangling off of each word.

"Nope. Especially not now." I cross my arms on a huff. This is supposed to be a fun date. It'll be easier to get whatever could be bothering him out of the way quickly.

The truck slows, shifting slightly into a ditch, far enough off the road to not get hit if someone's coming down at a good pace, but still on the shoulder. Will slams it in park as I reach for the buckle on my seat belt, hands shaking as if they know before I do what's about to happen.

"What's the matter? I can tell something's wrong. Is it your dad? I swear, if that man was an asshole again, I might lose my mind. Or is it Amy? Did something happen to Amy? Oh God." Rambling is one of my many tells on just how much I overthink. Spewing ideas helps ease my anxiety.

"It's not any of that. Look, can we just have a fun night? I don't want to talk about it." His eyes plead with me to let it go, but my heart is like a dog with a bone. I have to know what's going on, or I won't be able to have even an okay time.

"No. You know I can't do that. Just tell me, clearly something happened." Exasperation and desperation lace my voice in equal measure. *Please put me out of my misery here,* I silently plead.

"Fine! All I wanted was one more good night. One night to hold you, to kiss you, to just . . . be with you," Will shouts, covering his face with his hands while rocking toward the steering wheel. All I can hear on an endless loop is "one more good night." My brain is swirling with questions, fears, and denial—mostly denial.

"What do you mean? You aren't being specific. Why one more night? We are going to have all the nights at college. Fun trips to new bars, you're going to invite me to your frat house, and I'll sneak you into my sorority after-hours. There is so much fun in your future, it's honestly unfair to most." I'm being naive at best and a bit dense at worst. My stomach and my heart know what's coming but I refuse to believe it.

"I-I can't . . ." Tears pool in his eyes, threatening to fall. He bristles, wiping them away as if he refuses to let them take control. "I can't do this. I'm not going to college with you."

Seconds pass as I process my disbelief. We had a plan. I always have a plan, and this is not it. I can't fathom what he means. Did he decide to go somewhere else? Is he not going at all?

A single tear streams down my cheek as I ask, "What does that mean? Where are you going?"

"I joined the Air Force; I leave next week." Nine words. Ones that I know instantly will play on repeat for the rest of my life. Acid creeps up my throat as my stomach riots, and my heart feels like it is being ripped from my chest.

"W-why? We had a plan . . . I mean, we can make it work, but I need to understand. Make me understand because it doesn't add up, you've never even mentioned the military before. Do you not like the school? We can go somewhere else, but we both got into ISU. We could defer if you need more time." I'm rambling again.

Will grabs my hands in his, the first real touch he's offered since he picked me up. It should be comforting, but instead I feel the loss of him in a visceral way. Almost like he isn't touching me at all, even though there's barely an inch between us. "Cam, I-I don't have money for college. You of all people know how hard money is. I have to do something that doesn't strap me or my parents with mountains of debt. I also . . ." Will places his hands over his face again, like he doesn't want to watch my reaction to whatever's coming next. "I want to serve my country. I'm being called to serve, it's what I was made to do."

An anvil slams into my chest. How can he feel "called" to risk his life? Am I not worth staying for, not worth being kept safe? It's unfathomable to me that anyone is "called" to do anything. We make choices about what's best for our lives, it isn't fate or divine intervention telling us which path to choose.

"What does this mean? For us . . . I mean." I shift slightly, afraid to make eye contact, to see what waits for me there.

"It means. . ." A sob rips from his throat, echoing in the small cab of his truck. "We're done. I-I can't do this with you anymore."

My initial instinct is to go on the defensive. "No. No, no, no. We are not done. We are not done until we are old and gray in our beds dying together at ninety years old. I refuse." My tear ducts protest, not allowing me to shed one more drop. A refusal from my heart to believe that this is ending.

"I-I don't love you. It's time you see that, time to move on." The statement lacks conviction, but there's determination in his eyes. They aren't shining and bright anymore but rather dark, stormy pools that indicate this argument won't end in my favor. Heat seeps through my body as my skin turns clammy. I am going to vomit.

I throw myself away from him, lunging toward the passenger door and desperately pulling at the handle to escape the shrinking space before I lose my lunch or my sanity. I make it down into the grass before I hurl all the contents from my stomach. Tears flow freely now, as if I needed to shed my insides before the rest of me could unravel. Wiping my mouth with the back of my hand, I turn to see him staring out the window, stone-faced.

"I loved you! I planned my whole life around you, and you're just throwing it away? Did I ever mean anything to you? Did you think of anyone but yourself when you planned to betray everything we've worked for, every plan we built? Actually, you know what—don't answer that. Fuck you, Will Davenport. Don't ever contact me again." I shout every venomous thought I can at him. After all, I am the one who now has to start over; he has everything planned out.

Torn between wanting to fight, to scream, to claw my way into his heart and never let go, and at the same time wanting to run. I look at him one last time, tears flooding both our faces. I can't believe this is happening, can't process the betrayal. Because that's what this is, a complete destruction of every time I've held him while he choked back sobs over his dad abandoning him, every time he reassured me that I was enough despite never measuring up to my parents' standards. We found each other when we were broken, we healed together, and this . . . this is shredding me far more than I ever was ripped apart to begin with.

Knowing there's no changing his mind, I run. Back toward my childhood home and away from the love of my life. Each crunch of gravel beneath my feet congruent with the shattering of my heart. I vow to myself to move on but to never forget.

ONE

5 Years Later

Cam

"The Art of Starting Over" - Demi Lovato

"Elliott, why didn't you tell me that when they call it the Sunshine State, it's actually just a nice way of saying it's the armpit of hell?" I ask, fanning my face so my makeup doesn't melt completely off prior to my lunch date arriving, the one that is currently ten minutes late. I shift my cell from one ear to the other.

My brother lets out a throaty laugh, full of delight at my misery. "I think I did. Do you not remember me asking why the hell you would choose Florida for this grandiose rendezvous disguised as a career opportunity?"

"You act like I ever listen. It's your job to make me when it counts this much," I whine. Elliott is my big brother. Forcing me to obey his commands is in his job description, right next to noogies and throwing me under the bus to Patricia, otherwise known as our mother.

"Right, like I could ever command Madame Feminist Extraordinaire to do a thing. I gotta run into this meeting, and I shouldn't have to tell you, but it's not a good look to be on the phone when a date arrives. I'll see you later at the Crab Shack, and I better not get food poisoning there." He hangs up without giving me a second to reply to his quip.

As I wait for what is sure to be another dud of a date, condensation glides slowly down my glass, mesmerizing me and robbing me of my focus. Each drop represents the hellish Tampa heat, like the damp drops of sweat that roll down my back on a short jaunt to my car or into my apartment. I'm not lying when I say I missed the memo on exactly how hot it gets in Florida before I started this grand adventure. The beads run as if they're being chased down the smooth blue glass and can't escape fast enough. I'm envious of their swift and seemingly effortless movement. I'm desperate for an escape. Maybe it's a side effect of the new life I'm building, or maybe it's the decidedly self-absorbed man approaching. Either way, I'd like something—anything—to be as simple as running away was supposed to be.

This particular man, Andrew, is surprisingly gorgeous; his profile picture didn't do him a bit of justice. Dark hair flops delicately over his forehead, perfectly tanned forearms peek out from the rolled-up sleeves of his tasteful seafoam-green button-down shirt. And don't get me started on those brown eyes. Perfect chocolate drops that should have me melting, and yet—they aren't at all.

Seriously, I can tell from the swagger of his approach that my lady parts are obligated to be shouting from the rooftops. Instead, I'm calculating how soon a person can leave a date without being considered rude. Dating is not my thing. Can't we go back to the days of instantly falling in love over a shared affinity for the same apple at the grocery store? I want the kind of love that's unconditional, someone who wholly accepts me for who I am, flaws and all. It's just not that simple for me;

clearly, nothing is. Case in point, the man of so many women's dreams has just sat down across from me, and I feel virtually nothing. *Ugh! Why do I feel nothing?*

"Cam, right? It's great to meet you in person." Andrew grabs my lukewarm glass of water and takes a long chug. It wasn't icy cold like I prefer, but dude, get your own.

"Uh, yep. That's me. Andrew, I assume?" I reply, my face flushing further from my general awkwardness.

"You got it, babe. I gotta say, I'm relieved. You at least look like your profile picture. So many catfishers these days . . . Don't women know men aren't going to fall for them on the internet and then just overlook their flaws when they see them in person?" Arrogance radiates off of him in waves. I should've seen it coming with the far too many bro pics and shirtless photos on his profile. But this, this is another level. As someone who struggles with her body image, I'm annoyed.

"Well, maybe they aren't intentionally misleading you. Maybe there were other photos or signs, and doesn't it matter more what's on the inside of a person than the outside?" He shifts uncomfortably in his chair, not in a way that indicates guilt, more like I struck a nerve. Good. If he's looking for someone who won't call him on his bullshit, it's not me.

In deference to changing the subject, I say, "Anywho . . . tell me what you like to do for fun."

"Okay, yeah. Fun. Well, I fish. Let me tell you about my latest catch . . ." He launches into a story, and I zone out.

Glancing at the clock hanging haphazardly on the back wall of Antonio's, I can't help but notice the irony in the cozy, calming atmosphere blended with the war waging in my stomach. It's perfect here. Italian cold cuts a plenty, prim red-and-white checkered tablecloths, carefully curated family photos that honor tradition, love, and life. A warm breeze floats in *(finally)* from the open-air patio that sits perched against the white sand beach. I am a few good gusts away from resembling a human as opposed to the glazed donut I could currently be confused for. *Please bring on the salty air*, I plead internally.

The only thing out of place in the entire restaurant is my date. Andrew changed the subject slightly at some point while I've been mid-daydream, and he's now droning on about how to select the right bait for backwater fishing. Fishing is clearly a hobby of his, and not at all one of mine.

"Which do you think would be better, if given the choice?" he asks, bringing me begrudgingly back into the conversation. I'm not typically this unengaged on a date, but he lost me at "catfishing."

"Umm, sorry, can you ask me that again? I thought I recognized someone back there . . ." I say, pointing lamely at the back of the restaurant, where only an elderly couple and a waiter are occupying the space. *Smooth, Cam.*

I should've been listening more intently, but he just goes on and on. I mean, I grew up in a landlocked state. How should I know anything about fishing in the Intracoastal versus open ocean? *Not that he would know where I grew up*, I chastise myself.

"I asked if you think ocean fishing or backwater fishing is better, and which you would choose if you could."

"Oh, right . . . I'm sorry. I guess I would say ocean because I could maybe see some dolphins," I reply, putting all my effort into the answer. I'm trying here, give a girl a break.

He swiftly pulls his finger guns from their proverbial holsters, waving his pointers in my face as if to tell me I'm either onto something or completely hopeless when it comes to oceanic knowledge. The look on his face suggests the latter.

"Well actually, that's where you're wrong. You would be more likely to see sharks and dolphins in the Intracoastal Waterway. They frequent those for easy access to fish, kind of like it's the fast food restaurant of the sea," he rebukes, proceeding to mansplain the methodologies of porpoise and shark species as I go back to checking the clock.

He's a typical guy. Attractive (obviously), seemingly well-adjusted, and yes, clearly a grade A expert on fishing—which is great, just not for me. It's not that I have a vendetta against fishermen, there are likely a vast number of them who are perfectly suited for me. Just, not this one. He's asked exactly zero questions about me. Zilch, nil, none. Maybe he's nervous, but is it too much to ask for a little interest to be paid to your date?

I can't do this. I may be a lot of things, but fake isn't one of them. I thought I was ready to explore my options, and this guy was the best one, but at this point I'm looking forward more to waltzing out of here than to eating the basil pesto caprese sandwich I ordered. To be clear, very few things come between me and fresh mozzarella. I should've never come here, I realize. But since I did, an exit strategy is of the utmost importance.

"Listen, Andrew . . ." I say, cautiously interrupting him.

"It's Andy, that's what all the ladies call me," he quickly corrects me, winking as the words drip off his tongue. *Eww.*

"Umm . . . okay. This isn't working for me. I don't want to waste your time, and I'm sorry but I'm gonna go," I say, filtering all the determination and poise into my voice that I can muster while hoisting my purse on my shoulder and pointing with my thumb toward the door.

"Really? I thought I felt a real connection here." He seems genuinely befuddled as he swishes his hand back and forth between us.

"Look, it's not you, it's me. I'm just not as ready as I thought I was. Thanks for lunch," I reply, guiltily offering him a demure smile as I toss a few bills on the table to cover my meal. There is approximately zero chance of me sticking him with the bill. My incessant need to be liked, that all-too-familiar achy feeling in my chest, would never allow it. I intended on paying my way prior to even coming here, and I'm most certainly not going to be another "lady" he tacks onto his list of "all the ladies" to top it off.

"You know, just a friendly tip . . . if you aren't ready, then you shouldn't lead people on," he snarls out, disdain markedly etched on his face. Oh, the gall I have to turn down the self-proclaimed lady killer—*how dare I.*

"Excuse me?" Every ounce of guilt I had seeps out of my body in one swoop, and I'm left simply astonished at the bold statement coming out of Mr. Dreamboat's mouth. *Why did he have to be so hot?*

"You shouldn't agree to a date if you aren't looking for something. It's fucked up to lead people on." His lips quirk slightly up into a smirk as he says it. *Oh, come on, Andy.*

Plastering a pinched smile on my face, I spit back, "Thanks for the feedback. Here's a tip for you. Maybe don't only talk about yourself on dates." I turn to leave but stop short. "Oh, and Andrew—don't ask a woman to call you Andy just because all the other ladies do."

It's too much of a reply, I know, but really, can you blame me? I hustle off toward the door leaving him with his mouth agape and gulping air, looking eerily similar to one of the ten thousand fish he just described in excruciating detail. Somewhere in this world there is a beautiful, fish-obsessed individual for Andy, but it's not me.

—

The dream is always the same and today's no different. It's what I like to call the "Cameron Wright special" because like me, it's good on the surface but a complete mess underneath. Dim lighting, silky soft sheets, the scent of warm cedar filtering through the room. My senses are heightened; I can feel, taste, and smell everything all at once. His breath swirls warm and hot on my neck as he presses kisses into the tender spot of skin just below my ear. My whole body sings with awareness as he presses his hips forward, rubbing precariously close to the small aching bud between my legs. Softly, he growls in that mind-bending husky voice, "I'm leaving, Cam. It's over."

Gahhh! I startle awake from the dream—or should I say, nightmare—gulping for air. I'm covered in sweat with my arm placed perfectly between my thighs and my face jammed into my pillow. My whole body is an irritating mix of turned on and frustrated. Goddamn you, Will Davenport!

Fucking Will, the one who got away. The one I naively planned my life around as a dumbass eighteen-year-old. I'm totally over him, yet every time I get brave and go on a less-than-stellar date, I wake up like this. It's maddening. And to make matters worse, the dreams are getting more vivid as time goes on. What is wrong with me? Why can't I be like every other self-respecting woman in her twenties?

Collecting myself, I glance at my trusty clock radio perched at the edge of my nightstand. Shit! I have thirty minutes to pull myself together and get to the bar to meet my brother. I hadn't planned on taking a long nap, and I certainly hadn't accounted for what can only be described as a wet dream.

You are finally really losing it, Cam.

Bristling at myself, I throw on a pair of denim cutoffs and a black Rosie the Riveter T-shirt. After running a brush through my hair and grabbing my purse, I rush to my car. It's not a long drive but I've been looking forward to seeing my brother, and as my mother would say, if you're not ten minutes early, you're late.

My mother again—she's always in my head like this. Reminding me constantly of all her "rules" and laying on some good old-fashioned guilt without ever having to say a word. It's a good thing I remembered to gas up old Betty, my trusty green sedan. I can't imagine the guilt Patricia would cast upon me if she knew it went below a quarter tank. Betty's about five years past her prime, but I'm admittedly not the best at letting go of things—see the five-year-long crush on my high school boyfriend I'm definitely not still carrying around for reference.

I'm meeting my brother at the Crab Shack—a small seafood place known for all manner of delights, but for me it's the worn and weathered atmosphere, the locals, and let's be honest, the drinks that are most compelling.

Obviously, I need one right now.

Most people pass this place by thinking it's too dingy or it's a bad bout of stomach issues waiting to happen. For me, though, I like that it's got character. Tiny scraps of history ripe for the picking, like the paunchy old man at the end of the bar with leathery skin and a scraggly silver beard, the crooked but well-used dartboard, or the bartender who looks just slightly worse off than I am. There's a story here, a past I imagine that's not much different than my own. One of longing, or of love that's bore more pain than pure joy.

Having made it to the Crab Shack with nine minutes to spare, I plop down on a red faux-leather barstool that's seen better days. It's well-loved, and even shows signs of a few new tears forming, but it seems familiar and that provides me a slight bit of comfort. Almost as if this chair has helped people solve the world's problems longer than I've been alive. I find myself wondering if this chair has any valuable insight for a mess like me.

This is where I'm at mentally, latching onto things as minuscule as a chair that's had every butt in town plopped on to it at one time or another. I don't have time to dwell on my clearly suboptimal mental status though. Elliott will be here any minute, and I need to fix my face before enduring another one of my big brother's lectures.

I'm excited to see him, it's the first time any family has visited me since the big move. Not that this technically counts as a "visit" since he's just in town for work and making time to meet me for a drink. I should be thankful that he even made any time, but it stings that my family, including Elliott, isn't embracing this adventure more and encouraging my independence.

Taking a slow, deep breath, sucking in the mildew and yesterday's-beer-scented air, I quickly brush my hands over my hair to smooth it and collect myself. The humidity here is insufferable, which means no amount of time spent flat ironing or curling can keep this mane tamed.

A small jingle chimes as the door swings open, alerting me to the newly arrived guest. There's an audible gasp from the women in the bar followed by a bellowing of oohs and aahs, and I know Elliott is here without even looking.

He has this face, not so different from mine but less soft and more chiseled. A small dimple in his chin that I've heard all manner of, frankly, disturbing comments about. He isn't exactly tall, but not short either; he's average, I suppose. What he lacks in overwhelming height, though, he makes up for in physique. He works out and eats a ridiculous food regimen to stay in shape.

I wish I had his willpower, I do. But I also just enjoy life. Maybe if I was a little more realistic or determined, I could lose those fifteen pounds once and for all. I'm not a huge woman, but I'm curvy, and being on the shorter side doesn't help. Hell, I look at a donut and it practically staples itself to my ass.

Elliott sweeps up beside me, effortlessly sliding onto a stool, completely unfazed by the attention he garners everywhere he goes. I swear, it's like he doesn't even notice how he devastates women just by existing and tossing them a smirk once in a while.

"Cam, you could have warned me not to come overdressed. I didn't realize I was meeting you at a literal shack."

I gape at him. "I like it, it's cozy." He literally scoffs at me. *The audacity of this man.*

My brother, older than me by a few years, is not uptight or snobby, but he does appreciate the finer things in life and has worked hard to be able to afford them. Me, on the other hand, I'll just be over here slumming it in the Crab Shacks of the world, and frankly, I'm okay with that.

I've accepted that while my job is pretty exciting and has potential, it's not something I'm going to make a fortune doing, at least not anytime soon. Most of my money goes to my ridiculous rent. Lo, my roommate, can be a bit of a penny-pincher, so I'm not getting any freebies from her.

Elliott orders a Landshark, politely telling the bartender to keep the lime while simultaneously whispering to me about how he doesn't know what's been lurking around the cut fruit in this "shack." I ignore him and explain the menu, pointing out what I've been told is good, attempting to settle his nerves a bit. He levels me with a look and says, "Okay . . . seriously, Cam, how are you? You look great, the tan you're rocking is doing things for your face."

A snort sneaks out of me almost immediately; my brother has a way with words, ladies. In all seriousness, though, he kind of does, but we've never been all that good at compliments. I think it comes with the territory of being a Wright. You're expected to have a friendly-yet-stiff upper lip, a thick skin if you will.

"I'm good, great actually. Salon life is interesting but in the best way," I assure him.

"How's working for America's top stylist? Dreamy and delightful, or is he secretly a diva who claimed you for his peasant girl?" He mocks me by dramatically tossing his hand to his forehead—sarcasm is clearly one of his strong suits.

"Not at all. Daveed is good—he's like the parent I always wanted and never had. He loves us and takes pride in feeding me copious amounts of sweet potato fries. What's not to love?" Taking a glug of the cool, crisp tiki-inspired blueberry drink I ordered, I toss him a megawatt smile.

"Tsk-tsk, what would Patricia say?" He feigns disbelief, but I can tell he's joking.

"Honestly, I don't care. Should I keep a quarter next to me at each meal to help my waistline? Yes. Am I going to? No. I am burning calories just walking to my car in this sweatbox." It niggles at my brain, the fact that I've gained weight, because deep down I do care. I always wanted to be thin, modelesque if you will. But I'm not, and the reminder of my mother's insane method of shaming me doesn't serve me. It's hard enough to stop my brain from overthinking about each crumb I consume, I don't need any other reminders of my imperfections.

"Good. You shouldn't care what anyone thinks. But as a man who loves women, I have to say, in a very non-creepy brother way, that you are gorgeous. I hope you don't ever believe for a second otherwise." He shifts his eyes to a passing bartender, ever the flirt on the prowl.

"Thanks, El. Now eyes over here." I snap my fingers, recapturing his attention. "Tell me about your work, am I going to see you more often?"

"Maybe. Depends if I can close this deal first. If I do, there will be lots of routine visits. Better tell that roommate of yours to make room for the big bro." Winking at me, he sips down the last of his beer, standing to seek out a bartender for another.

"What's happening to your face?" Elliott breaks into my thoughts when he returns, fresh drink in hand. "Please do not tell me it has something to do with William Davenport again."

I feign shock and horror, probably overselling it. I suppose I shouldn't mention the very inappropriate dream I had no less than thirty minutes ago. "No . . . I was just thinking of how much I miss you and how nice it is to just grab a beer and breathe in the familiar. Why would you even think it would have anything to do with he-who-shall-not-be-named?"

"Cam, you know you can always come home, right? There are great salons downtown, and you wouldn't even have to be a shampoo girl." His beer is tilted toward me as if I should cheers him and finally give up the act I'm putting on for the family. Conveniently he doesn't address the comment about Will. I'm not sure if anyone in my immediate circle believes I ever got over him.

"I'm not a shampoo girl, even though that's what Mom probably tells everyone," I say, rolling my eyes. "I'm in training, I'm learning from the best of the best, and I need this time to find myself after dropping out of college and running straight into cosmetology school. Everything is a blur at this point."

"No, you need this time to find someone new. He's moved on, it's been five years. Cam, he isn't coming back and even if he did, you're not at home. So what, he's supposed to magically know you moved to Florida and come find you?" There it is, we've come full circle on my suspicion. Elliott shakes his head as if he's the one exasperated by this conversation.

Nothing infuriates me more than my family, especially Elliott, insisting that I'm still hung up on Will. Did it suck when he dumped me and ditched our well-laid-out plans? Yeah, I've got the scars to prove it. Do I have sex dreams about the dude after every date I go on? Also yeah. But I really am over him. If he walked in the door right now, I would not give him a minute of my time because I've walked that road before. I'm older and wiser now.

"Elliott, I promise, I'm moving on . . . I even downloaded a dating app. I'm getting out there, I had a date earlier today actually." I know I sound desperate, and maybe I am, but I really don't want to discuss this with him, or anyone else for that matter.

"Whatever you say, we all just worry about you. There is literally no way you could have met your soulmate in high school. Honestly, the girls I dated in high school . . . hard pass."

I should be offended by the utter disgust blossoming on his face—instead, I cackle, thinking about the girls he dated back then. The way he had his pick of the "best" ones was obscene. They were all beautiful and had absolutely nothing between their ears.

He's had a couple of girlfriends over the years that have been okay, but the current one . . . well, let's just say I've never really liked her. She's nice enough, but she doesn't seem to be all that into him, which frankly, how dare she. He's a catch compared to the available market I've seen. Thankfully, Elliott drops the hard-ass questioning routine, and we settle back into catching up on life.

He tells me why he's in town and says that if he can finally close this deal with Tampa General, he might be considered for a senior development rep position at work. I'm so proud of him. I don't know how a small-town Iowa farm boy turned into a hotshot sales rep who exudes swagger, but he did. I'd be lying if I denied the twinge of jealousy I feel, but he also gives me a shred of hope for myself.

After all, if he can ditch the shit kickers and Levi's, maybe I can transform myself a little too. Maybe living a stone's throw from the beach will help me pass on the fries, opt for a salad, take up running . . . Who am I kidding? I may be able to change some, but not that much. Honestly, even if I do make some drastic life changes, even more dramatic than moving thousands of miles from home, no one will take me seriously. No one ever has.

Exhibit A: My mother thinks I'm a glorified shampoo girl and doesn't understand why I needed space to spread my wings. When I explained moving for this opportunity, she told me all the space I needed could be found in the field out back.

It's not that she doesn't love and support me, it's just that this isn't what people from my hometown do. Good girls find nice country boys, get married, pop out a half dozen babies, and get on with life. Me chasing this "glamorous" lifestyle is foreign to everyone I know; they don't get it, or at least don't want to.

The sullen bartender (Sally, according to her name tag) approaches, tossing a beer-tinged towel down in front of us and placing her hands on her hips before asking, "You two want some food or what?"

I glance at Elliott for reassurance, before expeditiously saying, "We'll have the peel-and-eat shrimp, please. And I'll have another." Sally doesn't smile or nod, she simply grabs a couple of liquor bottles, pours them into a shaker, and goes to town. With a pointed look at Elliott, she places the drink down in front of me a little too hard before spinning around to hang our order ticket in the kitchen window. Pangs of empathy settle in. I want to tell her I understand. He was being impatient earlier and sought out a new drink from the younger, cuter bartender. It sucks to be the one overlooked. Instead, I shift my focus back to Elliott.

"Sooo . . . how are things with Michelle?" I ask with probably, no definitely, far too much disdain.

"She's great, working a lot and getting ready for that trip to Europe." Elliott has a smile plastered on his face, but as his sister and certified knower of all his moods, I can tell he's forcing it.

"The backpacking one? With the friend from college who's supposedly a best friend but you haven't met them in three years of dating?" I ask, raising an eyebrow at him.

"Yep, Samantha, who I'm going to meet. And you know what, I know you don't like her but I'm happy, Cam." The fire-filled reply indicates I struck a nerve.

I roll my eyes at his coy way of hiding what I can only assume is trouble. "Mmmkay, if you say so."

"Again, I came here on recon for Mom. I'm supposed to be finding out if *you're* okay. Did you say you've been on a dating app?"

I groan. Discussing who I'm swiping left or right on with my big brother doesn't scream fun for either of us, and to be totally frank, the options themselves aren't very appealing either.

Option 1: Dude with a big fish he caught.

Option 2: Military bro who thinks he's God's gift to women and the country.

Sally returns to deliver a steaming pile of shrimp tossed in Old Bay and dripping with butter. The interruption thankfully gives me a minute to think about how and what I even want to share. Based on my lunch date today, it's a no to all fishermen for me, and I'm not anti-military, but I just don't get the appeal after Will ditched me for his dream of becoming the next Rambo.

"Yep, I'm getting out there. So far it's mostly been gross dick pics from the bros of Tampa and people who are so totally in denial about general aging and how different they look than when they were twenty, but I'm trying," I say with a half-hearted smile as I lift a buttery crustacean to my lips.

"Don't you have friends at the salon who could set you up?" Elliott asks hopefully, while wiping his hands on a napkin like a civilized individual.

"Hmm maybe, but if I even hinted that it was fair game, Daveed would force me into shampooing every man that comes through the place. I can see it now . . . *You said you wanted to give them a head rub,*

Cam," I deadpan.

I love my brother, but he has no clue the lengths that a hair god like Daveed would go to so he can say he set me up. He takes meddling seriously, which I guess helps when you're a hairstylist (translation: a therapist who makes people look pretty).

We finish our second drinks and the shrimp in amenable silence. I can tell my brother is getting anxious to leave. I knew it wasn't going to be a long visit but that sharp pang of sadness still creeps in. After paying our tab and heading out, we make our way to our cars. Elliott hugs me tightly, and it hurts to let go. Seeing him is comforting—he's my best friend, partner in crime, and confidant in battling our parents. I also know there's more going on with him than he's letting on, but if he won't open up about it, my hands are tied. Reluctantly, I watch him leave, not knowing when I'll see him again.

I shuffle slowly to my car and duck in. Head against the steering wheel and eyes squeezed tightly shut to keep the waterworks at bay, I make a deal with myself right then and there: I'm going to embrace a whole new Cam. I may not be able to fix my brother's love life, but I damn sure can fix mine. I'm getting myself a new wardrobe, I'm getting in shape, and I'm getting back on the prowl. If I have it my way, Will is never going to be the leading man in one of my sex dreams again.

TWO

Cam

"Platinum" - Miranda Lambert

My feet hurt, my back aches, and I'm pretty sure I can't feel my fingers anymore. Working in a salon may look glamorous, but I'm here to report, it's anything but. Today alone, I've washed fifteen heads of hair—and I don't mean just lather, rinse, repeat. There's an art to giving a proper scalp massage, and a reason Daveed named the shampoo area the Lather Lounge. I've candled some ears *(gross)* and waxed more things than I care to explain. Some things just can't be unseen!

When I took a chance and moved here, I thought I'd be carefully styling the locks of the Tampa elite, not serving them butter cookies and cucumber water while mixing endless bowls of bleach and cutting thousands of foils. Heaven help me, I can almost hear my mother's smug remarks about me being a "shampoo girl" all the way from Iowa.

Apprenticeship is part of the gig, though, a rite of passage into this

profession. I'm fortunate that I get to train under the best. Daveed is world-renowned, as he likes to remind us whenever we complain about repeating any one of the various skills he's taught us. But it could be worse; I could be training under someone far less talented or far less caring.

Training with the best is only the first step to fulfilling my dream, though. I've wanted to be in the beauty industry for as long as I can remember. Not because I'm incredibly vain, or even one of those women with a knack for style, but because I truly love the feeling of making others feel good about themselves. Life is hard, and people often are dealing with struggles that can't be seen or identified at first glance. It's not always easy to love what you see in the mirror; I know I don't at times.

When I was about fifteen, my mom's friend Luanne opened up her own beauty shop in town. A small, three-chair boutique salon catering to women from all the neighboring towns. Luanne needed someone to answer the phone, schedule appointments, and fold towels on Saturdays, and I needed cash to save up for something other than the old farm truck to drive. It was a match made in heaven.

Working those Saturdays gave me one day a week that I could explore my more feminine side, without dirt under my fingernails or hay to bail. It fostered my independence, and I adored listening to all the small-town talk that ran through the place.

I remember one Saturday in particular. One of the stylists, Sara, had a client in her chair looking for a big change. She was recently divorced, had moved back into a small bedroom at her parents' house with her two-year-old, and was looking for work. The appointment went off without a hitch—the client raved about her new look afterward and left with an extra pep in her step.

As we were closing up, a knock on the already-locked door alerted me that she was back. Assuming she forgot something, I hurried to let her in and asked how I could help her. She immediately burst into thick sobs, wrapping me up in a fierce hug. When Sara rushed out to assist, the woman shared that she had planned to end her life that day. She explained how dark of a place she had been in when she came to the salon, and how Sara's willingness to listen, her ability to help her see the beauty and light in herself, renewed the woman's strength and hope that she could, in fact, keep going.

It was one of those moments that you know will forever change you. Like her story had been woven onto the very fabric of my heart, I understood right then the importance and power that we have over other people, even strangers—not just hairstylists, though it certainly gives us an easier way to build connections. But all people, if we allow ourselves to be open enough to truly see what someone else is going through without judgment. I wanted it then, and I want it now: to be a safe space, a judgment-free zone, a person people can turn to in their darkest hour.

I straighten my spine as the sound of the galley door swinging open jolts me out of my own head. Closing my eyes, I suck in a deep, renewing breath in an attempt to check my emotions.

Daveed saunters into the small room that's tucked in the back. As usual, he's dressed to the hilt in all black with skintight denim pants and a black satin button-down shirt. This room serves as a place for laundry, brush cleaning, washing out color bowls, and general bitching about clients. Daveed's aura and startling beauty, with his curly jet-black hair and piercing golden-brown eyes rippling with flecks of amber, don't fit in this space. He was made for the front of the house, where the magic and beauty radiate off of him like the rays of the sun.

"Cam, how's my favorite sweet girl doing? You have bags under your eyes, do we need to talk?" he asks, mock concern etched in between his brows.

His passive-aggressive way of telling me that I look like a bag of shit hits like a punch to the sternum, causing me to suck in a breath. It's fair—apparently, I look how I feel. I offer him a small smile in reluctant acceptance of his observation.

I could tell him the story I was just reminiscing about, but opting not to be too vulnerable, I say, "I'm great, just finished up the towels and I'm going to clean the brushes next. I was wondering, could I watch you do your men's cut at four? I really want to get better at blending, but my mind isn't letting it click for some reason."

"Oh, my sweet girl, of course you can. You know you're slaying this job, right? And you're adorable to boot. There's a reason I hired you. I mean, other than I'm clearly a genius and was doing you a favor," he says, rather self-assuredly—his usual vibe.

"Thanks, I've just been a little off recently, trying to reinvent myself and start dating again, which is just ugh . . . Why are men worthless?" I ask, sure my face is painted with weariness.

"Cameron!" Daveed crows loudly. "Not all men are worthless. I find them particularly delightful most of the time." He winks at me with a flirty grin.

"That's not fair, you haven't been on a dating app recently, and you aren't getting random dick pics from the bros of Tampa. It's slim pickings, as my momma would say." Pouting slightly, I cross my arms and lean back against the counter.

Daveed rolls his eyes and puts one finger to his lips, carefully considering his next move as my skin begins to tingle. I'm wondering if I just played too much of my hand. The goal was to avoid vulnerability, and here I am spilling all the beans. I mean, who openly admits their patheticness to their perfect, fabulous, probably D-list celebrity (don't ever tell him I said that) boss, especially when you know they're going to meddle?

Apparently, I do.

It came to me last night when I was lying awake in bed, staring at the ceiling to make sure Mr. Palmetto Bug didn't show up back in his favorite spot. Yes, we need an exterminator, and no, we can't afford one. Anyway, I made a deal with myself to be more open to possibilities and to be honest with those around me, like that client was with Sara and me back in the day. This is the first step, I hope.

"I've got it!" He snaps his fingers and twirls his index finger, pointing at my . . . face? No, my hair. "You're naturally blonde already, but as I always say, what doesn't kill you makes you blonder."

Welp, those lyrics are actually from a very famous country song, but I doubt he knows that or would even acknowledge it if I corrected him. I'm also unclear on how making me over is going to change the currently available dating pool—actually, cesspool. The currently available Tampa dating cesspool.

"Umm . . . that's great, but have you seen what you charge? And also what you pay me for that matter?" I ask, wearily.

A makeover by one of the most talented stylists in the world wasn't something I'd imagined in my wildest dreams. Certainly, it's not something I would have asked for, or am even sure I deserve. But if he's offering, who am I to say no? It can't hurt, and even if it doesn't change the dating options available, it may help me feel better about myself, which is something I desperately need.

"Oh, sweets, it's on the house. Come on, you can observe me finesse a man's hair even if you have a full head of foils. Plus, I've been wanting to discuss your career path. What better time than when I have scissors and bleach in hand?" There's that smirk again. He knows how embarrassing it is to work with a head full of foils, and yet, he couldn't care less with his idle threats aplenty.

Daveed saunters out as I trail behind, unsure what exactly I just signed up for but also unwilling to pass up the chance to have his skilled hands carefully crafting my new look. This is good—no this is great. Having Daveed Jones do your hair is on par with winning the lottery. Maybe my life's turning around already. Now, if only I could hit the actual lotto . . .

Two hours later, poised in Daveed's sleek black-and-gold styling chair under the static noise of a hair dryer, the beauty of this place he's built floors me. Every room is appointed with modern niceties, yet a relaxing calm envelops each client who walks in the door. The styling area was designed for the ease of our guests with comfortable hunter-green velvet couches to wait on, purse or bag hooks at each station, and crisp gold script lettering to label the doors leading into each adjoining room. Daveed also considered us, the stylists, by providing ergonomic work spaces, saddle stools, and top-of-the-line equipment. He's one of the best in the world not only because of his creative prowess, but also because of his ability to create an experience for guests and employees alike.

The dryer clicks off and he spins me around in the chair. Shock and awe strike me. I didn't believe adding foils to my already-light-honey hair would make such an impact, but I can practically feel my hair moving while my head is completely still. It's vibrant yet soft, and the way he molded a tiny bump to the ends makes them twist just a tad. Thank God he steamrolled me into it.

"Forgive me, but—holy shit. The movement and texture, you're a miracle worker. Thank you so much!" I squeal as I jump up to wrap him tightly in a hug.

Daveed gives me a cocky look that asks why I would assume

anything less than perfection. "It helps when you have a great canvas, and damn, sweets, you have hair for days. I'm actually considering going home with you for Christmas just so I can get some of that good Iowa grain in me and grow a beard."

Giggles erupt out of me. I can only imagine what Gram would think of my openly gay boss wearing a skirt to Christmas dinner. I love the woman, but she's far removed from the LGBTQ+ community. She's not judgy—believe me, Daveed and her would have quite the time laughing and swapping stories about all of their sordid affairs—but you never know exactly what's going to come from the woman's mouth. It's literal word vomit at every turn . . . Maybe that's where I get it from.

"I'll let Gram know you're coming, that will get her planning months in advance. The gays are coming for Christmas," I say with a quick snap of my fingers and a stifled giggle.

Daveed smiles slyly at me with that twinkle in his eye, confirming what I already know. He would have her eating out the palm of his hand in less than ten minutes. No doubt in my mind, Gram would trade me in for Daveed in a heartbeat, and I couldn't even blame her.

I thank him again with a quick hug and hustle back into the galley to pick up the tasks I left hanging for the other assistants. I appreciate what he did, but I don't need any of my coworkers thinking I'm asking for special treatment. I want to earn everything I'm given with no one helping me. Maybe I'm a badass bitch after all.

Will

"M.I.A." - Graham Barham

"Give me twenty more push-ups, dirtbags," barks Sergeant Montgomery.

"I swear to God, if Johnson doesn't get his chest to the floor this time, I'm going to kill him with my bare hands," I whisper quietly to Smith, so as not to be the one responsible for extended PT this morning.

It's Friday and it's been a hell of a week. The last thing I need is to have to lie face down on this busted excuse for a track for even a second longer than is mandatory. We've had nothing but problems with our surveillance feeds for the past four days, our computer network has shit the bed twice, and we're preparing to deploy at a moment's notice. Not knowing when it will happen is fueling my anxiety.

Coming off our last deployment, I thought getting moved as a group to Tampa sounded great. I thought it meant I'd actually see

a beach. Instead, I'm stuck in a constant state of darkness at work—literally. We work in a pitch-black room lit only by the hazy glow of hundreds of computer monitors. Then there's the fact that my mother decided last night would be a good time to tell me she ran into Patricia Wright at the market. Hearing about the woman who should have been my mother-in-law has my skin vibrating with regret.

". . . nineteen, twenty. Alright, you idiots. Shower and report to duty in twenty," barks Montgomery again.

Does that man ever speak any other way except in grunts and barks? I bet he walks around hollering about light switches being left on and who's signed up for trash duty when he's at home. It's reassuring that he found someone to marry though. There might be hope for the rest of us yet.

As we walk quickly toward the gym showers, Smith raps me on the shoulder. "Whaddya say, old Willy boy, wanna hit the Hole tonight?"

I groan quietly. I've been to the Waterin' Hole too many times to count in the last three months, and honestly, the place is dulling my senses. Don't get me wrong, I love country music, it runs in my veins, but every time I walk in that place, I'm transported back to dancing lessons in Cam's barn after school. The way memories of what we had seep into me and rip my heart out is becoming too much to handle.

"I don't know, man. I might just order pizza and chill tonight." A low-key night feels like exactly what I need.

"Willy boy, who gives a shit if no one can dance properly and if the music isn't the folksy shit you grew up on? Girls are girls and you need one, like, yesterday, my man," shouts Smith.

"Geezus, what I don't need is you announcing to the whole base that I haven't had a date in far too long. I don't need a woman, I'm fine by myself," I hiss back at him. He knows why I don't put myself out there, he just doesn't accept it.

"You need to get your mind off her and let go of all the ass-backward reasons you're holding on to for not putting yourself out there. You aren't your father. Never have been, never will be." He demands my agreement, grabbing my chin and shaking my head up and down.

As we step into the steam-filled locker room, he squeezes my shoulder and tells me to think about it, adding that I can hit him up at his apartment around nine if I want to grab a cab with him. He says it like it'll be this big endeavor when in reality, he lives across the hall from me. I could walk out my door and get in the cab when it pulls up, but that's just like Smith to lean into the drama of it all.

Shaking my head, I toss him an eye roll, grab my caddy, and head toward the shower. He's a great guy, a real man's man who will always watch your back in the field, but he's also loud and boisterous. Smith knows everyone and isn't afraid to make a scene, be the star of the party, and laugh his ass off—at my expense.

"Alright man, I'll think about it. Let's hurry here and get to work, so Montgomery doesn't make us do anymore push-ups today," I grumble.

We shower swiftly, put on our standard-issue uniforms, and rush to the secure facility we work in. It's not going to be a crazy day, but we're pretty busy and all on edge that we may have to head out soon. I can't stop thinking about what Smith said. Maybe I should do what the rest of the guys do, download Tinder and find someone to take the edge off quickly. It's not like I haven't done it before, it's just that I don't want to deal with what comes afterward. It's supposed to be quick and easy, but they always want more than I can provide, emotionally. The only person I was ever attached to I broke. These women don't deserve it.

To be frank, if—and that's a big if—I was going to get attached again, it would be to her. But I can't. It would be selfish to put her through what would inevitably be me making a mistake that costs both of our happiness. Not that she would even give me the time of day at this point. Cam is a no contest girl, when compared to anyone else she wins every category hands down and I screwed her over. Ultimately I did it to help her, she couldn't be a ray of sunshine stuck to my grumpy ass, but of course she didn't see it that way. Instead, she thinks I crushed her on purpose, and I let her believe it.

Smith rolls over, bumping into me with his desk chair, spinning like an eight-year-old entertaining himself on bring-your-son-to-work day. "So, the Hole? You in? Or are you going to sit around and wallow all night?" he chides me, knowing if he pokes long enough, I'll eventually cave. No one enjoys sitting alone at home on a Friday.

"I don't know, man, it's going to be the same shit as always. We go, I sit at the bar and drink while you pick up a girl, hook up with her in the bathroom, and then we leave. Why don't we go somewhere else?"

"Hmm . . . why don't you try not being a sad sack and finally give up on this no-dating rule?"

"You know why." I stare at him astounded that he doesn't feel exactly the same way. "I don't have a job where I can commit to being in one location. I am stubborn as a mule and struggle to say the right thing. I am sure that women are just waiting to line up," I deadpan.

"You know there's this thing you could try, it's called *just have fun*. Keep it light and casual with clear expectations upfront."

"Okay . . . so you want me to lead them on?" I ask, hoping deep down that's not actually what he's doing to the women he entertains. I may be dense at times, but I pride myself on being respectful in all things.

"No, that's the meaning of clear expectations. I just want you to quit moping around. Look, we all know that the elusive Cam is it for you, but that doesn't mean you're dead. We all also know that you don't even know where she is or what she's up to." He doesn't know my mom's latest update on her grocery store run in with Cam's mom is weighing on my mind.

"If I agree to go, will you never mention her name again?" I ask, impatiently.

"If you agree to stop pining away for her like a puppy that lost his favorite toy. You made the decision to drop her like yesterday's trash, you didn't want her, she would never have been able to handle the emotional toll, one of you would have eventually walked away, yada yada . . . Get over it, bro, it's been five years!" Smith throws his hands up and rubs them together, signaling my need to wash my hands of her. As if it would be so easy to forget the only woman I've ever loved.

"First of all, I didn't drop her like trash. I did want her, but I also knew what was best for her. Second of all, *stop* talking about Cam!" I raise my voice at him, immediately glancing around to see if anyone noticed. If I have to do another push-up today, my arms won't work at all tomorrow and it will be Smith's fault for provoking me.

"Whoa, dude, I'm just messing with you. But you really do need to find a way to break this spell. Let's hit up Venus instead. You can pay for a little action to take the edge off."

"Fine, I'm in, but I'm not buying you a lap dance. You gotta pay your own way," I say on a huff while I point my finger at him for emphasis, not that it will work. I don't typically enjoy frequenting strip clubs, but maybe he's right. Maybe I should try casual. I'm just afraid if I do, no one will ever measure up.

"Deal," Smith agrees, while trying to mask his sly smirk with his hand. He knows I'm paying, even though I literally just said I wouldn't. I always end up paying because I'm the only one who doesn't regularly blow the minuscule paychecks we get. I guess that's my penance for refusing to go dancing and for being stingy, saving every penny I earn aside from what's necessary for living expenses and the occasional stock up at the nutrition store.

—

Salty ocean air swirls around me, wafting hints of fish and sunscreen into my Jeep. The breeze is warm on my skin, not as refreshing as I'd like it to be with the temperature nearing triple digits, but it's moving air nonetheless. Lyrics honoring small hometowns and the people we take for granted vibrate from my stereo. Nothing like a classic country song to make you feel seen, or to sometimes deepen the ache for times, people, or places gone by.

I do my best thinking when driving, the silence allowing my brain to marinate on mistakes I wish I could change. I never meant to break Cam's heart; it's just, I've seen this all play out before. My mom was a devoted wife, but my dad felt like he missed his chance to sow his wild oats since he married his high school sweetheart, so to speak. He had never dated anyone else, never went to parties unless my mom was with him, and supposedly the dullness of never experiencing the things he "should" have wore him down. One day, my mom came into an on-call room at the hospital they both worked at and found him bent over a nurse with his pants around his ankles.

She wanted to forgive him—honestly, Valerie Davenport is the sweetest woman known to man, a real-life angel walking on earth. The problem was, he didn't want to stop giving it to Susie Homewrecker because she made him feel "alive," whatever the fuck that means. Getting his release was more important than his wife or kids.

I think that's why I fell so hard for Cam. Aside from her outer beauty, she taught me what it felt like to truly be loved, without exception. She met me where I was, and my scars became the roadmap to earning my heart. But I had to end it. Knowing I would never be able to give her as much in return as she gave me ate at me. Cam is sunshine, she's the most beautiful bouquet of flowers, the rainbow on a rainy day.

I am the man who wasn't even lovable enough for his father to stick around. Splitting up was easier than falling short of ever being able to lasso the moon for her.

"*Honk,*" a horn blares behind me, alerting me that traffic is moving once more and I'm carried back from my trip down memory lane. I turn into my complex, zip into my parking spot, and grab my gym bag from the back. Glancing at my watch, I have exactly three hours to eat dinner, relax, and shower before we're heading out. Rounding the corner to head down the hallway to my apartment, I grind to a halt. Something is off, out of sync, but I can't immediately place it.

Trained to trust my instincts, I slowly step down the long hallway. Ten paces away, I notice the edge of a suitcase peeking out from the alcove at my doorway. Anxiety ratchets up another notch within me—unattended bags equal bombs in my experience. My brain immediately races through scenes of how many cars are out front, which of my neighbors could be home, and where the hell is Smith? The acrid taste of gunpowder and the smell of pure dirt mixed with iron dance on my senses. Fighting the urge to panic or hurl, I place my hand flat on the wall, stare at a palm tree swaying in the distance, and repeat in my head the mantra I've practiced so many times: *You're safe, you're home, you're in Florida. You're safe, you're home, you're in Florida.*

When we got back from our last deployment, mandated counseling was one of the many prizes we won. Tina, my therapist, taught me to deal with the flashbacks or triggers by focusing on an object and repeating words to affirm my safety. I fought her on it—hello, it's me, not a big fan of therapy or talking about my feelings. But it does help, not that I'd admit it to most people.

I take a few deep breaths to steady myself, then place one foot in front of the other to close the distance. My younger sister, Amy, is perched carefully on a duffel bag with a rolling suitcase in front of her.

What the fuck is going on?

"Aims, what's wrong, why are you here, what the hell?" I huff out at a rapid clip, anger laced in my voice where shock should be. "I thought, well . . . I thought . . . never mind." I almost tell her the suitcase triggered an episode of PTSD, stopping only because she doesn't know I still have these episodes in the first place. And even if she did know, explaining why something as benign as a suitcase could send me into one doesn't make sense even to me. There is no rhyme or reason to it. It's easier to leave it alone.

"I can't take it anymore, Will. Mom is unbearable . . . she treats me like a child. I can't find a job. Rob is a cheating asshole. I dumped his no-good sorry ass, by the way. Ugh! Can we please just go inside?" she pleads with me, water dangerously close to leaking from her eyes.

"Yeah, of course, let's go." I sigh, desperate to bring her back from the brink of tears.

What does this mean? Is she staying? For how long? Does she expect me to pay for her to live, I mean obviously I would, she's my baby sister, but this isn't how I saw my evening unfolding. Hell, I only have a one-bedroom apartment, and I can't force my little sister to sleep on the couch in her current state. How the hell did she even get to Florida without anyone knowing—wait does Mom know? Questions flood my mind like a tidal wave crashing into the coast.

"I know it's Friday, Will. If you have plans, you can just go and I'll crash here." Amy withers.

"Well, I was going to go out with Smith and the guys from our unit. I am not leaving you alone, but if you think you'd be up for some dancing . . . it could be fun." Smiling at her and wagging my eyebrows, I'm desperate to make her happy. There's no one else in this world I would subject myself to a night out at the country bar for, except Cam.

"Yes! Dancing sounds like exactly what I need. Is Butler going to be there?" Her cheeks turn a vibrant shade of pink as she hides her eyes under those long lashes.

"He will but you know my friends are off-limits. These aren't the kind of guys I want you to be anything more than friends with." Bristling at the thought of my sister, the one who used to skin her knees trying to keep up with me on the playground, dating one of my friends—not happening, ever.

I shoot off a text to Smith letting him know Aims is in town and we will need to change plans. Of course he responds with heart-eye emojis, furthering the churning in my stomach. Looks like I'll be spinning my sister around the floor tonight to keep the hounds at bay.

FOUR

Cam

"Miss Me More" – Kelsea Ballerini

nserting my key into the deadbolt, I grab the door handle and push it open, drinking in the sweet relief of being home early and one step closer to being braless. The microwave clock glowing in its emerald green shows the time is approaching eight. It's a shockingly early time to be home after a Friday at the salon. Fridays are typically chockful of last-minute walk-ins trying to squeeze in a blowout or fresh cut before the weekend.

Daveed is headlining a big hair show in Orlando this weekend and needed time to prep, so we closed early, even turning a few guests away. Shows like this are pretty standard for someone of his caliber, and he usually brings all of us along. There's something awe-inspiring about watching him dazzle a room full of people while his hands magically transform the model's look. This time, he left Micah and me behind, opting to break in the less experienced assistants, since we've both been

with him for nearly a year.

I should be jealous of the assistants who get to go, but I can't remember the last time I had a Saturday off. Three days of no work is music to my ears—minus the fact that I won't be making any tips, which is remarkably bad for my bank account.

Slinging off my purse, abandoning it on the table, and toeing off my flats, I plop down on the edge of the well-worn blue suede sofa. This thing has seen better days for sure. Lo says it's in style and fits our mid-century modern meets boho meets Goodwill style, since neither of us is exactly raking in the cash.

Our apartment is small, a boutique sort of place with two bedrooms, a living room, and a small kitchen in between. It's not fancy. The cabinets could use an upgrade since best-case they were installed in the eighties. Yellow Formica counters add a unique and funky "vintage" flair. Lo calls the apartment "dated chic." In other words, it's fucking old.

She's always able to pick out the best thing about a person or place, always able to see the silver lining, which is one of the many reasons I love her. Being overly optimistic doesn't come naturally to me. I'm more of a tell-it-like-it-is, goofy kind of girl, who's a little fun and a lot self-conscious. I suppose that wasn't always the case, but you know . . . a heartbreak and fifteen pounds will have an impact on a person.

I lean back into the couch, trying to get into the coziest part of the corner. I have absolutely zero intent on leaving this position for the foreseeable future. All weekend, I'm going to sit here, look at my phone, and try to find inspiration for the new-and-improved Cam. Daveed suggested I create a storyboard to hang in my room, he wants me to really lean into who I want to become. But that would require things like glue, poster paper . . . Ugh, who even has the time for that?

Raising my hand to no one at all in this empty room, I admit it's me, I do. I'm just too lazy and maybe a little too worried about putting something out in the universe that I'm not one-hundred-percent sure about. Trying to decide who I want to be when I'm not even crystal clear on who I am—well, that's proving to be extremely hard.

Finally settling into my comfy spot, I hear a key slide into the doorknob and sigh, knowing I need to prepare for battle. I swiftly roll my shoulders back and get ready to list the pros to my butt not leaving this seat for at least twenty-four hours. In strolls Lo.

"Oh good, you're home. How's my favorite shampoo girl?" she asks in that sarcastic but loving tone she uses when she's giving me a hard time, otherwise known as mocking my mother. It's her favorite pastime, ever since Patricia and I ran into her conning one of the neighbors into taking her trash out on move in day. My mother thought she was lazy. But I knew based off of a single eye roll that the roommate I had secured through some diligent online searching would soon become my best friend. Lo and my mom have a fantastic relationship now, she just loves teasing me.

"Yep, I'm home, in my spot, not leaving for at least twenty-four hours, maybe even forty-eight."

"What? You don't have to work tomorrow?" Lo eyes me wearily.

"Nope, Daveed is prepping for that show in Orlando, so he closed the salon. I'm officially off work for three days straight. I know, it's a miracle, right?"

"Umm, you know what this means don't you?" she asks with a charming and devilish spark in her eyes.

"Nope, no, nada. You're not dragging me anywhere. I'm sitting here and contemplating my reinvention for as long as it takes," I whine, sounding slightly less decisive than I had hoped.

Lo eyes me suspiciously, as if some sort of alien life-form has taken over her roommate. She could never sit still in one place for days on end, and she would definitely never contemplate reinventing herself.

She's adorable, confident, and everything I wish I could be. Lo is tall, five foot nine to be exact, and has legs for days. She has curves but is also thin enough to pull off any outfit. Her long, thick brown hair has the perfect bouncy waves that she doesn't even have to try for, and she's an expert at makeup and always knowing what outfit is best for which occasion. Essentially, she's the opposite of me.

I'm on the shorter side at five four, I have curves that are only getting bigger with my emotional eating habits, and blonde hair. I guess I do love my hair, it's long and also thick, but it takes a lot of work and frizzes easily. I could never just wash it and let it air-dry like Lo.

"No, no, no. Don't do that, I can tell that you got your hair done today, it's perfectly styled, has lighter pieces, practically moves when you're sitting still, has so much dimension. For once, we're both single ladies, and we both don't work tomorrow, so you know what that means." She points her finger at me in shame.

"You want me to scoot over so you can sit with me for the foreseeable future?" I guess, knowing it's not the answer she's looking for.

"Absolutely not. It means we're getting dolled up, dancing the night away, and shooting back tequila like the real women we are!" she exclaims, so loudly that I'm ninety-nine-percent sure she just told all of our neighbors we're hitting the streets tonight and they can feel free to rob us blind because we'll be too drunk to care. It's not that I don't want a night out, I adore a carefully curated girls' night. It's just that seeing Elliott this week, the date with Mr. Fish that led to the nightmare about Will, and having a long-ass day . . . I don't want to spoil her fun with my crappy mood.

Lo deserves a better wingwoman, someone who will instigate her shenanigans, not be the Debbie Downer in the corner sulking.

"Please do not make me beg," she pleads, her eyes full of mischief.

If I'm going to transform myself, I need to start now, with the little things. And it's not as if I had even a hint of an idea for this vision board . . .

"Okay fine, let's do it. But I'm borrowing your clothes and your new lipstick," I bargain.

"Yes, that's my girl." Her arms shoot up as a sign of her clear victory. "Let me just think about this for a second . . . first we will get ready, then do a couple of shots here, and then go dancing." Genuine glee sparkles in her eyes, silently mocking me over breaking my commitment to the couch.

"Where are we dancing, not downtown again right? The place we went last time was kind of lame."

"Nope, we're going to the Waterin' Hole, momma. I'm taking you back to your roots where you can shake it like the backwoods country girl you are." She wiggles her eyebrows at me.

"A country bar? In Tampa? Where?" It's unusual that I haven't heard anyone at the salon talking the place up, but then again, the other assistants aren't really the line-dancing types.

"It's actually on St. Pete Beach. It's a whole vibe, and here's the best part . . . the Uber is the same. The bar has a fifteen-dollar sink or swim, and I plan on sinking, babe. Let me just get you my shortest shorts, and you can wear that fitted lace crop top I bought you last week at the thrift store. Get them old shit kickers out, we're going to have the men begging us for a dance."

I giggle at her enthusiasm because if there's one thing Lo can always do, it's make things a party. I love dancing and country music is my jam. Maybe this is the exact thing I need to get back to being the real Cam, and I may even snag myself a cowboy to dance with.

I hop up from the couch, making my way into my room to find the top I've been commanded to wear. Spotting it stuffed in my underwear drawer, I quickly grab it and yank it on. There is very little room for my boobs, to the point where I'm forced to go braless. At least that's one win for the night!

The top is bright red like cherry lip gloss, fitted around my ribs, and ends just above my belly button. It almost looks like a swim top; the lace pattern and hint of sparkle really pop. I dig around to find my black boots and then run into the bathroom to give my legs a quick shave. A bit of bending, cursing, and strenuous jumping is required to plaster myself in Lo's black denim cutoff shorts. I'm a half a size bigger than she is, but these things do hold in the small pooch I've been earning through diligent donut eating. Who needs to breathe, am I right?

I curl my hair just slightly, touching up those perfect tousled waves, and smear on some black winged eyeliner to go with Lo's red matte lipstick. Grabbing my black crossbody, I shuffle into the kitchen just in time for Lo to hand me a double shot of tequila. "Here's to being a real woman who shoots tequila, has fun, and rides a cowboy tonight!" she bellows.

I clink my shot glass to Lo's toast and head out the door at her heels, already feeling better about my choice to follow her on this adventure and about getting back to the real me again. As cheesy as it may be, I've missed myself.

FIVE

Will

"I Remember You" – Skid Row

Gravel crunches under the tires of the Uber van we commandeered as Smith, Ruiz, and Butler yammer on to Amy about the Waterin' Hole.

"So it's like this, Amy. It's a country bar with line dancing, but it's also at the beach. You can spin around while listening to the musical sounds of the ocean, sweetheart." Smith smiles at her, making my instincts shout in discomfort.

"Yeah, yeah. That's enough. She might be dancing, but it won't be with any of you knuckleheads," I remind them with a warning and a look that could kill.

"Oh Will, I can handle myself." Amy pouts from her seat, squished between Ruiz and me in the middle row.

When we arrive, we pour out of the van, making our way to the end of the line. There must be fifty people waiting to get in. I sit on an

old wooden pylon, making myself comfortable as this might be a while. The guys continue asking Amy questions about how long she will be in town, where she is working, really all the things I want to know the answers to. But for some reason I can't pay attention. The air is buzzing with something I can't quite put my finger on.

My eyes are honed in on people pouring out of various car services, some heading to the line like respectable folks, others trying to butter up the security guards in hopes of skipping. I grumble to myself about the lack of respect for others. What makes some people think they deserve to go in while everyone else waits is beyond me. The entitlement of it all has always rubbed me the wrong way.

"Dammmnnn. Do you see that?" Smith knocks me on the shoulder to get my attention.

"See what?" I ask, looking around for whatever's caught his attention.

"That." He points at a gorgeous tall girl in cutoff shorts and a sparkly tank top. She looks almost out a movie with her brown hair swaying in the breeze, long sculpted tan legs shifting easily with each step. Of course she and her friend are heading right to the door, not caring for the line of suckers, including me, waiting patiently to get in. Her friend has a magnetism about her. Maybe it's the way her long blonde hair swishes back and forth or the sashaying of her hips. I can't stop staring.

"Do you need a rag?" Amy snarks, rolling her eyes at me.

"W-what?" I snap my head in her direction.

"For the drool, bonehead. You are staring like a creep." She swats her hand across the back of my head to emphasize just how blatantly dumb I am being in her eyes.

"Who are we talking about? Going to clue us in?" Butler asks, crossing his arms like he doesn't want to be the one left out of whatever revelation we're having.

"He's staring at that girl. The one with the brunette. It's disgusting . . . I can practically see his eyes popping out of his head," Amy huffs, crossing her arms. Nothing like a younger sibling to call you on your shit.

"Bro, this could be the one. Get over there and talk to her." Smith shoves me, trying to push me out of line and in the blonde's direction.

"No." One single word, emphatic and definitive.

"Why the hell not?" Ruiz looks at me like I've lost my mind. It's unfathomable that I would find someone physically attractive and not be hounding her for a chance.

"What good would that do? I don't do relationships, remember?" Shifting my eyes to the back of the line, I notice it is getting longer by the minute. We picked the wrong night to come, crowded places amplify my anxiety.

"So, let me get this straight. We are just supposed to sit here and act like it's not a big deal that this is the first time we've seen you go 'moon-eyed' over a girl?" Smith makes air quotes to emphasize how ridiculous he thinks I am being.

"Yep, pretty much. Nothing good could come out of us talking." I defend my actions despite the protest happening in my belly. My heart is thumping out of my chest. I haven't felt the spark or desire to even talk to someone in longer than I can remember. Why now?

"What are you so afraid of?" My sister throws her arms up in frustration.

"You . . . You know the answer to that, and do not make me go there." I point at her in frustration. Of all the people in the world, she should know we are the castaways. The ones who will never be enough, my sister and I. I've heard it a thousand times: If we hadn't made life so painfully dull, he wouldn't have sought out something more exciting.

"For fuck's sake. Is this about dad? You seriously still believe that if you had been more perfect he would have stayed? Or is it that you're afraid to commit and end up cheating? Both are bullshit, by the way." Amy is practically shouting at this point.

"Enough, the line is moving. We aren't here to worry about my love life or lack thereof. Let's stick to the plan and nurse your broken heart back to health, Aims." We shuffle forward, silence radiating from our group. I know the guys don't understand it, but they don't have to. I'm not willing to risk it. Logically, I know there isn't any proof that I would be like my dad, but is it really worth finding out? I tried dating when I first joined up. It went okay but I always found myself wondering when the other shoe would drop, when would they find out I'm not all they hoped and dreamed of. The first time I pictured my ex when hooking up with another woman, I called it. I won't lose another person I care for, and I won't become my dad, longing for something or someone else.

—

After what feels like forever, we finally make our way inside, beelining for the bar with our sink-or-swim wristbands. While I love country music, and being so close to the ocean is a vibe, the best part of coming to the Hole is their drinking program. Fifteen bucks for bottom-shelf liquor and Jell-O shots. It's honestly criminal how much they are giving away. They'll try to get you, though, always asking if you want an upgrade.

"What can I get you handsome?" a cute-enough redhead bartender wearing a shameless low-cut top shouts at me.

"Whiskey and ginger ale for me, a beer for the lady," I say, pointing at Amy to indicate who the beer's for before realizing how much it looks like we're on a date. See, terrible with women, case in point.

"You got it." She goes to work preparing our drinks as I spin to take in the sights. My eyes search for the parking lot blonde, but she's nowhere to be found. I don't have any business looking since I'm not prepared to make a move. A little peek never hurt though.

"Here you go," Miss Bartender shouts, shoving drinks across the bar in a hurry. I slide a few dollars toward her, grab the drinks, and follow in the direction that Amy headed, finding her circled up at a table with the guys and watching the dancing ensue.

"Will, let's dance." She tugs me toward the floor while the guys follow.

We make our way through a few songs, laughing and talking over the music like we do this every day. The guys are bad at line dancing but Smith is by far the worst. My man has zero rhythm. During "Watermelon Crawl," I tried to show him how to do the famous slide onto his belly . . . He's going to have a bruised face tomorrow.

"We're gonna head back to the table, get a couple drinks," Smith shouts to Amy and me. We start following them, but then the classic barn-dance music begins to play.

"Will, please do this with me. It reminds me of nights at Chuck's with mom." The barn dance is a traditional partner dance where you form a circle and do a couple of stomps, kicks, and spins before switching partners. Our mom used to take us to Chuck's Dancing Dive on Sundays for lessons. I hated it and Amy loved it.

"Fine, but only because I don't get to see you enough, and you supposedly have a broken heart." Grabbing her hand, I move us into position in the circle. "You're buying my next drink though." We shake on it and she laughs.

"Deal! Cheapest one I've ever made." Throwing her head back, she giggles harder.

"What do you mean? Oh right, the drinks are free." I wink and begin to stomp with the beat.

"Will, thanks for bringing me out. I know we need to talk, but maybe tomorrow? I'm having so much fun." I twirl her for the first time, preparing to switch partners on the next one.

"Yeah, of course. I'm glad you're here." The final spin commences and off she goes to the man next to me. He looks harmless enough, a portly man with classic Wranglers and a flannel so tight on his beer belly he might pop a button.

"Hey, I'm Brittany." My new partner smiles brightly, introducing herself. She's cute in a girl-next-door kind of way. I could flirt with her, maybe I should, but that damn blonde is stuck in my mind.

"Will," I say on a nod. We go through the motions without more conversation, my eyes trained on Amy to make sure she's not about to be paired with anyone unsavory. Also so I don't miss the chance to leave if she's done strolling down memory lane.

After a few partner switches, I'm ready to be done. A break on the patio overlooking the crashing waves is calling my name. Shifting slightly to the right, I crane my neck toward my sister in an attempt to get her attention, and I don't notice my next partner approaching.

A dainty hand slips gracefully into mine, sending electric sparks up my arm. Whipping my head toward the unsuspecting stranger as if I've been burned . . . I am beyond stunned. The parking lot blonde isn't a stranger at all. It's Cam. Sweat breaks out on my forehead and bile races up my throat with my nerves.

"W-wh-what are you doing here?" Her perfect pouty lips are painted cherry red, accentuating their bow shape. Words are difficult to form. How is this possible?

"I-I . . . How? This must be a joke," she stammers.

"N-not a joke. Last time I checked anyway," I retort.

"Of course I would move away to finally escape the memories, and *you* would be here. Been haunting me for years, for the love of Pete. Can't I get a break? Why is this happening?" Cam rambles, I think to herself but maybe to me. I'm powerless to stop the smile that whispers across my lips. I've always thought it was adorable how she could go on and on to no one and everyone at the same time.

"I live here. The question is why are you here?" I ask, not as smoothly as I would have hoped. Not that I'm trying to be smooth. I am definitely not desperate to win anyone over, and I'm absolutely lying about it.

She scoffs. "No. I live here. You can't! And do not grin at me, Rambo. Not even for a second."

"Not grinning, promise." I force my mouth to form the straightest line possible, but I can't help it if my dimple insists on popping. Did she just call me Rambo? "I can't not live here. This is where I work."

"Well . . . ugh! Well . . . work somewhere else." A small giggle bursts free. She's always had an uncanny ability to laugh at herself when she says something immature or ridiculously outrageous.

"Sorry, no can do. Looks like maybe you're following me, Wright." If she's going to call me an annoying nickname, I'm certainly going to call her one too. She hates her last name, and giving her shit is my favorite pastime. I shouldn't do it but it's too easy. Too familiar.

"I-I'm not following you! I'm over you. You know what, fine. Live here, be around, it's fine. I'm totally unbothered." She's swinging our joined hands to prove how not bothered she is, but has she noticed she's clutching onto me like her life depends on it?

Neither of us has let go, our fingers are still meshed together as if they were always meant to be. She couldn't have not noticed. I'm not mad about it, I've dreamed of linking my fingers just one more time with hers for years. But I realize I have to let go, nothing has changed.

I untangle myself from her, dropping her hand. Understanding smacks her in the face as she looks from her palm to my face and back again as if she has been burned. One more glance, a silky sheen to her striking green eyes, hits me before she's turning to run. I can feel the absence, the loss in my soul. This is why I can't go back. Less than a minute of touching her and my heart has shattered all over again. I didn't break one heart that day five years ago, I broke two.

SIX

Cam

"Fake Names" – Priscilla Block

The Uber turns bumpily into a gravel parking lot nestled into the very edge of St. Pete Beach as I get the first view of a large . . . barn? It seems out of place, not your typical beachy vibe, but I can tell from the people crowding out onto the sand that it's open air. It's nothing if not unique, I suppose. Lo reassured me the "vibes" are good and they have a sink-or-swim program where you pay a flat fee and drink all night. If for no other reason than I live for a bargain, I'm willing to give it a shot.

The line of people decked out in true "country" attire stretches all the way down the side of what looks to be your average red metal pole barn and wraps into the parking lot. The barn is a decent size, but I can't fathom what the interior will be like. Maybe my country upbringing is swaying my judgment, but I'm fully expecting to smell a mixture of animals and manure with a side of hay as I walk onto a dirt floor. Actually, that wouldn't be so bad, it would smell like coming home.

As we exit our ride, I start heading toward the end of the line, but Lo quickly grabs my arm. "Where are you going, Jessie? I know someone. We aren't waiting in line," she coos at me.

"Umm, Jessie? Are we doing that thing where we use fake names again?" I ask.

"Please don't tell me you forgot the rules, *Jessie*," she says, with an emphasis on my name for the night.

"Nope, I'm good. And who are you going to be tonight? Steph, Val, Angelica?" I quip, raising an eyebrow at her.

"I think I feel like a Steph tonight, it's the most down-to-earth and, honey, I'm hoping to rope me a big bull to ride," she whispers while wiggling her eyebrows.

"Dolly would be so proud," I say with a grin and a chuckle.

I can't with Lo—she always has a plan and she never fails to execute. Her idea of coming up with fake names came on suddenly, about two weeks after I moved in with her. We had gone out downtown to one of the dance clubs, and Lo accidentally gave her name and number to someone less than ideal, to put it mildly. Of course, she had deemed him perfectly acceptable with her beer goggles on. It took her the better part of a month, and a couple very awkward grocery run-ins, to ditch Mr. Clingy. From that point forward, she decided we needed rules.

Rule #1: Never reveal your real name until at least the third date/hookup.

I had inquired about how the gentlemen might feel when finding out we had blatantly lied about our identities, but Lo just brushed me off saying that if they were "the one," they would understand the importance of safety. Gentlemen aren't the cause for needing the rule in the first place.

Rule #2: Never accept a drink from anyone unless we saw the bartender pour it, and the person hands it directly to us.

Hands down, this is the most sensible rule of all three since there are a veritable number of creeps and assholes looking to drug you at any minute. If you don't believe me—give it time.

Rule #3: Never leave the other person behind. If you want to go home with someone, then you both go.

I actually understand this rule and yet still despise it. It's about safety, which I champion wholeheartedly. But based on the number of times I've had to hangout on strange couches waiting for Lo to finish banging some dude, it's not my favorite rule.

"Hello, earth to Jessie. Are you ready to go in, or are we going to stand here all night while you space the fuck out?" Lo asks, waving her hand in front of my face.

"Shit sorry, I was just reminding myself of the rules, Lo—Steph," I quickly self-correct.

Taking a deep breath, I follow her to the well-built doorman and watch as she charms him into letting us skip the line. I don't know how she does it, she swears it's all about the slight arm touch and eye contact but I'm one-hundred-percent confident if I tried it, I would end up at the back of the line or even worse, barred entrance completely.

We pay our fifteen dollars, get secured with purple wristbands that let the bartenders know we're free to drink as much bottom-shelf liquor as we can, and head toward the bar.

The interior is a lot nicer than I anticipated. There's a large bar to the left with pool tables and darts lined carefully in front of it and roll-up doors opening to a sprawling patio overlooking the ocean. To the right is a huge dance floor with a rail on three sides for people wanting to sit and watch and for dancers to have a place to put their drinks. Small bar tables skirt the walls around the dance floor, and there's a DJ booth at the very far end.

It's dark and I can't imagine it looks this nice with the lights on, but it feels decently clean and people appear to be having a great time. "Steph" and I get drinks, "Steph" opting for vodka and cranberry while I go with the standard whiskey and ginger ale. My mom was always a Seven and Seven drinker—you could say drinking whiskey is in my blood.

We make our way to the rail and take in the dance floor. It's chockful of girls who couldn't be a day older than twenty-one, all in their shortest shorts trying miserably to do the Boot Scootin' Boogie. If this was a competition for line dancing, it would be like taking candy from a baby.

I down my drink pretty quickly, and "Steph" says we should do a Jell-O syringe before heading out to dance. I'm not exactly sure what's in said syringe, but it's bright neon green and tastes like I'm going to hate myself in the morning.

The first couple chords of "Watermelon Crawl" drift out of the speakers, my cue to race onto the dance floor, pushing past a swath of military men-children on my way. I could do this dance in my sleep—even the move where you do a running slide down the floor on your belly and "crawl" provocatively. This is my dance and there's no way I'm missing it. Lo hollers that she'll be right there waiting for me when it's over. I grin at her, baring all my teeth. I hate to admit it, but she was right—I needed this.

Several songs pass in the blink of an eye, leaving me on top of the world and shamefully out of breath. Beginning my trek to the rail, I notice "Steph" has company. She's surrounded on all sides by the exact group of dudes I nearly ran over earlier. I'm sweaty, drops rolling down my back embarrassingly, but I feel exhilarated from shaking my booty on the dance floor.

As I make my way over, barn dance music drums out of the speakers. *Maybe I'll take one more little spin*, I think. I can't pass up a barn dance after years of doing it at family weddings, school dances, and too many Sundays at Chuck's. I spin around grabbing the hand of a very burly man named Earl for my partner. His name may not actually be Earl, but he looks like it is.

Partner after partner, I kick, stomp, and twirl my way around the floor. Spotting the next man up, I can't see his face. He's turned away, maybe looking for someone? But his body, chiseled arms that are threatening to rip his too tight T-shirt, thighs so thick they make mine look small in comparison . . . This is my type of man—the kind I would feel small standing next to.

I slide my fingers into his, heat zapping up my body and turning to warm liquid low in my belly. He turns his head and—you've got to be fucking kidding me. Of all the men in the world, why does it have to be this one. Will and I exchange a few words, mostly arguing over who has the better claim to live here. I don't notice I'm clutching his hand until he lets go. The loss of that callused, rough skin against my palm gives me pause and pisses me off in equal measure. I run.

"Hey, St-e-ph, we need to leave," I demand, trying but failing to catch my breath when I finally reach our table.

"Oh hey, Jessie. I was just telling these handsome men that you're the best line dancer I've ever seen and—wait did you say leave?" I grab at her hand but I'd swear her butt is super glued to the stool she's sitting on. She doesn't budge an inch.

I quickly brush my hair out of my face and try casually to dab sweat from my upper lip with the back of my hand. "Yes, I said we need to leave . . . let's go," I say, stomping my foot and pointing to the door just in case she hasn't gotten the message.

"Whoa. Where's the fire? Did someone do something? We do not let people get away with treating women improperly," A tall, dark, and handsome guy says, interjecting with his hero complex.

"No. No one did anything b-but we just need to go." I cross my arms, contemplating leaving my friend behind. It's not something I would normally do (see rule #3), but my heart is pounding out of my chest and I can feel the tears starting to bubble up along with the knot in my throat.

I feel him behind me before I see him. "She wants to leave because I'm here," Will grumbles, presumably to his friends.

"Oh. My. God. Cam? Is it really you? You look fantastic. It's been, like, what? A year?" Amy's saccharine voice fills my ears as she grabs my arm to spin me around and into a hug.

My cheeks blossom into a shade of dark pink, a classic sign that I'm embarrassed, and I thank my lucky stars that it's dark enough in here and I've been dancing, so it's not too obvious. "Urm sorry. Yeah, probably about a year, but Lo and I were just leaving."

"Who the hell is Lo?" *This guy again, get a life, dude.*

"So, funny story . . . we use fake names like for safety and stuff. It's a whole thing, but actually, I'm Lo. Nice to meet you," Lo dazzles him with her megawatt smile and a quick rub of his arm. Ugh, the way Lo can work a man over is honestly a sight to behold. "Let me just take Cameron here to the patio for a minute, we will be right back. Do not move, soldier." Lo points her finger in warning at Mr. Hero himself and grabs my arm, practically dragging me toward the sand. I guess she isn't super glued in place after all.

We find an open love seat facing the water, both plopping down on it with heavy sighs. I stare out at the waves lapping the beach, willing myself to get lost in the mesmerizing drumbeat of the ocean.

"Okay, what the hell is going on?" She grabs my hand, squeezing but not too hard. If this had to happen to me with anyone, I'm glad it's Lo.

"That was Will." Three words, all I can muster. I must be in shock.

"Who's Will again?" She has to be kidding, we've talked about him about a million times. Sometimes I swear, I love her but she listens as well as a third-grade boy.

"You know, my *ex*. The one that broke my heart after high school?" I shift nervously on the seat. It's weird seeing him again. I mean, physically—good gravy, he's matured in a good way. But emotionally . . . what's the word for simultaneously feeling so much and nothing at all for a person?

"Ohhh. That Will. Well . . . we've been talking about moving on, working on yourself. Maybe now is the time to prove to yourself you can be around him and survive it?"

"Lo! I don't know if I can. Not to mention my body isn't what it used to be, I'm barely scraping by financially. Do you really think it's a good idea to subject myself to that kind of judgment?" I groan into my hands, leaning forward and putting my head between my knees.

"Honey, I think this is exactly what you need to prove to yourself that you are strong. You need to go in there and have fun. Maybe flirt with a few of his friends and show him that you do not need him." She snaps her fingers side to side with sass and confidence. "Where's the girl from all the stories you've told me? The sassy smart alec that could throw bales of hay better than the boys and always had a comeback?"

"No, you're right. If Taylor can do it with a broken heart, I can do this. Or at least I will try, but we need a signal if it's not working. And don't leave me to flirt with that alpha-male model in there," I say, pointing at her in warning.

"Oh my gosh, he is beautiful, isn't he? I might be in love." Her eyes are practically filled with hearts as she jumps up, grabbing my hand to rush back in.

This is a no good, horribly bad idea. I'm either going to hate him or love him, and honestly I don't want to do either. Time to put my game face on.

We sweep back up to the table, Lo scooching in closer to the latest love of her life. I squeeze in between two other guys, who I presume are Will's friends.

"What's it gonna be, Wright? Am I staying or going?" Will asks, eyeing me across the table.

"Listen up, Rambo. I'm only gonna say it one time and I'm only allowing it because of those two." I give a nod and wink to Lo. "You stay in your lane and I'll stay in mine." I muster confidence and sass for the reply, but inside I'm frantically pushing down the many questions my favorite friend, the overthinker, is tossing at me.

"Did you just call me Rambo?" He shifts his shoulders a bit higher and there's a twinkle in his eye.

"Yep! Sure did. Got a problem with it?" Crossing my arms and cocking a hip out in my power stance, I look at him in challenge.

He doesn't respond, just shakes his head and takes a long pull of his drink. I hate that I notice the way his throat works the drink down. The bob of his Adam's apple is infuriatingly seductive.

Turning to his friend, a tall blond drink of water who's a bit leaner than the others, I ask, "Want to dance, soldier"?

He looks at me, then at Will. Will shrugs nonchalantly, so he grabs my hand and off we go. It bugs me that Will was so casual about it. Guess I'll have to flirt harder with this new guy. Actually, no. I do not care one bit if Will cares or not. He broke my heart for no good reason and that's that.

SEVEN

Will

"Lonely Boy" - The Black Keys

Last night was interesting. Not only did my baby sister show up at my door unexpectedly, Cam danced right back into my life. Well, sorta. I wouldn't say she's in my life exactly, but we managed to be around each other for the better part of two hours.

The longest two hours of my life, and I spent them watching her flirt and fawn over Butler. *That schmuck.* We need to have a little chat about who's off-limits when it comes to dating in our friend group. Not that I have any right to stake a claim, but I've never not considered her mine after all we went through together. I pull up the guys' group text and see I've already missed an alarming number of messages.

SMITH

Yoooo, so I'll say it again. Last night was weird.

RUIZ

It's like a bad joke. Three hot girls walk into a club, Davenport walks in, and none of us get laid.

BUTLER

Your joke needs some work but I have to say, you're a damn fool, Davenport. That girl is special, man. I'm kinda pissed that she's off-limits.

SMITH

Remind me to show all you morons photos of my exes in case we ever end up in this situation again! I still can't believe you didn't recognize her in the parking lot.

RUIZ

I'm impressed you didn't throw out your man card, Butler. I'd have thought about it . . . wait Smith . . . you have exes?

SMITH

STFU, you know I have exes. I think we have one in common, Ruiz!

RUIZ

Don't remind me, at least I dated her first and not the other way around.

SMITH

👮👮👮 Seriously, we need a list. With photos so everyone knows who is fair game and so no one can sneak up on us.

WILL

Fuck you, Ruiz!

SMITH

Bro . . . seriously though, what are you
doing letting her get away?

WILL

Why do I have to keep repeating
myself? I don't date, not even Cam.

BUTLER

Based on last night . . . it doesn't look
like that's going to change anytime soon.
She looked like she was going to chop
your balls off and feed them to you for
breakfast.

WILL

Exactly! This is why I don't
do relationships . . .

SMITH

Well I do! I think I'm in love with Lo.

WILL

Of course you are! It doesn't take much.

SMITH

Would you prefer I date your sister?

WILL

Fuck you!

****DAVENPORT LEAVES THE GROUP CHAT****

****SMITH ADDS DAVENPORT TO THE GROUP CHAT****

SMITH

It was a joke, Willy! Come back to us! 🖤

"Um, are you going to wake up sometime today? I want—no, *need* food, like, right now or I'm going to start crying," Amy threatens weakly.

"Ugh, fine, it's not like I slept well anyway, what with an unexpected houseguest and the ghosts of girlfriends past haunting my dreams," I reply, my voice full of sarcasm.

"Will! I offered to take the couch. It's not my fault you insisted on being a gentleman and letting your baby sister have the bed. It was comfortable though." Amy throws a pair of rolled up socks at my head just like she used to when making me get up for school.

"Alright, alright. I'm up. You want to tell me why you're here now or should we eat first?" I ask, raising my eyebrow in challenge. I want to know the details, but I secretly hope she picks food first.

"Definitely food. Let's go to that one place . . . what's it called?" Twirling her hair, she's looking hard at me, as if she gave me any context at all. "You know . . . the one on the beach with the sandwiches and salads."

"Sal's?" I ask.

"Yeah, well, I think. Is that the one with the picnic tables in the sand?" Her eyes glisten with hope.

"Yep, let's go. They have the best double chocolate peanut butter cake in the world." My mouth is watering just thinking about it.

I quickly head into the bedroom, grab a change of clothes, and swiftly make my way to the bathroom. The shower spray is not hot, but it's warm enough for me to feel like I'm washing away the shock of yesterday. My sister showing up as a surprise isn't a bad thing, but I'm worried about our mom. I'd rather see my sister run off into the sunset with Smith than see my mom upset. I need Amy to call her and explain where she is today, if we accomplish nothing else. I rinse off and get changed quickly because that cake is calling my name.

—

Walking into Sal's is like walking into any classic deli you could stumble into in Brooklyn, except this one's right on the beach. The inside is plain with white walls and green tablecloths. A chalkboard sign lists the various sandwich and side options, while a cooling case displays an array of delicious treats.

"What should I get? You know I'm picky." My sister shifts from one foot to the other.

"Well, I have tried almost everything on the menu, but the classic turkey on pumpernickel is their most popular. That's what I'm getting. Oh, and dill potato salad, chips, and a slice of the cake."

Amy's eyebrows shoot into her hairline at my list of lunch items. "Okay, well . . . just order me the same. We can always bring the leftovers home."

I can't help the scoff that sneaks out; she's nuts if she thinks I'm not going to savor every single bite. I work out hard so I can eat what I want. I place our order, grab a number, and lead us out to a picnic table to wait. Burying my feet in the sand and moving my hat backward, I look at my sister, waiting for her to spill the beans.

"Sooo . . . are you going to tell me what you're doing in Florida?" I ask after what feels like an eternity of silence.

"I just thought it would be nice to spend some time with you. The teaching market is better in Florida because there are so many more openings than in Iowa. Oh, and also that shithead doesn't live here, but that remarkably hot group of friends you have do." She smirks, knowing she's going to get a rise out of me with that declaration.

"Ha. Very funny. No, but for real. What's the plan, Aim?"

"You're looking like Dad does when he's disappointed in me." She scoffs.

"Yeah, Aims, I am. Because you don't just fly cross-country with no plan, no job, and no Mom. It's not what we do," I reprimand her.

"O-kay, I know it looks bad, Will, but the truth is I've been thinking about it for a while. I needed to get away, start fresh, and I knew you would never turn me out on the streets. Finding a job is hard, and it's even harder when you have Mom meddling in everything. I know she means well, but the pressure and Pinterest boards she's using to mold me into the world's best teacher are too much. Also, it's an adventure. I don't have a plan; I just know that I couldn't stay there and I wanted to be here with you. I think if you admit it, you might enjoy having someone around since you're not exactly occupied, you seem lonely since . . . well, since Thatch." She folds her hands together then unfolds them, putting them under the table, clearly worried that she hit a nerve.

I'd love to say her assessment is wrong, but deep down I don't think it is. I'm surprised she brought up Thatch, she knows I don't like talking about him. She's also right in that I would like to have someone to hang out with other than the guys.

"Have you looked for a job?" I ask, right as a young kid dressed in all white and wearing a hairnet delivers our feast.

"Actually, I have an interview on Tuesday for a first-grade position in Tampa and an interview on Wednesday for a kindergarten one in St. Pete."

"Wow, that's great! Okay, sooo if you get a job, you will be here at least a year, and I assume you're willing to pay toward rent and shit you need?" I ask around a bite of my sandwich. Lettuce falls out of my mouth in a very unattractive way.

Amy, on the other hand, chews gracefully before answering, "Of course! I'm an adult . . . I would never make you pay my way . . . Please, Will, I don't want to find another roommate in a new city. Can I move in with you?" She's giving me puppy dog eyes. I've always been helpless against her puppy dog eyes. She knows it and has been using them against me for as long as I can remember.

"Fine, I guess you can stay, but I have conditions. First, you have to help pay the bills. Second, you have to tell mom *today*. And third but most importantly, you are not dating my friends."

I can tell she's relieved by the way she quickly agrees. I noticed her smile faltered a little when I said no dating my friends, but she will respect my rules or I will make her move out. Call me overprotective, but the last thing I need is Smith telling me all the ways he plans to bang my sister. Believe me, he would be relentless.

"Oh, and Aims, there's something you should know . . . I may be heading out soon, overseas. It's not set in stone, and I don't know when it will be or for how long, but it's coming and soon." Her smile dims, but she needs to know the truth. This is my job and it's not all sunshine and piña coladas on the beach.

"Geez, Rambo. Eating for two?" I look up from lovingly gazing at my potato salad to see Cam and Lo in their pajamas and carrying a to-go bag.

"Hey, Wright, forget to get dressed this morning?"

Cam rolls her eyes and pulls her sunglasses down from where they were pushing her hair back. "Actually, this is our tradition. We go out, drink our faces off, and go eat Sal's on the beach in our jammies the next morning." Lo scoffs, as if I should have known that it's normal for friends to be sporting matching pink flamingo pajama pants and turquoise tank tops out in public.

"I think that sounds so fun," Amy coos.

"It's interesting, I'll give ya that." I smirk at the ladies, not saying that I find it incredibly endearing. But what about Cam isn't. She's always had a way of disarming people with her charm.

"We aren't seeking your approval, Rambo. We just noticed your massive quantity of food, and I couldn't stop myself from commenting." Cam crosses her arms and turns to leave.

"Whatever you have to tell yourself, Wright. I'm flattered that you wanted to talk to me." That's it, I'll get the last word just for fun. It irritates me how little I seem to affect her, and I can't help but wonder if maybe she really did move on.

Cam and Lo leave as I begin my foray back into my potato salad. Damn, it really is so good. Simple, just potatoes, celery, mayo, and dill.

"Okay, what the fuck was that?" Amy sets her fork down and places both hands on the table, leaning forward.

"Wha-was-wha?" I ask, mouth full of a huge bite.

"You like her. It's so obvious. But why do you keep saying you don't date when the guys or I bring it up?" She's picked up her fork again and is pointing it at me like she's deciding if she should eat with it or stab me.

"I-I just can't," I say, shrugging noncommittally.

"Bullshit. That's utter grade A genuine cow doodoo. And you know it. The way I see it, you've got two choices. You either tell me and let me help you, or you die alone, a miserable sad sack."

"Option B." I pop the top on the cake's plastic container, preparing to dive into my final course.

"Nope. It was a trick question, I would never let you die alone, so option A it is. Start talking or I'm not letting you have this cake." Amy slams her hand down on the container, a force to be reckoned with if I want the sweet, salty hint of heaven.

"Fine. What do you want to know? This better not leave this table, either." I give in, glaring at her.

"Why did you really break up?"

"Ugh . . . not starting easy on me. It was complicated. Cam swooped in right around the time Mom and Dad split up. I was angry and lost but instead of letting me piss my life away, she bulldozed her way in and made me want to be better." Amy's looking at me with the tell-me-something-I-don't-know face, but I continue anyway. "It wasn't just that she was nice or pretty. It was the way I felt when I was around her. Like she was the sun, and for a minute I had a chance to touch that light. The way she could make me laugh, could get me to talk out the hard stuff. She didn't just tell me she loved me, she made me feel it. Believe it. I knew when I decided to join up that I was letting her down by leaving. I couldn't stand the thought of facing her disappointment, couldn't watch her cry every time I had to say goodbye if we did the long-distance thing. I would have ruined her life." Amy's mouth is hanging open and there are tears pooling in the corners of her eyes.

"So instead of feeling like you were a constant disappointment, the way Dad always made us feel, you ended it. Am I getting this right?" she asks, disbelief etched on her face as she chews her bottom lip.

"Yeah." I put my head in my hands, pressing the base of my palms into my eyes to chase away any emotion that may want to leak out.

"You really are a bonehead. You ran when it got hard. You were so afraid of making her feel like you did when Dad left, but you did exactly what he would have." I can tell she's disappointed, finally learning the truth I've known—I am just like our dear old dad.

"At the time, I guess so. But I did her a favor. Amy, my life, as a soldier, it's not easy. I'm gone at a moment's notice. I could never give her the life she deserves." Bri pops into my head, and all that she's had to endure with Thatch. It's not the kind of life that I could easily bring someone as good and pure as Cam into. The things I've seen would ruin her, they've ruined me.

"And what about what you deserve, Will?" Amy's ready for a fight now, face pinched in defiance.

"Look, I know you don't understand, but I-I just can't. I will always love her, but I can't hurt her more than I already have. And with losing Thatch, I can't risk letting myself fall just to lose her too when she gets sick of it."

"So this is about fear. You're afraid. Well that . . . that's something I can fix." Amy stands and takes our trash to the bin, returning to grab the two uneaten slices of cake and me. "Let's go, Will. I've got work to do."

EIGHT

Cam

"Brave" - Sara Bareilles

Waking up this morning, I am questioning all my life choices. My pillow has lumps in all the wrong places, I'm slightly nauseous, and last night is coming back to me in a slow rolling haze—the kind that reminds me of those pictures you see of places overseas where fog dances on cliffs. If my memories were cliffs, they'd be leading to things I probably don't want to remember, but the fog is just enough for me to pretend I don't, at least for a few more minutes.

My phone vibrates on the nightstand. *Who the hell thinks it's acceptable to call me at this hour?* I roll over, picking it up with a groggy hello.

"Camerooni! Guess what?" My brother's voice is far too chipper for . . . Shit, it's ten thirty already. I guess it's not a completely unacceptable time to be calling.

"W-what?" I clear my throat as I ask, rubbing sleep and yesterday's mascara out of my eyes.

"I'm coming back next weekend. Make room on your couch. I fly in Friday and decided to stay until Sunday, so we can hang out. I expect debauchery."

"El, that's great. I can't wait to see you." My reaction falls flat. I can hear it in my tone and hope he doesn't notice.

"What happened?" My brother groans on the other line. He knows me better than I wish he did.

"N-nothing. I'm half awake." I will deny that my world was rocked last night.

"Do not even think about lying to me, Cameron Jane. I know better. What is wrong with you?"

"Erm . . . fine. So Lo and I went dancing last night—"

"What kind of dancing? Did you meet someone? Tell me you finally met someone." I can tell by his interruption that he's intrigued.

"Elliott. Quit talking over me if you insist on forcing me to spill the beans," I reprimand him because come on, dude. I'm about to tell him the biggest thing that has happened since the one time Dad's prized bull got caught sneaking in to "visit" the mares in our farm's other barn, and he won't even let me get it out. "We went to this country bar on the beach. Everything was fine until I stupidly decided to do the barn dance, you know for nostalgia's sake."

"Oh no. Did you get paired with someone who didn't know the moves? The horror." He is mocking me.

"El, shut up. No, my partner knew the moves, that wasn't the problem. The problem is it was . . . it was Will." Silence. Pure, unadulterated, anxiety-riddled silence.

"What? You are fucking with me." I can't even say I blame him for not believing me. I think I'm still in shock too.

"No, unfortunately, I'm not. I didn't recognize him at first since he had his head turned away from me, but yeah. It was him."

"What did you do? Do not tell me you got back with him." I can hear him rifling around in the background, probably settling in for me to drop a juicy bomb on him.

"No! Of course not. I freaked out and ran away. Well, sorta." I sit up in bed, crossing my legs into a pretzel and punching the pillow to prop it up against the headboard with my free hand.

"What does 'sorta' mean?" I can tell he's up and pacing, I can hear him practically burning a hole in his apartment carpet.

"Well . . . Lo had been hanging out with his friends, not that she knew it at the time. So when I ran to her and demanded to leave, she dragged my ass to the patio and convinced me to stay. To not let him ruin my night with his presence because, and I'm sure you will appreciate this part, according to Lo, I've let him dictate my life for far too long." I huff out the last part. I don't necessarily agree that I've let Will control what I do, but if I'm really being honest, some of my decisions have been made by trying to try to eradicate him from my life.

"Good. I'm glad you didn't run . . . well, not completely anyway. You are the best thing that ever happened to him. I hope that he sat back and suffered, watching you have fun. Please tell me you flirted with his friends."

I snort laughing. "I did. I can't believe it, but I did. I went into full sass mode. Mom would have been horrified with my behavior."

"Fuck yes! And you know what, Mom loves you but she hasn't quite figured out how to marry her sense of duty with her ability to let loose. That's not on you." His reassurance has always comforted me when it comes to my mother-daughter relationship. My mom is really the best, it's not like she denied us love or anything. She just has strong values, and when we don't uphold them . . . well, she can be a bit judgy.

"Thanks, El. I mean it. I don't know if I have really processed everything yet, considering I was asleep before you called. But I think I'm actually okay." Bile nips at my throat, either from far too many drinks or the thought of Will living in the same town as me. Probably both.

"I love you. I'll see you in six days, and I mean it when I say, plan something fun. We are not sitting in your apartment all weekend." Elliott hangs up and I flop back onto my pillow, desperate for water—and a time machine to go back and skip last night. Well, one part of it anyway.

I can't figure out what bothers me more about seeing Will again. Is it the fact that I still have feelings for him, or is it that he saw me when I'm not feeling like my best self? It's not feelings, I decide. I mean, I will always care for him, I thought he was the love of my life. I just wish I had run into him after I lost the weight I've gained, after I had my own chair at the salon and a whole gaggle of clients waiting to sit in it.

Screw it. Monday I'm hitting the gym. I'm anti-workout. (I've always maintained that if I'm running, those around me should be too because something is trying to kill me.) Nevertheless, I can't continue on this way. I have to get my life in order, not because of Will, but in spite of him.

"How are you doing, sunshine?" Lo inquires while holding out a mug of steaming hot coffee. I didn't even see her come in. The girl would make a fierce cat burglar.

"I-I'm okay. I think." Shrugging, I shift to sit up again and take the mug.

"Want to talk about it?" Lo levels me with a look while plopping down on my blush-rose down comforter, sloshing hot coffee over the edge of my mug. I can't even be mad—caffeine is the only thing saving my ass this morning.

"Ughhh . . . fine. I was just thinking that if I had to see him again, I wish I was in a better place, physically and career wise. I absolutely am not ever getting naked in front of that man, or really any man, until I lose these fifteen pounds." I admit my feelings to her cautiously, knowing she will reprimand me the minute the words leave my lips.

"You went from 'I hate him' to 'naked' real quick, my friend. But you're joking, right? Cam, so you have a dump truck and more than a handful up top—you have a banging body, any man would be honored to see it clothed or otherwise." Lo's face is a mix of pinched annoyance and shock that I would think of myself so negatively.

"Okay, thanks, hype girl," I say, rolling my eyes. "But I'm being honest with myself, and I know I don't look like I used to. I've been binging too much, making unhealthy choices, and now I'm paying the price. It's karma really." I'm attempting to mask my vulnerability, but I know it comes off a bit rude.

"Nope, we're not doing this. You're getting your ass up out of this bed, we're going to Sal's, and then shopping. Put on your pj's, grab a change of clothes, and let's roll," Lo says this with such confidence, I'm forced to drop the argument that's begging to burst off my tongue.

Thirty minutes later, we're walking into Sal's just before the lunch rush. It's our little tradition: grab the world's best deli sandwiches and potato salad to soak up any remnants of last night's overindulging, and eat on the beach. We always wear matching pajamas—well, ever since the one time I picked up Lo from the side of the road on a walk of shame, and a pajama set of pants adorned with pink flamingos and a turquoise tank top my mother sent me was the only non-club attire in my car. It was hilarious and Patricia was delighted when we called to ask for another.

Lo and I order quickly at the counter, grabbing our to-go bag and heading toward the beach. I don't spot him immediately, but there's an uncanny shift in the air and my stomach knows before my eyes do. I glance around, sure enough, there's Will at a picnic table, toes buried in the sand, with Amy and enough food to feed ten people sitting in front of him. I shouldn't approach, but on second thought, why should I have to pretend he doesn't exist? Somehow we have managed to not run into each other in the year I've been living here, but it seems that my luck has run out.

"Geez, Rambo. Eating for two?" I ask, infusing my face with judgment despite the fact that I notice I've ordered the exact same lunch, minus the cake.

"Hey, Wright, forget to get dressed this morning?" he quips, a smirk blossoming on that smug, incredibly chiseled face. It irritates me beyond belief that he's calling me by my last name. He knows how much I hate it after the relentless jokes spewed in high school about how Cameron always has to do the "Wright" thing. Sue me for being a rule follower.

"Actually, this is our tradition. We go out, drink our faces off, and go eat Sal's on the beach in our jammies the next morning." Lo scoffs, she doesn't take kindly to anyone commenting on our attire. She's feisty at times, but this . . . this could actually work in my favor if I want her to be annoyed by him.

"I think that sounds so fun," Amy coos.

"It's interesting, I'll give ya that," Will says. I want to smack the smirk right off his stupid face.

"We aren't seeking your approval, Rambo. We just noticed your massive quantity of food, and I couldn't stop myself from commenting." I cross my arms and spin on the back of my heel, starting to walk away. I definitely don't think about putting an extra shimmy into my steps.

"Whatever you have to tell yourself, Wright. I'm flattered that you wanted to talk to me," I hear him call out after us. Ugh . . . he's the worst.

We find a spot about a five-minute walk down the beach, fanning out our beach towels just a few feet in front of a large swath of sea oats where the white sand is fluffy and undisturbed. Lo hasn't commented yet on why I walked over to Will, but I know it's coming.

"Sooo . . . were we looking for a fight this morning? What was the point of riling him up?" Lo asks around a bite of her Reuben sandwich.

"Honestly"—I huff out a long breath, taking a swig of my Diet Coke—"I just couldn't stop myself. There's something about giving him a hard time that feels too good to pass up."

"It felt like the feeling was mutual. You know . . . it's kind of poetic that you two are reuniting after all this time. Maybe it's fate." She fiddles with her hair, putting it up into a messy bun then taking it down again, refusing to make eye contact.

"It is not fate. It's a curse. Do you know how long I spent wondering what happened to him? If he was okay, why he did what he did, all of those things you aren't supposed to think about when you get dumped. It's actually kind of cruel that he's suddenly here and messing with my head again," I say, defending myself. I'm actually a little mad that she would even suggest this is some *Romeo and Juliet*, star-crossed-lovers bullshit.

"Look, you might not like it, or at least not want to admit it. But there was something special there between you two, or else you wouldn't have hung on for so long. The reality is, we had fun with that group of guys last night. I mean Smith . . . come to momma. If you are living in the same town, odds are you might run into each other again, and your going to need to figure out how you are going to deal with it. Do you go on hating him, be friends, or maybe something more?" She's wiggling her eyebrows at me, clearly not grasping the magnitude of all my pain.

"Hate, I choose hate. But because I'm the world's best friend, I won't stop you from pursuing your man. Just please don't force me to be around Will any more than is necessary. I can only keep from losing my shit for so long." Do I think she is being a little selfish, putting her needs before mine? Yeah, I do. But I love her, and I would feel bad about coming in between someone else's happily ever after. I'll just have to find a way to power through it if things work out between Lo and Smith.

—

After finishing our food and changing in the public beach bathroom, Lo and I shopped all day long. That girl gives new meaning to the phrase "shop 'til you drop." I think I modeled no less than seventy-five outfits, and I truly did come away with some remarkably smokin' choices. Most of them are not practical for daily use, but if I'm going to be getting back out there, then I need to freshen up my look. And that's the plan, I will be getting back out there despite my ex being back in my life.

My inner feminist is most excited about the lingerie I picked out. Something about wearing a little lace under your clothes gives you an extra sense of confidence. My mother always said your bra and panties must match because you never know when you might end up in the emergency room needing your clothes cut off, and there would be nothing more embarrassing than an orange bra and green panties underneath. Not that I'm delusional enough to believe your run-of-the-mill first responder would be truly comparing my skivvies to the next patient's, but I do love romance novels and crazier things have happened.

I suppose Patricia would be pleased to know that tonight I'm going out with a matching plum lace set, the bra practically playing peekaboo with my nipples, and I feel luscious in a good way wearing it. Smith invited Lo to a party at his apartment. Because of her rules and general ability to throw an immature temper tantrum when denied something, I'm going with her. For safety's sake, so she claims.

I opt to wear a flowy black sundress that hits just above my knees. It has thin spaghetti straps and the lace bra peeks out just a bit. Hey, there's absolutely nothing in the rule book about not dressing cute if your ex is potentially going to be somewhere. In fact, I think the saying is, "dressed to kill." I finish adding a quick bend to my hair so it's in those perfect tousled waves again, then I throw on some gold hoops and a smidge of my perfect lipstick shade, Saucy Mauve.

When I finish dolling myself up, I find Lo waiting not so patiently by the front door. How this woman gets dressed so quickly remains a mystery to me. She side-eyes me, her annoyance at my extended primping obvious. Shrugging off her attitude, I grab her hand, leading us out of the apartment and into our Uber. I'm not at all sure what to expect at Smith's. I know based on the address it's an apartment, but how does a single military man decorate? Should I expect total frat house vibes, or is Smith more sophisticated with actual furniture and décor?

The ride doesn't take long and Lo gives me a pep talk, citing things like my vivacious curves, killer lips, and hair that makes grown men weep. She's laying it on thick, and I don't believe most of what she says, but I appreciate the effort she's making to boost my confidence. Especially after she was annoyed with me for taking so long to get ready.

I can hear the music bumping as we approach the apartment; nerves turn my stomach. I suck in deep breaths and roll my shoulders back as Lo knocks on the door. Smith opens it, greeting her with a, "Hey, baby girl, so glad you could make it." She quickly responds with, "We wouldn't have missed it." To be clear, I absolutely would have missed it if she hadn't demanded my attendance.

We step inside and are greeted by a myriad of top ten terrorist posters littered with bullet holes adorning the walls, a cheap red futon that's seen better days, a TV on a cardboard box playing "Gin and Juice" by none other than Snoop Dogg himself, and a huge beer pong table. Honestly, I don't know what's worse: this place or a frat house. Either way, it's cliché as hell and reminds me exactly why I was avoiding the Rambos of the world.

At least it doesn't smell like vomit or stale beer. Smith has a single candle burning in the center of his kitchen island. The scent of vanilla cupcakes wafts into the air with each flick of the flame. *Why does this man own a candle when his décor style screams give me a tent and a gun?* I exchange hesitant looks with Lo in which I subliminally ask her if we should go, and she darts back at me a, *Hell no, you're staying* rebuttal. I am grateful for our ability to silently communicate except that she doesn't seem to understand the messages I am desperately shooting in her direction.

To think I was worried about seeing Will when in reality, I may need a blackout sleep mask to shield myself from the prying eyes of the terrorists dancing on the walls. *What the heck did I get myself into?* My anxiety spiral is interrupted when a firm arm wraps around my waist, pulling me into a side hug. "Hey, Cam, I'm so glad you came. Between us, I wouldn't have if I was you," Butler whispers to me as if we are conspiring partners about to unleash our evil plan. I like this one, he's a good egg.

"Heyyy, I wasn't going to miss a chance to see you again," I say, hopefully sounding a lot more at ease than I feel. *That's it, Cam. You're doing this.*

"You ladies want to play beer pong? Butler and I are reigning champs, but we can take it easy on you," Smith breaks in.

Okay, I can work with this. Will doesn't appear to be here, and they have zero idea just how competitive I am or how often Elliott and I used to practice playing with cups of Kool-Aid in the backyard just so we could beat everyone when we left for college. What can I say? Preparation is the key to success.

"You're on! Just please don't take it easy on me. A girl has to learn somehow, and watching the masters is the best way, don't ya think?" I reply, smirking at Lo.

Smith works on setting up the beer pong table while Lo and I quietly strategize about how we're going to let them think they're winning and then quickly take them down after we've each had three cups of beer. There's no world where I would allow anyone else to win without it being absolutely fair and square, but we're trying to get a little buzzed and we want them to believe it's beginner's luck.

The game gets going and our strategy is working even better than predicted. Who knew I could actually be pretty good at acting innocent and ditzy? I'm sure the blonde hair helps my cause. Butler sinks a ball in the cup closest to me, and I'm picking it up to drink when there's a knock at the door. Smith excuses himself, telling us he'll be right back and that I have to wait to drink because he doesn't want to miss it. Like I would need to cheat to win? Yeah, in his dreams!

I'm holding the cup firmly in my right hand, flirting a bit with Butler because it's fun and I can, when I hear Amy. I guess I'm not getting out of seeing the Davenports after all. Lucky me. This whole thing would be far less annoying if Will had gotten worse looking with age. Why can't he be like the other guys that we went to school with who I've seen back home, you know with beer guts and bad facial hair that grows in a little spotty.

No, instead he's sculpted like a Greek god. Think Thor swinging his hammer around. The muscles in his shoulders and arms are just begging to bust through his too-tight black T-shirt, and his brown hair is cut short but still long enough to be curly on top. Those perfectly coiffed ringlets that I used to love wrapping my finger around taunt me.

My gaze meets his against my will, and I'm struck still by those piercing blue eyes. They're the color of the sky on the bluest and most clear day, utterly mesmerizing. I could get lost in them for days and not even care about life passing me by. Except, wait—is he glowering at me? *I don't think so, buddy.*

"Wright, fancy seeing you here . . . with my friends." His comment lands with a thud. Oh, did he think this was his territory? Are we about to get in a pissing match over who is allowed to be here?

"I was invited, Rambo. Cool your jets and get a drink. If I'm not letting it bother me, then I don't see why you would." I down the cup of beer that I needed to drink for the game, tossing it gently onto a camping chair where all the other empties have gone to die.

"Oh, it's not bothering me. Just surprised to see you twice in one day. It's almost like you can't help but be around me at this point." He gives me that irritating lopsided grin, lifting one shoulder to shrug, and turns toward the kitchen, presumably to get a drink.

"Alright, ready to continue," Smith says, rejoining us at the beer pong table.

"She's hustling you, Smith. She knows how to play." Will's shout comes from across the room, causing Butler and Smith to eye Lo and me suspiciously while Amy takes off stomping toward her brother. *You go, girl. Tell him he's being an asshat.*

"Does it look like I'm hustling you?" I point to the even number of cups on the table to dissuade them from believing the truth Will can't seem to help himself from spilling. I roll my eyes at Will in annoyance. This is the side of Will I hate to love, he doesn't let me get away with any crap. Not in a controlling way, but when I was with him before,

I wanted to be better. Be less petty, less of an overthinker, and more open, more honest, more willing to show love. He made me feel proud to be who I was, not who my mother, or anyone else for that matter, wanted me to be.

Butler and Smith shrug and the game continues. The game that I am most definitely hustling them at. I feel icky inside. Like my own personal judge is sitting in the other room looking on at my behavior, knowing I'm only here to support my friend, that I am once again letting people talk me into doing things that I don't want to do just because I want their approval. Ughhh . . . . it's going to be a long night.

NINE

Cam

"Poker Face" - Lady GaGa

"**C**am, can you mix two scoops of lightener with twenty volume color developer for me please?" Daveed asks from across the color bar as he scrapes the bottom of a very empty bowl for his next foil. We are going on our third day of back-to-back color clients, and the exhaustion is settling into my bones.

"Coming right up," I call, grabbing the tub of bleach and bottle of developer to begin my task. This is par for the course with assistant life, always being at the ready and waiting to give Daveed anything he needs. Sometimes I'm pulling and tearing foils, shampooing a guest, or even occasionally doing a blowout. I'm ready for the next step though.

I walk across the room to where he is waiting patiently, handing him the color bowl and standing back to appreciate the finesse with which he slices and weaves this bombshell blonde. Doing hair is not as easy as the home color commercials make it seem. There's an art to

it, knowing the angles and where the shadows would naturally be cast from sunlight. It's easy to mess up, but I've been doing this for almost a year, and I've honed my skills on more mannequin heads than it should be legal to possess.

I start to walk away, off to check the towels and brushes, but Daveed calls out once more. "Cam, I'm almost finished here. Why don't you grab Micah and meet me out back." There's a seriousness in his voice, and I can't tell if I should be worried or excited.

I swipe a few empty bowls and nod at Micah to meet me in the galley on my way out. He stumbles in before I can even dump the bowls in the sink, the door nearly taking him out on the back swing.

"What's happening? You never nod at me. What do you know?" His questions aren't completely out of the blue. We've both been wondering when our turn to take the trials would be, he assumes I know something.

"I know nothing, so let's take the crazy down a notch. Like a half turn at least." I mimic turning a knob, which is something he routinely does to me when I'm overanalyzing, overstressing, or just generally talking too loud. "Daveed had me mix some bleach for him and then told me to grab you and wait for him out back. The way I see it . . . we are either both being fired, or it's our turn."

"Do you think? I don't know . . . Tori and Jenna had to wait eighteen months. But he isn't firing us, that's for sure. We do everything around here." Micah slumps against the counter.

"I think we've proven ourselves, and the salon is busier than it ever has been. Let's go outside and wait. Or actually, maybe we should get this stuff cleaned up first, so he doesn't think we are slacking off. But he did say to go outside. Shit. What are we supposed to do . . ." I'm flustered, and Micah's nerves are making mine worse.

"Let's go outside, and turn it down like half a notch, would ya?" He smirks at me, throwing it right back in my face, as he opens the back door and heads out with me nipping at his heels.

We both plop down at the patio table. It's times like this I wish I had an ounce of chill. I wish that I could just be told to come out here without nearly having a panic attack, overthinking what Daveed could possibly have to tell us. My mom used to say that there was no reason to be nervous if you haven't done anything wrong. That's easy to say when you are a Perfect Polly, but for someone like me—not so much.

Daveed pushes his way out onto the patio, sashaying up to where we are seated and taking a load off in one of the chairs. He glances back and forth between Micah and me, like he is trying to assess how on edge we are before he unleashes whatever he's going to say.

Steepling his hands in front of his mouth, he grins before saying, "Listen up. You two have been working hard for nearly a year. I never have to tell you where to be or what to do. Now, that does not mean you are perfect, but I do think you are ready for the next step." He shifts in his seat, straightening slightly, then leaning toward us. "Luka and I spoke about it, and we'd like you to begin preparing for your final trials. Although I know you both already know what I expect, I placed instructions in your mailboxes. I have all the faith that you will pass and will be successful additions to our stylist team."

"Thank you, oh my gosh, thank you. I am so grateful for the opportunity and won't let you down." I stand, leaning over to give him a tight squeeze.

"What she said. Thank you." Micah follows this by giving him a hug as well.

Daveed stands from his chair, looking between us. "It's five forty-five," he announces, before clapping his hands together in one single clap. Micah and I stare at him. Are we supposed to know what that means?

"Get out of here. It means leave. Go celebrate or something, my darling future fairy godmothers. The work to pass these trials starts tomorrow, and as I am sure you are aware, there are plenty of late salon nights in your future." With that, he walks away, heading back into the salon, as we stand gawking after him. I don't know that I've ever seen him send assistants home early. Let alone on a busy Thursday night after three straight days of back-to-back clients.

"Where should we go?" Micah asks, looking at me like I'd have a plan.

"Ummm . . . let me text Lo. She usually does a Thirsty Thursday trivia night somewhere. We could meet her and have a few drinks." I grab my phone from my back pocket and send off a text.

"I'm not very good at trivia, but I also don't have a life sooo . . . send me the details." Micah heads inside to collect his things. I forward him the location Lo sends me and a text telling him to meet me at seven sharp at Tiki Tonga.

—

Palm trees sway with the evening breeze skating off the Gulf as flashing green and purple spotlights wave back and forth, lighting up the pavement at my feet. I'm standing outside of a very packed Tiki Tonga, waiting for Micah and Lo to show up. I told them both to arrive at seven, which apparently meant show up at seven fifteen and skate in at the last minute to sign up before trivia commences at seven thirty.

Maybe my mom wore off on me a little too much in the punctuality department. I remember her saying that the cows weren't going to feed themselves and asking how I would feel about waiting for my breakfast every morning. It didn't make getting up and doing two hours of farmwork before school any easier, but I am chronically on time for everything now as a result.

"Wright? Is that you, standing all alone in the dark?" a familiar husky voice asks me.

"Rambo? What are you doing here?" I retort, as Will steps into the bar's glowing entry light. I attempt to mask the eye roll I can't help from happening—clearly he is just bound to be everywhere I am now.

"I have a feeling I am here for the very same reason you are. Trivia, right? Lo convinced Smith that we all needed to participate, and he twisted my arm." Will shrugs while I curse out Lo internally. *That meddling little shit wants me to think fate is playing a role here.* She's determined to make me run into him over and over. I'm going to have words with her, but I'm not going to let him know it bothers me this much.

"Ah, I see," I respond. "Well, I hope you weren't coming to win. I happen to be very good at knowing useless facts." I shift from one foot to the other, bracing for whatever comeback he throws my direction.

"I remember."

That's it? That's all he's got?

"You don't know anything about me, and let's not pretend you do." I let out a harrumph in frustration and defiance.

"Okay, Wright. Sure. I know nothing about you . . . You can tell yourself that, but it doesn't make it true." He smirks at me, heightening my annoyance.

"Well . . . since you apparently know *everything*, want to make a bet?" I should not be engaging with him at all. I don't trust him as far as I can throw him, which is to say not far. But, for reasons I can't explain, I just need to drive him crazy.

"What kind of bet?" He looks at me cautiously, putting his hands into the back pockets of his light denim jeans. The ones I'm definitely not noticing accentuate his thick man-muscle thighs.

"Hmm . . . if I win trivia, you have to avoid all friend group activities that I could potentially be at for two weeks." I don't love the queasy feeling that rises in my belly at the thought of not seeing him, and I don't understand why it's even there. I can't stand the smug smirks he gives me or how he always seems to be doting on his sister. He's a jerk of the worst kind. A hot jerk, but still.

"That desperate to get rid of me, huh? What do I get if I win?" He shifts his baseball hat lower on his head, shading those piercing blue eyes, thankfully.

"What do you want?" *Why did that come out so breathlessly? Stop it, body. We do not like him, we do not find him attractive in the slightest*, I remind myself.

"Oh, there are so many things. Let me think of the best way to torture you." Will touches his finger to his lips, and I'm overcome with jealousy that his finger is the one whispering over those full pillows. *What the fuck is wrong with me.* I need a drink or five.

"I've got it," he says. "If I win, you have to sing karaoke tonight." The stupid smirk is back in place. But he has no chance of beating me, so it's fine.

"Deal. Too bad you won't be hearing these pipes any time soon, Rambo. Best of luck to you." I reach out to shake his hand and seal the deal, which is a horrible, no good, terrible idea. His palm is rough and callused as it rubs against mine. I do not want to like it, but I do. Warmth seeps into my belly, followed by a flurry of flapping butterfly wings. Thankfully, I spot Micah approaching and stop myself from feeling anything I shouldn't be.

"I show up a few minutes late, and you already have a handsome suitor waiting for you? Your life is so hard, Cam." Micah bumps his shoulder into mine before extending his hand to Will saying, "Nice to meet you, gorgeous. I'm Micah."

Will chuckles, reaching out to take Micah's hand and giving it a firm shake. "I'm Will. It's a pleasure to meet you, Micah. Although depending on how close you are with this one"—he points at me, *the nerve*—"I'm not sure how long you will be a fan of mine." With that, Will turns and walks into the bar, leaving us standing on the sidewalk.

"Umm . . . explain. Now." Micah is still blushing from the touch of Will's hand and is fanning his face to cool off.

"That would be my ex." I shrug, trying to act like I don't understand Micah's visceral reaction to being in Will's proximity.

"So you're saying I have a chance. Noted." He winks at me. Micah and I have become pretty close over the last year of working together. I know he would never cross any lines, but I also know that he is absolutely going to tease me about this for the rest of my life.

"Go for it, but don't say I didn't warn you when you get your heart broken in the worst way." I huff, crossing my arms over my chest. "Should we just go in and get a table since Lo is clearly running late?"

"I'm not late, I'm right here." Lo walks up in between us and wraps an arm around each of our shoulders, steering us toward the door and into the bar. "Why are you both blushing?"

"I'm not," I say at the same time Micah chimes in with, "I met Will."

"Hoo-boy, I know, right? Tell this one she should stop acting like fate didn't bring him back into her life for a reason."

"Maybe fate brought him into my life." Micah winks at us both and we laugh.

Tiki Tonga is every beachgoer's dream destination. With sand-covered floors, swings in lieu of barstools except for at the tables, and a giant tiki statue in the corner lit by a colorful array of spotlights. The ambiance screams give me a piña colada, some sunnies, and a coconut bra. It's packed to the gills in here with patrons spilling out onto the ocean front patio while the Beach Boys blare from the sound system.

We spot our group, Smith, Ruiz, Butler, Amy, and of course Will, holding down a table with exactly three stools open. Smith waves, as if we could have possibly missed him in his neon pink Hawaiian shirt. We each grab a stool and a beer from the bucket on the table at the same time that a balding middle-aged man—with skin so leathery, he has clearly been laying off the sunscreen for the better part of twenty years—says, "Welcome to Tiki Trivia, where the questions leave you twisted and tangled more than the tiki bar." He chuckles to himself as the microphone makes a loud screech..

I can't help the bubbling burst of giggles that rips out of me. The trivia host is adorably endearing in the worst way. My table mates look at me like I've lost my mind—well, all of them but Will, who is also laughing. *Don't laugh at the things I think are funny.*

The host, who I am calling Larry for no good reason other than it feels right, explains the rules and tells us to refer to the guidelines and game answering devices on our tables. Glancing down, I see the rules list:

All teams must have four players.

Questions must be answered on the game answering device within thirty seconds.

Team rankings and results will be posted on the projector screen above Tonga the Tiki God.

The winning team earns a free round of drinks and first choice for karaoke.

I look up from the paper to see a smiling Will, who has traded places with Ruiz to sit directly across from me, presumably for no other reason than to try to throw me off my game. He knew that one of us would end up singing tonight before we even made our stupid bet. I plan on winning though. Snooze ya later, Rambo.

"How should we split up the teams?" Lo asks, disgustingly holding hands with Smith across the table. Get a room, lovebirds.

"Cam and I need to be on separate teams." Will dodges the elbow that comes from his sister as he says it.

"Okay, let's just do the three of us and Amy. Does that work?" Lo points to Micah and me as Amy happily hops off her stool and carries it over to our side of the table.

"Alright Tiki Trivia contestants, the first question is loading in three . . . two . . . one,, goooooo!" Larry announces as our devices light up with the first question.

What crop is traditionally produced on the Kona Coast of Hawaii's Big Island?

We huddle together awkwardly, and I tell my group I know the answer. It has to be coffee. They nod in agreement, and I type and submit *coffee beans*, watching the board to make sure we got it right. That was an easy one, so I'm not surprised to see that most teams answered correctly.

"Looks like we are off to a great start. The next question is loading . . . now," Larry bellows.

Which two states do not observe daylight saving time?

Amy grabs my arm, whispering in my ear that it's Hawaii and Arizona. We huddle with Lo and Micah, confirming they agree, and submit. Yes, another one is correct! I shift slightly, wobbling on my stool as I reach for my beer.

"Had too much to drink already, Wright?" *Of course, he noticed.*

"Not even close, Rambo. Just a wobbly three-legged stool, but nice try." I shake my head and take a long, refreshing glug of icy cold beer— my attempt at washing away the bitter taste he leaves in my mouth.

Suddenly, Will stands, grabbing his stool and walking around to our side of the table as the next question pops up. Does he think I am dumb enough to let him see our answers? I quickly submit an answer without consulting my teammates. "Don't be coming over here to get a glimpse of what we are submitting, Rambo. It doesn't count if you cheat," I chide him.

"Stand up, Wright." Will's voice is commanding, along with his broad shoulders and hulking frame.

"No. I will not be told what to do." I turn away from him toward Micah, rolling my eyes.

Will taps me on the shoulder. "Stand up. I'm giving you my stool, so you don't fall off this one and get hurt." Amy and Lo swoon while Micah clutches his chest in deference to the sweet gesture. I can't refuse without looking like a completely petty bitch, so I comply. Taking his solid, not-at-all-wobbly stool reluctantly.

Will smirks as he makes his way back around the table and plops down on what was once my unstable chair. I may have a firm and steady place to put my caboose now, but mentally, I'm even more unstable than before.

We work our way as a group through more questions, and the race to win becomes tighter and tighter. Will's group and mine are tied with only one question to go, and I can feel Will's eyes boring into me from across the table. "What's it going to be, Wright?" he asks.

"Huh?" I turn away from chatting with Micah about work and look at Will.

"What song are you going to sing after I win?" He winks and takes a long pull of his beer, awaiting my answer.

"You aren't going to win, so it doesn't matter. What are you going to do with all your upcoming free time?" I point the end of my beer bottle in his direction; it's been empty for some time now, but getting a refill in a place this crowded is like trying to climb Everest in a tank top. Not happening.

"What is going on?" Lo asks glancing between us.

"Your friend made a bet with me. If I win, she has to sing karaoke." The guys pop off in an uproar of hysterics, slapping Will on the back in glee.

"If he loses, he doesn't get to come to any group events for two weeks. I can almost taste the freedom and alone time I'm going to have with the three of you," I say, sweeping my arm to indicate the friends of his I will be commandeering.

This causes the guys to laugh even harder, hooting and hollering for all to see, as Larry announces the final question of the night, adding that there is a planned tiebreaker if needed. Seconds feel like minutes as I wait to see the last question pop up on the screen.

Which state utilized a UHF wireless packet network to connect its residents?

My vision goes blurry for a second while I try to decipher what the fuck that even means. I pull Amy, Lo, and Micah in close asking, "Do you know anything about this?"

"No, what the hell is a wireless packet?" Amy asks.

"If it's not about hair or Taylor Swift, don't look at me." Micah holds his hands up in surrender.

"Come on, it has to be tiki related, so it has to be Hawaii, right? That's the only thing that makes sense. Lo, back me up," I say, the realization that I'm likely going to be singing karaoke churning in my gut.

"Sure, sounds good to me." She shrugs and goes back to rubbing her thumb softly over Smith's hand.

I type the response and attempt to hit submit, but a flashing red bar says time's up. I don't want to look across the table, but maybe they didn't get their answer in either. Groaning, I glance from under my lashes, darting my gaze across some very-pleased-with-themselves faces and landing on the smuggest face of them all, stupid Will's.

"I'll go get another round from the bar. Oh and I'll sign you up to sing, Wright. Better start warming up those vocal cords." Will walks off toward the bar, staffed with beautiful bartenders flaunting their assets in booty shorts and too-tight, cropped Hawaiian shirts.. I might throw up from the loss and the stage fright.

TEN

Will

"Ever Since You Left" - Priscilla Block

Walking toward the bar for another bucket of beer is just the break I need. When Cam was waiting out front alone, in her sage-green cotton sundress, it was all I could do to stop myself from wrapping her in a hug. I know it's not a good idea to get involved with her, and I'm not ready to open myself up to being hurt or, even worse, potentially hurting her. But she looked lonely and maybe a little sad out there all alone. I do still care about her. I mean, truthfully, I will probably love her forever, even if I can never tell her that.

I shouldn't have stopped to talk to her or made this silly bet. But like a moth to a flame, I am powerless to keep my distance from her. There's something about being around her, this sense of being wholly

seen and accepted. She puts people at ease, and it's not just me, it's everyone. Butler was right when he said that she's someone special.

I'd contemplated letting her win tonight, although knowing she doesn't want to be around me hurts more than it should. This is exactly why nothing about dating her, or anyone else for that matter, is a good idea. The people I love always leave: first my dad, then Thatch. It's a never-ending cycle that is bound to repeat itself—not to mention, I'm still fucked up from what happened overseas. I can't bring anyone else into that shit.

"What can I get you, handsome?" a cute bartender with braided brown pigtails asks, drinking me in aggressively.

"We will have a bucket of beer and eight shots of tequila with salt and limes," Cam shouts across the bar, her face twisted in displeasure as her hand grasps at my inner arm, gentle fingers wrapping around my bicep. *Is she . . . jealous? No, she must just be mad that she lost.* My skin tingles where she's touching me, heat and comfort seeping into my bones.

Cam pulls on my arm to turn me toward her, then drops her hand. The tingling from where she grazed my skin lingers. "Are you really going to make me do this, Rambo?" she asks.

"A bet's a bet. When have you ever been one to not hold up your end of a deal? What would Patricia say?" She looks like I just struck her, cheeks turning slightly pink in shame.

"You know what . . . fine." Cam huffs, and spins around to walk away. I grab her hand, pulling her back to where I am standing by the bar, electricity pulsing up my arm when our hands meet.

"I can't carry all the drinks by myself, Wright. Also, what did I say wrong, because you're clearly pissed off."

"N-nothing, it's fine." She blows me off, refusing to tell me if she's mad about more than having to sing in front of a couple hundred people.

The bartender places our bucket of beer on the bar along with a tray of the shots, limes, and salt. I grab the bucket in one hand and start to reach for the tray with the other, but Cam swoops it up, her hand placed perfectly center under the tray, and lifts it above her head. She starts walking back toward our table and I follow, wondering when she learned to carry trays like a waitress. I guess I have missed a lot in the past few years.

"Who wants a shot?" Cam shimmies and shakes in a little dance, setting the tray down gently on the table and passing the shots out.

"No can do, I'm driving tonight." Butler puts his hand up to decline politely.

"Two for me then," Cam says as she brings the back of her hand to her mouth, licking the tender skin above her thumb. *Geezus, stop looking at her.* She sprinkles salt onto the wet spot and grabs the first shot to do a toast. I hurry to my spot, grabbing my shot glass and raising it, nervous about what Cam's toast might be.

"Alright, I'll take it old school, in honor of my brother's favorite toast. Here's to you, here's to me, friends we will always be, but if the day comes that we are not, then fuck you, here's to me." Her gaze is pointed at me, laced with anger and betrayal.

"That's the best toast I've ever heard," Smith claps his hand on her shoulder, pulling Cam into a side hug. One that, based on his face, is his way of saying, *I'm sorry my friends an asshole.* I mean, he isn't wrong, and I'm glad she has this new-found family in my friends, but it hurts a little, how easily I am being shoved out.

Screech. The trivia host grabs the mic, sending off an ear-splitting noise for the second time tonight. I can't help but laugh, I've always thought it was funny when that happens. It's embarrassing in the way that, you clearly couldn't control it from happening, but you have to take the judgment and responsibility anyway.

"Well, I guess this thing is still on. Who's ready for some karaoke?" The crowd cheers in excitement, Lo and Amy turning quickly into "woo girls" while Cam sulks and takes down her second shot. "Get on up here winning team, and pick your song."

"Looks like you're up, Wright. Better put on a good show, give the people what they want."

I see the shift in her attitude as it takes place, the forced smile blooming on her face, the straightening of her spine. "Don't worry, I don't let people that are counting on me down." *Ouch!*

She walks around the group and toward the elevated stage without another word. Shit. She is not messing around, and if I was a gambling man, I'd say she's mad at me right now for more than breaking her heart. But for what? I have no clue. This whole bet was her idea.

Cam takes the stage, carefully climbing the three steps at the side and gliding over to the DJ to tell him which song she would like. While he cues up the music and lyrics, she walks to the front of the stage, where the trivia host turned karaoke emcee is waiting. Rainbow-colored spotlights illuminate her, painting a pattern of streaks and shadows across her flowy dress.

"While we cue up your song, can I ask you something?" He looks at Cam like he wants to eat her for lunch. Eyes trailing from her toes to her hair and back down. I want to punch him in the face, yet I have zero right to.

"Sure, ask away." Cam smiles her megawatt smile at the crowd and does a little swing of her dress.

"How did you manage to be the one singing tonight? You aren't on the winning team, I noticed." He winks at her, as if to say, *I've been watching you.* She bristles a little, wrapping her arms around her waist. I don't think anyone else noticed, but I did. He is creeping her out.

Leaning in to speak directly into the microphone, she says, "Well, here's the thing. I got my heart broken five years ago, and not that long ago, my ex randomly showed back up in my life. I made a bet with him tonight, and well . . . I lost, so now I have to sing."

"Wow, that's rough. Ladies and gentlemen, did you hear that? This beautiful girl lost a bet and now has to sing karaoke in front of her ex. Let's show her some love." The crowd roars with several combinations of "Whoo!" and "Knock 'em dead!" and "He's an idiot!"

After getting the signal from the DJ, Cam grabs the microphone, moving the stand out of the way, and shoos the emcee off stage. As the music begins, she looks right at me with laser focus, pointing her finger directly at my chest. "This one's for you, Rambo."

As the first lyrics roll out from the speakers, with Cam's voice perfectly aligned over them, I hear, "ever since you left" on repeat a few times before the song moves into more lyrics about how the singer/Cam went right back to living. Unfazed by the breakup, moving on, not wanting to go back, all these themes are spiriling around in my head and in Cam's words as she dances, swings her skirt, spins, and plays to the crowd's delight. They are eating up everything she's serving, and suddenly, although I won this bet, I realize the joke's on me.

By the second time the chorus rolls around, Lo and Micah have joined her on stage, singing with her as if this is their bedroom and they're belting it out with a hair brush. Cam points at me again before singing something about knowing I want her back and how she does not give a single fuck. She makes a kissing face before smacking her right ass cheek and spinning around.

"I'm not sure exactly what you said to that girl way back when, but I don't think she's getting over it anytime soon." Ruiz smacks my shoulder playfully. He has no idea how spot-on he is.

"I disagree. If she didn't still care, she wouldn't be up there singing a breakup song at the top of her lungs. I think you have more of a chance than you think." Smith squeezes his way into our conversation, rubbing his hand over my curly hair, undoubtedly messing it up.

"It doesn't matter either way. I've told you both, she's a no-fly zone. It's not happening. Ever." I don't notice that someone new has taken over karaoke.

"Well, that's one thing we agree on, Rambo. Not. Happening. Ever." Cam walks past where we are standing, grabbing her purse from the table and giving what I presume is a goodbye hug to Butler.

On her way out, she walks back by us holding hands with Micah and laughing about something he said. "See ya around, Wright!" I shout after her.

"Maybe in your dreams, Rambo."

ELEVEN

Cam

"Red Bowling Ball Ruth" - The White Stripes

Pulling up the arrivals ramp to the passenger pickup area at Tampa International, I idle waiting on the curb for my person. And that's truly who Elliott is, he's my person, the Cristina to my Meredith, my man in a storm. After the past couple of weeks, especially last Thursday, I can't wait to talk it out with someone who gets it. Someone who will be on my side, not in my ear talking about fate and true love like Lo and Micah keep insisting on.

ELLIOTT

Walking out now, door 7

I pull my car back into the drive thru lane, inching up toward where Elliott is waiting. When I see him standing on the curb, relief washes over me like a tidal wave. I roll down the window and squeal the biggest, warmest hello I can muster. Elliott grins, waving and heading

toward the trunk to put his massive suitcase in the back. If I didn't know he was quite the fashionista, I would think he was staying for a month.

He opens the passenger door and plops into the seat. "Finally! I didn't think I was ever going to get off that plane. People are gross, I need to shower immediately."

"Ugh, they really are the worst. How was the flight though?" I ask, slowly easing back into traffic to leave the airport.

"Ehh. It was okay. What do you have planned for me? I told you that debauchery better be included."

"Oh gosh. I do have a few things planned. But I think I've had enough of that recently to last me a lifetime." I'm not looking at him as I merge onto the interstate, but I can tell he wants a full debriefing.

"We are going to get into all of that. But I'm starving. Food first?" he asks, almost like he's reading my mind.

"I thought you'd never ask. I'm taking you somewhere really good. I found this authentic Mexican taqueria a little while back with Daveed. It sits right on Bayshore Boulevard, with scenic views of the bay and the best birria tacos you'll ever have anywhere," I say, hitting my blinker and turning down MacDill Avenue—we're almost there.

"Yum, so I can grill you about your love life over a margarita? Even better." He smiles at me, that arrogant I'm-going-to-find-out-everything look plastered on his pretty face.

We pull into the small gravel parking lot, get out of the car, and head inside to request a small patio table. The taqueria is quaint, crisp, and clean inside, and the patio has an amazing view of the water, with red, purple, and green umbrellas shading the tables.

Our server brings over the taco menu, an ordering form, a pencil, and a couple of waters. "Do you want something else to drink?" he asks, getting his notepad out.

"We will take a pitcher of your signature margarita, thank you," I order the standard, making sure we'll be covered for the conversation we're about to have.

"A pitcher. That bad, huh?" Elliott raises an eyebrow.

"No, it's really only three margaritas, hardly enough to get drunk on when we are sharing and eating," I say, unnecessarily justifying my need for tequila at a moment like this. Some things are just easier to talk about when you have Jose Cuervo on your side.

We scan the menu, opting to share six different tacos so we can try a variety. We also put down an order of chips, salsa, and queso dip for good measure. Our waiter, whose name I've learned is Marco, brings the margarita pitcher and two chilled glasses, snagging our order form on his retreat back to the kitchen.

"So, Will Davenport lives here . . . What were the odds of that?" Elliott slurps his margarita, shaking his head at the coincidence of it all.

"Yeah, yup. Sure does." I shrug, following his lead, licking salt from the rim of my glass and slurping some ice-cold Jose, hoping it infuses courage into my veins.

"That's it? That's all the reaction I get after all this time?" He's astonished, but there's not much else to say. Other than a few moments of trading barbs, there isn't anything going on between me and Will. Okay, maybe that's not entirely true, but I'm working up to it.

"It's just . . . Honestly, it's so weird. Like a part of me could so easily just fall back in step with him. We bicker and banter like we always have. But then I also hate literally everything about him. I hate his stupid beautiful face, the way his hands are the right amount of rough and soft, the way he insists on being nice to me and doting on his sister. It's disgusting and fake, and I know that there's this whole other side of him, the side that just throws people away like they mean nothing.

So yeah, it's fine." I down half my margarita, afraid to look my brother in the eye.

"That's a whole lot to unpack. What are we doing after this?" Elliott shifts in his chair as Marco drops a platter of chips, salsa, and queso in front of us.

"We are going bowling. Why?" I ask, a chip halfway to my mouth dripping salsa down my shirt, because of course I'm spilling red sauce on a white tank top.

"Just trying to gauge how many margaritas it's going to take to unravel the shitstorm of red flags you just laid down. Didn't want to jump in now and miss something important later." He chews thoughtfully on a chip. "Let's start with the fact that it doesn't sound like hate at all. It sounds like a whole lot of tension of the sexy variety, but definitely not hate. Which is concerning because it means your heart is already involved, whether you want it to be or not."

"My heart is absolutely not involved. I hate him, I promise." I pull my leg up under me, leaning in, ready to defend myself against what is turning out to be a conversation with another skeptic.

"Okay, let's pretend that's true. If we hate him, then why does it even matter if he's around? Like, why is it affecting you so much? Just pretend he's a gnat and ignore him." He grabs the pitcher, refilling our glasses with what remains and signaling to Marco to bring another.

"Ugh . . . I can't because he insists on either being nice to me, which is just so . . . so typical of him that it's infuriating. Or he's giving me a hard time, and you know I can't back down from a fight." I put my head into my hands, fighting back tears of frustration, tears of longing, tears of pure despair. Five years of my life have been wasted on this, five years that I will never get back. "How am I supposed to deal with caring about him as a person but at the same time wanting to throat punch him repeatedly?"

"My dear . . . that right there is what I like to call sexual tension." Elliott pauses, presumably trying to be thoughtful about his response. "And normally I would advise you to just take him for a roll in the hay, but in this case, that's too dangerous. For your heart, I mean."

"I know that. I just wish he had . . . I don't know, aged poorly?" Marco drops off our tacos and we dive in.

"Let me ask you something." Elliott has his serious face on, except he's got a smidge of crema on his cheek making it difficult to meet him there. "Do you trust him?"

"No." It's an easy answer, one that I can give emphatically and without reservation.

"Well, that's the answer then. Regardless of how much you want to jump his bones—which by the way, gross—it won't work if there isn't trust. Without it, you don't stand a chance." He takes another bite of the birria taco, hogging the rest of it. So much for sharing.

"So I hate him. Okay. I can do that." I reach for some queso, pouring it onto a chicken taco.

"I didn't say that." He shakes his head. "We both know you don't. But there's too much history, too much baggage. It's like . . . do you remember when our house burned down? We loved that house, and then the fire came and ripped it to shreds. Mom and Dad rebuilt and we both liked the new place but it was never the same, you know? I think you could be friends-ish. Not too close but, like, acquaintances, since you share a group of friends."

"I don't know, El. That sounds easier than it actually is." I sip the last of my margarita.

"Listen, you don't have to decide anything right now, you just have to trust your instincts. Do what feels right and don't overthink it—which I know you will, but you have to admit that it's got to be fate bringing you both here. It's too much of a coincidence otherwise."

Elliott waves to Marco, likely to request the check.

"It's not fate. I don't believe in that. But maybe you're right, maybe I needed this, needed to see Will again, to finally let go and move on." My brother nods his agreement.

I don't know why Will is back in my life, but I do know one thing: It's time for me to get closure. It's time for me to move on.

—

The smash of balls hitting pins echoes all around us as Elliott, Lo, and I walk into the Alley. After our fiesta lunch, Elliott and I headed back to my apartment to change before our evening plans and pick up Lo. The Alley is a classic bowling alley that's been renovated to be provide modern amenities with a vintage flair. The carpet is a kaleidoscope of colorful swirls beneath our feet as we make our way to the lane we reserved. The very one that's already occupied by my three new friends and the Davenport siblings, one I love and one I hate.

"Hey, Cam! Bring a date?" Smith hollers when he sees us approaching.

"That's her brother." Amy elbows him in the ribs. "Hey, Elliott, how are you? It's been a while."

"Little Amy Davenport? It's been forever. I'm great, you?" Elliott and Amy start catching up. There's nearly a ten-year age gap between them, but Amy was around a lot when Will and I were together.

"Wright, good to see ya." Will nods a welcome in my direction. If I was guessing, I'd say he's a little nervous with my big brother around. Serves him right. "Elliott, been a long time, man. Good to see you." He reaches out a hand to shake my brother's, interrupting Elliott's conversation with Amy.

Elliott looks at him, really assessing him, before saying, "If it's all the same to you, I'd rather not shake hands. Not until you've made things right with my girl."

"I respect that, but if it's all the same to you, I'd like to steal a moment of your time." Will points toward the patio. Apparently he'd like to talk outside, man to man.

"What is this, the 1920s, Rambo? You don't need to talk to my brother." I stomp my foot and prop a hand on my hip. I do not need him to chat up Elliott and come to some big understanding. If he wants to talk to someone, he can talk to me.

"Cam, it's fine. I'll be back in a few. Order me a drink." Elliott leads the way out toward the patio. If I didn't know better, I'd say he puffed out his chest a little as he walked away. Men are so dumb!

I say hello to the rest of the group, pick out a red, sparkly bowling ball, and set up our names in the computer to keep score. Then I order a couple of fishbowls, which are advertised to contain sixty-four ounces of blue punch with more than enough alcohol to hate myself in the morning, and slump into a chair at one of the two tables skirting the red pleather horseshoe-shaped bench seating. It's been like ten minutes, and there's still no sign of my brother or Will.

"Hey, you okay over here?" Butler bumps his shoulder into mine, gentleness etched in his brow.

"Yeah . . . . But actually, what the hell are they doing out there?" I groan before taking another sip of punch. *Yep, I am going to hate myself in the morning.*

"It's a man thing. He just wants to clear the air with your brother. It's fine." Butler shrugs before grabbing one of the ten straws sticking out of the giant (literal) fishbowl and sucks. "Davenport is an honorable man. He's doing the right thing by owning his mistakes."

"If you ask me, he's owning those to the wrong person," Lo quips before also grabbing a straw to drink her fill.

"Cut him some slack. You loved him once, in case you forgot. He's not a bad person. He got dealt a bad hand, and you know he thought he was doing the right thing at the time." Amy points her finger at me, challenging me to tell her she's wrong.

"You know what, you're right, Amy. I did love him. But that's old news. Everyone needs to chill and stop acting like this is some bullshit love story." I take another large gulp, trying not to groan as the sugar-filled drink hits my stomach. "Will and I aren't meant to be. It's fine. We've moved on and so should everyone else."

"Hidey ho, Winslow! I'm back. Oh, this looks like a deliciously bad decision." Elliott wraps his arm around me, reaching for a straw and sucking. Is it gross that we are all sharing this drink? Probably. Do I care? Not in the slightest.

We grab our balls and proceed to bowl, the competition and the puns getting stiffer as we go. Will and I avoid each other for the first two rounds, like two caged lions circling and staring but never engaging. I'm pissed that he would talk to El and not to me. Not that I want to talk to him, but if anyone deserves an explanation or a clearing of the air, it's me. Right?

"What did he say out there?" I ask when Elliott comes to sit by me in between turns.

"Don't worry about it. Just wanted to clear the air. It's fine." He grins at me and shifts in his seat like he knows something I don't. I hate being the one left out of a secret.

"It is not fine. Don't you think I deserve to know?" I protest.

"You don't need to know. He didn't say anything that would change the way you or I feel about things. I think he just was afraid I was going to kick his ass." Elliott flexes, showing off an impressive bicep.

"I'm not sure you could take him in a fight, El. But good to know you'd try." I can't help but size up Will while I'm talking about him. He's dressed in a navy Air Force T-shirt and light jeans, and his hair is a little messy. The shirt is snug against his broad chest and strong arms, which definitely does not make my stomach flip when thinking about what he could do with those muscles. When he laughs with his friends, his eyes are such a bright shade of blue against his suntanned skin. If I didn't hate him, which I absolutely do, I would want to drag my fingers through those messy curls.

"You're staring, Wright. Like something you see?" *Shit*. He caught me gawking and now he's going to be even more insufferable.

"Not a chance, Rambo. Keep dreaming," I quip back, turning to grab my ball and take my final turn of the round.

When I picked this ball, I had two criteria in mind: one, it needed to be light enough to throw, and two, it had to be pretty. I didn't account for how small the finger holes would be; it's probably a child's ball. I've managed to play with it up until this point, but the more I drink, the more my fingers swell, which makes holding on to the ball a challenge. If I was thinner, this wouldn't be an issue, but I have the slightest bit of sugar, and my fingers become less dainty and more precooked breakfast sausages.

Walking carefully up to the line, I balance my ball with my left hand as I jam my pointer and middle fingers in a little further for good measure. I wiggle them back and forth, just to make sure I don't lose feeling, and secure my grip. Glancing over my shoulder at the group, I wink at the lot of them. If I get a strike, which I fully intend to do, I will win the game. Have I mentioned how much I like winning?

I refocus on the task at hand, lining my feet and ball up with the center arrow, pulling the ball back with all my might, and lunging forward to release it. Except, it doesn't release—it takes me with it. Suddenly I'm barreling down the lane like a bull in a china shop, like a potato shooting out of a launcher, like one of those pumpkins soaring through the air during the annual Punkin Chunkin' competition. I can feel the wind beneath me, as if I'm flying for the first time, before I crash with a thud and slippery-slide through grease to what I hope is my eventual death.

I close my eyes, willing myself to disappear through the hole at the end of this long lane. *Please, for the love of Pete, let me go through that mystery tunnel and never return.* I hear a myriad of shrieks, laughter, and one "holy shit that was awesome" coming from the peanut gallery. Not that I thought I was going to be sleeping with anyone in our group, but I hold a brief funeral in mind for my barren vagina anyway. Someone definitely got that on video. I'm probably going viral and doomed to a life of abstinence forever more.

Pounding footsteps approach down the lane followed by the now familiar sliding-swishing sound that I'm positive my body just made. I'm hit on my back with something heavy and hard. Wait, not something. Someone.

"Hey, fancy meeting you here." Will grins, turning on his side and propping his head up on his hand like we both didn't just slide down a bowling lane and aren't covered in grease.

"What the fuck are you doing, Rambo?" I glare at him. He's the last person I needed to be down a lane—no, up an alley with.

"I could ask you the same thing, you know. I came to rescue you, Wright. Take the win." He smiles at me with a lopsided look, showing all those infuriatingly gorgeous white teeth.

"I didn't need rescuing, and how did that slide work out for you?" I shift, trying to pry my fingers out of the ball they are still stuck in. Nope, not coming out. I am now one with the ball.

"Here, let me." Will shifts to a sitting position, inching closer to my hand slowly, so he doesn't slide any further than necessary, I presume. He swipes his hand down the greasy lane and gently grabs my fingers to run the oily substance along where they are stuck. As he circles each one, I feel the chill bumps erupting down my arm, that tingling sensation low in my belly. Gently, he tugs each finger and my thumb free, helping me sit up and steadying me.

"All better, Wright." The words come out gravelly like he's just as affected by touching me as I am.

"Th-thanks for, um . . . for, um, rescuing me, I mean," I say, breathlessly, before righting myself and attempting to scoot to the nonoily lane divider. I crawl up and work my way to standing before turning to face our group with my head hung. Talk about a walk of shame. Stepping off onto solid ground is the best thing—I'm closer to finding the nearest exit and never returning.

"Well, that's one way to win the game, kid." Elliott wraps an arm around me, careful to avoid the brown streak of grease that's surely ruined my favorite pink "Ask Me About My Blow Job" T-shirt that has a cute little hair dryer on it. "Ready to get outta here?"

"I thought you'd never ask." I wink, thanking him with my eyes for a solid escape plan.

We quickly say goodbye to the group, settle our tab, and hustle to the car before bursting into laughter over my ridiculously clumsy bad luck. Only me, I swear it, this shit only happens to me.

TWELVE

Will

"I Can't Explain" - The Who

Last night was interesting, almost like an out-of-body experience. In the military, they train us to have a "bulletproof mind," which essentially means nothing, no situation or person or action, can rattle you. It sounds good in theory, and I've been through so much of the training that I like to pretend that it's true for me. And honestly, in most situations it is. I'm calm under pressure and don't let things affect me. My mind is locked carefully behind an impenetrable steel vault, and there isn't anything that can enter it if I don't want it to. That stupid ache in my chest, though, apparently didn't get the memo.

As soon as I saw Elliott walk in the door with Cam, I knew that I had to talk to him. When Cam and I were dating, Elliott and I were close. He was the brother I never had but always wanted. I didn't realize until I saw him yesterday just how much I missed our friendship. That dude has an unbelievable ability to make me laugh and to call me on my bullshit, not unlike his sister.

I asked him to talk mostly to clear the air. Not that I'm delusional enough to think things would ever be the same between us, but because I wanted him to hear it from me, man to man, what my truth is and what I intend to do about it. I've had a lot of time over these past few days to think, and I've realized, with the help of my sister, there are a few things that I know to be true. For starters, I care about Cam and I always will. She isn't going away anytime soon, with Lo and Smith now a pair. Second, I can't be with her. Not that she would want to be with me anyway, but I can't. I am not willing to risk hurting her again or getting hurt. I made this decision five years ago for a reason, and I have to trust that it was the right choice. Finally, I would like for her and me to be friends. I'm not sure it's possible given all the history, but she's magnetic to be around. She's funny, hardheaded, sassy, and the most genuinely caring person I've ever met. She's a good friend, and I'd like to be one to her in return.

I asked Elliott if he thought it was possible that Cam would want to be friends. He said he wasn't sure but that he thought it would be good for both of us to be able to get some closure and finally move forward. He even confirmed I still have the right phone number for her. God knows how many times I've almost called it over the years but stopped myself, not knowing who would be on the other end of the line. Now's the time. I need to bite the bullet and text her—or should I try to call her? No, definitely text, that way if she's sleeping, I don't wake her up. And if she doesn't want to respond, at least I'll know if she leaves me on read. There's a churning in my stomach and acid creeping up my throat as I open her contact.

WILL

> Hey, Wright. Hope the grease rinsed out of your hair okay.

I hit send and hop out of my bed like it's on fire. I can't lie here to see if she responds, the wait will kill me. And if she responds immediately, I know I'll get a sense of false hope. This is precisely why I don't deal with dating: I can't do it. My anxiety over a stupid text message where I hope to ask a girl to be my friend has me ready to spin out.

I wander into the kitchen and start making coffee when Amy pops up from behind the peninsula looking ornery as all get out. "What's the look you're giving me, Aims?" I ask, rolling my eyes.

Of course, my sister just had to be in town, and suddenly become my new roommate, when all this went down. She will never let it go, and I can't deal with disappointing her either. Amy always loved Cam. She looked up to her, and I'm sure I broke her heart as much as I did my own when I ended things.

"Soo . . . were you asking Elliott for her hand in marriage?" She chuckles.

"Amy, no, what the hell . . . She hates me!" I exclaim while chucking a wadded-up coffee filter at her.

Amy looks at me like I have three eyeballs and a snaggle tooth. "Are you serious, Will? You cannot think for a second that Cameron Wright actually hates you. The girl practically swoons every time she sees you. She may trade barbs with you out of anger, but there are hearts in her eyes when she does it, and there always will be," Amy says defiantly.

"I texted her," I admit at an almost inaudible volume.

"Wait. Why? Did she respond?" Amy asks before I even finish my sentence.

"I don't know. I hit send and then ran out here to make coffee," I say nonchalantly, when in reality, the words *cool*, *calm*, and *collected* aren't anywhere near to describing me at the moment.

Amy stares at me, mouth gaping like I just admitted to the crime of the century. Before I can even register what's happening, she leaps up and darts into my bedroom, presumably to grab my phone. I continue making my coffee because I suspect she's going to be highly disappointed when she sees no response from Cam, but then I hear her gasp. "William Jessie Davenport, did you seriously think it was a good idea to remind her of what I assume is the most humiliating moment of her life?" she shouts from the other room.

I shrug and carry my steaming mug into the bedroom with me. Amy is perched on the edge of my bed looking smug as hell. "Do you want to know what she said?" she asks, guiltily.

"Give me the phone, Aims," I demand, holding my hand out palm side up.

"Nope, not unless I know that you aren't going to be a total man about this and write something back that's just as lame as your first message."

I take a deep breath and run my free hand through my hair. "Fine, you can help me think of something to say, but first I need to know what she responded with." Amy hands me the phone, and I see for myself.

CAM

Can we just pretend that the whole thing never happened, Rambo?

I shoot back a quick message. Amy smacks me when she sees what I am typing but hovers over my shoulder nonetheless.

WILL

I mean, maybe, but you do have five million views on TikTok so it might be a challenge.

CAM

Shut up, no I do not. You better be joking!

CAM

By the way, are you just texting me to remind me of Grease Gate? Or is there another reason why are you messaging me, Rambo?

WILL

I was hoping we could make a truce.

CAM

????

WILL

Let's agree to be friends, for Lo and Smith.

CAM

I know you don't want me in your life, and frankly, I'm not sure I want you in mine. I care about you and that will never change, but I think it's for the best if we don't pretend this is some weird twist of fate or that it means something it doesn't. It's purely coincidence that we ended up living in the same city. We don't need to be friends just because our friends are dating.

Wow, I feel like I might throw up. Cam really doesn't want me in her life. I always knew I would have a hard time if I ever ran into her and her husband, the fictitious one that lives in my mind, back home. I never imagined that I would run into her here and that she would be single and still want nothing to do with me. Bumping into her anywhere outside of our hometown hadn't ever crossed my mind as a possibility. I assumed she was living in Iowa with Mr. Perfect, not living thousands of miles from home with a roommate.

I should just respond and say yes, we can forget it all, but deep down I know now that I've spent time with her, I can't do that. I'm jealous of every minute my friends spend with her that I don't. It makes my skin itch when she razzes Butler or Ruiz, or when she does something nice or gives advice to Smith. I should evaluate what that means, but it doesn't matter. I won't go there. I will not let myself think about the possibility of being vulnerable just to have someone walk away.

I know that I'm not the guy for her. I can give her pleasure for sure, but I can't make her happy—not, like, truly happy, white picket fence and two-point-five kids happy. How have I been going through life without her all this time?

"What are you going to say?" Amy asks, interrupting my thoughts.

"Honestly, I have no fucking clue. What should I say?"

"Say *no*! Ugh . . . tell her you absolutely are not going to forget it and that *yes*! Fate did bring you back into each other's lives, and you aren't entirely sure what that means, but you'd like to try being friends," Amy rattles out, sounding completely exasperated by this entire situation and me.

"I don't know, maybe there just really is too much hurt there. I mean, I want to be friends, that's why I sent the message, but if I'm being honest, I'm not sure I even really know how to just be friends with her," I admit.

"Well duh! I swear some days I think you're the smartest person alive and others I think you're more on par with a caveman. You aren't actually going to end up friends, but too much time has passed. You need to live in the friend zone for a little bit until I can get you back into the boyfriend zone, Will." She rolls her eyes and crosses her arms, just like she did when we were kids and she meant business.

"I don't want to be out of the friend zone, though, Aims. I can't."

"Shut up, Will. You can lie to yourself all you want, but I see the connection you two have. It's like watching two magnets orbit around each other until they eventually crash together under the weight of the pull. You always start out in separate corners, but don't forget big brother"—she pats me on the shoulder—"I've been with you every time she's around, and you both end up trading verbal punches as an excuse to be near each other."

I'm probably going to live to regret it, but I let Amy type the message out and send it. I can't forget Cam lives here, and I also can't justify rushing back into things. Maybe Amy's right, maybe being friends with Cam is the way to go, and maybe we can end up just being cool with each other.

She always was my best friend and it would be nice to have that back, even if it scares the living daylights out of me. I tell Amy I'm going to head to the shower and beg her not to respond to any new messages without my approval. A long, hot shower is what I need to get my mind clear and figure out my messy life.

THIRTEEN

Cam

"Boyfriend" - Ariana Grande

To say it's been a weird couple of weeks would be a gross understatement. Of course, there was the excitement of spending some time not working when Daveed had his show, which I thought would be a good time to figure out how exactly I was going to reinvent my life, but instead it turned into a night of drinking far too much coupled with William Davenport trying to waltz back into my life.

Then there were the run-ins, first at my favorite deli with Lo, then at trivia, and finally at the Alley with Elliott. How is it possible that I've lived here a whole year and never seen Will once, and then suddenly I see him three times in less than that many weeks?

I can't even picture the little green syringes or the giant blue fishbowls without facing a bout of nausea. And I don't have any clue of what to think about this Will situation, which also makes me nauseous. Basically, I've spent the last ten days living in a weird

space-time continuum of intensely needing to vomit and being utterly dumbfounded over my incredibly terrible luck.

The problem is my best friend is cuddled up with his best friend. Avoiding him is almost impossible at this point. I came to Tampa to have a fresh start, to become the Cam I've always been destined to be, and I don't know if reintroducing the Cam from my past is really helping with that mission. *Hello, old friend nausea, I'm so glad you only took a five-minute break.*

"What's going on over there, sweet girl?" Daveed asks, intruding on my thoughts.

"Just thinking, nothing, I'm fine, totally cool over here," I reply nervously.

"Mm-hmm, sure sounds like it . . . I'm almost finished up here. Can you take these bowls back to the galley and wash them out for me? I'll be back as soon as I get Ms. Martha here under the dryer, and we're going to talk it out." He directs me with a point of his index finger and a reassuring nod.

Great! Fantastic! No biggie! I've tried so hard to keep it together. Coming to work, asking great questions in preparation for the hair trials I will be facing to earn my chair, and keeping my head down. I should've known that Daveed would poke and prod it out of me at some point.

I puff out a deep sigh and quickly round up all the dirty color bowls before making my way to the back. Maybe I can distract him with a conversation on color waste, seeing how some of these bowls are nearly full. It's pretty apparent there's some overmixing going on.

Rationally, I know it won't work. Daveed is good at sussing out the goings on of his employees; he looks at us like we belong to him—not in a controlling way, but in a loving, you're-my-family kind of way. Aside from his four fur babies, his stylists and assistants are the children he and his partner, Luka, never had.

"Staring at the bowls won't clean them, Cameron," Daveed chides, sounding a little annoyed but more concerned than anything as he walks into the galley.

"So-Sorry, I was just thinking this is a lot of waste. People must be overmixing, and you know, maybe we should do something about it," I say, trying to convey my one-hundred-percent loyalty to his bottom line.

"Oh, so that's what we're doing now?" he asks, crossing his arms and leaning back against the counter.

"What?" I play dumb.

"Evading, trying to drum up some financial woes to distract me from my sweet girl and why she's been acting like a distracted mess for days," he murmurs.

"Fine, I'll spill. But can we go out back? It's kind of personal," I plead, playing to his inner drama-loving queen. The last thing I need is the salon gossip mill spinning, though I'm sure Micah has done enough sharing as it is.

Daveed opens the back door and sweeps his arm, directing me to go out first. My butt hasn't even finished settling in the chair when the events of the past couple weeks come spilling out of me.

"So, remember the ex I told you about? Well he . . . he lives here."

"What? This is a sign," he gasps, clutching his heart.

"No, it's definitely not a sign. It's just my shitty luck," I groan, covering my face with my hands.

"How could you say such a thing, sweets? The universe is always giving us exactly what we need." He's clearly offended by my lack of faith in fate, but it feels like a cruel joke.

"And what about this is exactly what I need? Do tell." Challenging Daveed is never wise. He always has some pesky truth bomb hidden up his sleeve to make you question life.

"Let me ask you something. Did you love him?"

"Of course I did. And I think a part of me always will. But he said he didn't love me. He threw away our plans." I plead my case, but I can tell he isn't convinced.

"Did he? I seem to recall you saying that he dumped you when he chose the service over college. There was something about money involved, was there not?"

"Yes, but that doesn't explain how one minute he could love me and the next we're just done."

Daveed raises a single eyebrow and asks, "How's he been acting when you've seen him lately?"

"Fine. I guess." I'm not exactly sure how to answer that. It's not like he's been rude to me. I mean, we have banter, but that was always the fun part of being around him. It's just that seeing him is so random and piles on top of my already anxiety-riddled, uncharted course in life.

"Let me get this straight. The love of your life, the one that got away, *the* William Fucking Davenport, saunters back into your life, and all you can muster is fine, you guess?"

"Okay, so it's been infuriating. He's as gorgeous as ever and here I am, not at my best. But then, I also don't care what he thinks because I'm mad and I don't think I could ever trust him again," I admit.

"What does Will think?" he asks, slyly.

"How should I know? He's the king of mixed signals, flirty and protective or bantering one minute, and then cold as ice the next. I mean, he seems like he's the same Will, but then again, he's not. He's so much harder than he used to be, more tentative, cautious, not trusting . . ." I trail off with a sigh.

"That's Uncle Sam for ya, always hardening up the boys for battle."

Laughter bursts from my lips, and Daveed hits me with a funny look before he hears it too. "Should I start calling you Uncle Sam? You know, since you also have a way of hardening up the boys, Daveed?" I ask, giving my eyebrows a wiggle.

He cackles. "You absolutely should, but it has to be our little secret." He presses a finger to his lips. "I don't know how Luka would feel about being called a mere boy."

"Noted, you're secret safe with me." I zip my lips and mimic throwing away the key.

"In all seriousness though, Cameron. I know you're on some mission to reinvent yourself, but I don't think that means you can't also reconnect with the past. People come into your life for all kinds of reasons. Relationships all have beginnings and ends, could be a breakup or a death or simply just deciding to pursue other avenues, but you have to remember one thing. The only, and I mean the *only* thing that matters is how you conduct yourself in the middle. If you're his friend, show him the love and support that you would give any other friend you have. Then if he walks away, you can hold your head high knowing you were the best you could be while it lasted."

Daveed's truth bomb lingers heavy in the air, exposing my soul. I don't think I did everything right the last time I was with Will. I didn't understand him when he said he was joining the military. I was so desperate to hold on to what we had, I didn't consider his circumstances. Yes, he said he didn't love me, but I remember the look on his face when he said it. He didn't mean it.

Maybe that's why I've held on so long, it's unfinished business, a wound that never healed. While I know I'm not ready for anything more than friendship, maybe this is my chance to redo it and right those wrongs. I feel gutted. I've been on a high horse for five years, alternating between wanting him back and being so hurt that now even the most basic of things make me doubt myself.

My phone dings and I hesitate, not sure if my conversation with Daveed has come to an end. After some awkward eye contact, Daveed excuses himself, telling me I better look at it—and that I most certainly better keep him in the loop or else I'll be solely on ear-candling duty for the foreseeable future. You would not believe the weird shit that people have inside their ears—my stomach turns at the thought. Ugh, will I ever not be nauseated again? The jury is still out.

WILL

Hey. I kind of need a favor, and Lo told me if I didn't ask you she would kill me. She's scary, by the way.

CAM

Yeah, okay 💀 That girl couldn't hurt a fly. What is it, Rambo?

WILL

So, I know you don't really like "sporty" things, your words not mine, but there is this fundraiser my squadron does every year, and up until five minutes ago Smith was my partner. But you know LOOOOOO got involved and I can't participate alone and it's mandatory sooo . . . wanna be partners?

CAM

It's not something Amy can do? If it's, as you say, "sporty," I'm not sure I would actually be doing you a favor. Remember the bowling alley incident? Actually don't. Please forget that.

WILL

I don't know anything about a bowling alley, actually I've never even been to one, Wright. And nope, Amy's busy. I promise you will be fine, and I'll be with you the whole time. I wouldn't ask if I didn't really need a friend. Please say yes! I'll pick you up Saturday at noon.

CAM

I work on Saturdays. I guess I can sweet-talk my way into getting off an hour early, but you will have to come to the salon. Also, what am I supposed to wear?

WILL

Just wear athletic gear and bring a change of clothes. Thank you, I owe you my life. It's a date.

CAM

You got it, dude! Also, not a date . . .

WILL

It's just a figure of speech. Thanks again.

CAM

You owe me, Rambo.

I don't know what the hell I just signed myself up for, but my stomach is doing somersaults at the thought of spending more time with Will. Why did he call it a date? It's not a date. Also—"you got it, dude"? Who am I, Michelle Tanner? I know I better get my butt back inside to fill in Daveed, but first I need to send Lo a hate text. She seriously owes me for this. Sports and I don't mix.

FOURTEEN

Will

"Closer" - The Chainsmokers & Halsey

Saturday rolls around, and I don't know why I'm so nervous. I've done this obstacle course multiple times, Smith and I usually win the whole event. This year is different though. I'm partnering with Cam. Cam who says she isn't into "sporty things" but who I also know is the most competitive person on the planet and can hold her own physically, when the opportunity arises.

I told her to bring a change of clothes, but I wasn't exactly forthcoming about the amount of mud she's going to face today. She's going to be pissed, I know it, but Amy insisted that this would be a good opportunity to show her that we can be friends.

I stopped by a little sub shop to get us some sandwiches before I headed over to the salon to pick Cam up. I have no clue what I'm about to walk into here, but I imagine it's going to be the biggest challenge of the day, at least for me. Pulling up to the address Cam gave me, I notice

it's a house. I wouldn't have pegged a salon to be in this seventies-style bungalow, but Google Maps hasn't let me down yet, and based on the sign, I'm in the right place.

Walking up to the door, I can smell the aroma of what I assume is hair dye and hear the low drum of hair dryers mixed with laughter. Taking a deep breath, I twist the knob on the front door and walk into an onslaught of chaos.

It's not actual chaos, but it's almost like one of those ballets you see—people moving about in some weird, coordinated fashion, hair being swept, pulled, and tugged into perfectly coiffed styles. I'm so out of my element. This is a far cry from the Mickey's barber shop that I visited as a kid. Walking into Mickey's was like walking into a bar during the day. It was sort of dingy and filled with stale cigarette smoke. This place is high-end, with blow-dryers dropping from the ceiling and stylists sitting on what look like horse saddles.

A man starts toward me, and I hold my hands up like I'm about to be accosted. *What the hell is wrong with me?* I'm a complete fish out of water here.

"Hey, can I help you?" the man asks while sizing me up, like he wants to remove my clothes and lick my body from head to toe. I shiver a little. I'm not used to being checked out so blatantly by anyone. This guy's game must be strong for him to have that kind of confidence. "Umm, I'm here to pick up Cam," I respond, sounding a little more growly than I intended.

"Sooo you're *the* Will Davenport we've heard so much about. Sure, I'll grab her—but just know that Cam belongs to Daveed and me. If you mess with her, we will both come for you!" Mr. Guy-Who-I-Thought-Was-Friendly-at-First exclaims.

"Oh Luka, stop it. We all know I'm the most threatening one here," Cam breaks in with a giggle. She looks at me with a brow raised, like she knows I'm at a total loss here. It's almost comical that she can read my inner monologue and figure that I have absolutely no clue what I'm doing in a place like this.

"Hey, Micah, good to see you again." I wave at the one other person I know besides Cam when I see him near the blow-dryers. "Are you ready?" I blurt out, wanting to get the heck out of here as quickly as possible.

"Yep, let me just grab my stuff from the back. Oh, and change real quick," she says. I give her a look that I hope conveys, *Please make it quick.*

While I wait for Cam, which feels like the longest four minutes of my life, I continue to get side-eye from Luka, who's perched at the front desk, and inquisitive looks from everyone else. Right when I hear the door swing open, I expect to see Cam, but instead a good-looking man saunters out and heads over to me.

"Hello, William. My name is Daveed, I'm the owner of this salon and also Cameron's biggest fan," he says, definitively.

"Nice to meet you, sir. This is a really nice place, impressive." I clasp and unclasp my hands, shifting from one foot to the other with nerves.

"Cameron is a real talent; I hope that you will not damage any of her God-given gifts today. I have big plans for her future, and I expect her to be physically and emotionally intact on Monday," Daveed warns.

"Yes, sir. Cam's . . . Well, she's important to me. I intend to take very good care of her," I explain, stumbling over my words. He just raises his brow at me in a look that tells me no matter what I say, he already knows I'm in really deep trouble with this one.

Cam sweeps into the lobby slash hair-doing area (I don't know what the hell it's called). The air whooshes out of my lungs. She has on those legging things that women like to work out in, except hers are camo and there are sections that look like mesh, so you can see parts of her skin through them. She's paired them with a fitted black tank top—I guess that's what I'd call it, but it's practically a freaking bra. It stops about an inch above where her leggings start, exposing a sliver of milky soft skin. Her hair has been thrown up into a flowy ponytail. My palms itch, wanting to reach out and grab it.

"Okay, I'm ready now. Lead me to my impending doom," she says with a grin. *Her* doom? I was screwed just by asking her to do this, and now she shows up like some Rambo Barbie ready to compete as my partner. The worst part is, I know she's even more beautiful on the inside.

Friends, man . . . We are just friends. I need to lock down my feelings. Today is too important for me to get distracted by things I can't even begin imagining how to handle.

We get in the car, and I gently toss Cam her sandwich before taking off.

"Oh, Antonio's. I love this place . . . Well, I used to anyway." Cam's voice falters.

"Is there something wrong with Antonio's?" It's always been reliable and delish as far as I've known, but she looks like she might be sick.

"Oh no. It's fine. Great, actually. I just had an epically bad date there not too long ago, and I may not be able to show my face there for a while." Glancing at me tentatively, she dives into her sandwich, moaning about how good it is. My heart is beating erratically from her admission—and from the sounds she's making. I bite down on my lip to keep myself from saying anything about her dating life. *She's not yours. She can date if she wants to.*

Cam and I walk up to the registration tent, and the look on her face tells me it was a mistake to bring her here. Her skin has turned three shades of pale, and her cheeks are puffed out like she may throw up as she assesses the obstacle course sprawled out in front of us. I tell the lady at the check-in table our names. She gives us race bibs and thanks us for participating.

Of course, I'm going to participate. This charity provides much-needed mental health services and supplies to soldiers struggling with PTSD. I used to think that was weak and that this fundraiser was some sort of ploy to help the guys who just couldn't hack it. But that was before we lost Thatch. I've seen first-hand the damage that being overseas can do to a person, and I'm more committed to doing this race than ever before. Cam doesn't know that, of course. She thinks this is just something I'm required to do for work.

"Why didn't you tell me I was going to be facing the endurance challenge of a lifetime prior to my wolfing down an entire sub?" Cam asks, clear annoyance etched across her beautiful face.

"You didn't ask," I respond, trying and failing to look clueless.

"Are you freakin' kidding me? Is this some weird version of *Punk'd*? Where's Ashton Kutcher?" she spits back at me.

Oh boy, she's pissed. I didn't think this through. I just thought she would show up and her competitive side would kick in. I assumed she'd be a boss like always.

"No Ashton here. Just you, me, and about four hundred other people. I didn't think I'd ever see the day that you'd shy away from a challenge." I wave my arm around, pointing out all of the other racers.

"Excuse me? I'm not shying away from anything, Rambo. But don't blame me if I puke all over you." She huffs and crosses her arms in defiance. There's my competitive girl. *Correction: not mine.*

"I guess if you throw up on me, we'll have to rinse off." I wink just to rile her up. and my stomach fills with a flurry of butterflies at the mention of showering together. A whoosh of anxiety quickly follows, making my vision go blurry. I have to stop thinking about her in that way. *I can't go there*, I remind myself.

"You have fun with that shower. It'll be a lonely one," she scoffs, then mumbling something about not being able to fit with another person since she's gained a little weight.

I opt not to mention it, but Cam thinking that she is anything short of perfection is so unfathomable to me. She's the kindest person I know—I've seen her literally give the last dollar she has to a friend who forgot their lunch money. When did she get so unsure of herself? She's never been one to be arrogant about how downright breathtaking she is, but she also never talked badly about herself. In fact, when I used to put myself down after my parents' divorce, she half-heartedly threatened to beat me up *(like she could)* if I didn't immediately treat myself better.

Cam always said that if you can't be kind to yourself, then how could anyone else be expected to be kind to you. She has a way of making people want to be better versions of themselves. She talks about weird shit, like seeing a light in you and your ability to change the world, one person or smile at a time. Did I damage her so much that she became more like me? Does she hold these insecurities now because I broke her heart? Or did something else happen to Cam along the way, after I left? I need to get to the bottom of it, but right now, it's more urgent that I convince her somehow to compete and help me win this thing. For Thatch.

Risking pissing her off further, I gently put my thumb under her chin, coaxing her to look up in my eyes. "I'm sorry I didn't tell you exactly what we were doing here, but I thought you'd assume given the attire I told you to wear . . . Oh, and the fact that I referred to it as 'sporty,' which is something I don't say, like ever. You'll do fine. I need you to harness that rage and help me win, can you do that? You can be mad at me later," I negotiate, my fingers tingling from where they touched her skin. The physical connection between us is undeniable, even though I vow to deny it.

"Fine, but I was serious when I said you owe me, Rambo. The only reason I'm doing this is because you seemed desperate, and I'm just nice enough to not let you flunk out of this . . . well, whatever the hell this is," she says with the most dramatic eye roll. It should worry me, but instead I am reassured that she still won't back down from a competition.

We make our way over to the starting line and catch up with the rest of the group. Lo tells Cam how hot she looks. *Yep, I agree, Lo. Thanks for noticing and reminding me.* Butler gives her a hug, apparently also noticing this blonde smokeshow next to me, and mouths, *You owe me*, over her shoulder. He doesn't want me to forget how he backed away from flirting with her that first night at the bar, because of bro code. I grab her hand just as the gun sounds, and we're off. Here's to hoping we actually make it through this. And that she doesn't kill me when it's over.

FIFTEEN

Cam

"Under Pressure" - Queen & David Bowie

Remind me the next time a friend asks for a favor to absolutely and without hesitation say *no*! We aren't even ten minutes into this race, and already my lungs are burning. I'm having to resist the urge to toss my cookies, and we haven't even attempted a true obstacle yet.

I estimate we'd run maybe half a mile when we came up to the first stop, which required us to dress in the attire of our troops, putting on helmets and heavy bulletproof vests. I also have to carry a plastic gun resembling one of those toy weapons that shoots Styrofoam darts, except this one doesn't shoot anything and is just another thing for me to keep track of.

Of course, Lo looks like she's having the time of her life. She loves working out and adventures. She's probably ecstatic to be participating in something like this. Meanwhile, I'm trying to cycle through all

the things my middle school track coach taught me back when I was attempting to transition from being a sprinter into someone who ran longer races, like the eight hundred meters and the mile.

Breathe in through your nose, out through your mouth. An oyster has a piece of sand inside its shell that hurts, and it's similar to the pain in your side. When you run, that sand turns into a pearl. If you just keep going, your body will be a beautiful pearl, Cameron. Unfortunately, it didn't work then, and it isn't working now.

"You doing, okay?" Will huffs out at me.

"Yep, great. This is a breeze," I wheeze at him. Will flashes that million-watt smile at me, and for a second, I believe I can actually do this. We stumble up on our first true obstacle, a set of door-like apparatus that have the top parts cut out, which require you to boost yourself up and through the hole. I manage it pretty easily, but Will rushes through like it didn't even faze him. *Jerk.*

I'm not sure if I'm relieved, but the next obstacle is only about twenty feet ahead, and there seems to be a bit of a backup. I'm thankful for the wait so I can catch my breath, but Will spots an opening just wide enough for one person. I look at him ruefully, since I don't think I'm tall enough to even hoist myself up over this barricade wall. Even if I had the arm strength, the height disadvantage has me thinking I might be qualified to skip this one.

Will smirks at me, almost like he can hear my thoughts and knows I'm looking for a way around this one. "The only way through is *over*, Wright," he says, chuckling at me.

"And how exactly am I supposed to get over it?" I ask.

"Oh, that's easy. I'm gonna give you a boost." He actually fucking winks. My swampy backside is going to be right in his face. I hate him, it's decided.

We quickly navigate over to the spot, and he asks if I'm ready. I level him with a look that screams that I'll never be ready, but he doesn't hesitate. In a flash, he's hoisted me up high enough that all I need to do is get a leg on the top of the wall and then I can straddle it and lower myself down the other side.

Did I mention his face is literally parallel with my right butt cheek? Maybe I should flex and really give him a show. Ugh, I need to get it together and just get over this wall before he drops me.

I carefully swing my leg over so I'm sitting on top of the wall. Then I make a big mistake: I look down and realize I'm perched nearly six feet in the air. I'm not afraid of heights typically, but something about the possibility of falling from this position has me paralyzed with fear. I glance down at Will, and he motions for me to keep going so that he can make his way over.

I shake my head furiously, letting him know I'm completely stuck. He sighs and tells me to hold on a minute, and the next thing I know, he's climbing up and over the wall a few feet down from me. Once Will has cleared the obstacle, I motion for him to go on without me: I've decided that this is my home now, and I will live the rest of my days like a bird perched upon this wall, overlooking the park.

Will runs over to where I'm content in my new resting place and asks, "Do you trust me?" Trust him? The answer to that is a resounding hell no. Now is not the time, but the question sends me unwillingly into deep thoughts about how my answer was always a resounding yes prior to our split.

"Cam, I need you to trust me. I'm going to reach my hands up, and I want you to grab them and then jump from the wall," he shouts.

"I'm good, I'll probably just stay here . . . You can't catch me, anyway, I'm too heavy," I shout back.

"Cameron, I promise I will catch you. You will not fall, just trust me. We need to keep moving if you want to win," he pleads with me.

Of course, I want to win, and he knows it. This is the disadvantage of doing this sort of thing with someone who knows me better than anyone—he knows exactly how to kick me into full gear. Against my better judgment, I nod.

I huff out a breath and ask if he's sure he's ready. He gives me a nod and reaches up to me. I can see the muscles in his forearms and shoulders bulging. It's actually unfair how distracting they are, but him being forced to catch me gives me an opportunity to gasp at them in a completely friendly, non-sexual way. Or at least that's what I'm calling it.

I grab his hands and hoist myself off the wall and over to him. He quickly wraps his arms around my legs, just under the globes of my backside. He lowers me slowly, as if he's taunting me; I can feel every muscle ranging from his broad, strong shoulders to his tree-trunk thighs. As I make my descent, I unintentionally smooth my hands down his hard chest and stomach, feeling nothing but solid, granitelike muscle. He's the one who caught me, but somehow I'm the one intensely short of breath.

I'm blushing from my chest to the tips of my hair, and I'm positive it's obvious. If my rosy cheeks weren't a dead giveaway, there's the fact that my nipples feel like they could cut glass. Thank God for thick-padded sports bras. The smell of Will lingers in my nose, a mix of sweat and cedar, simple, intoxicating, and ridiculously irritating. He should not smell this good. Will grabs my hand, and we begin running again. I can see Lo and Smith just up ahead. They're making us work to catch up.

The next obstacle is about a quarter mile up the path, and it actually looks pretty appealing right now. It's a mud pit with barbed wire strung neatly across it, about two feet above the crawling area. I don't know why I'm excited for this, but I surmise it's likely because I've never been afraid of getting a little dirty. And also, the mud is sure to cool down my overheated skin.

"Stay low and don't lift up until your whole body makes it out the other side," Will reminds me.

"I got it. This isn't my first rodeo, Rambo." I smile and dive into the mud.

It's thicker than it appears and proves more challenging to crawl through than I'd imagined, but we make it. Standing up on the other side gives me a sense of pride and accomplishment, like I might actually have a chance of surviving this thing. Will grabs hold of my arm and turns me to face him. Gently, he swipes his thumb through the mud caked to his chest and makes a quick swipe under each of my eyes.

"Now you look like a real Rambo Barbie," he says, with a bit of a catch in his voice.

I stare at him intensely, my voice turning mute and the tingling where his thumb just brushed the tops of my cheeks settling into a light vibrating rhythm. I am giddy over feeling this sensation after far too long without it. Should I really be getting this feeling from Will though? He was always a safe place for me, and we decided on being friends. But the heat that's covering my body from head to toe doesn't feel friendly at all.

Our issue hasn't ever been chemistry. Putting Will and me together is synonymous with lighting a match over a bucket of kerosene . . . but that's not what we are anymore. Together, I mean. How am I supposed to be his friend when he acts like there's more to it? And why does he even act like there's more to it? He didn't want me five years or fifteen pounds ago, so it doesn't make sense for him to act like he wants me now. Unless this is all just a game to him. *It's something to evaluate later, after I win*, I tell myself.

We muster on through the rest of the course, tackling some tires that have to be flipped, a set of wooden balance beams, and a series of calisthenics challenges. I run side by side with Will, having my second wind kick in. Occasionally, I catch him glancing at me with a shy smile and a look of pride on his face.

Finally, we approach the last challenge, neck and neck with Lo and Smith. There are tables lined up with puzzles that must be assembled in the right order. Will and I are assessing the pieces and starting to move things around to see how they might fit together when it hits me.

I've seen this puzzle before! I've watched almost every season of the popular game show where contestants compete to win prize money, and this is directly out of season three's final challenge. I toss a glance at Lo to see if she remembered too, but she looks clueless.

"Rambo, do you trust me?" I whisper.

"Umm, I guess . . . Do you know how to assemble this thing?" he asks.

"I think so. Give me the piece that looks like a star first, but don't make it obvious or you will give it away to Lo," I say quietly.

Will does as instructed and continues to hand me piece by piece discreetly. Every time Lo or Smith look over, we fake acting frustrated so they don't try to copy us. Will hands me the last piece, and I slide it in place, looking for a judge to come see. Everything checks out, we grab our flag, and run like our lives depend on it.

At the finish line, we run through a giant red ribbon. I'm elated—there's nothing like the feeling of winning, especially when you started out wondering if you'd even be able to finish the dang thing at all. More than that though, winning with Will feels like getting a gold medal. Proving to him, in a small way, that I'm worthy and strong. Well, that's the whole reason I was ever with Will in the first place. He gave me confidence; I felt sure of myself when I was with him because I never had to wonder if I could be loved. His belief in me gave me the boost that I never got from my parents. His appreciation for all the pieces of me, even the flaws. Although we are just friends now, it feels good to bask in the glory of it for a short second.

The crowd of spectators is cheering, and we dance around in celebration to the hoots and hollers. Will sweeps me up into a hug, lifting me in the air and twirling me around. Oh, good lord. If I thought the slow, taunting slide down his body earlier made me flush, it's got nothing on this. I shouldn't be letting him hold me . . . but I can't resist.

His breath is hot and sweet on my neck as he thanks me for helping him win. My lady parts cry out and rejoice like they are the winners now. I can feel how strong he is, holding me as if I'm light as a feather. His body is pressed so tightly against mine; it feels like this is where I'm supposed to be, and also like I could possibly have an orgasm just from hugging him. We fit together perfectly, like I was made specifically to melt into his hard, defined body. *It's official, I'm pathetic or desperate. Maybe both.*

No, my brain shouts, *don't do this again.* I push away, taking control of the situation, forcing him to put me down. The separation feels cold, but necessary given our friends status.

Lo and Smith run through the finish line next. "I can't believe you beat me." Lo hip checks me.

"You should've spent more time watching game shows with me on the couch." I shrug and smile at her. "You wouldn't be a loser if you had."

"I'm not sure that's something to brag about, honey." She pats me on the arm.

The four of us head into the beer tent to grab a drink and cool down. I'm eternally grateful for the portable AC units they have pumping in cold air because the sweat and exertion is catching up to me. We sit in amenable silence, gulping down crisp IPAs, which I should add taste great but are definitely not helping with the electrolyte imbalance I'm certainly suffering from.

Something to the left catches my eye, and I quickly glance over to see a life-size poster of a soldier with his story posted at the bottom. Excusing myself, I wander over and start reading about PTSD, learning how it shows up at random times and is often unidentified until it's too late due to the stigma surrounding mental health in this country.

The story talks about a soldier named Thatch, who served in the Air Force. He was a member of a joint special operations communications team. It explains that joint operations are common and necessary in our ability to fight our adversaries, both foreign and domestic. Thatch was twenty-three when he took his own life with prescription drugs.

He had been in a harsh situation overseas and never truly came home, not emotionally anyway. The storyboard is punctuated with a quote from his widow, Bri, saying, "I will never get back the love of my life, the person I believed would be the father of my children, but through groups and fundraisers like this one, we can all raise awareness and bring light to the battles our loved ones' fight even after returning home."

I'm struck by her statement. Tears pool at the corners of my eyes thinking of this stranger and how alone he must have felt, how alone his wife must feel now. How could I look down on Will for signing up to serve when it's the biggest and most selfless act that anyone can do? He signed up to lay down his life so that I could do anything in the world I want, and I yelled at him for it. I feel his large hand on my shoulder, and I turn to see he has tears in his eyes, too, and a fresh beer in his hand.

"Di-did you know him?" I ask, my voice coming out a little strangled.

"The greatest man I've ever known, he was my best friend," he says with a muffled voice and a nod.

Will places the beer at the foot of the poster. "This one was Thatch's favorite." I look at him from under my lashes, afraid to see the pain that I know is lingering there. Seeing Will in pain over the loss of his friend makes my heart thaw the tiniest bit. Will simply gives my shoulder another squeeze. "I'll tell you all about him some other time." I nod and we return to Lo and Smith.

SIXTEEN

Will

"Free Fallin'" - The Cadillac Three & Breland

Saturday went better than I was expecting. Cam and I ended up winning the event, despite her initial fears. Winning wasn't the goal, but doing it with her by my side made it that much sweeter. Spending time with her feels like a missing puzzle piece of my life is finally clicking back into place. It's calming to be near her, like I can finally come up for air after far too long.

I'm terrified that the closer we get, the closer I am to drowning for good. I can't lose sight of what's at stake for both of us.

Aside from winning, there were some other highlights of the day for me. Well, one highlight, really—when Cam slid down my body in the slowest, longest descent ever. I felt every soft curve of her as I set her down. Her body is tight yet supple, with curves in exactly the right places. I had to bite my cheek to keep myself from palming her round, full backside. My hands are still itchy from wishing I could have snuck

even one more brush against her skin.

I'm trying to play it cool, but the more time I spend with her, the more my feelings come back. Who am I kidding? The feelings never went away, I stuffed them down hard, like the trash you keep pushing down until the bag gets so full you can't get it out of the can.

Loving Cam has never been the issue though—it's being good for Cam. I've seen not only what my parents went through from not having had their own life experiences, but also now what Bri has to deal with in the wake of Thatch leaving us. I gave my life to my country; it's difficult to fathom how I can also give it to Cam. If I did, what would she be left with when something happens to me?

It may be selfish, but my identity is dictated so much by my profession at this point. I'm caught in the middle of a cataclysmic game of tug-of-war, holding on desperately to the little bits and pieces I have left that are just for me. And weighing the options of my future, whether I could bring someone into it with nothing to offer but unknowns.

Aside from me being scared of losing her, I can't open Cam up to the heartbreak that would inevitably come when something happens to me while I'm deployed. Not to be morbid, but it's only a matter of time until I'm physically damaged or emotionally scarred enough to not ever be the same. She doesn't deserve to become my caregiver or to watch my soul fade away like Thatch's did.

Thatch . . . I miss him more than words could ever describe. Thinking of him is one of those things where it feels good doing it but also leaves you twisted up afterward. Seeing the poster and reading the words spoken by Bri wounded me. Loss like this is similar to a knife being plunged just deep enough and then turned to enhance the pain. Thatch was a good man, and he didn't deserve to go out the way he did. The guilt, more than anything, eats at my soul when I remember the events playing out. They flash through my mind like a black-and-white movie playing on reel.

"Will, did you want to share today?" Brad, the chaplain in charge of leading our mandatory small group discussions, breaks into my thoughts.

After our unit got back from overseas, they made us start going to these group sessions with a bunch of other people around base. Some are from the Air Force, and some from other branches. The purpose for us all is the same: learn to cope with what happened. My therapist says these sessions are good for me, but they have a special way of bringing up all the things I desperately want to forget. We just sit around sharing heartbreaking shit—talk about pouring salt in a wound. We have to do it though, it's either agree to this or not be cleared to return to work.

"Ugh, not really. But I know you're not gonna let me out of it so here goes . . ." I mumble. "We were working a mission with our unit . . ."

The guys and I belong to a joint tactical airborne unit, so our group is comprised of members from multiple branches of the service. Our mission is to provide early entry and airborne communications. This means we're often the first group on the ground, sometimes dropping in via parachute to remote locations.

"Thatch was watching the video feeds, remarking about how dull of a day it had been, when our position was compromised. It wasn't compromised by your average terrorist looking to engage, but by a child. The girl couldn't have been more than seven or eight years old, and she was strapped with enough C-4 to blow most buildings. The other unit we were with moved to try to communicate with her and tell her they could help by disabling the weapons. But the vest she had on must have had a remote operator because she never pressed the button and yet it still blew up. Most of us were far enough back that injuries were minimal, but the image of that innocent girl, one who was likely not even given a choice, reverberated through our team the way shock waves linger after a large earthquake. You're never the same after you've been through something like that, and yet here we all are, minus Thatch, getting ready to go do it again."

"How does that make you feel, getting ready to head back, minus your buddy?" asks Brad.

"It's the job, Brad. You act like we have a fucking choice," I spit back at him, annoyed that he would even ask the question.

Smith chimes in, saving me from ripping innocent Brad's head off. "We all miss Thatch. Hell, he was a better man than most of us . . . But like Davenport said, we have a job to do. Rehashing it all isn't going to make any of it go away, and it sure as shit isn't going to make the enemy fight fair the next time."

Brad looks at us over the rim of his standard-issue, thick-rimmed black glasses, his brow furrowed a little. I'm sure he's seen this too many times to count, and there isn't an argument for it. We signed up for this exact thing, to fight against all enemies foreign and domestic when no one else will. Hell, Brad signed up to try to give us some hope and peace as a chaplain. I'm sure he didn't expect the horrors of war to fill his days. He probably envisioned us all sitting around in a circle singing each other's praises for a job well-done.

"Since we don't seem to be making any progress toward a resolution of what happened, is there anything else you'd all like to talk about today?" Brad asks, looking at his watch and frowning distinctly as the realization that we have thirty-eight painful minutes left smacks him on the cheek.

"Can we talk about the stunner that Davenport brought to the course this past weekend?" some dude named Shoemaker pipes in.

Brad's face shifts immediately from a state of surrender to intrigue. I know the line of questioning that's coming my way, seeing that I never bring female friends to anything work related for this very reason. I have to say something quick to shut it down. There's always someone looking to cozy up to your girl and keep them comfortable while you're overseas. I've seen it too many times, and it's something I strictly avoid. Cam, however, is my friend, and while I knew I shouldn't have opened her up to this scrutiny, I couldn't help myself. When it comes to her, I can never help myself. I'm starting to need her close all the time, and that scares the hell out of me.

"Cam is not open for discussion or dating!" I shout definitively, scoring me a couple of raised eyebrows from Smith and Ruiz. Butler is so damn lucky he doesn't have to come to these sessions since he wasn't on our last mission.

"Fair enough. Gibbs, you're up. What do you have for us today?" Brad gives me a nod of solidarity.

I try to pay attention to the stories that Gibbs recalls. I do believe people get something out of sharing their feelings, and I don't want to see anyone else end up like Thatch. Even so, sitting through these sessions is never easy. The meeting drags on until Brad finally declares us free to go, and I sigh in relief that the conversation never made its way back around to me.

Now that our group session is over, Smith, Ruiz, and I head to the base exchange, which is basically a glorified food hall, to get some lunch before going back to work. It's inevitable that they're going to bring up what I said about Cam. It's more a matter of when they're going to call me on my bullshit. We grab tacos, since that line is the shortest and we're running low on time. I'm working my sauce packet open when the tension mounts to an almost unbearable level.

"Okay, out with it. Smith. I know you have something to say," I mutter.

"Dude, laying claim to a woman you won't even fess up to liking . . . bold move," he says, snickering at me.

"What was I supposed to say? What would you have said if that guy chose to comment on Lo?" I demand, pointing my finger at him and raising a brow.

"Relax, I'm just giving you a hard time. But seriously, what's the deal with the Cam situation? She's all we heard about for years, and now that she's finally here, you're acting like a wimp. Why won't you ask her out?"

"We're just friends, Smith. I don't do relationships, remember? We've been over this!" I practically shout. He's pissing me off now.

"Okay, okay, okay, but hear me out . . . I know you don't do relationships, but you don't even know if Cam wants a relationship. Maybe she'd be cool with a few friends-with-benefits sessions, you know, until we leave. Keep it light, casual," he explains.

"Yeah, a little Netflix and chill, man," Ruiz adds, crunching down his taco.

"It'll never work, we have too much history, too many feelings. It's best if we're just cool with each other. That way once we leave, it's no big deal," I say around a mouthful of taco. I'm not about to open up and spill my heart out to these two town gossips anyway. It's better if I downplay any feelings I may or may not be having. They wouldn't understand where I'm coming from. They've never lost people, at least not in the way I have. Thatch was close with them for sure, but we were best friends. He was the first person I let in after my dad walked out and I dumped Cam. He was the only other person besides Cam that I let all the way in.

"Fine, if you say so, but let the record show that I think she's exactly what you need. She makes you better. I even saw you smile at the race, and my dude, I haven't seen those pearly whites since long before our last deployment. I even poured one out on Thatch's grave telling him about it. We all just want you to be happy," Smith admonishes.

I chuckle and shake my head because while he means well, Smith is relentless. I've been happy and smiled prior to the race day with Cam. He's just playing up the drama for his own enjoyment. Does she make me happy and want to be better? Yeah, of course! Is it possible for us to be together without one of us getting hurt? That's still a big, fat no.

SEVENTEEN

Cam

"Pretty" - Lauren Alaina

What is it about working out that makes you infinitely hungrier? You start this mission to become healthy, fit, in shape, sexy, whatever you want to call it. You're dedicated, like seriously all in, killing yourself, and yet all you can think about is eating. It seems really counterintuitive, like my stomach should get the memo that we're supposed to be eating less, not more.

It's unfair! I think this is why people pay big bucks to get hypnotized into not wanting to eat. It's got to be some sort of weird mind fuck that your brain is playing on you to keep the status quo. I don't buy into the whole "you're burning energy so your body wants more" bullcrap. My body has access to an assorted array of donuts, pastries, and french fries stored freely around my hips and thighs.

Since the fundraiser, I've been all in on getting fit. Doing the race gave me a good burn in my lungs and made my muscles feel that raw

ache that hurts but also weirdly feels magnificent. I decided that night, while soaking in an Epsom salt bath in my too-small bathtub, that this was the push I'd been waiting for. Since Saturday, I've been getting up early and working out at the little gym in our complex. I don't pretend to be an expert at the machines, but I've been trying to do at least thirty minutes on the treadmill and then some free weight exercises that I picked up from my mom's old Cindy Crawford workout tapes in the nineties. Patricia would be proud.

Will seems excited by me working out. On one hand, it's cute that he's being supportive, sending me workout ideas and protein powder recommendations. On the other hand, it's becoming pretty evident that he wants me to reshape my body. Last night he sent me one of those cliché thirty-day ab transformation challenges. I've been finding myself spending more time looking through our text thread trying to glean clues about his motivation than actually reading the messages for what they are—a friend trying to help.

WILL

Hey, Wright . . . want to do this ab challenge with me?

CAM

Erm . . . I feel like those things don't ever work.

WILL

Trust me! They work . . . Smith and I did one a few months ago, and I spent weeks rolling out of bed because I couldn't sit up fully.

CAM

You're really not selling it the way you think you are, Rambo.

WILL

Come on, it'll be fun.

CAM

Said no one . . . EVER.

WILL

I'll buy you a milkshake if you make it further than I do.

CAM

Hmm . . . add in some french fries and you got a deal.

As far as food goes, it's been all protein and salads for this girl, and let me tell you . . . I *hate* salad. It's rabbit food! Anyone who tells you they love salad is lying to your face. Well, unless it's doused in ranch dressing, then I suppose that's fair. I could eat a ranch dressing–covered flip-flop if push came to shove. But seriously, I've been dedicated. It's a real triumph in my opinion. I even turned down maple bacon sweet potato fries from Daveed at work, and he checked my temperature to see if I was coming down with something. *Asshole.*

For the most part, my friends at the salon have been supportive, and Lo is on board since she primarily eats healthy anyway. She's been helping me by making sure I have a healthy dinner to come home to and encouraging my workouts by either coming with me (that's if Smith didn't spend the night, of course) or making me a post-workout protein smoothie when I'm finished.

The scale, however, is not my friend. Rationally, I know it's only been a couple of days, but I still expected to see some progress. The amount I'm peeing should've at minimum reflected a pound gone. But nothing. Lo keeps telling me that it takes time and I'm building muscle, but I don't like it. I want to see the fruits of my labor pay off, and quickly. This is why I've never stuck to a fitness routine in the past. The process takes too long and it drives me crazy.

Did I mention Smith has been around . . . *a lot*? He's at our apartment practically every night, coming in from work with all this swagger, wearing his uniform. He's a great guy and he makes me laugh, but hearing Lo's lovemaking sounds all night is not helping to boost my ego. Seriously, someone should get the girl a gag or something to make it stop. I'm happy she's found someone who matches her over-the-top energy, but I'm starting to see cross-eyed from lack of sleep. Also, it feels kind of pervy for me to be listening, but my less-than-noise-canceling headphones aren't a match for her.

"Hey, can you text my boy and tell him to cover for me? I'm gonna be five minutes late to PT, and I forgot my charger," Smith asks, pulling me from my inner bitch session.

"Uh, yeah . . . You know we have chargers, right?" I deadpan, shooting off a text to Will.

CAM

Lover boy is running late because apparently he forgot this is the 21st century and we have our very own phone chargers.

WILL

Thanks! Good morning, by the way. How was your run this morning?

I leave him on read. At this point, it's becoming a little too obvious that he's invested in my workout plan for ulterior motives.

"Your girl's distracting . . . What can I say?" Smith quips, smirking and pulling me away from overanalyzing Will's response. "So when are you gonna give Davenport a chance to break outta the friend zone?" He looks at me with a nosy yet innocent sheen in his eyes.

"Last time I checked, he didn't want out of the friend zone," I respond with every ounce of annoyance I feel. What happens with Will and me is none of his business.

"Yeah, *okay*. My boy might be too stubborn to tell you, but he's been pining away for you for as long as I've known him." Smith rolls his eyes.

"Is that so? Well, if that's true, why doesn't he tell me that or make a move?" I ask defiantly.

"Cam, look, I have to run since I'm already late, but you're gonna have to trust me. My boy loves you, like big-time love, and he thinks he knows what's best for you, all that 'keeping you from hurt and harm' bullshit, but the love is the same. If you have any feelings for him at all, it's gotta be you who makes the moves because he's too stubborn," Smith rattles out as he's headed for the door. And then he just leaves.

Shit! What am I supposed to do with that? Smith is a meddler. He means well, but he doesn't understand all we've been through. He doesn't grasp that Will had his chance and blew it. But he also doesn't know that if Will made a move now, my willpower has waned and I'd likely give in. Even though I don't fully trust him, Will's been funny, sweet, and easy to be around.

"What was that about?" Lo asks, looking sheepish.

"Oh, you know, just your boy toy trying to get me in Will's pants, so he'll have more surfaces to bang you on around here," I say sort of joking, sort of not.

Lo blushes and huffs out a puff of air. "While I can admit that he probably is a little selfishly motivated, he does know Will better than anyone—well, next to you, that is—and there might be something to what he's saying, Cam."

"I don't think so . . . Will has never held back when it comes to getting what he wants. He loves the chase, the adrenaline of working hard for something and achieving it. If he wanted me, and that's a big *if*, he would make a move. He wants to be friends; he doesn't want someone who can't even lose weight when she tries," I say. I'm being way too vulnerable for this early in the morning, but if I can't open up to Lo, then who can I talk to.

"Why do you do that?" she asks.

"Do what?"

"Oh . . . I don't know, act like you're some horrible, ugly, giant ogre that no one could ever possibly want? What happened to being body positive and a badass feminist and all that other empowering shit?"

"I don't do that. I know what I am, Lo. I'm realistic. Honestly, you, Will, and Smith have to stop!" This might be the first time I've ever yelled at her, but in my defense, this conversation is becoming insulting.

This morning has been exhausting. First, there was Will being way too overinvested in my workouts, then Smith saying it's on me to make a move, and now Lo. I don't get it. I'm not trying to beat myself up, and I know I have some good qualities, but a life's worth of comments and directions have given me evidence enough to understand what I am. I'm not perfect. My parents always made me wait to see if my stomach felt full enough before getting seconds. I wasn't enough for Will to want to stay with—and believe me, if I looked like Camille Kostek, he would have.

Patricia and Dale Wright don't sugarcoat things. They always told Elliott and me that we were replaceable. Not replaceable as their children, but in the sense of our society as a whole: You must work hard, be the best, and even then, there will always be someone better than you. It's a good lesson actually, and one that's helped me along the way in school, work, and in my personal life. It's similar to what Daveed says about being the best you can in the middle: You have to give everything one hundred percent but also be realistic enough to know that even that might not be enough.

"Okayyy, so I know what I've said, and I heard what Smith said this morning, but what did Will do exactly?" Lo asks. I can feel the tension and disdain rolling off of her.

"Ugh . . . can we not? I need to get ready for work," I say dismissively.

"You can get ready while you tell me," she demands.

"Fine. I spilled the beans about my new fitness lady lifestyle, and now he keeps sending me workout ideas and asking about my morning runs. It's pretty obvious that he thinks I need to lose weight. Why else would he care this much?"

"Are you crazy?" She looks horrified.

"I mean, maybe. But it's just so obvious. If he didn't think that, why wouldn't he say something like, you're perfect the way you are?"

"Tell me, Cameron, when was the last time you went around telling your *friends* that they were perfect out of the blue?"

"Well . . . I guess, I don't. But he knows . . . he knows how much this has always been a struggle for me. The fact that he's not being reassuring tells me everything I need to know," I say with a shrug.

"Cameron. Jane. Wright. That boy couldn't keep his tongue from lolling out of his mouth for half the race and it wasn't from being out of shape. You are gorgeous. Inside and out, although this conversation is making me question the inside of you a little bit. When you walk into a room, men practically drop whatever they're doing and stare, you're just too dense to notice it. Furthermore, you haven't given him any reason to be nice to you, and yet he still dotes on you all the time, like when he saved you from the bowling ball or switched out your stool at trivia so you didn't fall. You are cold or callous toward him most of the time, and I know you think it's witty banter, but to me it just looks like a mixture of hurt feelings and jealous rage."

Lo shrugs and puts her hands up in the universal symbol of surrender. "There I said it, he needs someone strong and confident, capable of handling the shit they go through in the service and supporting him afterward. Propping up your ego isn't something he's going to want to do, and if you want a chance with him again, you need to get over yourself and quickly. He isn't going to wait around in the friend zone forever. You need to make a choice—and don't even think about saying you don't want him back. As for the text messages, did you ever think maybe he is just looking for a reason to talk to you?"

Lo stomps out of my room without giving me a chance to respond. She's never been mad at me over anything, not like this anyway. Maybe there's something to what she's saying. I've been actively practicing my self-demoralization skills a little more than usual lately. Since I saw Elliott, actually. Why am I doing this? How long is Lo going to be mad and throw this tantrum? More importantly, if she is right about Will, do I even care if he moves on from me?

I love Will, but I don't know if I'm in love with him. Yes, there is a difference. You can love a lot of people and impact their lives with that love. But being in love is a whole different ball game; it's more than just showing up, demonstrating kindness, and sharing memories. Falling in love is a joining of two souls, an experience after which you no longer have to carry the burdens of life alone. In many ways, it's not a choice in the beginning, hence the falling part. It's an all-encompassing need to be connected with that specific person, like our need for water or breathing. After time, it becomes a choice. The choice to keep going, to fight through the strange, murky waters that life continually plunges us into. Will and I have so much history that it's easy to confuse whether that love is the deep-friendship kind of love or the over-the-moon kind of love. I know I made mistakes when he was leaving for the military. Is this just my inner self trying to right those wrongs, or is it possible to fall twice? What would being with Will for real even look like now?

I know nothing about his job, other than he works on base and is a soldier. Truthfully, I don't really know a lot about him as a grown-up. Our texts have been entirely surface level, mostly gossiping about Lo and Smith, or him talking about how it is to live with Amy. I have a budding career, sort of. How long is he even going to be in Tampa? Don't they move around a lot in the military?

There is far too much pressure coming from our friends right now. Will and I should probably talk, but I don't really want to. I need to figure out my own crap first, starting with apologizing to Lo and trying to tame my inner voice. Body confidence issues are such a bitch.

EIGHTEEN

Cam

"Whether You Love Me or Not" - Meghan Patrick

Wednesday 7:45 AM

WILL

How bad would it be if I intentionally hid Amy's straightener this morning? I accidentally grabbed it to put it away after she left. Spoiler alert: it was plugged in and I burned the shit out of my fingers.

CAM

She might kill you in your sleep, Rambo. . . I would.

WILL

I may never have identifiable fingerprints again . . . it feels like justice to me. You would miss me if she killed me.

CAM

In your dreams, Rambo.

Thursday 6:56 PM

WILL

I just had the best taco I've ever eaten in my life. What are you having for dinner?

CAM

I don't think it can be the best in your life when you say that about literally any taco you've ever met. I had chicken and broccoli 😊

WILL

How was your day? Still getting the silent treatment from Lo?

CAM

Yep! She glared at me from across the room for a minute and then got distracted by Smith . . . surprise, surprise.

WILL

I'm sorry, that sucks. Want to watch a movie tonight? We can time it so it starts at exactly the same time.

CAM

No thanks, Rambo.

WILL

Let me know if you change your mind.

CAM

I won't.

WILL

I watched a movie with Ruiz once, at the
same time over Skype.

CAM

Cute, still a no.

It's been another long week at work, and Lo has been giving me the silent treatment for days. But Will has been texting me nonstop, and to be honest, I'm relishing it. I haven't made any decisions on how I feel about him yet, but with this fight between Lo and me still going on, it's good to have someone to talk to. Not that I can tell Will what we're fighting about . . . I'm pretty sure he thinks it's about Smith always being over.

The longer the fight goes on, the more I consider what my best friend was trying to say. I've been crazy hard on myself when, instead, I should be my own biggest fan—though that's easier said than done. I also need to make a decision about Will. Each time we talk, the lines get blurrier, and it's not healthy for anyone.

Daveed and I had a long talk about it today, and no surprise, he agreed with Lo about my need to stop being so hard on myself. He went on and on about how many clients have requested me to do their scalp treatments, and he made sure to throw in that a few have been asking for my number, which obviously he didn't give.

The kicker is, I don't know how to make myself feel better. How can someone miraculously love how they look? Can I buy confidence on Amazon? My self-esteem hasn't always been an issue for me. Of course my parents were realistic with my brother and me growing up, and I never thought I was a model. But Will broke me, and it wasn't just when he dumped me.

Will has always been spectacularly above average—I'm talking walking dreamboat. Like Elliott, he can turn all the heads in a room without even trying. He never consciously played up his looks, but I never believed for a second he didn't love the attention he garnered. A couple of weeks before he ditched our dreams and me, we had gone on a college visit.

Will seemed pensive during the entire tour, but right when we were going to meet my mom at the dining hall to head home, we walked past a sorority house. Some of the girls were tanning themselves on the front lawn wearing little more than scraps for bathing suits. Will's eyes were glued to them. I tried mercilessly to get his attention, but it was like I wasn't even there. Repeating the question I had asked him three times before he even heard me catapulted me into a serious spiral.

By the time we reached the dining hall, I was so furious over the blatant disrespect, I didn't say a word to either him or my mom the entire ride home. Later, my mom came up to my room and pried until I spilled the beans. Have I mentioned that Patricia isn't one to sugarcoat things. She told me that if I wanted the body guys dream of, I would have to work a little harder. And curse my grandmother for my bad genes.

I realized that night that I would never be good enough for any man, let alone Will. It didn't matter the hundreds of times I tried sculpting my body into something resembling a stick figure, I was destined to have curves. Part of me wept for the adoration I would never experience, and the other part got pissed off. Truthfully, it's probably why I begged Will not to leave me that night. I thought he was my only shot at some semblance of attraction. I didn't want to be alone.

When I shared this all with Daveed, he sympathized. He said he used to struggle with similar issues, and it wasn't until he decided to embrace himself for who he was, to stop wishing to be someone else, that he began to really come into his own. He explained that even if we aren't coupled up with someone, it doesn't mean we are alone.

After a fair amount of grumbling about Will's brain cells not all firing, Daveed said something that struck a chord, something that gave me a new way of viewing loneliness. I've been repeating his words in my mind all day: "Cameron, just because someone is single, it doesn't mean they are lonely. True loneliness comes from not having others to help carry you through life's messes. You have a family that loves you, friends who think you walk on water, and me. Don't settle for a relationship with Will, or anyone else for that matter, because you think it will bring you the self-acceptance you're seeking. True happiness, fulfillment, and acceptance of one's self comes when you let go of the fear you're carrying about being enough and about being alone."

It was such a profound statement, and so far removed from any angle I'd ever viewed my insecurities from previously. We strategized together on the best way for me to start moving past the stories I'm telling myself about how I'm perceived. My homework assignment was twofold: the next time I go out, don't let anyone else pick my outfit, pick something I feel good in, and essentially fake it 'til I make it. And second, call my therapist for a session.

I agreed to try it, to try to not pay attention to the voice in my head that's telling me what I think people believe, and to sit back to actually observe instead. There's nothing to lose by giving it a whirl. The only problem is it's Saturday afternoon, and I have no plans in sight for me to take my new perspective out on a test run. Speaking of plans, I'm desperate to make up with Lo, and I'm hopeful she will come home soon so I can give her the biggest hug, grovel on my hands and knees if I have to—oh, and also give her this bottle of tequila I picked up.

As if I summoned her, Lo waltzes into the apartment and slams her purse down on the table with a huff. Unsurprisingly, she's been drawing out the drama of this fight. The girl gives major pissed-off-mom vibes when she's upset.

"Lo, can we talk?" I ask hesitantly.

"Have you learned your lesson?" She stares at me, eyes practically bugging out of her head and hands on her hips.

"I think so? Is the lesson that you love me and don't appreciate me bad-mouthing myself because I'm your best friend and you wouldn't be friends with someone who isn't a body-positive feminist?" I hedge.

"Yes! I do love you, but I won't tolerate that bullshit, Cam."

"Okay, I can't promise that I won't ever feel insecure, but I can promise to stop talking badly about myself."

"Well, I guess that's a start, but you should know this is about more than just the negative self-talk. I want you to feel like you can come to me, confide in me about anything, not just feed me the surface-level shit that you share with the guys. I know there is more to this story. You have never been this self-conscious in the whole time I've known you." I notice a tremble in her voice. "I feel like you're shutting me out while tearing yourself down."

"I do know that. I really do." I jump up immediately, sweeping her into a hug. "I promise to be more open instead of keeping all my fears to myself."

"Good, now are you going to tell me what you're so afraid of with Will?" She looks at me with tears in her eyes. I guess it's now or never.

"It's complicated. I care about him a lot. I think I always will. But, as much as he was my person back then, he hurt me along the way too. He always got so much attention . . . I mean, look at him." I stop for a second to gather my thoughts. "There were times that I could tell he was noticing other girls. I don't think he would have ever acted on it, but when he dumped me it was so cold and calculated, like he knew he would have better options than me where he was going." Telling her this makes me feel a little guilty, since I don't want her to hate Will.

Lo reaches out to hug me a little tighter. "Do you know for a fact he was doing that, or is that just the story your very hormonal teenage brain told you? Because from where I'm sitting, I don't see a man who wants someone else."

I smile at her. She might have a point there. "Well, maybe I was a tad hormonal at the time. But you don't see a man who wants me now either."

"Cam, when was the last time you really looked at him?"

"I look at him every time I see him. Since we are telling the truth, I might as well admit, it's hard not to look." I shift a little out of her embrace. This is becoming a long conversation for holding on to each other through.

"Tell me what you notice about him, aside from the physical stuff, because phew . . . I have eyes." She shakes her arms out like she can feel his attractiveness. I get it. Boy, do I get it.

"Well, he's funny and kind. He seems a little sad or tense, like there's always something on his mind right out of reach that he doesn't want anyone to know." Walking over to the couch, I plop down, tucking one leg up under me.

"And what do we think that is?" she prompts me to spill, like I have the answer. I shrug because I really don't know. Lo keeps going. "I'll tell you, it's fear. That man went through some bad things after he left you. I'm not going to give you details because it isn't my story to tell, but there is a reason he's afraid to be vulnerable. According to Jackson, it started with his dad and continued to pile on from there. Will loves you, it's plain as day, but he's scared to death."

"What if I don't want him to love me? What if I'm not good enough?" A tear drops down my cheek, and I wipe it away quickly.

"You are better than good enough. You are everything, I just wish you could see it. And as for what you want, well, only you can decide that, but I think you do want him to love you."

"I don't think I could ever trust him again. Without trust what do I have?" I shift anxiously on the couch, biting my fingernails and fighting tears.

"Will you ever know if you don't try?" Lo approaches, sitting down next to me and wrapping me back into a hug. "Having insecurities isn't foreign to anyone, everyone has them, even if it seems like they don't. Relationships are never guaranteed to work out. Make me a deal, though. When you feel the worries coming on, tell me. I would never lie to you. Case in point, the new sweater you bought looks like it belongs to a grandma. Whatever you decide about Will, I've got you."

"Two things. First, you have a deal, and second, how dare you slip a dig about my new grandma sweater in that beautiful speech." I scoff at her while gently grabbing the bottle of tequila from where I stashed it behind a pillow, slipping it between us and making her laugh uncontrollably.

"So . . . you're buying me off with booze?" she jokes.

"Sorta. Also, Daveed gave me an assignment, and I really need my best friend to come get drunk with me." I give her puppy dog eyes for good measure.

"Sounds like my kind of assignment, what is it?"

"Well . . . I have to pick out an outfit that makes me feel sexy, get all dolled up, and then go hit the town."

"Yes! I knew I liked him!" Lo shouts, releasing me from the hug, then standing and spinning around.

I don't tell her about the other part of my assignment: sitting back and seeing how people react to me, instead of telling myself stories about how they see me. She would eat it up. But she'd also almost certainly spend the evening trying to point things out to me, and I need to observe everything unadulterated, for myself. Maybe I'll share with her later, when I'm hosed on tequila. That'll be entertaining!

She quickly tells me we have plans, already scheduled. In exactly forty-five minutes, I need to be ready to go to the beach, and I need to bring a change of clothes for whatever happens after. It's almost like she knew I couldn't stand her silent treatment any longer. She's such a brat!

I scurry to my room, searching for a bathing suit that makes me feel good. Twenty minutes later, it looks like a wind storm swept through and tossed clothes around my room. There are bikini tops hanging from the ceiling fan and panties strung on the lampshade. The good news is, I selected a black sequin bikini. It's got a standard triangle top, but the bottoms are cheekier than I would normally dare to wear. I'm looking for reactions, and this is the best bet for real, honest feedback since almost nothing is covered. Thank God I let Micah give me a Brazilian when it was slow at the salon on Thursday.

My beach bag is packed with the essentials: sunscreen, my favorite towel, the new Ray Riley book, and of course, my sunnies. In my overnight bag, I throw a bodycon red halter dress, my curling iron, a toothbrush, my makeup bag, some heels, and a lavender tank top. I have no idea what we're doing later, so with my distressed jean shorts over my bathing suit and my favorite sandals, I'm pretty sure I have all the bases covered.

I spend a few minutes braiding the front of my hair into a headband braid, so it'll stay out of my face in the heat, and give the rest of my hair beachy waves. I slick on some lightweight tinted sunscreen and peachy lip gloss, just because. I'm gathering the last of my things when Lo peeks her head in and says our ride is here. *Wait? Who's picking us up?*

Lo hands me a travel cup, and by the smell of it, I'm one-hundred-percent sure it's mostly tequila. I take a big swig . . . Oh boy! I think it's all tequila. I attempt a muffled cough as she grins.

"You weren't supposed to drink it until we added the mixer, ding dong," she cheerily tells me.

Off to a great start! We head downstairs and sweep up to not one, but two Jeeps with their tops down, doors off. Excitement vibrates under my skin; I love convertibles! Sweeping my eyes over the vehicles, I notice there's a spot for Lo in the first one, front seat since Smith is driving and Ruiz is already sprawled out in the back.

That's when I hear it, a growly, almost unrecognizable, "Wright, you're with us!" Is Will sick? It sounds like his tongue is stuck in his throat. I make eye contact with him, not that he can tell since I'm wearing my sunnies. Oh . . . he's not sick. There's heat in his eyes, and he looks possessive as fuck. I glance quickly around me and then it hits me—he's looking at *me* like that. My stomach does a backflip, but I don't dawdle. I hop into the stunning black Jeep, deliberately shimmying a little extra to get comfortable while I greet Amy and Butler, before turning to him. "Hey, Rambo."

—

Waves crash against the shore in a rhythmic and soothing beat, and white sand is buried between my toes. I'm relaxed, thrilled to be spending the afternoon at the beach with my friends. Having an actual group of people I can refer to as my friends is so refreshing. I've had people I can rely on, but feeling like I actually fit into a group for the first time since moving to this city is exhilarating.

The ride here was the most fun I have had in a while. Will and I bumped the music and sang like idiots at the top of our lungs to some nineties throwbacks like LFO and my girl Britney. Will belting out all of the words to "Space Cowboy" by everyone's favorite boy band though . . . epic!

Lo made us drinks as soon as we arrived, and I've been chilling on my towel, soaking up the sun and the view. I'm not talking about the ocean, ladies. Being with a bunch of dudes who are required to be in shape for their job is far from a hardship. Will has the best body, I get goose bumps just looking at him wearing his low-slung blue board shorts, the kind that show that perfect V, pointing like an arrow directly down to other admirable parts of him. It's been a long time since I've seen my old friend down below, but I can recall what he looks like vividly, much to my dismay.

Will is flaunting every curve and swell of his perfectly tanned muscles. He's throwing a football with Smith. If I was a betting woman, I'd say he's flexing a little harder than needed with every toss. Thank the good lord that I chose my darkest sunglasses—I'm rapidly approaching creepy stalker territory with how much I'm starring.

Lo smirks knowingly at me from her towel. "Are you going to take off those shorts and go for a swim with me?" she asks. I silently weigh my options: I could sit here and read my book and leave it all to the imagination, or I could take the shorts off and walk down to the water and see if anyone even notices. Daveed's voice, like a little devil on my shoulder, whispers to me . . . *"Cam, shake that ass, girl!"*

"Yeah, sure, let's do it," I tell her.

I make my way to stand and slowly pull off the shorts. No one is looking, so I'm not sure why I'm moving in slo-mo, but whatever. I take two big gulps of my drink, make sure I have a hair tie in case I go in deep enough for my hair to get wet, and adjust my top for maximum lift.

We make our way down to the water, snaking directly across the boys' throwing area. *Thanks, Lo.* I pass by Will, and he grumbles almost inaudibly, "Ohhh fuck me," or at least I think that's what I hear. Smiling to myself, I wade into the warm water with Lo, taking extra care to shuffle my feet. Stingrays are no joke!

Suddenly, there's a huge splash beside me, and something latches on to my leg. I scream, jumping like my life depends on it, prepared fully to pull a Michael Phelps and haul ass out of the water. Bulging, strong arms wrap me up before I can make my great escape. Will's vibrating laughter is sealed against my back, his hot minty breath wafting on my neck when he utters, "Gotcha."

"Rambo! You about gave me a heart attack," I shout breathlessly.

He tugs at my hand, pulling me out a little deeper in the water. "You in that suit is giving every man on the beach a heart attack, Wright. I was just doing a public service." He feigns innocence, but the darkening pools of those cerulean eyes paint a very different picture.

I roll my eyes, the corner of my lips turning up into a shy smile. He pulls me toward him, sucking me into one of those hugs in the water where one person essentially holds the other up weightlessly.

"What are you doing?" I ask, splashing water at him.

"Just hanging out with my friend." He shrugs, a lopsided grin blooming on his face.

I grab on, wrapping my legs around his waist. "I'm a little glad we are friends," I admit.

"That so? Coulda fooled me, Wright." He winks. Shit, this is a very bad idea. Warmth fills my belly, then slips down lower.

"Nah, just fucking with you, Rambo. I am completely unaffected by your friendship," I lie, as an impressive steellike rod pushing against my inner thigh makes an appearance. Umm . . . well, let's just say it doesn't seem grossed out, and it also doesn't feel friendly, but I'm still not sure if it's a win or not.

Will holds me for a few minutes, waves bobbing against us as we ignore the clear way our bodies react to each other. I tuck my head under his chin, listening to the sounds of the ocean mixing with his heart beat. He's so strong, he smells divine, and I want him more than I've wanted anything in a very long time. I'm not sure what's going to come out of my mouth, but feeling brave, I lift my chin to say something, anything. As I do, he sets me down on my feet with a splash.

The water is startlingly cold outside of his embrace, goose bumps returning to my skin for completely different reasons. "G-gotta get more sunscreen," he mumbles, as he shuffles his way to the shore without another word. Gahhh! We were having a moment. Did I do something wrong? Was he just being playful and my cuddling him in a non-friendly way became too much? It didn't feel like too much, but we did agree to be friends.

I steal a glance at Lo, expecting her to be fully wrapped up in Smith. Instead, they're both looking at me with pained sympathy in their eyes. To hell with it. I head back to my towel, my tequila, and my book. At least Ray's mystery romance featuring a hot Hispanic man won't let me down!

NINETEEN

Will

"Love You Again" - Chase Matthew

Why did I suggest going to the beach? Oh yeah, because it's all I've wanted to do on my day off for weeks. And yet, it was an incredibly stupid idea. The worst possible idea in the history of all ideas because we invited the girls. Cam in a bikini . . . well, that just might be the best thing I've ever seen. Frankly, her body has changed since we were last together. Gone is the girl from my youth and firmly in her place is a curvy, luscious woman.

Seeing Cam strut down to the water with most of her perfectly round, delectably plump backside hanging out made me forget my own name. All the blood instantly rushed from my head down south, and I acted without thinking. Playing with her in the water was nonnegotiable, a must-have, at the time. Her body was like a homing beacon drawing me in, I was powerless to resist her. I held her in my arms as the water gently rocked us back and forth, lost in the flowery smell of her lotion

mixed with the coconut shampoo she must use and the salty ocean air. Someone should bottle that scent and sell it, it would fly off the shelves. Cam felt amazing in my arms, she fit perfectly against my body. I savored every second of having her there until, embarrassingly, my body reacted in a visceral way. Leave it to my stupid brain to take over. As frustrating as it is, I had to put her down and remove myself before I did something impulsive like kiss her.

I can't though, the mere thought of crossing the line with her sends me spiraling. She's everything I've ever imagined in a partner. She's kind, funny, smart. She has no problem giving me shit—hell, she riles me up more than the guys. But, I absolutely can't cross that line.

Lucky for me, working to avoid kissing, or any of the other hundred things I'd love to do to her, isn't over today. When I asked Smith to do the beach thing, of course he took it to the next level, convincing me to rent a little place on the Intracoastal so we could take full advantage of the bar scene. Staying down here didn't save me money, an Uber would've been far cheaper. Unnervingly, he convinced me with just two words—Drunk Staycation!

I'm hopeless.

I rented a bungalow equipped with three small bedrooms, two bathrooms, a tiny galley-style kitchen, and a living room. The garage was converted into a game room, with a pool table and darts. There's also a hot tub outside, which I would love to use but have decided to strictly avoid in order to keep myself safely in the friend zone.

Butler and Ruiz have one room claimed, Smith and Lo will take another, and Cam is getting a bedroom as well, which leaves Amy and me relegated to the living room. I plan to give Amy the couch, and I'll sleep on my military-issued cot, which is essentially a one-inch pad that inflates and provides minimal cushion to the floor. I've slept on worse though.

"Hey, pizza's here!" Smith shouts.

My stomach growls in response. I didn't eat much all day and desperately need to tear into something before heading to the bars. Keeping myself in check around Cam requires not being overcome with alcohol. The three bulk-store bottles of liquor waiting on the counter mock me, and I know my attempt is likely futile. The guys dig in while lazily looking around, wondering what our lady counterparts are up to. If I had to guess, there's a flurry of hairspray and makeup flying around in the master bathroom as they prepare to head out. Amy begged Cam to style her hair. Of course, she didn't say no. It's her day off, but she would never turn down a friend in need. I'm positive Cam's elbow deep in some sort of fancy-curling-iron-meets-aerosol-can debacle.

We eat about three quarters of the pizza before deciding we better leave some for them, or we're going to have tears and throw up to deal with later. I realize they're all grown women and can handle themselves, but I've also seen what happens when too much tequila goes down without food. Hell, I've had a moment or two myself, crying to Don Julio about my problems.

Making quick work of it, I shower, change, and head back out to the living room, where still no signs of life from the girls can be found. Did they all pass out from fumes?

I settle into the couch, knowing that this may be the only reprieve I get for the rest of the night. Going out will be fun. I'm genuinely looking forward to some downtime with my buddies and a change of pace from our usual haunts. The bathroom door swings open crashing into the wall, flooding the entire house with lady smells a thud so loud I'm worried I may not get my deposit back. There's hairspray, obviously, mixed with perfume, and something else I can't put my finger on.

Exchanging looks with Butler, I slowly turn around to see Cam, Lo, and Amy tumbling out in a fit of giggles. It's contagious, the laughter and joy on Lo's and Amy's faces makes me chuckle to myself. Clearly, whatever they were doing in there was far more fun than what's been happening out here.

Amy sashays down the hallway first, wearing a black skirt that's too tight and too short with a purplish sequin crop top. Her outfit is way too provocative, and my big brother instincts are on high alert, causing me to scowl at her and raise an eyebrow dangerously close to my hairline. She notices me glowering and gives me a look while flipping me the bird. That settles that. I'm not allowed to comment on how my sister is dressing, apparently.

Lo follows after her with a skintight black dress on and heels that accentuate her smooth, defined legs. Not that I'm checking her out, it's just facts. Smith looks like he could bite off his tongue as sweat begins to bead on his forehead. He is so screwed or lucky—I'm not sure which, maybe both.

She looks us all dead in the eye, which should be impossible since we are spread out around the room, but she somehow manages and says, "Line up the tequila, boys!" A stifled cough rolls out of Smith as he saunters to the counter to obey her orders. Call the fire department, the man is toast.

Facing back to the hallway, waiting for Cam to appear, makes my stomach do those weird flip-flops. She's the last one we're waiting on, which makes sense since she likely helped the other two get ready. I take the shot Lo hands me graciously as she whispers, "Prepare yourself, she's dressed to kill tonight." Is Lo conspiring with me now to make a move? I hate to disappoint her, but it's not going to happen.

Cam rushes out of the bathroom and down the hallway, apologizing that she took an extra three minutes longer than the others, and all I can do is stare. That's so typical Cam, worried about inconveniencing others. It's absurd and charming all at the same time. I'm paralyzed by the fire-engine-red dress Cam has poured herself into, leaving nothing to the imagination. It has one of those ties around her neck and pushes her cleavage up, offering a delectable view of her curves. Her legs are not exceptionally long, but the heels she's wearing make them seem lengthy, sculpted, and tan. She's still rocking that braid that looks like a headband, but her long blonde hair is wavy and hanging loose over her shoulders and back.

Cam heads to the kitchen, giving me a view of the back. My mouth is rapidly turning as dry as the Sahara. I swallow hard, trying to forcibly make my salivary glands work once more. The dress is so short that her ass is barely covered, and the back of it is completely open. Who the hell makes clothes like this? It should be illegal. She tosses back not one, not two, but three shots of tequila before sucking tenderly on a lime. My pants feel too tight, and I adjust myself discreetly before walking over to her.

"You, uh . . . you look good, Wright." I stumble on my words, moving next to her at the counter.

"Not so bad yourself, Rambo." She bumps her shoulder into mine, unleashing a chain reaction of tingles up my arm. "Although, this is getting a little long." She ruffles my hair with her fingers, twirling to walk away.

"Maybe I'll call Micah, get in for a fresh cut." I grab her arm gently, rubbing the smooth skin on the inside of her wrist with my thumb.

"You could try, although . . . I'm not sure he gives as good a head rub as I do, Rambo." With that she pulls away, walking toward Lo and heading out the front door. I groan. She isn't going to make this easy on me at all.

___

The military has reformed some of their interrogation methods, ones that were deemed too harsh or inhumane for the treatment of our enemies. Things like waterboarding and other forms of torture are not used widely anymore, at least not according to the mainstream ideals of what goes on in interrogation rooms.

I won't confirm or deny if those things still happen, just that we are trained to say they don't. Where am I going with this? Well, call up Mr. President because I've just discovered the best way to get a heterosexual man to answer questions and bend to every demand: Cam in this damn red dress. Well, really her in anything, the way she commands a room without even trying is like nothing I've ever seen before. People gravitate toward her, and she welcomes them each with friendly conversation or open arms. It's why I know she will be successful in her career, she's got that magic aura about her. It's why I know, no matter what I want deep down, I will never be deserving of her attention. I never have been.

We made our way through a couple of bars, having a drink and appetizer at the first. By the way, eating shrimp shouldn't be sexy, but apparently it is. If I could get Cam to slurp something off of me the way she carefully lapped at the butter dripping off the crustaceans . . . *Fuck, I'm hard again just thinking about it. Stop it, body, we aren't going there.*

We're at the third bar on our crawl now, and it's getting pretty late. The girls are all dancing to some not-so-good cover band like it's the greatest concert they've ever been to. Fun is one word for what they're having, but it has been supported by several shots of tequila.

Cam has been flirting with me all night—actually, she's been flirting with everyone all night. She danced too closely with Butler at the last place. He apologized to me afterward, but I could tell it was equal parts awkward and hot for him. She even made a play at Ruiz, which was pretty funny, seeing how shy he is. He blushed for twenty minutes after she kissed him on the cheek and playfully called him her "Latin lover."

I would be lying if I said the green-eyed monster hasn't been sitting on my shoulder all night. Seeing Cam all over my friends made my stomach turn sour. I stopped drinking at the last bar, just so I could be coherent enough to make sure she didn't end up in the wrong bed, and I didn't end up in jail for killing one of my friends. I have no claim to this girl, but I can't help feeling protective over her, like she's mine even if she isn't. She's messing with me, because logically I know she doesn't seriously want to be with either Butler or Ruiz.

"You gonna sit there and scowl all night, or you gonna do something about it?" Amy asks, putting her hands on my shoulders, gently kneading the knots that live there and breaking into my jealousy trip down pity lane.

"What am I supposed to do here?" I ask, rolling my eyes.

"Quit being afraid of everything that might go wrong and just let it happen, Will," she responds, annoyed.

"Why are you mad at me, Aims?" I scoff. I didn't do a damn thing wrong here.

"Let's see . . . you've wanted another chance with her for years, and now she's right here and you're letting your head dictate what happens, not your heart. You don't know how it will turn out, but you can't protect her at the cost of your own happiness. You can sit here and say you're afraid of losing her all you want, but that ship has sailed. Even though you're just friends, if she walked out of your life right now, it would hurt just as much. So for the love of God, just go with it, see what happens." She says all this with a vehemence that gives me chills, reminding me of our mom.

"Amy, stop. You don't understand, and you never will." I'm about to get up to take a walk, go to the bathroom, do something to clear my head, but a firm hand on my shoulder stops me.

"She's not wrong. Thatch not being here broke you, buddy." Smith's voice is gruff. "I see it, fuck, we all see it. But here's the thing that you keep failing to understand. He didn't leave because of you, just like your dad didn't leave because of you. They left for different reasons, but they both left because of their own issues. You didn't cause any of it, and nothing you did or didn't do would have changed it. Just like nothing you do, aside from maybe cheating, would be the reason she walks away, if she ever does."

Smith moves in front of me, pushing the table back and out of the way so he can get right up in my face. "You aren't the only one who lost a best friend that day, and do you want to know what the most fucked up part is . . . I lost two. You might be able to hide from everyone else, but you can't hide from me. I've seen you in the bathroom wiping your mouth off when you throw up from the anxiety or the flashbacks. I've seen you go for a run at five in the morning because I'm up doing the same thing. He would want you to live, to soak up every moment you can while you can because he couldn't. He would tell you that you've seen horrible shit and that nothing, not even fear is worth wasting a minute of your life because one day you are going to take that last breath and you don't want to regret the shit you didn't do."

"Fine, fuck. I know you're right, but . . ." I run my fingers through my hair. Can I do this? Should I do this? "She's different. She's the only one who's ever seen all of me. I'm not the same as I was back then. If I was damaged then, I'm obliterated now," I whisper to Smith, and Amy, since she's now crowded into my space too.

"She doesn't strike me as the type to walk away from damaged. She's the human equivalent of duct tape, stick her on you and suddenly you're all patched up. I mean fuck . . . I didn't even know you knew how to flirt until she came around. Quit fighting it."

"Fine . . . I'll try, but you two are responsible if this backfires. And it'll be your ass picking me up off the floor." I point at Smith. I know he would be there for me a million times over.

"Deal, but Will, don't take it too far . . . just enough to see if you still have something there. I don't want either of you getting hurt," Amy admonishes. What happened to throwing caution to the wind?

"Deal." I smirk at my sister. She has no clue how strong the connection is and that I already know there is enough heat between Cam and me to start a forest fire the likes of which the modern world has never seen. Chemistry has never been our problem; it's been emotions.

I've hurt Cam before, and I don't want to lose another person, but maybe things will be different this time. Or maybe the alcohol is leading me down a path I shouldn't take. But hey, wouldn't be the first time, and torturing myself by not finding out sucks.

TWENTY

Cam

"Bad Idea Right?" - Olivia Rodrigo

'**ve** been dancing for hours. I'm drenched in sweat, and I don't believe for a second that my playful flirting with Will's friends has gone unnoticed. He's eyed me warily all night, the scowl he's been sporting for the better part of the last two, maybe three, bars is almost comical. He's making this more difficult than it has to be. It's not like making a move on me isn't something he hasn't done before. And while a few days ago, hell, a few hours ago, I would have reasoned his lack of response toward me was because he wasn't interested, I know better now.

How am I suddenly so confident? For one, feeling his hard length against me in the ocean was a dead giveaway. Second, he hasn't so much as looked at anyone else, and trust me when I say there isn't a shortage of drool-worthy girls to go around. It's the beach after all, it's practically a walking porno mag everywhere we turn.

Amy has been giving me shit all night about not making my move.

The thing is though, even if I can tell he wants me, there is no way I'm acting first. Will has always loved the chase. Plus, my newfound understanding of his feelings is not enough for me to open myself up to rejection from him, or from anyone else for that matter. I guess I still don't fully trust my intuition or his supposed feelings for me, as told by Amy and Lo.

I spotted Amy and Smith talking to him earlier. They must have said something about the stick he had lodged up his ass because he started drinking again—not enough for him to be drunk, but definitely enough to be bold. I, on the other hand, started the night strong, but the food I plowed through and the dancing has made it nearly impossible to get anywhere beyond that warm, hazy buzz that happens after the first two drinks. Honestly, I'm thankful. I hate feeling out of control or hungover.

Slow beats bellow out of the speakers, lulling me into a euphoric state. I slowly swing my hips as the music takes a slightly more subdued turn. Music has always been fuel for my soul: a quick, happy song with the windows down to celebrate the fresh spring air, a soul-wrenching breakup song that drowns your tears better than any girls' night or pint of ice cream. Songs like this are so much more than just music; it's therapy, soothing me and carrying me through any situation imaginable.

I close my eyes, taking a deep breath, content to let the melody carry me through this weird night, and really, this entire weird situation of being caught in the middle. I don't want to admit that I have feelings for Will, but it's something that won't go away. Like a splinter you work at but can't seem to pull the last bit out.

"You okay, Wright?" Will's smooth, soothing voice sweeps over me, hot breath on my neck as his big, strong arms wrap tightly around my waist sending sparks up my spine.

My eyes pop open, and dammit, I can't help but grin. "I'm great!

Letting the song take me away from it all. What are you doing over here, Rambo?" I ask, sweeping my arm toward the dance floor.

"Just checking on you. I can think of some other ways to carry you away from it all, you know," he says with a sultry smirk.

"I–is that a good idea? I thought we were just friends, Will," I ask, a little breathless and puzzled, all at the same time.

"You called me, Will." He leans toward me and smiles. I can feel his lips turn up as they coast across my neck.

"Don't get used to it. What are we doing?" I turn in his arms, fully enveloped in him, wrapped in his cedar scent.

"I was told not to think, to just go with it." His words come out gravelly as his chest heaves, sucking in breaths.

"We have to think about it though, don't we?" My mind is spinning. His lips are inches from mine, our breath intermingling.

"You are all I've thought about for five years. I just want one minute to not think, just to feel with you. Only you." He closes his eyes, pain and sorrow nipping at my resolve.

Do I want to go down this road? Should I let myself become vulnerable to what is surely going to be a road of heartbreak and pain? But the feel of his warm, strong body wrapped around me creates a fictitious sense of security. I'm feeling safe, protected, even a little loopy.

I glance at his lips quickly, then dart my eyes back to his. He takes a minute to stare deep into mine, like he's searching for something, but what it is, I have no idea. He whispers, "Fuck it," and I feel his lips crash down on mine.

Will's kiss is soft and tentative at first, just a simple press of his lips against mine. I feel the rumble of approval in his throat, and I dart my tongue gently out, licking carefully across the seam of his mouth. He parts it slowly, and we gently take our time exploring each other's taste, almost tentatively.

It's not awkward, it isn't our first time kissing each other. Instead, it's comforting, similar to saying hello to someone who was important to you but who you lost touch with for a bit. Kissing Will is tantalizing. Goose bumps pepper my whole body, and there's a wet heat thrumming down my belly and into lower parts that sends shivers up my spine.

He nips at my lower lip, and I take the advantage by delving in, pulling the kiss deeper. I'm not sure when I wrapped my hands around his neck, but I can't seem to get him close enough. At the same time, I can't breathe because I'm wrapped so tightly against him. Our tongues tangle, searching, exploring, tasting everything we can. He's pressing my favorite steel rod into my belly as my hips work to gain leverage and I grind against him. I break the kiss for a second, gasping for air.

"Th-that was . . . nice," I huff out breathlessly.

"Nice? Hmm . . . I think I would choose a different adjective," he says, his lips curling up adorably into that smirk I've come to love so much.

"I mean, yeah, obviously. I don't think my brain is working right now. Lack of oxygen, you know?" I say, pink dusting my cheeks.

Steering us away from a debate on descriptive words, I hastily grab his face and pull him into another breathless kiss. He is heaven and hell wrapped up in one excruciatingly devastating package. He smells all male, warm ribbons of fresh cedar waft in my nose. His lips know how to mesh perfectly with mine, infusing his kisses with just the right amount of teasing and depth. I could stay here for hours—not at this bar, just with Will.

I shift slightly, bringing myself even tighter against him. I'm practically rubbing myself on him and whimpering, like a cat mewling for attention. His hands slip down to my lower back, dangerously close to my ass, when the hooting and hollering breaks out.

"Thank the sweet lord, it's about damn time." Smith's roar bellows out across the dance floor, shattering the bubble we were in.

Will leans in again, pressing one soft, chaste kiss to my lips and whispering, "We're busted, Wright."

Giggles burst free. "Thanks for, um . . . Thanks for that, Rambo." I grab his hand, walking back toward our group.

Lo floors me with a look, a mixture of pride and wariness. She's not unhappy with this development, but it's apparent she isn't sure what her reaction is supposed to be, as my friend. The rest of the group appears ecstatic that the awkwardness is finally over. Little do they know, this all just got a lot more complicated.

—

We hang around the bar, allowing everyone to finish up their drinks, before heading back to the rental. Will keeps me close, but the kissing seems to be over, and aside from a few stolen glances or light touches, we are mostly acting as friends. Will was never much for PDA, so it shouldn't be surprising. Still, I can't help but wonder if maybe the kisses felt better to me than they did to him.

On the walk back, Will makes sure that he is walking on the outside, chivalry and all. We joke and laugh when Ruiz wobbles a little too much and ends up face-planting in a bush. No one realized he drank so much. I certainly wasn't paying much attention, with all the dancing and kissing.

Speaking of kissing, I can't help feeling a little let down. I mean, it was amazing—hands down the best make out I've had in years. But it also feels like a mistake, and I'm not sure why. My walls are going up faster than one of those prebuilt stick homes. Will is acting casual, maybe too casual, and I wonder if it was all just a drunken, meaningless thing to him. He's made it clear he wants to be friends.

After stepping into the cool air conditioning of our rental, everyone seems to become aware of how late it is. Lo and Smith give quick waves and make their way into their room. Amy immediately bolts to the bathroom, and Ruiz passes out face down on his bed with his door open. That leaves me, Will, and Butler standing awkwardly at the counter, sharing some leftover pizza.

I'm picking at my pepperoni. It doesn't taste good, and I've mostly sobered up from dancing and walking back, but I also know that my tomorrow self will thank me for putting something in my stomach.

I can't help but overthink every minute of the evening. There's a knot in my stomach twisting and turning, screaming at me. I'm not sure how to just go to bed after how the night ended up. Even though I'm not ready for things to go to the next level, I want Will to come to bed with me. I've always loved cuddling, and having that warm, chiseled body snuggled up tight with mine sounds simply exquisite.

Realistically, I know it won't happen. The little voice in my head is telling me it was a one-time thing. We kissed, we leaned into the attraction that had been brewing over the last couple of weeks, and that's it. I refuse to open myself up or believe that there is more to this. Will wants to be friends, and I know he only has the capacity to hurt me. I should never have kissed him. *Gahhh! Stupid, stupid, me!*

I need to get out of this situation. I'm not strong enough to go through another heartbreak at the hands of Will Davenport. Sexy he may be, but when it comes to relationships . . . he's nothing but red flags. So why do I always act like a bull and run straight toward them?

Quietly, I slink off, acting like I'm headed to the bathroom. At the last minute, I duck into my room as quietly as I can, closing the door. Lying down, I force myself to think of how much fun I had tonight instead of wallowing in self-pity.

Having this group of friends, people like Butler and Ruiz who are just genuinely funny and easy to be around, is extremely comforting.

And Smith and Lo are something else. Looking at them, one would think they had been together for years. Relationships like theirs are what people dream of. A unique and uncanny ability to complete another person so wholly. I'm not an expert on Smith by any means, but I can tell from the short time I've known him that Lo is his person. She's everything he isn't, and yet they mesh so well. There's no fighting over differences or wishing the other person would be into the same things they are. They simply accept each other for who they are, without trying to change a single thing about the other.

Being around them is not always easy, they're both a handful. Smith is boisterous and loud while Lo is a blast but a little bossy. They're a power couple, and yet the smallest things have them glancing at one another, almost like they're communicating through their eyes. It's what I want, what I had with Will once. That connection isn't the same now.

I never know exactly what he's thinking, I dream of being able to look into his eyes and see his soul. Don't get me wrong, there have been glimpses of it here and there, but he's different now. He's matured, hardened, and he's not open to anything more than the occasional pet name and stolen kiss at the bar. I can feel it in my bones that this is as far as it goes. Maybe it's for the best.

Walking this path with him only leads to one place: me being alone, broken, and hating myself even more than I did the first time. No, I will not allow him to do this again. It feels good to know he is physically attracted to me, but I refuse to give him my heart. Too much has changed, too much time has passed. I have a career, a life without him. That's precisely what I wanted, and that's the way it needs to stay.

A faint knock on the bedroom door startles me from my spiral. It's probably Amy wanting to snuggle in with me instead of taking the couch. What if it's Will, though? I can't do this with him. I won't do this with him again. Kissing him was a warm balm to my soul, but I will not let it be the warm-up for the eventual cooldown of the harsh reality that awaits.

I pretend to be asleep, deciding that letting Amy in would only further this ache and unravel me. She cannot know my feelings because she will absolutely tell her brother, and that would only complicate things more.

The door creaks open a smidge, and I hear not Amy, but Will.

"Cam, are you awake?" he asks softly.

Instead of reacting, I remain still and keep my eyes tightly shut. It's dark enough, he won't be able to tell I'm faking. I need him to leave, and in the morning, I need to get the hell out of here. It was fun while it lasted but I need space. I need to focus on my life, my health, and my career. Heartbreak is not on the agenda today, folks.

TWENTY-ONE

Will

"See You Again" - Wiz Khalifa & Charlie Puth

Last night was heady. A myriad of emotions went through me, which is unusual since I aim to never feel most of them. At first, it was like a three-piece special, nervousness with sides of anxiety and lust. Cam looked indescribably good in her little red number. Then, my old pal jealousy came back with a vengeance. It's been a while since we've tangoed, the last time I felt his presence was with Cam. Smith and Amy really got in my face about how scared I've been. It sucked, but also I think it was the wake-up call I needed. They weren't wrong—I'm in too deep as it is. She already has the power to ruin me.

The final feeling of last night's emotional buffet was pure, unadulterated need. Kissing Cam was the closest I've felt to being home in longer than I care to remember. Her soft lips so perfectly in sync with mine, I would have gotten lost in her forever had she not pulled

back the reins. It's unclear if she was embarrassed by the outburst from our friends, or if she simply decided she wasn't into it. By the time we reached our rental, she was in her head and cold as ice.

My attempts at trying to talk to her were met with more stonewalling. Cam pretended to be asleep when I knocked and peeked in her room. Does she seriously think I can't tell when she's actually relaxed versus lying there stiff as a board? Images of her curled slightly on her side, softly breathing, are burned in my mind. There isn't a more beautiful sight in the world. I know how she looks when she's soundly asleep and lost in a dream as well as I know my own name.

Today, I'm simply befuddled, if that's even a word I could use to describe my feelings. I laid on my floor mat last night thinking this morning would give us a chance to talk. I planned to ask her to walk with me for coffee so we could hash everything out, except at just after six in the morning, I was awoken by the quiet sounds of her sneaking out and getting into an Uber. She's always been a magician when it comes to executing an Irish goodbye, but this was different. Cam was running full steam away from me. It's exactly what I knew would happen, and why I never should've listened to my sister.

After she woke up, Lo hit me with a million questions about where Cam had gone, and frankly, all it did was piss me off more that I didn't have answers. I nursed several cups of coffee, packed up my shit, and made my way back to my apartment with Amy in tow. Amy is being cautious around me; she can probably read my mixed feelings. Either that or she's afraid I'm going to take out my frustrations on her, since it was her idea for me to act on my urges last night.

A soft knock on my door sounds, and Amy pops her head in.

"Are you feeling okay, want some soup?"

"I'm fine," I huff at her.

"Do you want to talk about it?" She eyes me cautiously.

"I don't know, Aims. You tell me, have you ever put yourself out there and been rejected so coldly?" I ask with vehemence that's unmatched.

"Well, first of all . . . you can't claim to have been rejected when everyone saw that kiss, Will."

"What do you call her icing me out and then running away this morning like her ass was on fire?" I scoff.

"I call that fear. She has reasons to be scared, and I can't say I blame her, not completely anyway," she rebukes.

Fear, I know fear. Okay, I can work with fear. But Cam doesn't need to be afraid of me. What does she think is going to happen? *Oh yeah, maybe that you're going to break her heart again, dumbass.* Well, she might realize it, but she's the one holding all the power here. I've fought tooth and nail, tried everything I could to keep my distance and keep it light, but I can't. Cam is the only thing that's exactly right in the world, at least for me anyway.

"She doesn't need to be afraid of me. I won't hurt her again," I say in a hushed tone.

"That's the thing, you may not intend to ever hurt anyone, but you did hurt her. Your whole argument against this thing between you two has been that you didn't want to be a burden to her, that you were afraid she would get sick of all the unknowns that come with your career and leave. Can you honestly tell me that a couple of kisses has changed your mind about staying in the friend zone?" What is this, the Spanish Inquisition?

"No, yes, I don't know." I run my fingers through my hair for what feels like the thousandth time. At this rate, male-pattern baldness should top my list of concerns. "I've been keeping a distance from everyone for so long because I didn't want to hurt anyone. Having her around, though, is like breathing fresh air for the first time in years. I wonder if maybe I need her just as much as I want her."

Amy's face becomes slightly marred with pity. "Will, you need to think long and hard about this. I've heard every excuse you've told yourself and, well, everyone else for that matter. The thing is, love defies logic. It isn't ever convenient, and there's always a risk of getting hurt or hurting someone else. The magical thing about it is that when you find it, none of the risk outweighs the reward. If you don't believe me, ask Mom. She would tell you she would marry Dad all over again, even knowing how things turned out, because the years they had together meant something. They shaped her into who she is today, and she is stronger for having had that love. It's why I want to find someone so badly. I don't want to get hurt, but I want to touch the sun, even if only for a little while." Tears prick her eyes, making me feel empathy for how lonely she is.

"Thanks, Aims. I will think about it, I promise. Now did you say soup?"

Amy sniffs then chuckles. Rolling her eyes, she quickly goes to the kitchen and returns with a steaming bowl of broccoli cheddar soup and a crusty piece of bread. Amy is an angel. She's annoying sometimes, but having her here has made me feel better, and it's a bonus to have someone constantly feeding me.

—

I spent most of the afternoon holed up in my room, vacillating between being determined to make Cam see that what we have is worth giving another shot and talking myself out of it because it's destined to go up in flames. After giving up the argument with myself, I decided to head to the one place I haven't been often enough. To go see Thatch.

Walking up here feels surreal. While it isn't the somber and austere sanctuary that is Arlington National Cemetery, it's still a military graveyard honoring those who've paid the ultimate sacrifice. Identical white headstones mark those that answered the call, those whose loved ones still live in agony without them.

The grass is kept neatly trimmed, and some plots have the flowers or wreaths of a loved one's visit. Thatch's always has flowers since he and Bri loved to tend their garden together, but there is also always a bottle of his favorite whiskey on the side or one of his favorite beers. Between myself, Ruiz, and Smith, we've likely spent an entire paycheck bringing along extra alcohol to drink with Thatch.

Today, I brought a six-pack. He can't actually drink with me, of course, but it wouldn't feel right to not at least pour one out for him. Approaching his site, my stomach always gets a little twisted up, and today is no different. There's a sturdy tree at the base of his plot, slightly to the right, and it's my favorite spot to settle into. Taking a deep breath, I lower myself down, cracking two of the bottles open.

"Hey, buddy, sorry I haven't been here very much lately. It's not that I don't want to visit, I just still can't believe you're gone, man."

I feel immensely guilty about how long it's been since my last visit here. When we first lost him, I vowed to visit at least once a week, but lately it's been less and less frequent. I recognize that it's normal to move on with life, but it can't be right to move on from someone that's practically family.

"My life is kind of a mess without you keeping me in line. I don't understand why you had to go." Shaking my head as the words come out, I feel embarrassed and ashamed that I'm giving him crap for leaving me. "Work is the same, we head out soon, but who the fuck knows when. Smith is all kinds of whipped with his new girl, and I'm sure he told you Cam lives here. Can you believe that shit?"

I chuckle to myself, imagining how big Thatch's grin would be hearing the whole story of me running into Cam again. He would have found that whole debacle hilarious, and he would've loved giving Bri all the dirt. Probably would've had a betting pool over how long it would take for me to fall for her again.

"Smith relished breaking the news to you, I'm sure. He's such an asshole. I miss you every day, Thatch. I know you'd give me the most shit over this situation with Cam, but you would've also known exactly what to do . . . I sure as hell don't."

Thatch was never serious, he was always the first to crack a joke or make you laugh. But somehow, he just knew what to say, he would come out of nowhere with some profound advice that would leave you wondering if you were ever going to get it together and grow up like he had. He seemed to always have it all figured out. But then he was an anomaly. Never scared on missions, yet the most affected by them.

I knew he was struggling when we got back, haunted by what we'd seen, but I thought it would pass. He had the love of his life, and he had us, his friends. It was never going to be an easy road, it just never dawned on me it would end like this. Me sitting at his grave, pouring a beer into the grass, talking to a ghost.

The worst part of all of it is that I get it. I'm not angry. There have been moments where I've thought to myself it would be easier to end it too. Moments when I wake up drenched in sweat, grasping for the weapon by my bed, only to realize the door isn't an enemy, the lamp isn't someone lurking, the fan isn't an enemy chopper overhead. And don't get me started on fireworks. They're beautiful, symbolic, and torturous for people like me. Action movies, completely out of the question. I've tried to watch them and usually end up face down on the floor panting to catch my breath. Once I heard some music that was reminiscent of the music played in Iraq; I broke out in a cold sweat and my vision got cloudy.

I'm not looking forward to going back. The dreams have eased some with being home, but I know what I'm in for this time. If I'm being honest, I'm scared. Not for myself, but for my teammates, my friends. I don't want to lose anyone else, and yet I live for the job. I love it. Rock meet hard place, that about sums it up.

"What am I going to do about, Cam? Thatch, she's all I've ever wanted, but I'm scared to hurt her. I don't want her to see me shaken and scared after a bad dream. She doesn't deserve to have to take care of my ass when I come home broken or maimed, and I couldn't bear it if she walked away when I became too much."

"Have you ever asked her what she thinks about those things?" Bri speaks softly beside me, scaring the crap out of me and also stunning me with the question.

"Bri, holy shit, where did you come from? I didn't even hear you walk up," I wrestle out.

Bri chuckles at me, putting a hand over her mouth softly. "I really did scare you. You should be more aware of your surroundings, William."

"Oh sure, laugh it up. I wasn't exactly expecting anyone to talk back to me here, Bri," I say, eyes practically bugging out of my head as I gesture to the ghosts we are surrounded by.

Bri's amused, and I have to admit, it's really nice to see her smile. I haven't seen much of her recently. We all took turns checking in on her when Thatch first passed, but after a couple months, she kindly told us to get a life and quit hovering. She knew we were dealing with our own grief and that it was weighing on us more than we let on. She's perfect that way, knowing what others need and always helping where she can.

"You gonna answer my question?" she prods.

"No, I haven't asked her. I think I'm afraid of the answer," I admit.

"Afraid because you think she won't be up for it, or because she will?"

"I-I don't know. Maybe both."

"It seems to me that this girl has been on your mind for quite a long time. Thatch used to tell me how you pined away for her. Will, no one can predict what the future will be. If she's half as smart and amazing as you've always said, she will make the right choice for herself. The kicker is, you my friend, have to be willing to accept that choice, whatever it is."

"Did you make the right choice?" I ask, knowing that I shouldn't. I'm fully aware it's not really a fair question seeing as she would never admit regret over a dead man.

"For me there wasn't ever a choice. Thatch was a foregone conclusion. We came on strong and quick and loved with all we had. I never stopped to think that hard about it. I'd like to say if given a choice, I would do it all over again, but I'm not there yet. I know I miss him with every breath and fiber of my being," she says, sounding sad and remorseful.

"Thanks, Bri. Really . . . I appreciate you telling me. We don't just miss Thatch, you know. We miss you too. You need to come around more," I say trying to be encouraging but also sounding a little sterner than I had hoped.

Bri wraps me in a hug. It's fierce despite how little she is, and I feel the warmth of a true friend. She's one of the strongest people I know, and I wasn't lying when I said we miss her. She laughs softly and hoists herself up on tippy toes to ruffle my hair.

"I'll make you a deal. I'll come around when you get the girl. Now give me two of those beers and get outta here. I'm trying to have a date with my husband." She smirks and raises a stern eyebrow at me.

I oblige by giving her the remaining beers. "I don't take orders from you, but I know he would want the alone time." I nod toward Thatch's headstone, laying a hand on it and willing myself not to cry.

I begin walking back to my car when Bri shouts, "Hey Will!" I turn to look at her. "Call your therapist, work it out before you go get her." I give her a salute and continue on.

Plopping down in the driver's seat, I grab my phone and call Tina, my therapist. She answers on the first ring. "Will, what's wrong?"

"I-I need help. Can we meet?"

"I'm at the office, come on by."

"I'll be there in ten." I hang up and put my truck in drive. Time to do the hard work, time to make some decisions.

TWENTY-TWO

Cam

"This Feeling" - The Chainsmokers & Kelsea Ballerini

Will is applying a full-on takeover mission this week—the dating kind. I practically hauled ass out of the rental Sunday morning, running like my life was on the line. In some ways, it was. My heart has never been more unsure of something: Do I see what happens and risk it all, or do I draw inward and ensure my safety? When I left, I had essentially made my mind up. And my mind told me to get the heck out of dodge, pretend the kiss never happened.

Will has other plans, though. I didn't hear from him yesterday, but this morning when I opened the door at six to head to the gym, there were a dozen bouquets of peonies, a protein shake, and a note letting me know it was game on. I almost couldn't believe my eyes; it was early and I hadn't had coffee. If it weren't for nearly tripping over everything and slamming my arm into the doorjamb to catch myself, I would have thought I was dreaming.

The note was simple.

Cam—

A couple of things for the most beautiful girl in the world. I'm all in, I want to see where this goes. Meet me at Amore at noon if you do too.
—Will

Now I'm sitting in my car like a coward, wondering if I should go in the restaurant or ditch this whole thing and pretend I didn't see the note. It's perfectly reasonable to claim a raccoon or snake ate the gift before I came out to hit the gym this morning, isn't it? No, it's not. How the hell would they take down that many flowers? But how else do I play off not showing up? Ditching him wouldn't do much for proving I'm not cold and heartless.

Lo made it clear that she thought Will's gesture was adorably sweet, albeit over the top. And that I would be the biggest dumbass on the planet if I didn't take him up on the free lunch and at least hear him out. Our apartment looks like a glorified flower shop now, and she is in heaven. I am too, the flowers are beautiful. Part of me does want to know where this change of heart came from. Was the kissing as good for him as it was for me? Or is this just some ploy for Will to have his fun for a bit and then drop me when something better comes along?

I can't help but wonder if what I am feeling is just left over from the past. Nostalgia, like when you think back to a childhood memory and it's the greatest thing ever, but then you experience it as an adult and are sorely disappointed. Have I been holding on to the memories of what we had for so long that I've convinced myself there are feelings here? Or is this actually real, with potential to become the all-consuming love that people spend their whole lives searching for?

I'm not usually this much of a nervous Nellie, I swear I'm not. I moved halfway across the country on my own, for God's sake. Love is something I desperately want. The feeling that you have someone in your corner, someone pushing you to be better and supporting your dreams. Do I really not want to take this chance and place my bets on the creepy Tinder options instead? Ack! I wish there was a way to do this and still make sure I don't get hurt. Dammit. I'm going in. I owe it to him to at least see what he's going to say, right?

I push out of my car with a deep breath. I dressed for the occasion, opting for a light blue romper that accentuates my best assets. My hair is down, pin straight. I have my small crossbody purse, and I quickly apply another coat of peach lip gloss in my car's side mirror. Here goes nothing.

I nabbed a sweet parking spot right out front, so the front door is a quick three steps from the curb. Gently pushing it open, I'm greeted by the smells of freshly baked bread and house-made tomato sauce. The garlic and herbs practically roll over me as I step inside, and it's impossible not to think of all things romance . . . and how bad my breath is going to be after this. Thank goodness for breath strips.

The host asks me if I'm meeting someone, and I politely nod. I've barely finished when Will sweeps up beside me, leading me to our table on the back patio with his hand placed gently on my lower back. It's something out of a movie out here. Perfectly placed bistro tables with a view of the water. Fresh flowers on each table, and water in one of those classic glass bottles. Ivy climbs every which way up a wrought iron pergola overhead. It's breathtaking.

Will smiles at me, and I'm enraptured by him instantly. So much for playing it cool and seeing what he has to say. My nipples are turning into tight peaks, and I'm breathless from the mere sight of him. His tall, muscular frame and delicious brownie-colored curls. I could eat him up. That's how honestly delectable he is.

He has on a blue button-down shirt with the sleeves rolled up, revealing his insanely chiseled forearms. Matching chino shorts and boat shoes indicate he went all out for this. He isn't sporting his casual look, and it appears he even attempted to style his curly hair.

"You look beautiful, Cam," he says with a hint of a smirk in those ocean-blue eyes.

"Thanks, you clean up pretty good yourself, Rambo," I say, the words coming out breathlessly. *Way to play it cool, Cam.*

"Have you ever been here before?" he asks, a hint of nerves lacing his words.

"No, I've wanted to come, I hear so many great things about it from clients, but it's not exactly in budget at my current salary," I explain.

"I'm so glad we're here then. It's amazing and I remember how much you love pasta." He winks and my panties immediately melt. *Down, girl.*

"Thanks for asking me to lunch, and for the gifts. What is all this, though?" I motion with my hand between us.

I can't help but dive right in. I've never been good at surprises or mysteries. I have a serious need inside me to know what's happening and be in control at all times. My family teases me endlessly about being OCD, but seriously—I need to know what to expect, or I will for sure disappoint someone. It's less OCD and more a compulsive need to people please, if you ask me.

"This is me, hoping you'll give me a chance. Again," Will says with a bit of sadness in his eyes.

"A chance for what, though? Things can't just go back to how they were before. I don't even know you anymore, not really anyway," I say, urging him to explain what he wants.

"Exactly, I want a chance to see if this is something. Look, I'm not asking you to be sure or to make any sort of commitment to me. Hell,

I don't even know if I can make a commitment. All I'm sure of is that being with you is like breathing fresh air for the first time in years. You make me happy, you make me laugh, and you make me feel things I had long forgotten how to feel. I don't know if it's nostalgia or something more . . . please don't make me go back to suffocating alone," he pleads.

Our waiter comes over as relief washes over me. Will just spilled everything right out there in his impassioned speech. Maybe that's what's so confusing about it all—we both remember how we used to feel, and focusing on that is clouding what's true in the present. Honestly, I'm relieved I'm not the only one who's thought of that.

We order, spaghetti and meatballs for him, and shrimp Fra Diavolo pasta for me. At the last minute, Will adds on an order of homemade mozzarella sticks and a bottle of rosé. He knows I'm a sucker for any form of fried cheese, that hasn't changed. The rosé surprises me; it is my most recent favorite, but he wouldn't know that since I've never drank it in front of him.

Lo must have tipped him off, cue my internal groan. Her and I are going to have to talk about not giving Will any hints in the future. If this is real, it needs to be authentically him and not the him that's had someone telling him how to win me over. Also, it's not at all fair for her to help him—no one's giving me a Will guidebook.

"So, tell me what you're thinking in that pretty little head of yours," he says, and I can tell just how nervous he is.

"I-I think you're right. I've been in my head, wondering if this thing between us is past feelings coming up or if there is something more. I want to see where it goes, but I'm also terrified. I still don't understand what happened back when . . . well, you know, when you dumped me." I'm fighting the knot lodged in my throat, willing myself not to cry.

"I know, I owe you an explanation. The thing is, I don't even know if I really have one." He shifts in his seat, nervously playing with his napkin.

"Just try, Will. I'm the one taking all the risk here, you have to give me something." Pleading with him, I take a big gulp of water to ease the tightness in my throat.

"Is that what you think? That I don't have anything at risk?" He rears back as if I slapped him, stunned at my statement. "Cam, I never stopped loving you. I-I know that I said I did back then, but I didn't mean it. I was scared and young, and so stupid. I thought that if I ended things, I was saving us both, protecting us from whatever harm was to come."

"I-I don't know if I believe you." Tears well in his eyes, I can see the defeat taking over. "I want to believe you, I want to try. It's just that you walked away when things got hard. You didn't trust me to tell you what I needed or wanted. You just decided, and that was that. I'm not that young, naive girl anymore. It's going to take time for me to adjust, and you can't keep things from me or make decisions for me. I won't have it."

Will reaches around under the table, grabbing the seat of my chair and pulling me closer over to his side. He wraps his hand around mine and stares into my eyes. "There is no one else that lights up my world the way you do. You are the brightest spot in all of my days, the one that I think about when my days are tough or the nights are long. I don't know why fate brought you back to me or what I did to deserve it, but please, I'm scared to death. Give me a chance."

"I don't believe in fate, but tell me one thing. Why are you scared?"

"I can't lose another person. I won't survive it." He hangs his head, silent tears coasting down his cheeks.

"You won't lose me. Even if this doesn't work out, I will never not be your friend. I will always care for you. Why do you think I didn't make you leave the bar that first night? I couldn't do it." I grasp his face gently with both of my hands, coaxing him to look at me. "But if there's going to be a we, I mean it, I need total honesty. You broke me, and it's not going to be easy for me to trust you."

"I can work with that. I will do whatever it takes, babe. Just please, don't give up on me." Will's eyes twinkle as the realization that we're actually doing this hits him. I press a quick kiss to his lips, chaste and sweet. I already feel myself wanting more, and at the same time I'm worried that I just made the biggest mistake of my life.

"Geez, Wright. I didn't take you for the type that kisses on the first date." He pokes at my side tickling me, mischief written all over his face as he eases us back into fun, light territory.

"Mmm . . . there's a lot you don't know about me, Rambo. Maybe I am that kind of girl," I say with a wink.

A husky laugh billows out from him, and it's apparent I'm in serious trouble. Being near him makes my insides melt into this squishy, gooey mess. That beautiful melodic laugh makes shivers run up my spine and other places down below.

We spend most of the date talking about work, of course. I give him a load of crap for taking the day off to bring me on a date, but it's honestly pretty sweet and thoughtful since he knows I'll be working long days the rest of the week. I fill him in on all the salon gossip and what it's really like working for Daveed. I tell him how nervous I am for hair trials this week and all that's riding on me passing my exams. He's tight-lipped about his job and I don't pry because I assume he can only tell me so much.

The food is utterly divine. I force Will to try mine and beg to taste his, which results in us essentially sharing both meals because we can't decide which is best. Before I know it, we've finished up our food and polished off the wine. I have a warm buzz running through my veins and feel lighter than I have in months, maybe years.

Several times throughout the meal, Will reached over to touch my hand or gently brush my hair off my face. My body is in overdrive, and I have to shift awkwardly to alleviate the ache between my legs.

I don't want the date to end, but with him paying the bill, I know it has. I'm a little sad, but I remind myself that this has to be like any other first date. I have to protect myself, a little anyway. I can't rush into being with him all the time.

Will sweeps me up from the table and into a gentle hug, offering to walk me to my car. On any other occasion, the amount of wine I had would prohibit me from driving, but the mass amount of food I ate has absorbed every bit of it. I walk as slow as possible, prolonging the inevitable, but my car is so close it takes less than a minute to get there.

"Thanks for a perfect first date, Will," I say quietly.

"When can I see you again?" he asks, looking deeply into my eyes. We're standing so close I can feel his heart beating against my chest, and I have to strain my head back to hold his gaze.

"I have a really busy week with my client demos. I'm not sure when I'll have time," I admit weakly.

Gently sliding a finger down my cheek, he says, "I'm proud of you, Cam. It's okay if you're busy, just promise me you'll try to make some time for me."

There's hope, lust, and a bit of trepidation in his expression. My heart bursts with the nervousness I can so clearly read on his face. Maybe he really does care. "I promise. Now kiss me, Rambo," I say boldly.

He doesn't hesitate. He carefully places one hand gently on my face, using his thumb ever so slightly under my chin to guide my lips up to his. The kiss is a featherlight, chaste brush against my mouth, but I feel it in the depths of my soul. I pull at his shirt, dragging him in for one more, trying to infuse all my emotions into a simple kiss before he pushes me away slightly.

The corner of his mouth tips up in his signature pantie-dropper grin. "Call me anytime, day or night, Wright. I mean it." He waves as he walks away.

Fumbling with my keys, I unlock the door and get in my car. It takes me a few minutes to collect myself before I turn the ignition and prepare to head home. That was the best first date I've ever had. Will is funny and attentive. It feels like he genuinely wants to hear about my life and my work.

He said he was proud of me. I don't know if anyone has ever said that, but if they have, it didn't make my stomach fill with butterflies like when Will said it. Will is all grown up, a real red-blooded American man. I might live to regret everything about this, but right now I can't find it in me to care.

I'm doing this, I'm dating Will Davenport. Elliott is going to lose his shit!

TWENTY-THREE

Cam

"9 to 5" - Dolly Parton

Some days are just better than others. There are days when everything is falling into place, exactly how it should, and then there are days like today. Similar to a bad hair day, today has been stressful with performing my assistant duties at the salon and trying to confirm models for my trials.

Daveed has a rigorous training program. Part of that program is bringing in a model for each function of a stylist's role and demonstrating that you can meet his standards. This must be done before a stylist is given their own chair and allowed to start booking their own clients. There are six tasks that must be demonstrated:

#1 Perform a Blonde Bombshell Service: Full foil highlight with no breakage and optimal tone.

#2 Perform a Bake-like-a-Brownie Service: Full head of color, level 5 or darker.

#3 Perform a Men's Cut & Style

#4 Perform a Women's Cut & Style

#5 Perform a Waxing Service: Must have optimal shaping and desired result.

#6 Perform a Full Lather Lounge Experience with a Blow-Me-Beautiful Finish: No heat tools, must only use blow-dryer, product, and round brush for finishing.

To make it easier, some of the skills can be combined. For example, if I do a full highlight on someone and then give them the Lather Lounge experience with the blowout after, that can be graded and check two items off the list. Knowing this, I planned accordingly and condensed as many tasks as possible. I set up Lo to get #2 and #4, one of our salon sales reps to get #1 and #6 (she's processing now), and Elliott to come in town for #3 and #5. I am nothing if not efficient, after all.

However, today, I'm striking out. Not on the actual skills part, but on the models keeping their word and showing up part. My list consisted of my two closest friends, Lo and Elliott, whom I thought were reliable enough, or at the very least, desperate enough to agree to free services rendered. Thank my lucky stars, Anita showed up.

Lo suddenly can't make her appointment because her boss went on a tirade, letting several people go, so she's swamped with her own work. Elliott had a sales opportunity come up and has to be in Maryland for an important meeting. Elliott was always a long shot, I knew that going in. My backup plan for that situation has always been to call in one of the guys and beg them to help me out.

None of it is a deal breaker, Daveed is one of the most patient people on the planet and will do whatever he needs to in order to ensure my success. However, I wanted to do this the right way, follow the rules, and get a successful score without any help. Making matters more complicated, Will has been so sweet to me all week, and I've been short, unavailable, and frankly, downright grumpy when talking with him.

I'm not the picture of newly dating bliss right now, let me tell you. I'm surprised he hasn't run kicking and screaming yet. I practically blew him off when he came by with a coffee last night at nine thirty. It was a sweet gesture, and I simply said, "Thanks, now scoot. I gotta practice." I've spent very little time responding to his texts or talking to him when he calls. Lo thinks I'm avoiding him because I still have walls up, which may be a little true, but I would like to see him some.

Instead, I'm desperately trying to figure out fill-ins for the four services I no longer have models for. I could ask Will to be Elliott's replacement, but somehow, I think cutting his hair would make me nervous, and I don't think he gets anything waxed. Does he get anything waxed? Nope—I can't let my mind go there right now, I need to focus. Okay, Amy has brownish hair, but I'm not sure she colors it or wants to start. Resigned that I have very few choices, I shoot off a text to Smith.

CAM

Hey, buddy . . . I need a favor.

SMITH

What's up, roomie?

CAM

Just to be clear, you do know we don't actually live together right?

SMITH

I love you too! What do you need?

CAM

So . . . you know how I'm doing hair trials this week? Can I cut your hair and also maybe wax something on your body?

SMITH

Yo for sure! I never turn down a free cut,
and you know I keep my brow game tight.
When?

CAM

When are you available?

SMITH

I could come today at 5ish.

CAM

Sounds good, thank you
so much! I owe you.

Thank the heavens above, that's two more off my list. Well, almost. I have Anita, the sales rep, under the dryer now, working on lifting those beautiful highlights to the perfect shade. Now it's just a matter of finding a replacement for Lo. Her cheapskate butt is going to be so mad that I replaced her, but she also can't commit to an appointment, so what's a girl to do?

Ding! Time to take Anita out from the dryer and give her the best Lather Lounge treatment of her life. Maybe I'll end up with some free samples out of this deal or a giant tip that could allow me to exist on something other than ramen for the next few days.

I check her foils and her hair lifted beautifully, so much so, I won't even need to apply a toner. I verify with Daveed, and we head into the lounge. Once she's settled in the bowl, I begin the arduous task of removing what seems like eight thousand foils and getting the water to the exact right temperature.

I've set Anita up with a hot towel on her face—yes, her makeup will be ruined but it's worth it. The hot towel with soothing lavender essential oil is exquisite. Exactly, what is needed for the optimal relaxation experience. This is where I thrive. My shampoo girl game is strong, and I know I will give her a great experience. I spend extra time on the head and neck massage, to the point that I'm not entirely sure if Anita is awake when I finish. I nudge her up gently and welcome her back to the land of the living.

We make our way out of the lounge and to my chair. That feels weird to say. Gosh, I hope this is my chair when everything is said and done. Daveed cuts her hair because he's the only one she trusts, but she has me beaming from ear to ear with all the praise from the color experience and the Lather Lounge. Daveed promptly gives me kudos, noting that even he hasn't ever made Anita doze off. I'm soaring in the clouds with all this positive feedback.

The signature blow-dry that's up next is something I could do in my sleep. Most people think you need a flat iron or curling iron to get that frizz-free, effortless, wavy look, but you definitely don't. The barrel of a round brush is metal, and when heated by the blow-dryer paired with proper positioning, it is wildly more efficient at smoothing flyaways and adding shape or curl to the hair.

I finish her up and call Daveed over for his assessment. He takes a chopstick off my station, examining her highlights to ensure there weren't any bleeds or lines of demarcation. He runs his hands through her hair to ensure it's completely dry and won't frizz the second she steps out into the sweltering Tampa heat. Finally, he gives me a sly smirk and tells me it's perfect. Sweet relief. One model down, two to go.

I'm ecstatic to be done with two of the six trials. It's a huge weight off of me, even if I do have several more to do. I will finish two more on Smith today, and then it's just a matter of working out the last client for tomorrow. I want to call Will and let him know. It's weird but he is the very first person that I want to share my excitement with. I'm not sure I should, though, he may be upset that I didn't ask him to fill in for Elliott.

Realistically, I know he shouldn't be, but there's a small nagging feeling low in my belly that this is the exact thing he would expect to help with. He is very proud in general and wouldn't appreciate me seeking the help of one of his friends when he isn't even aware I'm having an issue in the first place. Now I'm second-guessing myself, should I have asked him? I don't think so because it would have been harder for me and my potential to fail would have gone up by an exorbitant amount. Ugh!

Making a snap decision, knowing I have twenty-ish minutes until Smith arrives, I pick up my phone and call the one person I know will give it to me straight: Elliott.

"Hey, I'm walking into a client meeting in ten minutes, what's up?" he says, sounding annoyed that I would dare call him while he's working.

"Hi, umm, so I kind of have a teensy tiny little problem."

"Oh God, this ought to be good. What did you do?"

"Well, so, uhhh . . ."

"Geez-us, spit it out, Cam!"

"Will and I . . . well, we're sort of together now."

"Wow . . . uh, okay? And why is this is a problem?"

"Well, no, not exactly . . . but you know how you couldn't make the trip down for my hair trial, and so I sort of asked his friend to fill in for you, and now I'm wondering if that was a mistake and if he is going to be mad," I ramble out without taking a breath.

"Cam, seriously? He is lucky you are even giving him the time of day, in my opinion. I like the dude, don't get me wrong, but he kinda fucked you over. You should not be sitting there worried about making him mad over a freaking free haircut. This doesn't sound like a very healthy start, if you ask me. Also, why the hell did you not call me the minute you got back together?"

"I know, I'm sorry, I should have called you. I just didn't know if, well, I still don't really know where it's going. I don't know if I trust that he's in it for real, but I'm giving it a chance."

"Listen, I gotta run into this meeting, but we are going to talk about this. You need to be careful, and I don't love that you're already keeping things from me. I love you, Cam."

"I love you too. Call me later. I'll tell you everything, I promise."

Welp, I thought Elliott would help me work out my dilemma, but instead I just feel worse than I did before calling. I love my brother; he is right that I should have called him right away when I got back with Will. I'm not even clear on why I didn't. Maybe I was worried he would think I'd officially lost it, or that I am so desperate for the past that I'm settling. No, that's not right, Elliott isn't like that. He might not agree with all my decisions, but he's always there for me. No matter what. Ugh, I'm the worst!

"Cam, your appointment is here," Micah says, looking like he is up to absolutely no good with the shit-eating grin he's giving me.

"Wow, okay, I guess the military is all about being punctual, am I right?" I say trying not to reveal the bout of nausea that just swept over me.

"Something like that, I think. Hopefully they don't all come prematurely," he quips.

"Oh my God, Micah." I laugh hysterically and he looks amused as we round the corner—oh crap. Smith didn't come alone. Will is sitting right next to him on the small leather sofa in the waiting area, sporting a cocky look.

"Heyyy . . . I didn't know you were both coming," I say breathlessly as I shoot Smith a confused and somewhat exasperated look. Just the sight of Will in my space makes my head spin and the spot between my thighs heat. At the rate things are going, I'm going to need to start packing extra panties in my purse.

"Well, I'm not going to say that I'm not happy to see you, you look gorgeous as ever. But I'm actually not here for you, Wright," Will says with a satisfied smirk.

"Oh, okay . . . ready, Smith? Wait, who are you here for then?" Confusion forces my feet to stay put.

"He's with me, lovebug. He heard about the amazing head rub I give and simply couldn't resist," Micah pipes in, grabbing Will's arm to lead him over to his chair.

Will's face has transformed from holier-than-thou to pinched with confusion, and Smith is about to die laughing. It's going to be an interesting evening, that's for sure. Will has no idea what can of worms he just opened. Micah has been lusting after him since trivia night. I get it, I couldn't agree more with every downright naughty thing he has said about Will. I should be jealous, and maybe I am a little, if I'm honest with myself. However, I've seen and touched that coarse, curly hair before, and there is absolutely no way I would attempt blending a high and tight on him. My skills aren't to that level, yet. Also, it's going to be fun watching Will squirm under Micah's advances. Micah does not do subtlety well.

I quickly move through Smith's haircut. There isn't much to cut, but it's enough to count and get me a passing grade with Daveed. Then I take Smith into the Lather Lounge and give him the full treatment. Waxing his eyebrows is a once-in-a-lifetime experience—he whimpers more than most women do during a Brazilian. I wish I could have recorded it for Lo, but that's against the rules and also probably would have been slightly incriminating. I may or may not have pulled a little harder than necessary as payback for all the sleepless nights I've had recently, thanks to him.

After Smith is waxed to perfection, I give him the warm towel treatment and wash his hair with peppermint-scented shampoo, spending extra time on his scalp massage so I can keep an eye on Micah and Will. We finish up about the same time, both Will and Smith looking completely relaxed, drunk on it, actually.

"Davenport, if you fuck this up, I'm going to sweep in and steal Cam for the head rubs alone," Smith says, pointing at Will to let him know he's serious.

"Don't worry, William—or should I call you Rambo? Your bed will never be cold and empty unless you want it to be," Micah winks at Will before grabbing his arm to help him sit up in the shampoo chair. Smith and I cackle until Daveed comes in and tells us to get a move on and that all the laughter is killing the vibe. Micah and I roll our eyes, but hustle back out front to finish them up.

After Will settles his bill, he asks me for a minute outside. Micah kills me with a look that says if I don't go, I'll never hear the end of it. So I agree. I was going anyway, but the added pressure didn't hurt. Smith has already headed out and when we reach the front porch, he dips into his car to give us privacy. Will reaches out to brush a hair off my face, tenderly.

"Hey, you holding up, okay?" he asks sweetly.

"Yeah, much better now that almost all the trials are done. I only have two more to go."

"Why didn't you tell me you needed help?" His brow is furrowed in concern.

Blowing out a breath, I admit the truth to him, "I was afraid. I would be really nervous cutting your hair in general, and I knew doing it for the trial would make it worse. Are you mad?"

Relief washes over him. "No, not at all. Why would I be mad? I've just been worried about you this week, and when Smith told me you reached out for help because some people have canceled . . . well, I guess I felt guilty that I didn't even know you were in a bad spot."

I can see it in his eyes. He isn't mad, he's simply sad that I didn't rely on him. If the roles were reversed, I would feel the same way. Why did I question him, why did I think something so small would upset him?

"I'm sorry. I just didn't want to weigh you down with all this. I know I've been really short this week. I've just been under a lot of stress and haven't been sleeping well. I've never wanted to succeed at something as much as I have with this." I grab for his hand and give it a light squeeze before intertwining our fingers.

"I understand, but you can count on me. Don't be afraid to ask me for help, if you need it. I want to support you, babe." His lips tilt up with a small smile.

"Thanks, Will, truly. I'm really glad I got to see you tonight. You've been so good to me, I swear I'll make this week up to you," I reassure him despite my own reservations. If I can count on him, why do I feel so unsure?

He kisses me lightly, just a brief brush of his lips on mine, and yet the electricity instantly hits me like a jolt of espresso coursing through my veins. I can't help but pull him into a hug. He's comforting, and being in his arms is all that's right in the world.

"I better let you get back in there. Call me when you get home, Wright." He squeezes just a little tighter to let me know it's not a request. He cares, I think.

"Okay, Rambo. I'll call ya, I guess."

"Friday, I want to spend some time with you . . . if you can swing it."

"Sure, I'll make it work. I'll call you later," I say as I press another soft kiss to his cheek and brush past him, heading back inside to resume my duties. I don't want to walk away right now, and I may be done with clients for the day, but I'm not done with cleaning brushes, sweeping up my mess, and talking with Daveed about my trials. Duty calls.

TWENTY-FOUR

Cam

"Call Me" - Blondie

I sling off my purse, letting it drop in the entryway of our apartment as I bend to untie my boots. My feet hurt so bad from standing the last three days, they may never recover. You would think I would be used to it by now, but no matter the shoes, the ache never goes away.

"Hey, you're home. How did the trials end up?" Lo twists herself like a pretzel, untangling herself from Smith on the couch.

"Great. I think I passed, but Daveed will give us the final word tomorrow." I step gingerly, wincing at my protesting big toe, as I walk into the kitchen and peer into the fridge.

"There's a surprise in there for you, top shelf," Smith says, proceeding to tickle Lo and kiss her neck. They are disgusting.

I pull out a clear plastic Tupperware that has a yellow sticky note on top.

I spent three hours on the phone with my mom to make this. Hope you enjoy it, Wright!

—XoXo— Will

He made me dinner? I open the top and see his mom's famous chicken pot pie waiting inside. The smell wafts to my nose, comforting me; it's almost like I'm home. Popping the container in the microwave for a minute, I grab a fork, a big glass of water, and two chocolate stars for dessert. When I get to my room to enjoy my dinner in bed with some trash TV, I text him.

CAM

You made me dinner, Rambo 💀

WILL

I was worried you didn't get to eat all day,
don't make it a big deal, Wright.

CAM

It's sweet. It's almost like I should give
you a reward for being so nice.

WILL

I mean . . . I could think of something 😏

CAM

I said almost, Rambo.

I'm laughing to myself about riling him up when my phone starts ringing with a FaceTime call. I pick it up, mid-bite. "Don judge me for eating." My mouth is full in a very unattractive way.

"I'm glad you like it. You do like it, right?" Will shifts, and I can see he's lying in bed, shirtless. I swallow and grab my water, taking a big gulp to stop myself from panting.

"It's delicious, seriously, thank you. I probably would have been eating half a bag of stale cheese puffs without it." I set the Tupperware down on my nightstand, shifting lower into my pillows to talk to him before I finish my meal.

"How was your day?" He's looking at me so intently, those bright blue eyes peering into my soul.

"It was good, finished up the trials and then just normal assistant work after that. How was yours?"

"Better now, just therapy and work. Did you pass?" He moves so he's lying on his side, propping the phone up on something, who knows what. *Did he say therapy?*

"I don't know yet. I think so, but Daveed will do his final assessment tomorrow. I'm a little nervous. Did you say therapy? What kind?" I shrug, shifting to sit up and rub my feet with my free hand. They hurt so bad, but I want to know more about what Will decided to casually mention.

"What are you doing? You moved, not that I'm complaining about the view." I look at the small picture on my phone that reflects back to me what he sees—my silky sleep dress has creeped up my thighs, revealing a hint of panties and a lot of leg on the screen. Whoops.

"Shit, sorry. I was trying to rub my feet with my free hand. They hurt so bad from all the standing. By the end of the week, I'm usually toast. You can't distract me from the comment, Rambo. What therapy?" I move the phone, propping it against a pillow, strictly positioned on my face.

"Do not apologize, you're the most beautiful fucking thing I've ever seen. I'm irrationally jealous of a silk pair of panties, for God's sake." He shakes his head, bristling at his own admission.

"Why would you be jealous?" I'm playing coy. I know what he meant, but I still don't mind hearing it.

"I wish I was that silk pair of panties, so I could be buried in you."

"Oh . . . um . . . wait, what are you doing?" I can tell by the flexing muscles in his left arm that it's not something sweet or innocent, and at the same time, the thought of him seeing me for two seconds and having to touch himself—well, it's fucking hot.

"You know what I'm doing, Wright. Do you want me to stop?"

"Erm." My cheeks heat, turning my face three shades of pink. I'm not usually so shy about these things, but it's different with him. There's more at stake.

"I'm not going to apologize, Wright. You're beautiful, and since we shared that kiss, you're all I can think about, all I dream about. But I won't do it with you here if it makes you uncomfortable."

"Oh . . . um, I mean I can't stop thinking about you either. I just, I've never done that. On the phone, I mean, obviously." Why am I so nervous? I'm sweating and panicky, yet there's an ache down below that I need to fulfill.

"Do you want to? You don't have to, but obviously, I'm in if you are." He smirks with his adorable lopsided grin, like he didn't just get caught pleasuring himself with me on the phone.

"We could, we could try. I'm not sure I know how this is supposed to go." I lie back further into the pillows, sliding my hand down my belly to touch myself.

"Tell me what you're doing. Tell me how it feels." Will's eyes search mine, the dark lusty pools leaving me breathless.

"I'm touching myself, rubbing tiny circles around my, oh . . . it feels so good, Rambo." He moves the phone so I have a view of him stroking his beautiful cock. It's long and thick, so hard I can see the veins jutting out as it stretches toward his belly.

"Are you wet for me, Wright?"

"I-I'm soaked." I practically pant the words around soft moans. I don't even care if Lo and Smith hear me, lord knows it's payback at this point.

"Good girl, you're such a good fucking girl." His praise and dirty mouth send both of us over the edge. I come so hard I think I scream. I for sure can't see straight.

"That was . . . it was incredible. I'm embarrassed to admit I've been dreaming about that for years," Will says, with a shy smile on his face.

"I shouldn't tell you this either but uh, I've had these dreams about—" I stop, instantly regretting that I'm stating this out loud. "—about you. After all the bad dates I've been on." My cheeks turn bright red at the admission. *Why did I tell him that?*

Making things even more awkward, Will tells me to hold on a second, walking away from his phone to presumably clean himself up. I do the same, jogging into my bathroom to wash my hands, wipe off, and panic a little hoping he wasn't paying attention, before snuggling back into my bed.

"As distracting and satisfying as that was, I still want you to answer my question." I raise an eyebrow at him as I attempt to steer the conversation away from my admission. I'm trying to be serious while also quickly falling under the mesmerizing spell that is his strong jawline, straight nose, and those fucking blue eyes.

"Uh . . . okay. I-I'm not really sure where to start, but I've been seeing Tina for a while. She helps me with some mental health stuff." He looks away, almost like he's ashamed to tell me.

"Will. Look at me." Will turns his phone back to his face and I beg him with my eyes to really listen to what I have to say. "I'm proud of you for getting help. I talk to someone too. And I'm not going to force you to tell me why, not until you're ready. But you need to know I get it, I understand, no judgment."

I don't know if it's because of what we just did together or if it's because he's just Will and I will always care about him, but I mean the words. I don't want him to tell me what's going on until he's ready. Maybe because I'm not ready to tell him my shit, or maybe because I know I will get invested and I don't fully believe he's going to stay this time.

"I promise I will tell you at some point. I just don't think it should be over the phone." He pulls his blanket up higher on his chest, a big yawn sneaking out.

"I understand, it's okay, I promise. You are tired, though, and I need to finish this delicious dinner my boyfriend made me. Talk tomorrow?" I grab my dinner to show him there is still a hearty portion left and I plan to eat every bite.

"Your *boyfriend*? Shit. I'm going to get my ass kicked if he finds out what we just did, Wright." Will smiles wide, flashing all his pearly whites and making me giggle. "Come over for a date tomorrow, after work."

It's not a question, more of a command. But I already can't say no to him, and that scares the living shit out of me. "Okay, Rambo. Good night."

"Good night, Wright."

We hang up and I attempt to take a bite of my dinner before slinking back down into my pillows. It really is delicious, but I'm suddenly not hungry. A date at his apartment comes with all sorts of strings: What if he doesn't like what he sees if things go in the direction we took tonight? What if he leaves or ends it? I pull a pillow over my head and scream into it. I have a long, sleepless night of overthinking ahead of me.

TWENTY-FIVE

Will

"Sucker" - The Jonas Brothers

Amy and I spent the better part of yesterday evening planning and preparing for Cam to come over. I was nervous that I was putting the cart before the horse since I hadn't officially asked Cam yet, but Amy was convinced she wouldn't say no. She had all kinds of wildly elaborate ideas on what we should decorate with and how to make my obviously bachelor pad apartment look romantic. There were mentions of roses and a candlelit dinner plus massage oils and other very presumptuous things. I think all the talk of what could potentially happen led me to initiating the phone sex we had. Well, that and those damn silk panties.

My sister is a romantic through and through, the perfect blend of wedding planner and hook-up arranger. While I am thankful for her support, I woke up decidedly focused on keeping things more simple, more relaxed. The goal is to not scream that I'm trying too hard, but

also to appear like I put some effort into the night. Limiting myself helps keep my expectations and feelings under control, according to Tina. She told me that the best way to manage my fear about losing Cam or fucking things up was to manage my expectations and my view of reality. Essentially, not to get swept away and throw out the rest of my life and things I care about.

Cam's had an intense week at work, trying to prove she's worthy of having her own spot as a stylist. I know in my soul that she's meant to be there, at that salon, and based on what I saw her do to Smith, I'm positive she's earned her spot. Anyone who can make that dude look semi-decent must be great, right? He wouldn't shut up all day about how good her head massage was. I had to stop myself more than once from throat punching him.

After thinking about it all day and texting to confirm plans with Amy, I decided on skipping the flowers in lieu of a few candles, lavender-mint scented, like the ones in that shampoo area at the salon. It may seem counterintuitive, as she probably wants to escape work, but that scent was like magic. You can't help but relax as soon as you smell it.

I have about thirty minutes before Cam's set to get off work. Once she texts me, all I have to do is pop the popcorn for the movie I hope we watch and wait. I already spent far too much time getting ready, with all the outfit changes and manscaping. It's hard to know what the right thing to wear is. I consider this a date, so sweatpants seem too casual, but again, I don't want it to seem like I'm trying too hard or trying to be someone I'm not.

Amy went to her new friend Joy's house for the night. She met Joy at her job interview and they hit it off, which, fortunately, for me means she won't be home tonight and has a job lined up to teach kindergarten come fall. My sister is funny and great to have around, but she needs something and someone else to keep her busy for exact times like this.

I owe Joy a drink, if I ever meet her.

My phone buzzes in my pocket.

CAM

On my way! Can't wait to hang out 😊

My stomach does that flip-floppy thing that feels like it may have lodged accidentally in my throat. She got off earlier than I expected.

I quickly light the candles to get the scent going and throw the popcorn in the microwave to start popping. No, I'm not making it homemade because who the hell knows how to do that. Everything else is set up. Let my anxious pacing ensue—from the kitchen to the door, the door to the living room—geezus, I'm a fucking wreck.

Is it better to wait on the couch and take a second to answer the door, or should I be prepared to open it at the first knock? Why am I so nervous? I run around making sure everything looks good, double-checking the bathroom to ensure it's clean and Amy didn't leave anything lying around. I smell myself and make sure my nerves are properly masked by my deodorant and cologne.

A soft knock sounds at the door, causing my pulse to ratchet up another notch. I'm going to have a goddamn heart attack if I don't chill the fuck out. I take a deep breath, pumping oxygen into my lungs, and open the door. The sight of Cam nearly knocks me on my ass. She's so gorgeous I choke on the words as I greet her.

"H-h-hi," I say. I'm blocking the doorway, holding on to the doorframe so I don't crumble to the floor. She's stunningly beautiful after a long day of work.

"Hey, you gonna let me in?" she asks, one side of her mouth shifting up in an adorable lopsided grin. I scoot to the side slightly, sweeping my arm as I welcome her in.

Cam is wearing a black overall-style dress that cuts off an inch or two below the swell of her backside. She has on a black short-sleeved T-shirt that is skintight and sheer black leggings with black combat boots. My eyes shamelessly sweep over her whole ensemble before meeting her gaze. Her body is fully on display and yet covered completely in the weirdest mind trick I've ever experienced.

"Sorry, I didn't have time to go home and change," she says, almost self-consciously as she slips out of her boots.

"You wore that to work?" I choke out.

Hello dear friend, jealousy. Nice to see ya again. I don't want her to look this good for other people, especially not when she has to get so close to them, touching them, running her fingers through their hair.

"Umm, yeah. We wear black so none of the stains show when we make a mess coloring someone's hair," she explains.

"I guess that makes sense, it's just . . . you look gorgeous. Clients are going to line up to sit in your chair," I say, masking my insecurity, hopefully.

A husky laugh bellows out from her. She raises an eyebrow and says, "Oh please, like you don't have women lined up when you're in uniform?"

"Not really, come here." I grab her hand and pull her into a hug, molding her tightly against my body. A thought about not wanting to ever let her go flashes in my mind, and I force a deep breath so I don't blurt it out. *Reality. I have to maintain a sense of reality about where this is going.*

We stand there for a few minutes, simply holding on to each other. It feels like this is where I'm meant to be, wrapped around her after we both finish work for the day. Is it hot in here?

Peeking up at me from under her lashes as she gently releases her hold, she asks, "Sooo, what are we gonna do?"

"Well, I thought we could start with a shoulder rub and a foot soak, since you said your feet hurt so bad." She walks past me, out of the entryway and into the open-concept apartment.

"Oh my gosh, shut up. Did you set up a tent and twinkle lights for me?" She grabs my hand and bounces up and down in excitement.

"Amy will be glad to know she was right about you liking that, but yeah. So we can watch a movie after you relax." I can feel my cheeks heat in self-consciousness. I'm relieved Cam likes it, but also I feel a little vulnerable putting myself out there like this.

"Seriously, this is perfect. I've been wanting to set something like this up forever, but how lame to make a movie bed for a party of one," she crows. *Thank you, Amy!*

I lead her to the kitchen and open a bottle of rosé, pouring her a glass and grabbing myself a beer.

"Are you ready to relax?" I ask with a bit of seduction in my voice that came out of nowhere.

A husky laugh and another raise of her eyebrow compliments her slow nod. I motion for her to put her feet in a heated pedicure footbath that I set up next to the kitchen peninsula as I bend down to hit the button that makes it bubble.

"Umm, I-I have on tights, Rambo. Slow your roll," she stutters out.

"Oh, um, okay . . . we can skip the footbath."

"No . . . I just need to take them off. Do you mind turning around?" she asks, her cheeks turning the faintest shade of pink.

I turn around and face the textured white apartment wall. It's not like I haven't seen her in all her glory before, but if she wants modesty then that's what she'll get. Consent is important!

"All good, you can turn around," she coos, a small touch of excitement in her voice.

She's already propped on the stool and lowering her feet gently into the water. I shift behind her, gently sweeping her hair forward so I can properly massage her shoulders. My hands begin in tender movements, kneading and pressing into the knots but being careful not to exert too much pressure.

A low moan rolls softly out of her mouth, and I hesitate for the briefest of seconds. I did not prepare for her soft noises or the proximity. I can feel my growing shaft pressing against the zipper of my jeans offensively. *Dammit, I didn't think this through!*

"Is that too hard?" I ask before realizing the way the words sound coming out.

"Last time I checked, there's no such thing." Her laughter melds with the sounds of her practically purring.

Thank God the footbath has a timer on it and shuts off after ten minutes. Not only are my hands tired, but I need to put a little distance between my cock and Cam or I'm going to embarrass myself. As if on cue, her stomach rumbles so loudly we both are stunned to silence before doubling over in laughter.

"Hungry?" I ask.

"I'm sorry, oh my gosh, how embarrassing. I didn't get to eat lunch or dinner since I was finishing my last trial today." Her cheeks blush, hinting her embarrassment, but she still smiles sheepishly.

"Hey, it's okay. I will feed you, but you need to make sure you're eating. I have popcorn, but I could also order pizza?" I say, wondering if she needs something more substantial.

"Pizza sounds great. I can pay, I made tips today." The words tumble out of her mouth, yet there's an edge to them, like she really can't afford to pay.

"Wright, when you're with me, you don't pay. I got you, promise."

I tip her chin up and press a gentle kiss to her lips before making my way over to the kitchen to grab my phone, ordering a pizza plus mini cinnamon-sugar donuts, because I can.

While we wait for the food, we decide to snuggle up in our makeshift movie theater bed. Twinkle lights dance overhead as the tent walls and blankets make a sort of cocoon around us. Cam mentions she would rather talk than watch a movie, so I set the TV to play some soft, soothing jazz tunes. A glittering, bright giggle rolls out of her. "Did you steal this playlist from Dalton?"

"Oh my gosh! Do you remember how awkward that double date was? Dude seriously thought he was getting lucky, serenading her with love songs." We both laugh until we have tears rolling down our faces. Senior year, one of our mutual friends, Dalton, took us on a double date for his first time out with this girl. He played love songs the whole way to the restaurant. I'm talking about Marvin Gaye's "Let's Get It On"–style of music. It was so awkward that his date ended up leaving before the appetizers came, and we had to spend the rest of the night cheering him up.

After our laughter has settled, I brush the remaining happy tears from her face with a swipe of my thumbs and ask, "So . . . did you pass your trials?"

"Yes, I did. Ugh, it's such a relief, except now I have to actually build my clientele and money is even less guaranteed since I won't get an assistant's salary." She throws her head back and rubs a hand roughly down her face.

"You're amazing, everyone you meet adores you. I'm sure it won't take long, and if you ever need help, you know you can ask."

She presses her soft lips to mine, just once. "While that's incredibly sweet and generous, this is something I have to do on my own. Prove to myself I can, you know?" I'm proud of her. I wouldn't mind helping her out if she needed it, but the fact that she wants to be self-sufficient is really hot. If this works out between us, it will be because she wants it to, not because she needs me.

"Tell me something, Rambo . . . What do you do at work?" She snuggles in a little closer, using my arm as a pillow.

"Well, there isn't much to say. We do communications, but you know that already. Most of it we can't talk about since it's classified. Is there something specific you want to know?"

"Umm, I guess . . . do you like it? Is it dangerous? Do you have to move around a lot?" The fear in her eyes is crippling. I should've seen these questions coming. Cam has always been an overthinker, and we haven't discussed my job much at all. She knows about Thatch, but only the basics.

I puff out a breath of air and run my hands through my hair. "I love it, it gave me a sense of purpose when I really didn't have one— no offense." I eye her suspiciously for any hint of anger over our past bubbling up. When I don't find it, I continue, "Danger is relative. My job's not always safe, but bad things happen to people walking down the street. I may have to move at some point, but not anytime soon. My team is here and we relocate as a unit, so it's unlikely that they will want to send us and all of our belongings to live somewhere new." Moving and deploying are two different things, I keep the possibility of the latter to myself, for now.

I'm downplaying the risk, obviously, but there isn't a point in scaring her. It's not a lie to say that danger lurks no matter where you are in life. Bad shit happens to good people all the time. Do I run toward it more often than others? Yeah, I do. I will explain more to her at some point if things progress, but right now, I'm trying to make sure things actually do progress. I also don't want to give her any excuse to run.

Knock, knock!

I head to the door to grab the food, then make my way back into the tent with the pizza box, the bag of donuts, and some napkins.

"Dinner is served, milady." I hand Cam a slice of pizza and bow my head.

"Do not quit your day job, Rambo. That wasn't very good acting." She eats her pizza tentatively, taking small bites.

"Do you like it?" It feels like she doesn't want to eat it, but I don't really know why.

"It's so good, thank you. I'm just not super hungry." She fiddles with one of the blankets, looking down at her half-eaten slice.

I take the slice from the napkin on her lap and plop it back in the box, moving it to the opening of the tent. "Wright, look at me. What's up?"

"What do you mean? Nothing." She dismisses me, moving to grab the pizza and pull it back toward us.

"Nope." I grab her hands, turning her to face me. "You are hungry, I know you are because your stomach told me. Why are you picking at the pizza? I can get you something else."

"Stop, Will. It's just . . . well, you know I've gained weight since you last saw me, and I've been trying really hard to lose it, but I don't know. I guess I just thought that after the phone call, maybe something was going to happen tonight and you . . . well, you know."

"I what? I wouldn't think you're attractive if you eat?" I'd had a hunch that she struggled with her body image, but honestly, she's never been more beautiful in my eyes. Her curves could kill a man.

"Well, I mean, yeah. Realistically, if I was thinner back then, you probably wouldn't have left. I have these stupid athletic knees and wide hips. I just . . . I don't know."

"Is that what you think?" She can't be serious. But she looks at me, tight-lipped, unwavering in her assessment. "Cameron Jane, you are the most beautiful woman I've ever laid eyes on. You're not even close to being overweight, but even if you were, I would still choose you a million times over because what's in here can't be beat." I place my hand on her heart.

"Still, I'm not where I want to be. For myself." She plays it off like she believes me, but I can tell she's not a hundred-percent sold. I make a mental note to keep reminding her.

"That's okay, you know I will help you, I've already been trying to. But promise me one thing. If you feel insecure, tell me. It would be my pleasure to show you just how much I adore your curves." She rolls her eyes but grabs the bag of donuts. I consider that a win, for now.

"Mm-uh-gosh," she moans around a mouthful of sugar as her eyes practically roll back in her head. I get it. I could live and die by these sweet balls of fried perfection, and her eating them.

Once we finish eating, we settle back into our makeshift bed. Cam snuggles in close, resting her head on my chest, under my chin, and her leg intertwines with mine. She's soft in all the right places, pressed in close, fitting like she was made just for me. I don't want to move her, but after going so long without her in my life, I'm desperate to kiss her again.

I slide my hand under her chin and shift her head slightly so she's peering up at me. There is molten lava in her eyes, and I can tell she wants this too. Her breath catches just slightly. I press my lips to hers, swallowing the small sound.

Cupping her face with one hand and running the other up and down her arm, I swipe my tongue out, running it along the seam of her lips. An invitation for more, if she wants it. She scoots higher, deepening the kiss. Moaning softly, she opens and grants me access. I take my time exploring the lingering taste of cinnamon sugar on her lips. It's an intoxicating mix of sweetness and raw need.

Cam shifts again, slowly moving her hand down my abs and chest. She's exploring my body as much as she is my mouth; her touch is not tentative, but confident. Her arms are covered in goose bumps, and every stroke of my hand makes her shiver in a delightful conformation that she's as affected as I am. Cam inches her hand further down, gripping my cock through my jeans.

I break the kiss, grabbing her wrist. "You don't have to do that, Cam. We can take things slow." I don't want her to feel pressured to do anything, especially after she told me how she's been feeling. But also, I would love the opportunity to show her what she does to me.

"I want to, Will," she says, looking me squarely in the eye with a ferocity and heat I haven't seen . . . well, maybe ever.

"I just don't want you to feel pressured, you know, because of last night. You are the funniest, most thoughtful, caring, and generous person I know. I love that you are so self-sufficient and determined with your work. I just don't want you to think this is only physical, remember it's much more about what's in here and up here." I place my hand over her heart and then gently swipe my finger across her forehead. It's the truth, this is about so much more than the physical for me, it's about what's in her soul.

"For me too, but I want this right now." Her eyes glisten with the faint sheen of tears beginning.

I lean in to kiss her again, whispering against her lips, "Okay, but if you get to touch me, Wright, then I get to touch you too."

I reposition us both on our sides, facing each other, so we can easily touch but still kiss. Cam slides her hand over me again, gripping firmly, and then unbuttons my jeans, sliding the zipper down carefully. I lift up slightly so she can slide my jeans and boxer briefs down. Her breath hitches as she gazes at me with big, round appreciative eyes.

"Hey, you still have on your dress, not fair." I pretend to pout as my hands shake from the thought of finally being able to touch her.

"Just lift it up a little, and we're even, Rambo." She winks at me, continuing to use that ridiculous nickname that I'm sort of starting to love.

Holy shit, does she not have on underwear? I mean, she did remove the leggings, but I thought people still wore something under those. I must look confused because she giggles, taking my hand and sliding it up to her wet, hot heat. She's soaked.

"Christ! Is that all for me?" My words come out in a husky growl.

She doesn't answer, just leans in, sucking my bottom lip in between her teeth, returning her focus to my straining erection. She grips me firmly, stroking me tightly in focused movements. This is not going to last long; her small hand feels too good wrapped around me.

I get to work rubbing her nub with my thumb, rotating between slow and fast circles. I take a chance and dip one finger into her hot center—holy fuck, she's tight. She's squeezing one finger so snugly, I'm not sure I can fit another. I feel her heating up, getting wetter by the second. Our mouths mingle in languid, lazy movements while we focus on other efforts. I need to get her there quickly because I'm seconds from bursting.

I struggle to add another finger but finally manage. I turn them to crook them at that perfect angle and hit her sweet spot. Her body trembles, and I know she's close. "Will, oh God, I'm coming," she cries out.

"Right there with you, baby," I say right before I release, spurting hot liquid on my belly and the sheets below. It feels like I come forever, her name on my lips. We are both completely satiated and wrung out. She presses a soft kiss to my lips, then rolls onto her back laughing.

"You okay over there?" I ask with an eyebrow raised, but my face is surely amused.

"More than okay, happy." She giggles again, placing the back of her hand over her mouth.

I shake my head and get up to clean myself up, returning with a couple of damp washcloths, one to wipe off the sheet and one for Cam. This girl and her laughter are quickly becoming my favorite things. After everything is tidied up, I snuggle back into her, pressing my lips to her temple.

"I missed you this week. Thank you for tonight, you're so sweet." She yawns, burrowing deeper into me.

"You earned it, Wright. Now rest. I set an alarm, so you'll have time to go home and change before work tomorrow."

"Thanks, Will," she whispers, and I can tell she's falling asleep by the soft puffs of air faintly escaping her lips.

I lie here awake, simply watching her sleep, thinking of all the ways this is probably going to blow up in my face and all the reasons I couldn't care less. We didn't exactly take things slow tonight, but I'm not complaining. I probably should've been more honest about the dangers of my job, but it would have ruined the mood. I wanted her to relax and have fun without adding to her stress. I care about her, far more than I've admitted. Tonight was fun, perfect, relaxing, and hot as hell. I'm falling for her all over again, which feels familiar and different all at the same time. She is different now but better, stronger in so many ways, and that raises the stakes even more for me. She doesn't need me, she could easily walk away taking my heart with her.

TWENTY-SIX

Cam

**"You Look Like You Love Me" - Ella Langley &
Riley Green**

spent the night with Will! He was endearing, sweet, and fun and made me feel safer than I have felt in longer than I can remember. Being around him, no matter the setting, relaxes me in a way that's more than soothing. It feels nice to have someone look after me, and the lengths he went to ensure I could unwind after a long couple of days were exactly what I needed.

We hooked up! Well, kind of. I guess you would call what we did "rounding second base," maybe third. I'm not sure which base means what exactly in that whole analogy. All I do know is it was hot with a capital H. Kissing him is not awkward at all, it's like our mouths already know exactly what to do, and if I let go, it just happens and it's perfect.

Speaking of perfect, Will has a holy, chiseled-by-the-gods body. It's seriously unfair, and yet I'm over the moon with gratitude. His chest and stomach look like replicas of Michelangelo's *David*, while his manhood is far above average.

More than his body, though, his face and heart draw me in the most. He has perfectly straight white teeth and those ocean-blue eyes that sparkle unlike anything I've ever seen. He has secrets and pain hidden behind those deep pools, and I find myself longing to discover each and every one of them. I want to take away the pain I see, and the pain I know is buried in that tender heart. I am desperate to give him peace the way he has given it to me recently.

I worked today. It was light for a Saturday. I spent the majority of the day setting up my new chair and station since I haven't officially booked any clients yet. Filling Daveed in on my evening was a much more in-depth conversation than I'd expected. He practically threatened me that if I messed things up, he would sweep in and steal Will away. Gosh almighty, so much for his loyalty. Between Micah and Daveed, the competition is stiff—pun intended.

All in all, last night was everything I dreamed it would be: romantic, relaxing, and downright sexy. At the same time, though, it makes me nervous. He's so good at this part, the wooing, but I've done this before. What if I can't recover from the fall this time, the one that I know will inevitably come?

Tonight, I want to see Will, and I want to have fun, let loose. We need a minute to enjoy each other without the feelings and heated moments clouding our judgment. Don't get me wrong, I'm really in it with him, but I need to slow down on the heart side of things, for my own well-being. I texted Lo on my lunch break and asked her to help me out. She obliged, after demanding all the details, and now we are set to meet up with the whole group at the Waterin' Hole "for some drinks, dancing, and debauchery"—her words not mine.

Glancing at my phone, I see that I have roughly one hour to get glammed up before the guys arrive to pick us up. Ruiz volunteered to be our designated driver since he has a large SUV, and I couldn't be more thankful. Money is getting even tighter now that I won't have my steady income, and while walk-ins are pretty frequent, I'm a bit nervous about how I'm going to make ends meet. Spending extra money on ride shares is just one more thing I need to be cautious about in the interim while I build my book of clients.

"Hey . . . whatcha thinking of wearing tonight?" Lo pops her head in my room.

"Haven't decided yet, you?" I ask, shrugging nonchalantly.

"I'm either going with that little turquoise dress or shorts and a cropped tank . . . but I was thinking . . ." she starts, eyes twinkling with mischief.

"Should I be worried?" Amusement dances on my face.

"No! I was thinking you should wear this." She chucks a gray shopping bag at me.

I open the bag and pull out a green cropped, thin-strapped tank top that's got lace and sequins. It's unequivocally the most beautiful shade of emerald I've ever seen.

"Lo! This is stunning, you shouldn't have," I scold her, even though there is no way I am giving it back.

"Really, it was nothing. I saw it on clearance at the mall and I knew it would bring out the green flecks in your eyes perfectly."

I hop up, strip off my T-shirt, and pull it on—holy smokes. It's a little snug but hits in all the right places. My boobs look great and I don't even need a bra with it, which makes it a winner in my book. I'll do practically anything to avoid those torturous devices.

"Are you sure it's not too much?" I ask, glancing in the full-length mirror carefully propped against the wall by my dresser.

"Cam, you will never be too much. If anyone ever tells you that you are, then they are not enough," she says matter-of-factly.

"Thanks, you're my best friend, you know." I reach out to pull her toward me and into a hug.

"Yeah, yeah . . . Now get a move on." She smacks my backside. "We don't have long, and I know you're going to fret over what to wear for bottoms so I already decided. Wear your black high-rise jeans, the ones that flare at the bottom." She winks at me, slipping out and heading toward her own room to get ready.

I don't dare go against her advice after she gifted me yet another stunning piece of clothing so I do as she says and put on the black denim pants. I re-curl my hair and throw it in a braid on one side to keep it out of my face. Flicking on some mascara and opting for lightly tinted ChapStick, I'm ready to go.

Since I have plenty of time before we need to leave, I venture into our kitchen and set about making Superman shots. I am inexperienced at best when it comes to making drinks, but this is one I have mastered. I shake the blue curaçao and vodka with ice, pouring it carefully in the variety of shot glasses I was able to scrounge up from the cupboard. Using a straw, I layer in the grenadine slowly, so it's the perfect ombré of red fading into a slight purple where the two liquids meet and then into solidly bright blue.

Just as I finish, there is a heavy knock at the door. Lo rushes out to answer it, giving me a slight eyebrow raise when she notices my concoctions. I hit her with a lopsided grin, silently communicating that I'm trying to impress.

Our knights in shining armor along with Amy, filter into the quaint kitchen.

"Wright," Will says, sliding his arms around me from behind.

"Hi, you look handsome. Got a hot date, Rambo?" I turn to face him, fully knowing I'm letting my insecurity show, but handsome is an understatement. He looks lickable. His soft black two-sizes-too-small T-shirt shows off his ridiculously chiseled arms, and I can't help myself from wanting to climb him like a tree. His denim is worn and faded, accentuating his muscular thighs and squeezable booty. *Down, girl.*

He winks at me and I know he's reading my very dirty thoughts right now. He presses his lips to mine quickly and I groan a little, chasing his mouth as he pulls away. He chuckles and whispers, "Later," so that only I can hear.

Reluctantly, I turn back to my shots and explain them to the group, my voice laced with anxiety. "I call these Superman shots because, obviously, they are the right colors, and I had a borderline-obsessive crush on Clark Kent as a teenager. Not in a creepy way. Just, I m-mean . . . I mean, have you seen the movie? Henry Cavill is a brilliant actor. He should have won an Oscar for that role," I blurt out nervously.

Will squeezes my hip, chuckling to himself softly, causing me to look around the room at the array of raised eyebrows, smirks, and a single eye roll from Lo. I may or may not have done a little overexplaining due to my nerves and desperate attempt to make my friends love the shots as much as I do.

"I promise they are delicious and go down so smoothly," I say, willing them not to tease me about this.

"I don't really care what you call them as long as there's liquor in there," Smith says, winking at me.

"To Clark Kent," Butler toasts.

After the shots are done, we pile out of the apartment and into the SUV. The guys all chime in to thank me for being the one girl Will is willing to go to the country bar for. There are a minimal number of comments about me being his kryptonite. Yes, I deserved every one of them . . . Why did I give that whole explanation and not just tell them it's a shot like a normal person?

—

Waiting in line is the worst. I don't usually have to do it when it's just Lo and I attempting to con our way into a bar, but the whole group thing seriously cramped our ability to flirt our way past the bouncers. We spent close to half an hour waiting to get in! It's obviously more crowded than the last time we were here, but the vibe seems good and I'm over-the-top excited to dance with Will.

I made a mental decision before coming tonight that I would avoid the green syringe shooters at all costs, and so far, I've been able to pass without anyone truly noticing. I'm nursing a whiskey and ginger ale while we all gathers around a small table to take in the atmosphere and get our liquid courage up. It's not a big enough space for a group this size, but there isn't any room on the rail around the floor, and at least we still have a decent view of the dancing.

The first couple of chords to "The Devil Went Down to Georgia" stream out from the speakers. I turn to make eye contact with Will. He doesn't have to say a word, he just simply nods and I know it's time to head to the dance floor. I'm amped because not only do I love the song but we just successfully pulled off the whole silent communication thing that I've been jealous of Lo and Smith over.

I make my way to the center of the floor with Will nipping at my heels. We both get in the rhythm of the beat and quickly fall in step with where everyone else is in the dance. I'm jumping, kicking, stomping on cue, lost to the music, letting my body perform the moves from muscle memory. This . . . here . . . with Will by my side. There's nothing better.

"Oh my God, I can't keep up. How do you know how to do this?"

Lo yells, as she sashays up beside me.

"Just look at my feet and follow my lead. There wasn't much else to do in the small town we grew up in!" I shout back at her over the music.

She's trying, but, my gosh, she's so bad at it. It's honestly a little embarrassing and exciting at the same time that I finally found something I can do better than her. I know, I know, I should be all supportive because she's my best friend, but it's nice to excel at one thing over her. Sue me!

The music fades out and just as quick the starting beat of the famous "Footloose" song rolls on. I look at Will. Yet again, I'm on the receiving end of a self-assured nod. I tell Lo to stand aside and watch, which irritates her and makes her laugh in equal measure.

Will grabs my hand, dragging me to the very front of the dance floor, where we perform every move to the song flawlessly. He hits every step and spins me at exactly the right times. We're having so much fun that I'm completely engrossed in the moves. I don't immediately notice the crowd that has gathered around to watch and cheer us on.

When the song ends, I'm drenched in sweat with giggles bursting from my lips. Will whispers, "Want to give them a show, Wright?" Heat flashes up my neck, painting my cheeks even redder than they would have been from the sheer exertion. There's a round of applause as we take a bow and Will spins me backward, dipping me suspiciously low to the floor before curling me into him for a heated kiss. The crowd lets out a round of hoots and hollers as we head back over to where our group has commandeered some space at the rail that opened up.

"Holy shit . . . Who knew you had moves like that, we coulda had chicks begging to come home with us this whole time," Smith says pointedly to Will. Lo promptly smacks him on the arm.

"Don't be jealous, it's all my partner. Couldn't do it without her." Will shrugs and points at me with his thumb.

"Ha, you have no idea how many times he stepped on my toes when we spent weeks learning that dance in the barn after school," I say winking at Will.

"Oooh, burn. She got you, bro." Smith laughs huskily.

"She didn't mention how long it took her to learn the two-step," Will responds, his face morphing into a goofy, lopsided grin.

He's not lying. It did take me a ridiculously long time to figure out a really simple dance. I've always been an overthinker. Trying to go too fast, then too slow, it was a real miracle the day I finally got it down.

"Okay, fine, that's fair—ooh, let's take a shot!" I point at the approaching server, steering the conversation away from my shortcomings.

I know I made myself a deal, but fuck it! I grab the waitress and we all take two Jell-O shooters each, down the hatch. Ruiz returns with a round of drinks, which also go down way too quickly.

We stand around singing some of the songs as they come across the speakers, taking turns dancing on the floor in different groups. Sometimes it's just the girls, and other times it's Will and I trying and failing to teach Smith and Butler the moves to various dances. I notice Butler glancing at Amy more than once . . . I need to explore that but don't want to miss out on spending as much time with Will as possible. The night is progressing quicker than I had hoped, but it's true that time really does fly by when you're having fun.

A slow song descends and couples line up in pairs, forming an oval around the dance floor. Will extends his hand. "Shall we?"

I link my fingers in his and we get in position. I haven't two-stepped in close to five years, but I know with Will leading it will all come right back.

Boy, does it. I glide around the dance floor with one of his strong arms carefully positioned at my lower back and our hands locked in front of us at each of my hips. It's not intimate in the normal sense of slow dancing, but the occasional spins and dips he manages to put me in are just as intoxicating. Or maybe it's the alcohol that's intoxicating. Probably both.

We end the song with one last spin and dip, Will pressing his lips to mine and thanking me for the dance, like a real gentleman. I move to head back to the table and he playfully swats my backside. Fine, maybe he's not completely a gentleman. But I'm more than okay with it.

Our group oohs and aahs with a round of applause as we approach. It's a good thing I love them all. If I didn't, they would be getting serious talks from me about how embarrassing they are.

We take a couple more shots and dance a little more before the swaying and blurred vision settle in. Lo and I have both obviously had more than we should have, and Amy is passed out on a stool, her face plastered to the railing holding her up. Butler is suspiciously close by, ensuring she doesn't fall . . . I think. Lo and I look at each other, silently exchanging our need to find out more about that.

"Looks like it's time to hit the road." Will snaps his fingers, twirling his pointer in a circular motion in an effort to round up the group. I lean into him, intent on giving him a kiss, but I clumsily miss, ending up a little closer to his chin. I can't feel much at this point, but the slow rumble of his laugh is comforting.

The next conscious awakening I have is that I'm home. Ruiz thankfully lived true to his word and expertly performed his designated driver duties. Will and Smith help Lo and me to our apartment and into our separate rooms.

"Come heeere, Ramboooo," I slur from my position, perched on the edge of the bed.

"I'm gonna tuck you in. Do you need pajamas?" he asks, grabbing my shoulders to stabilize me.

"Not if I'm sleeping with you." I bonk my finger to the tip of his nose.

"As much as I'd love that, not when you're drunk, Wright."

I put on my best puppy dog eyes and beg him to stay with me. Instead, he chuckles, helps me pull off my jeans, and expertly tucks me in like a burrito. My eyes are fluttering and I know I won't be awake, or maybe alive, for long, but I do notice him placing a trash can and bottle of water by the bed.

Will kisses me on the forehead and tells me to call him in the morning. I huff an "Okayy fine, sur losssss," and then he's gone, quietly closing the door. I faintly hear him and Smith exchange a few laughs and then head out the front door.

I wish he would have stayed. We had a blast tonight, and yes, I definitely drank way too much. Cuddling would have been nice, although the thought of lying on my side stings the back of my throat with the precursor to what is surely bound to be vomit. I guess it's good he didn't stay for the disgustingly unflattering night and morning coming my way.

TWENTY-SEVEN

Will

"Miles on It" - Marshmello & Kane Brown

've faced down bullets, seen enemies do all kinds of radical shit, baled hay for hours upon hours, and spent more time than I care to admit studying; I'm no stranger to hard work. Raised to put my head down and push through the pain, the heat, the mental strain that inevitably exists. What's the one thing I wasn't raised to do? Plan a date when your significant other is surely going to be hungover. I'm at a loss here.

Sundays are one of Cam's usual days off, and seeing that I don't know when exactly the call will come in for me to leave, taking advantage of every available moment in our schedules is paramount. The trouble is, she deserves better than me just snuggling in bed with her, even if it's likely the one thing she feels like doing today.

I called her to check in this morning and was met with a few groans and questions as to why I would allow her to once again take those

"little green syringes of death." Reminding her that I am not, in fact, responsible for her decisions and that she's an independent woman went over about as well as if I had suggested she was on her period during a fight. Note to every significant other out there: Do not bring up periods as an excuse or supplement to any argument, ever!

So here I sit, pondering how to steal time with her while also not aggravating the world's worst hangover; yes, I know because I've been there—those Jell-O shooters are no joke. The beach would be nice, the salty air and breeze usually makes me feel better. Packing a late lunch, maybe some hair of the dog, and a nice soft blanket to lay out on . . . This would be semi-close to lying in bed all day but would also eliminate any of the pressure that being in bed brings.

Not that I don't want the pressure, I'd give Cam almost anything she asked me for at this point, but I still feel a little guilty for taking things so far the other night. I know that she was into it, but at the same time, there's a nagging feeling in my stomach that when she finally sees the real me, the scarred version, she is going to run.

Deciding a beach picnic is the way to go, I call Cam and confirm that I can pick her up around three. Planning for later in the day gives me time to renew the pass that allows me to drive on the beach, plan food, pick up some wine, and hit up a Target for the softest blanket I can find. It also gives me time to prepare for the conversation that I desperately need to have with her but have been strictly avoiding.

Until now, we have kept things simple, not too serious, but reality is quickly setting in. I'm going to be leaving, no clue when, and she doesn't even know that's a possibility. Honestly, it's highly likely she doesn't even know what I really do. She knows about Thatch, but not the details of how, when, why. If I had to guess, she assumes he always had mental health problems, not that he won them as the ultimate prize of war or that I have them too. We briefly talked about therapy the other day, but I didn't tell her *why* I go. I haven't been honest enough, and that alone sends my stomach clawing into my throat because she has every right to tuck tail and run.

It's possible Lo has given her some sort of warning; she's facing the same very cold reality with Smith. He hasn't mentioned talking about it with her, though, not that he tells me everything that goes on between them. On the other hand, maybe Lo didn't tell Cam anything because she knows Cam will overthink it. I think Lo knows this is fate bringing us back for our second chance. I think she wants us to make it and I'm grateful.

Adding to the dilemma, I'm questioning if Cam will even care. I want her to care, and on some baseline human level she will, I know that. What I mean is, I want a reaction that makes me feel more secure in this relationship. Is that messed up? Yeah, it is.

Cam's never been one to hide her feelings, and even though she's different than she used to be in a lot of ways, I anticipate this going one of two ways: It will either drive us closer or it will end us. Maybe it's better to find out sooner rather than later.

—

"Will, I swear to all that's holy, you are a genius!" Cam shouts from her spot on the navy blue knit blanket I brought to the beach.

She's sprawled out, on her back, wearing a peach-colored bikini, with her head resting comfortably on her pillow. Yeah, she demanded that she bring a pillow to the beach despite my efforts to explain that the sand will ruin it. She said she needed it for maximum comfort. I could only argue so much when she offered to bring one for me too. Pillows on the beach—not something I've done before, but it does seem remarkably comfortable.

"Oh really? What did I do that makes me the next Einstein?" I make my way over to her with the basket of food and drinks.

"Hmm, let's see. You took the girl with a hangover from hell and made her a bed on the beach. Who needs a sound machine blasting ocean waves when you can have the real deal?"

Smiling at her, I shift down on my side of the beach bed and carefully put my hand on hers.

"You want to guess what else I brought?" I ask cheekily.

"Hopefully food . . . Please say there's food in that basket."

Chuckling, I reach inside and pull out a bag of empanadas I picked up, as well as some pickles, olives, cheese, crackers, and fruit.

"Shut up! You got me Miguel's?" She smacks my hand in disbelief.

"They are the best and nothing cures what ails you better than some beef and fried dough." I give her a playful pat on the thigh while rummaging to pull an empanada out for her. She bites into it faster than I can fully pull my hand away.

"Mmm . . . muh gawd," she says around a mouthful. "If I didn't already like you, this would have for sure sealed the deal, Rambo."

"Glad I could take care of you. I'm happy you're happy. It seems like you're feeling better?" I ask hesitantly.

"You make me feel better," she chimes and presses a soft kiss to my cheek.

Her lips are butter soft. Either from an intense moisturizing routine or empanada grease. Could be both. They feather across my face almost like a whisper and yet leave me feeling like I've been hit by a Mack truck.

"Umm . . . we should talk." I choke out the words because I know this sounds bad but also need to bite the bullet.

"O-kay? What's wrong? Look, I'm sorry for drinking too much last night and for propositioning you. It wasn't fair and, again, it was stupid and I'm sorry," she blurts out in a rush while looking positively adorable as she turns three shades of pink.

"Cam, it's not that. Believe me, if you hadn't drank so much, you wouldn't have had to beg me to stay. It's about my work."

"Oh God, you called me Cam. This must be serious. Are you moving, tell me you're not moving, you're freaking moving after we just reconnected. Just my luck. I finally find the guy and then, of course, he would move away. Fuck a duck," she rattles out in quick succession.

"Whoa . . . you done? Can I explain now?" I'm trying with all my might not to outright laugh at her clear spiral.

She looks at me with wide eyes, and I can tell she's embarrassed that she just blurted out her inner thoughts, but she nods for me to continue.

"So, I'm not sure if you really understand what I do, for work I mean. But um . . . we are part of a unit that goes in to set up communications for special operations teams."

Again, she nods and waves her hand for me to continue, looking equally interested and scared to death.

"We usually go into a place before anyone else. Sometimes we have to parachute in and sometimes we can drive. Either way, there isn't anyone there typically, so we get everything set up for the teams to come in and carry out missions."

"Are these places dangerous?" she asks.

"Not always, but it's hard to ever say or know exactly what we will walk into."

"Okay . . . what else?"

"Well . . . we don't always know when we will have to go. Sometimes things are pre-planned and we have warning, can make arrangements, stuff like that, and other times it's spur of the moment and needs to be done quickly and quietly."

"So, you don't always know when you're leaving. But you must get some notice. I mean, they can't just expect you to be available at all times. What if you were on vacation?"

"No, there have been times when we didn't have any notice. We keep a bag ready at all times and keep it with us. Vacation doesn't really happen; we have to be able to make it to base within two hours unless we have special approval."

"What? That's insane. How do you know when you have to go?" Her face is a perfect picture of annoyed and confused at the confines of this job.

"There's a chain of command. I get the first call and then I call the next person on the list, Smith. It moves on from there. We can complete the list from start to finish in six minutes if everyone answers." I say this with too much pride, but that shit takes lots of practice to perfect.

"What happens if you don't answer?"

"We always answer." I look at her matter-of-factly because the consequences of not answering would be dire. It's not even something we can allow ourselves to think about.

"I call bullshit. You can't possibly be saying no one has ever missed the call, fallen asleep, been in the shower, for fuck's sake?"

"No, not since I've been here. If you miss the call, there are consequences. We make sure we never miss the call."

"Hmm, okay. Are you telling me this for general awareness, or . . . Why are you telling me this?" There it is, the understanding settling in that I'm not having this conversation just to rile her up about the demands of working for the government.

"Well, believe me, if I could avoid it, I would. But there is something coming. Not sure when or for how long, but it's going to happen and it'll be soon. It's been a while since they called us up, after Thatch we got a break, but it's our turn."

"Wait, hold up. I thought Thatch, um, uh . . . committed suicide.

Did he get hurt on the job?"

Wincing a little at her phrasing, I respond, "He did. We had a really rough mission our last time out. It stuck with all of us. But Thatch . . . well, let's say, he came home with some scars that wouldn't heal."

In a split second, she went from irritated to concerned. "What happened, Will"?

"It's a long story. I don't . . . It's hard to talk about," I murmur quietly.

"Rambo . . . I care about you a lot, always have. You don't have to tell me, but as someone who has known you a very long time, I know it's changed you. I can see it in everything you do, it's a burden weighing you down, but you don't have to carry it alone. Let me help you." She squeezes my hand, that simple touch like a warm blanket wrapping around me.

She wants to know the demons that haunt me, to help me slay them. Surprising? Not in the slightest. It's just not a burden I want her to carry. It's my job to protect her, and how do I do that if she's the one picking up my pieces?

"Wright, what do you want me to say? It's an ugly world. There are people who do things so unimaginable it would break your heart, and the very last thing I want to do is hurt you—again."

"Just trust me. If this is going to work, we have to talk about things deeper than our favorite foods or gossiping about our friends. I want to be your shelter, your safe place." Her eyes glisten with tears as she pleads with me. I want to tell her, but the trust part is a little hard; she's never broken it, but I still wonder when she will wake up and realize this is all too much to handle.

"Okay . . ." I say, pulling her a little closer and linking our fingers. Bri's words from the cemetery give me confidence to push through this.

"Our last mission was rough. We had to set up comms under heavy enemy presence. We almost finished and were about to make it out when a little girl, maybe seven years old, approached, strapped with explosives. Some of the guys tried to convince her to let us help her disarm them, but before they could get close enough, it detonated. We believe it was remote detonated by someone a good distance away. She was innocent, like a kid sister, it wasn't fair. These assholes use kids all the time, I know that, but the image is burned in my memory, in all of our memories."

Cam shifts her head in her hands for a second and then quickly crawls into my lap wrapping her arms tightly around my neck. I can feel the slight shake of her shoulders as she's crying. Damn it! I didn't want to upset her, but I had to tell her. She wanted to know.

"Hey. Talk to me." I gently rub my hand down her spine to console her.

She pulls back, revealing those big blue-green eyes soaked with tears. "I'm okay. I'm sad. I mean, for you and Thatch and that poor baby. But mostly . . . I'm scared."

Pressing a tender kiss to her lips and one to her forehead, all I can do is reassure her.

"Look, I will never lie to you. My job is dangerous at times, but a lot of it isn't that bad. We don't have to stay gone for as long as many other people in the military do, and we make a big difference. When we came back, we were all torn up. I had nightmares, still do sometimes, that's why I see Tina, but I've learned ways to handle it and I go to a support group. I didn't start this conversation to drudge up the past, I just wanted you to know in case I get called up and have to leave."

"How long? Where will you be going?" she asks.

"I don't know. Hopefully only a month, maybe two at the longest. I can't say where."

"Okay." She looks at me, tears still threatening to fall from the corners of her eyes. She's breaking my heart and mending it all at the same time.

"I know this is a lot to ask of someone, to deal with this life, I mean." I run my fingers through her hair then grasp both sides of her face so we are eye to eye. "Think you can handle it? Will you be okay?" My voice shakes as I ask her this. Bri assured me that Cam would make the right choice for herself, but I can't help worrying she won't choose me.

"I'll be fine, Will. I'm more concerned about you being safe and coming back to me."

I make the one promise I can't guarantee I can keep: "I'm always coming back to you, baby."

She sucks in a breath, and I think she's going to call me out on it, but instead she grabs my face with both hands and plunges deep into a passionate and emotion-filled kiss. It's like she's communicating her thoughts and feelings all in one kiss. Conveying everything that has gone unsaid between us.

Cam swipes her tongue against the seam of my lips and I shudder but open to her exploration. She's squirming in my lap, turning me hard instantly, and grasping on like it might be the last kiss we ever have. She breaks contact but peppers me with little kisses down my face and throat. My body is alive and buzzing from the chemistry between us.

Slowly, she moves her hips in little circles, causing me to stiffen beyond what I thought was possible. We are touching everywhere, exploring each other without abandon. She's fucking amazing, I can't think of anything other than being with her, in this moment, forever.

A cool splash of liquid hits my outstretched toes, bringing me painfully back to reality.

"Shit! The tide's coming in, we need to move," I say, panting and breathless.

"Oh, umm . . . okay, yeah . . . okay, let's move." She stumbles trying to jump up from my lap quickly.

We rush to get everything thrown into the Jeep before we turn into a soaking wet mess. We are on a narrower stretch of sand and unless we want to lay down in the sea oats, it's time to move.

"Do these seats lay down?" she asks randomly. Though based on the mischievous look in her eyes, maybe not randomly at all.

"Umm, yeah. Pull the lever—wait, why?"

"Rambo, we weren't done. Hurry, get this stuff in and move the Jeep up the beach a little farther where the water hasn't reached in this far." She waves her hand at me like, *Get a move on*.

"Yes, ma'am." I hit her with a salute, sending her into a fit of giggles.

I move the Jeep quickly and see her walking up to it with a sultry grin.

"Get in the back, Rambo. I'll close the tailgate and crawl through the front seat." It's a demand, and a damn sexy one at that.

I cannot believe this is happening. Actually, I'm not even sure I know what is happening, but my growing erection assumes it's going to be good. I do as I'm told and settle into the back. Cam closed the tailgate, just as she said, and is shimmying her way in next to me from the front seat.

"I'm really thankful you have tinted windows," she huffs out as she makes her final hoist into the back.

"Oh yeah? Why's that?" I play it coy, not one to assume, even if it's a pretty safe bet what's about to happen.

"I've been dying to taste you, all of you, since the other night. Is that okay?"

Is she for real? What kind of idiot would I be if I said no.

"Of course, it's okay. Just remember, there are things I want to do too."

On that note, she tugs at my swim trunks and I lift a bit to help her. Cam settles between my legs and gently wraps her small hand around the base of my shaft. She makes quick work of licking me root to tip, spending extra time and attention on the crown. My brain is going foggy, and I may actually be seeing stars. She takes all of me, letting out a small hum of satisfaction.

"Oh God, you have to stop or I'm going to embarrass myself," I half whisper, half shout.

"I want you. Have you been checked out recently?" she asks quickly.

"Yeah, you? Birth control?" My hands are roaming every curve of her body.

"Yes, and yes." She's climbing up on top of me, my cock positioned perfectly between her legs and her delectable tits hovering right above my mouth. Taking a chance, I move her bikini top to the side and suck one nipple into my mouth until it forms a tight nub. Laving on her, I move to the other one and give it a similar treatment. Holy shit, the soft gasps and taste of her is enough to make me blow, and I haven't even sank into her yet.

Letting out a little sigh, she grabs me and puts me in the perfect spot, sinking down ever so slowly. She gasps a little as I stretch her to accommodate me. She is tight, extremely tight, gripping me like a fist. She pushes herself down the rest of the way, fully seating herself on me.

"You, okay?" I ask, concern mixed with need as the words filter out.

"Yeah . . . oh fuck . . . you feel so good. I need to move," she moans.

I grab her hips gently, helping her find her rhythm. She bounces and circles in a perfect motion, and I lift slightly with each bounce, sinking deeper and deeper. She's getting close, I can tell by the slickness coating me and the uneven breaths she is puffing sweetly against my neck. Quickly, I move my thumb between us, over her sweet spot in light vertical flicks. She tightens instantly and lets out a strangled scream, drenching me. The sound and sight of her falling apart sends me crashing after her with a growl.

I hold her tightly against my chest, soaking in the aftermath. Completely sated and semidelirious. Running a hand down her hair and back, I ask, "You good?"

She lets out a small laugh, kisses my cheek, and nuzzles into my neck. "I'm pretty sure I just saw heaven, met God, all the things."

"God, huh? That's high praise, Wright." I can't help but smirk and raise an eyebrow at her assessment.

"Oh sure, laugh it up. I'm not operating on all cylinders, but seriously . . . I now understand the term *mind-blowing*, if you must know." She swats my arm.

"You were amazing, Cam. Truly, even better than I remembered."

"Ohhh . . . so you've been remembering me? Is that why I noticed you keep my picture in your wallet?"

I lightly smack her on the backside. "Damn it, I knew you saw that last night. I was hoping you didn't notice. But the answer is yes. I never stopped thinking about you, missing you, lo—" I'm interrupted by a loud knock on my window.

"Beach Patrol, everything okay in there?"

Shit! I know he can't see us, thank fuck for the window tint.

"Yes, officer, just taking a break from the sun," I shout back as Cam scrambles off of me and adjusts her bathing suit.

"Can't just hang out in your vehicle. It's about to get dark and the tides are coming in. Get a move on." He taps the window once more.

"Yes, sir," I shout as he starts to walk away.

"Oh my God! We almost just got caught having sex on the beach," Cam says through a fit of laughter.

I smile at her shyly. "Worth it."

While I'm a bit annoyed that the officer broke up our post-coital snuggle, it dawns on me that I almost told Cam that I love her. I do, I know I do, but it's too soon to say it. Thankfully, the officer showed up when he did.

"We better get a move on, like he said. I don't want Elliott to have to bail us out of jail." I kiss her cheek one last time. "Thanks, Wright."

"For what?" She looks at me like I'm a puzzle she's trying to decipher.

"For understanding about my job . . . for uh, for being supportive."

"Sure, Rambo. I've got you." She smiles at me, a soft tentative smile. It's full of reservation, but I can't tell if it's from her own fear or because she isn't actually planning on sticking around. She promised she could handle it, and at this point, only time will tell. I'm too in love with her to resist the risk.

TWENTY-EIGHT

Cam

"Two Things" - Kelsea Ballerini

Have you ever heard the expression, if you want to make God laugh, tell him your plans? Plans are my thing. I make lists, set goals, overthink every possible outcome and yet my follow-through, virtually nonexistent. No one would call me type A, organization is not my strong suit, cleaning—meh. Good intentions should count for something though, right?

Good intentions are exactly how I would label every interaction I've had with Will so far. I intend to go in, be fun, and protect my heart at all costs. My follow-through. . . in serious jeopardy. He's too kind, too sexy, too funny, too badass, too everything. The kryptonite to my Clark Kent. The very things I wished for back when my mother used to tell me you could have too much of a good thing. Except it's not too much, I want it all.

At this point, I can't even pretend I'm trying to be unaffected by

him. I like being with him. It's simple—well, not really, but it feels easy. He makes me brave and also calls me on my shit: The perfect balance of building me up and bursting my bubble when necessary.

And then there's the sex. When the dictionary was written, it should've had a picture of Will next to that word. No definition needed, just a picture, people would get it with a mere glance. I thought it was good back when we were younger, but let the record show—like fine wine, it got better with age.

Aside from the phone sex, I initiated both times things went further than kissing, which I should regret. But I can't help it that Will turns me into a glorified floozy. I can't resist him. My mother would be mortified to know I had sex on a beach. Well, technically in a Jeep on the beach. Same difference.

Was it worth it? A million times over, absolutely, hands down. The man knows how to make my body come alive with a simple caress of his hand. He's efficient and skilled and, lord almighty, gives me earthquake orgasms. You know, the ones that give you aftershocks a day later just thinking about the experience.

Yes, *experience*. Sex with most people is an act. Something that, based on my previous history, you do while tightly squeezing your eyes closed and praying for it to be over. Not with Will—that shit is like one of those immersion experiments where you're blindfolded in a dark room and eating odd foods but nothing has ever tasted better in your life because your senses are fully activated.

It's addicting, and I'm shamelessly desperate to do it again. The problem is, while I'm ridiculously into him, I'm also scared out of my mind that I'm letting myself slip right back into what we had. I am trying to let go of the past and these fears that haunt me, but it's still really hard to fully trust him. I keep thinking that the more time I spend with him, the easier it'll get. Fake it 'til you make it, if you will.

Unfortunately, today's a workday for him, so hanging out is basically off the table. Speaking of his work, our conversation yesterday was pretty intense. On some level, I knew his job wasn't simple, safe, or easy, but I had no clue how involved it was. No vacation without special permission, leaving at a moment's notice, walking into unknown situations. It's *a lot*.

I can't quit thinking about what happened the last time they went on a mission. What kind of sick world exists in which someone would hurt a child? That girl was someone's baby, maybe a sister, definitely a friend. Thinking about it has me choking back sobs, and I wasn't even there.

It's unfair and yet that's life. If I could change what happened, I would. Not just for her but for the guys too. Wrapping my head around how they could have witnessed such horror and yet still laugh and smile and joke . . . It's incomprehensible.

I like to think I'm strong, but I know I couldn't have come back from that. I can empathize with why Thatch didn't. Often, since reconnecting with Will, I've wondered why he seemed hardened or different. Now I know. His heart has scars from being haphazardly stitched back together. Not all wounds are visible, but that doesn't make them any less real.

Hell, my heart has a permanent bruise simply from hearing him recount what happened. He asked me if I could handle this life, his life. What kind of question is that, and who would I be if I said no? I'm not delusional enough to think it will be easy, but taking even a bit of pain, fear, or worry from that man—it's not even a question, I will do it without reservation every single time. I will be my own kind of warrior; I will fight every battle to protect his soul.

Over the past several weeks, I've pushed and pulled, ignored and evaded, trying desperately to keep my true feelings at bay. I refuse to do that now. I love him! I'm not ready to tell him that yet, but acceptance is the first step, right?

It terrifies me in the worst way, the soul-crushing, anxiety spiral, aching-in-my-bones kind of way. Somewhere inside, buried deep, I know he has the capacity to hurt me. He's walked away before, and even though he was young, it doesn't mean this is guaranteed to work now, just because we are older.

Love to me is not logical. It's not something you choose, at least not in the beginning, but rather something that happens to you. Like how the strike of a match causes it to ignite: All relationships have the potential to set sparks ablaze or to burn out. It simply depends what type of ignition device you're working with. Is it a cheap match that was a free giveaway at your favorite bar? Or is it a refillable Zippo lighter that you can top off when the flame gets low? If it's the latter, you can make that choice and reignite the flame as it ebbs and flows through the years.

My daddy always told me the key to a lifelong love was finding someone who pushes you to become the best version of yourself. He said you don't need a yes-man; you need someone who isn't afraid to tell you the stuff that's hard to hear. The guy who will tell you that you do indeed look bad in that dress, but that you are still the most gorgeous woman on earth. Someone who will walk beside you during a storm, not run off for shelter, leaving you to follow behind. I want to believe that Will is that man.

A knock on the door drags me sluggishly out of my warm bed. Ugh! Who is here? This was supposed to be my lounge day.

"Delivery for a Ms. Cam Wright," the paunchy old man with a scraggly beard bellows from behind a bouquet of what must be three-dozen pink, white, and red peonies.

"That's me, thank you," I say, taking the bouquet and turning back to the kitchen, closing the door with my foot.

What can I say, the man knows I love peonies. I set the flowers gently in a vase that I filled with water and reach for the card.

> Cam—
> These flowers are beautiful but not anywhere near as gorgeous as you. I can't stop thinking about our "WSOTB."
> —Will

Shut the front door! He sent me sex flowers! Flowers come with all kinds of meanings. Sometimes they're "I'm Sorry" flowers, "Thinking of You" flowers, or "I Fucked Up, Give Me Another Chance" flowers. These are "We Had Hot Steamy Jeep Sex on the Beach" flowers.

Grabbing my phone, I shoot off a text.

CAM

Rambo! Did you just spend a small fortune on flowers just to thank me for having sex with you?

WILL

I mean it was mind-blowing, if I recall.
Worth every penny!

CAM

It was life altering! TY for the flowers
Can u meet for lunch?

WILL

Sorry, can't today . . . super busy.

CAM

Bummer . . . call me later.

Well, that sucks. He doesn't get a lot of time for lunch, but it would've been fun to bring him a sandwich and see him if only for a few minutes. I've been dying to try this new burger place that's close to base. Daveed won't quit talking about it, he's borderline obsessed with their truffle fries and I'm equal parts concerned for him and curious.

You know what makes a lazy day even better? Eating a giant greasy burger and fries while binge-watching my favorite show in bed. I shouldn't, it's financially irresponsible and certainly not going to help my waistline. On the other hand, I've been working out every day, pinching pennies, and I passed my trials. That settles it. Since Will isn't available, I'm ordering takeout and making my own joy today.

—

Stepping into Patty's Patties is like entering a different era. Daveed told me about the fifties diner theme and how it's the perfect mix of cool and cliché. His description of the atmosphere alone had me itching to try it. I live for a novelty experience. Sit me smack in the middle of an old-school diner, and I'm instantly Sandy from *Grease*, ready to squeeze into leather pants and belt out, "You're the one that I want!"

Similar to my music addiction and how it can carry me away from any situation, a novelty like this restaurant is the perfect place to let my mind roam and dream up any number of fictitious stories about the people who work and dine here.

I intended to take my order to go, but the perfectly appointed décor, Elvis strumming on the jukebox, and insane-looking milkshakes have me second guessing myself.

"Hi there. Can I help you?" asks an older-looking waitress wearing a mint-green dress topped with a white apron. Her hair is piled up on her head in a bun being held together by a pencil stuck through it. It's mousy brown but large streaks of shimmering white would place her somewhere in her sixties if I had to guess.

"Hi. I placed a carry-out order, but now that I'm here . . . I think I'd like to stay. Is that okay?"

"Of course, honey. Do you want a seat at the bar or a booth?"

Stealing a glance around the restaurant, I take in the jewel-toned plastic barstools and cushy-looking booths.

"Bar's fine. Can I have a seat at the end?"

"Whatever tickles your fancy, toots."

Flashing her a grin, I make my way toward the last stool and plop down. I wanted this seat because it provides the best view of the restaurant but also gives me enough cover to be unsuspecting in my examination of all the other guests. It's close to the jukebox, and my need to play a few songs is as visceral as my need for a cheeseburger at this point.

Rhonda, the waitress whose name is clearly embroidered in black stitching on her dress, delivers my order, asking me if I'd like to try one of their famous milkshakes. After I order the Chocolate Peanut Butter Bliss, she scurries off and I dig into what can only be described as a gooey, buttery, cheesy explosion of delight.

Daveed was not lying! This is unquestionably the best burger I've ever had, and the truffle fries elevate the otherwise basic french fries to near perfection. Rhonda returns, sliding the milkshake across the bar to me at the perfect moment. The chocolate mixed with peanut butter in the milkshake cuts the grease perfectly. I'm quickly approaching food coma status, so I toss my napkin on my plate and drizzle some milkshake on it to stop the temptation of going back in for more.

It's been a while since I took myself on a date, so to speak. I generally don't love eating at restaurants alone. Soaking in this atmosphere, though, is enough to make up for any lack of conversation or awkwardness.

Peering around, I see there is a mix of business people grabbing a quick bite for lunch, couples sharing milkshakes in the most swoon-worthy way possible, and a couple of families. Rhonda and her fellow employees bounce from table to table carrying armfuls of plates, shakes, and baskets. Listening to the hum of the music, the clanging of silverware, and the sizzle of the grill mimics a live-action play evolving around me.

Every time the door jingles with the sound of a new guest coming or going, I'm swept up wondering who will enter next, why they are coming here, what's their story. This particular guest entering is breathtaking. Flowing chestnut-brown hair that's perfectly coiffed with tendrils falling effortlessly down her back. An emerald-green sundress that hits just above her knees paired with strappy chestnut-colored sandals. She's petite but has killer curves, the kind of woman every other woman wants to hate because she's simply stunning.

I realize I'm approaching creepy stalker status, but I'm drawn to watch her as she talks quietly to the host and follows effortlessly to a booth on the opposite side of the restaurant. Noticing the host has placed down two menus, I can't stop myself from fixating on the door in anticipation of who is meeting her. Will it be her lover or a friend for lunch? Perhaps a business meeting or a first date.

I steal another glance at this mystery bombshell when the jingle of the door chimes again. In walks Will, all svelte and macho looking in his uniform. He's beautiful and breathtaking, but what the hell is he doing here? I sit up a little straighter preparing to wave when he turns away and heads toward the gorgeous girl I've been obsessing over for the last five minutes.

What in the actual fuck?

She slides from the booth with ease, wrapping her arms around his waist in a hug. He hugs her back and smiles at her with that dazzlingly sexy smirk that I thought was reserved for me at this point. They sit down and chat comfortably while looking at their menus. It's obvious they know each other as neither seems tense or awkward like they would be on a first date.

This isn't happening—I'm the other woman. How did I not know he was seeing other people? I mean, we haven't discussed being exclusive, but I assumed when he said he was "all in" to see where this goes that he wasn't dating anyone else. I wonder if Smith knows—wait, does everyone know but me? How stupid am I to think a man like him wouldn't be playing the field? I need to get out of here, *now*.

Cautiously slipping a twenty on the counter to cover my milkshake and tip, since I prepaid for the carry-out order, I slink off my stool. I head toward the door walking as quickly and quietly as possible to go unnoticed. Damn it, I can't help but steal one more look. Hand on the door handle, I peer over at the table and immediately lock eyes with Will.

He looks confused and a little stunned. The milkshake, burger, and fries are rioting in my stomach, like a brick sloshing around and battering my insides. My heart is pounding against my rib cage, and yet it feels like it might stop beating all together.

I push my way out into the fresh air and sprint to my car, quickly unlocking it and ducking inside with a slam of my door. I need to move, get out of this parking lot, go home, bury myself in bed for the foreseeable future, but all I can do is put my face in my hands and cry. The sobs sound more like screams from a wounded animal, but I guess that's kind of what I am.

I fucking love him and he's seeing other people. I knew better, dammit, this is why I didn't want to get involved. How could I be so stupid and reckless?

A knock on the car window startles me, and I peer up to see who it could be. Freakin', Will.

"Cam, it's not what you think," he says through the glass.

Deep breath, keep it together, don't show him you're in pain.

"I'm fine, Rambo. Just leaving now, have a nice day!" I shout back through the window.

"Wright, seriously, dammit. Let me explain," he pleads.

"It's all good, Rambo. Have the chocolate peanut butter shake, it's great. Please move so I don't run you over," I respond, trying to sound normal despite wanting to throw my lunch all over my lap.

He steps aside looking defeated and sad. I flip it in reverse, peeling out of the parking lot. Time to go start over . . . again!

TWENTY-NINE

Will

"High Road" – Koe Wetzel & Jessie Murph

That did not go well. The knowledge of it is slinking its way through my body like venom, easing into every pore, vein, and muscle. Guilt is rioting in my stomach, and yet my mind is protesting that I did nothing wrong.

"Sorry about that, I just, I didn't want her to get the wrong impression about . . . well, you know, about us," I say, stumbling over my words to Bri while sinking back down into my side of the booth.

Bri and I had agreed to meet for lunch today. I've wanted to catch her up on how things have been going with Cam since seeing Bri at the cemetery. Cam had mentioned this place was close to base, and it seemed like the perfect spot to meet since it's halfway between there and Bri's office.

"It's okay, Will. How'd it go out there?" she asks, looking concerned but also not having a problem scarfing down her burger.

"It didn't. She just told me to have a nice day and said it's fine."

"Like a real *fine* or a disgruntled girlfriend *fine*?" Bri inquires while dipping a fry in an alarming amount of ketchup.

"Pretty sure she's pissed. It looked like she was crying."

"Look, Will, what's the matter with you?" Bri's face makes it evident that she's a bit annoyed and disappointed with me.

"What's wrong with me? I didn't do anything wrong," I snap back, aggressively shoving fries in my mouth.

"Ohhh okay, this is what we're doing? Fill your mouth with fries so you can avoid talking. Tell me one thing . . . how did you find out about this place?"

"Cam told me about it and how much she wanted to try it." It doesn't matter how I discovered it. I'm still unsure of what Bri's getting at.

"Hoo-boy . . . Did you tell her we were meeting for lunch or did you forget to mention it?"

"No, I don't need to ask permission to see my friends, Bri. This is exactly what Tina said for me to do. She told me not to let myself drown in something new." I huff out a deep breath. I'm trying to do the right thing, follow the steps, face the fear.

"Right, you shouldn't, but as an outsider to this situation, it looks like you kept our meeting a secret and took me to a place you knew she desperately wanted to go."

"It's not like she has a lock on good restaurants. I'm allowed to go wherever the hell I want to go for lunch." Now I'm getting mad, this is not my fault. I don't think I did anything wrong yet this burger is going down about as good as a brick of chalk.

"Will, let me ask you something. When's the last time you talked to her?"

"This morning. I sent her flowers and she asked me to lunch. I told her I was busy and couldn't—ohhh shit."

"Yep . . . there it is." She points at my face as if she can see the realization blooming in my cheeks. "Now you're getting it. She wants to meet you for lunch, but you tell her you can't because you're busy. That's fine, so she takes herself to lunch at a cool place she wants to try and then to her surprise you show up, hug another woman, whom you probably appear comfortable with, and you can't figure out how this went wrong."

"Yeah, I fucked up. But so did she. If she had just let me explain who you are, she would've understood." Scrubbing my hand down my face, I plead my case.

"Will, seriously? Come on. You've hurt her before and for all intents and purposes you lied to her today," Bri admonishes me, an accusatory finger pointing at my chest.

"Shit. What do I do, Bri? You have to help me here."

"Do you love her?" she asks, raising her brows in consternation.

"Yeah. Unequivocally."

"Then you do whatever it takes. After work, go talk to her. Make her let you explain, and for fuck's sake, don't lie to her about seeing me ever again," she huffs.

"I'm sorry I put you in the middle of this. I ruined our lunch and messed everything up. I wanted to meet up with you to fill you in on how things are going with Cam, but also to tell you we're leaving soon. I know it's not the same for you, but I wanted you to know. In case . . . well, I thought in case Cam needs you while I'm gone."

Bri swallows hard then places her hand on mine gently. "Will, thanks for telling me. You know I'll support her and I'll be praying for your safety. You may want to fix this, though, so she actually takes my help."

There's my girl, Bri.

"Very funny. I'm gonna try, promise."

Bri and I finish eating and catching up. She's the best kind of friend. Calls me out on my crap and supports all of us even though she lost her soulmate. I love her, in a friendly way, which is exactly why I need to fix this mess with Cam. I know she will love her too.

I feel shitty about what happened. Hurting Cam was unintentional, it never crossed my mind that she would find out or that I was even keeping something from her. I've been doing my own thing for so long that running a lunch date by her or even just telling her for the sake of awareness wasn't a thought. I sent the flowers and haven't been able to think of much else besides Cam for weeks. Apparently, my feelings for her are not obvious, though, and I'm running out of time to make things right before I leave.

—

My stomach is flipping and flopping in the worst way. It has been since I ate that burger for lunch. Well, and potentially ruined the best thing to ever happen in my life. It would be easy to blame Patty of Patty's Patties, but I doubt the greasy burger is the cause of my current state. No, that would be my own idiocy in not being transparent with my girl. This is what I was afraid of, that I would make one mistake and she would run. The people I love always leave.

I didn't think about how having lunch with Bri would look from anyone else's perspective but my own, and that's on me. I simply wanted to meet a friend, so I made plans, and when Cam asked, I said I was busy. I wasn't trying to lie or avoid the truth—truly, it didn't cross my mind. I don't know if being a dumbass man is an excuse, but it's what I have to go with.

Full disclosure, I have no clue what I'm going to do if she won't forgive me. I'm essentially a ship floating aimlessly at sea right now. A ghost ship with no captain, abandoned to ebb and flow with the changes of the tide. I have to fight for her, I can't lose her and myself with a mission approaching. Actually, to hell with the mission—I can't lose her period.

Taking a deep breath and closing my eyes, I knock on the door. Three slow but sure taps that announce my arrival. Still deep breathing through my nose, I'm almost startled when the door swings ajar. My eyes fly open and I huff out, "Cam, I'm so sorry."

"Slow down, cowboy. Cam isn't talking to you," Lo spits out, frosty disdain dripping off her tongue.

"Lo, please let me in. I need to explain. It's not what Cam or you think. I swear," I plead with my hands up in full submission.

"Yeah . . . hmm. Let me get this straight. She caught you on a date with a gorgeous woman—I mean, seriously a model—and it's not what we think?"

"Bri's not a model. Although, I can see why Cam would say that." My lips quirk into a grin absentmindedly. Thatch would've loved hearing that his wife was model material.

"Not helping your case, Davenport." Lo rolls her eyes and starts closing the door in my face.

"No! Stop. I didn't mean . . . Bri is Thatch's widow. Yeah, she's pretty, but she is practically my sister. Please let me explain it to her, Lo."

"Wait, Thatch's widow, like *the* Thatch?"

"Yeah." I sigh and drag my hand through my hair. My curls were already sticking up like crazy from all the times I've worried my hand through them today. This isn't helping, but I'm losing my patience.

"Rambo? You can come in," Cam hollers from somewhere inside the apartment.

Lo rolls her eyes again but steps aside, allowing me to enter. My eyes track over the disheveled mess. A bottle of wine, a pint of Chunky

Monkey that's half eaten and been left to melt, and a bag of Doritos litter the counter. Cam is nowhere in sight, so I head to her room, slipping inside and closing the door quietly.

"Uh, Wright . . . you in here?"

"Yeah. Say what you need to say." The lump of a comforter gives a muffled reply. The thought of Cam holed up and hiding under there makes me smile. Just a little.

"I didn't come here to talk to your comforter."

"Well, I guess don't talk then, just get the fuck out." Another muffled and surprisingly fiery response.

I ease my way down to the edge of the bed, slowly peeling back the covers. The image unfolding shatters my heart into a million pieces. A mess of blonde hair, black streaks on the pillows, and a tear-stained Cam wrapped up in one of my military-issued PT shirts that I didn't even know she had.

"Hey, where'd you get this?" I ask while sliding my hand gently up and down her back.

"I stole it. Not that it matters now. I'm sure Miss Model McModelson has one of her own," she says faintly.

"Th-That was Bri. Thatch's Bri."

"What? Why? How?" She shoots straight up into a sitting position, confusion etched on her face.

"Well I . . . I saw her a little while back at his grave site. I told her about you. She told me not to contact her until I got the girl, and . . . well . . . I feel like you're my girl. I wanted to see her because she's a good friend who has been through a lot, but also because I wanted to ask her to look out for you and be a friend to you when I leave."

"Ugh! Rambo, you big dummy. Why didn't you just tell me? I mean, when I saw you . . . I thought . . . well, you know," she says on a sob.

"Babe, I tried. Please don't cry . . . You wouldn't let me explain." I gently wipe tears off her cheeks, each one a tiny shard of glass cutting me in pieces. I hate it when anyone cries, but Cam crying is another level of gut-wrenching. I'm well and truly fucked.

"No, Will. Why didn't you tell me when I asked you to lunch?" She's positioning me uncomfortably in the hot seat.

I rub my hand through my hair again before saying, "Honestly, it didn't cross my mind to explain. You asked and I was busy, and I just . . . it didn't dawn on me to tell you. I wasn't trying to hide it, I'm just a dumbass."

"I don't mind that you see Bri," she admonishes. "I think it's good she still has you. I mean, she's been through so much. But I need to know what this is. I've been thinking all afternoon how we never said we were exclusive, and you know, I just feel stupid."

"Wright. We. Are. Exclusive," I say while peppering her tear-soaked face with kisses.

"We are?" She looks at me with those big aquamarine eyes.

I cannot tell her I'm in love with her. And I am, absolutely, without a shadow of a doubt, but it's too soon. I refuse to force my feelings on her if she isn't there yet, and knowing her, she would feel obligated to reciprocate. I'm treading on delicate ground here. I have to keep my words in check while still making sure she knows I'm in this, for real.

"I know we said we're just seeing where this goes, but I'm falling for you. I told you I'm all in. You're my girl and I don't intend to share you with anyone else, so yeah, we are—you're mine . . . I hope."

"I'm falling for you too. I mean, I fought it really hard. But I can't help it anymore, you're mine too. I think you always have been. You have to be honest with me though. No more unintentionally secret lunch rendezvous. Trusting you is really hard. I'm terrified I'm going to get hurt again." I can see she's trying to act serious, but there's a hint of a smirk playing at the corner of her lips.

"I promise, no more secret lunches where I beg my widow friend to take care of my girlfriend. Scouts honor," I say holding up my middle finger just to tease her a bit.

"Come here, Rambo. It would be a whole lot easier to hate you if you weren't so dang attractive and sweet, you know," she murmurs, pulling me closer and pressing her lips on mine for a deep, sultry kiss.

I reach my hand slowly to her ribs and lightly slide it up, leading her to believe I'm about to cop a feel, but instead I move in for the tickle attack. Cam bolts and wiggles and writhes away, laughing hysterically and swatting me back.

"That was so unfair!" she huffs out while trying to regain composure.

"I mean, you did steal my shirt. Who's the one really playing dirty here?" I feign innocence.

"Okay, you know what . . . it smells like you, and all the talk of you leaving . . . I just, I wanted something of you to keep, Rambo."

"You can have whatever you want, babe. But I do have a question," I say while gently sliding two knuckles down her cheek.

"Good! Now, come snuggle me while you ask me whatever it is."

"Why do you call me Rambo?" I pull her into my side and continue stroking her face.

"Because it's hilarious." She snickers to herself. "But actually, I always told myself that you ran off on me to become the next Rambo. When I saw you again, the name just reminded me to hate you."

"And now?" Acid creeps up my throat at the thought of her hating me.

"Now . . . well, it's just kinda funny and cute, I think. Like you calling me Wright. It drove me nuts at first, but now, it feels good. Like a warm and inviting but funny hug."

"I guess that makes sense. Hearing you call me Rambo made me crazy at first, but now, it sorta makes me feel like a badass."

"Oh for fuck's sake, don't let it go to your head." She swats at my arm while desperately trying to hold in a laugh. "Are you staying to hang out?"

"I didn't bring an overnight bag, but I'll stay right here as long as you'll have me." I snuggle in deep with her as she clicks on the TV, firing up Netflix and scanning to find something to watch.

I'm only half paying attention to the British baking show she selected. I can't help but feel perfectly content wrapped up with her in her bed. The smell of her sweet shampoo and the feel of her soft skin. I'm going to miss her beyond words when we ship out.

It's not just having someone to do the physical stuff with, or even just having a friend to talk to. It's being with her that makes me whole. She can look at me and see the innermost depths of my soul without me ever having to say a word. She knows the things I wish no one did, without ever having to discuss them.

I could tell when we talked about my job that she wasn't scared only for me but for us both, because we're knitted together. On paper we don't make a lot of sense. We're the patchwork squares that seemingly don't fit but when bound together make the most beautiful quilt.

She's a gorgeous, independent feminist who wants to work for everything she has. She's the light in the darkest room, the one who can make anyone anywhere feel like they are the single most important person in the world. I'm a grumpy, war-torn, scared-to-death man. Somehow, someway, we found each other against all odds, and I'm never letting go.

THIRTY

Cam

"Woman's World" - Katy Perry

Vanilla bean candles mixed with the scent of stale beer, Ping-Pong balls clinking and clanking off of hard and soft surfaces, eyeballs adorning the walls that follow me everywhere I walk. Yep, I'm at Smith's bachelor pad again. Although, he's not really a bachelor anymore. I'm unclear how my neurotic and lovable Lo hasn't made drastic changes to this place yet; everything is eerily the same. *Oh, that's right, they are always at our place.*

Will and I spent most of the week alternating between his place and mine after work. Spending this much time together, and so soon into our budding relationship, feels right, and at the same time I can feel myself slipping deeper into this relationship, making my fears multiply. Obviously, there's history between us, but he makes me happier than

I have been in so long. It's hard to justify putting distance between us when there's a chance I could be wrong about how this ends.

I'm also afraid he is going to leave and that something will happen to him. Savoring every moment has been my primary focus, and yet it feels like waiting to die. That may sound dramatic, but how is someone supposed to deal with their loved one preparing to head off to God knows where when God knows who is trying to kill them? Or when you know you are just waiting for the other shoe to drop . . .

Feelings like this must be par for the course for military spouses all over the world. Fortunately for me, Will did say he isn't usually gone as long as others, so I suppose I'm lucky. The thing is, whether it's ten days or ten years, the worry is the same. Of course, I'll miss him either way, but the sheer angst over the possibility of him being hurt is unbearable to think about.

In the meantime, we're all trying to blow off steam with this party. Beer pong and bad decisions. Nothing screams rational like a bunch of anxious dudes, overly emotional and worried significant others, and alcohol. Very mature. Patricia would be sooo proud.

Opting to stop thinking about our impending doom, I suck down a long pull of light, refreshing and a little skunky beer. Beer is never my first choice, but when I do indulge, it has to be foreign or an IPA.

"Hey, you wanna be my partner next round?" Lo wiggles her eyebrows at me.

"Sure. I don't know if they will want us to team up after the last time, though." I gently knock my beer bottle with hers and throw in a wink for good measure.

"Think we can beat them?" she asks, nodding toward Smith and Will.

"Duh. In my sleep. Should give them something to talk about on their little vacay."

"Nope. That's off-limits. We are not talking about it or thinking about it before it happens. For all we know, it could be months." Lo gives me her serious face, but I know deep down she is low-key freaking out too. She doesn't love change, but who does? She also is head over heels, borderline disgustingly in love with Smith. At least we'll be in misery together when they leave.

Cheering breaks out from the designated "pong area," indicating the winners have finally claimed their victory. For a group of people who play enough to have a set up permanently installed in their apartment, these guys aren't very good. I can win in far less time and with far more style.

"We have next!" shouts Lo.

Pulling myself off the couch to join her is far harder than it should be. My body is tired from all the worry, anxiety, and sexy time. Not to mention, standing all week at work; that doesn't help either.

Will saunters up, all charming and swoon-worthy, trying to throw me off my game.

"Wright, don't think I've forgotten how much you practiced this game with Elliott. No funny business," he whispers softly in my ear.

"Please, Rambo, would I dare pull one over on you?" I give him my most innocent puppy dog eyes.

"Yeah. You absolutely would, and I know you're up to something." He smiles as he says this matter-of-factly.

"What's going on you two? No trading secrets . . . she's your enemy right now, soldier," Smith chimes in, wrapping an arm around each of our shoulders.

"Don't worry, Smith. Will's just trying to woo me into going easy on him." I give Will a little shove away from me and toward the table.

He knows I would never go easy, but it's nice to have a little witty banter back and forth. Keeps things interesting. Smith looks appalled at the idea that anyone would have to ask Lo and me to take it easy, which is going to make beating him that much more fun—he still thinks the last time was beginner's luck. Will eyes him cautiously, giving him the *dude, you don't know what I know* look.

Lo steps up to the table, grabbing a ball for herself and handing me one. We wait patiently as Smith and Will refill the cups; if I didn't inherently have the drive to always win, the low-end domestic light beer would have done it. *Gross!*

The table is set. I toss one little wink at Will, draw my hand up, and with a flick of my wrist, I sink the ball directly into the first cup. He chuckles a little at me and then tosses one our direction while drinking his cup. It's a perfectly placed ball, landing in the cup directly in front of me, causing beer to slosh out at just the right angle, spraying my shirt. Arrogance and sass are written all over his face. He actually thinks I might let him beat me. The audacity! *Game on, buddy. I'm coming for you now.*

"That was cute, Rambo. Too bad your friends will all be able to see through my white shirt now." I turn toward Lo and throw the ball without even looking. Before I can finish downing the beer in my hand, Will is at my side pulling his hoodie over my head.

"Not anymore." He races back to his side, challenging me with a look to take it off. I won't and he knows it. If this helps him feel more secure, then fine. But it's a tad dramatic seeing that the only part of my shirt that actually got wet was below my belly button. Not much to see, but a part of me likes the protectiveness he's displaying.

We continue tossing balls at breakneck speed. Lo is playing so well, neither of us has missed. Smith is completely confused; he was so sure we were horrible, but as of now, he's the only one who can't sink a ball. As for me, my competitive streak has given me precision-level focus. I could make any ball in any cup I wanted right now.

We each have three cups remaining, and since Lo and I threw first, we're going to win, as long as we don't miss. I'm trying to decide which cup I want to aim for when there's a knock at the door.

Okay, seriously, everyone is here. Who could be showing up when I'm about to win?

"Hey, Butler, get the door wouldya?" Smith shouts across the room while I sink another ball.

Instead of drinking, Will immediately walks away toward the door, leaving the rest of us to stand and wait. Lo tosses me a skeptical look, and even though I know where we stand, my skin is covered in goose bumps and my stomach starts to churn. It's a woman's voice I hear first; greeting Will and Butler like she's known them for years.

Finally, they round the corner, and I see her. The girl from Patty's Patties. Bri. She's wearing a casual pair of jeans that are rough cropped at the bottom, exposing just a tad of her perfectly skinny ankle. She has on a pale teal tank top that hugs her slender curves, and her luminous hair is flowing down her back in perfect waves. She's breathtakingly beautiful, just as she was the other day, and she makes it look effortless. It's incredibly unfair to be that magnificent.

Jealousy should be the furthest thing from my mind, because I know who she is. I know what she's been through and what she means to the guys. It's not rational, but I can't help wondering why she's suddenly back in Will's life right when we've reconnected.

"Hey . . . you ladies must be the ones who've swooped in and stolen these knuckleheads' hearts. I'm Bri," she says sweetly. Her voice is slow and smooth, like dripping honey.

"Umm . . . yeah, I guess so." I'm not able to contain my nervous smile. "I'm Cam."

"Oh Cam, I've been dying to meet you! I'm sorry Davenport is such an idiot and didn't tell you about our lunch the other day. I kicked his ass over it. I swear, men are *sooo* dumb sometimes." She pulls me into a hug, and while I'm a very physical-touch kind of person, it startles me a little.

Just going with it, I squeeze her back.

Have you ever hugged someone and just known instantly that they're a good person? Like you could just feel their soul, see and know everything about them from something so simple?

I have now. Hugging Bri back, the mixed feelings about her swooping in to Will's life unexpectedly from a minute prior vaporized and vanished. There wasn't anything particularly spectacular about it, it was just a hug, and yet it felt like being in the arms of a best friend I didn't know I had.

"It's okay . . . about the other day, I mean. I'm very glad to meet you." I stumble over my words a bit, still shaming myself for being such a raging jealous bitch on the inside. He made me this way, though, this is the result of me still not fully trusting him.

"Same. This one hasn't shut up about you in years." She nods toward Will while giggling to herself.

"*Years?* Really? Tell me everything!" I smirk at Will, raising an eyebrow.

"Honey, you must have a magical lady cave because my boy here has been pining away for you as long as I've known him."

This sends Lo, Bri, and me into a fit of giggles at her use of the term *lady cave* and makes Will look adorably shy, like he maybe just swallowed his tongue. I may want to hate this girl, but I think it also might be love at first vagina joke.

"This is greeeeat. I take back every nice thing I've ever said about her now. She is the worst and you two should not be friends. Come over here with me, Wright." Will throws this last bit in for good measure, which just results in more laughing from the three of us.

Will leaves us to our own devices, and the three of us spend time chatting about the guys. Bri, being the goddess she is, brought a couple of bottles of wine and a wine opener, so we find a spot to perch at Smith's high-top table.

"So, how did you fall for that big lug?" Bri points at Smith, who is crowding Will and whispering, likely about us.

"It was love at first sight. I don't know how it happened, but there was just something about him." Lo has hearts in her eyes. It's still insane to me how over the moon she is for him.

"More like love at first Jell-O syringe," I quip.

"Well, I can see it. He's a good guy, deep down. Maybe way deep down . . . I've seen that man pull some stunts, so I can't give him too much credit." Bri twirls her wineglass before taking a long pull, savoring it.

"Okay . . . I need you to tell me at least one story. He practically lives with us, I need dirt." I say, as Lo and I both lean in conspiratorially.

"There was this one time . . ." Bri begins laughing to herself, struggling to get the story out. "He met this girl, and sorry if this is weird for you, Lo . . . but he met this girl, and we could all tell she was completely off her rocker from the second we met her. He went home with her and then what do you know, at three in the morning, Eric's phone was ringing with the fire department calling us to pick him up. When we got to the station, Smith didn't have any clothes on and he was soaking wet." Lo's eyes have grown ten sizes, and she's carefully covering her mouth so as not to laugh or cry, who knows.

"Wait, why though?" I ask, I have to know.

"This girl wanted him to sleep over, and he was ready to leave, so she burned his clothes. Wadded them up, tossed them in her trash can, and lit it up. The sprinkler system in her apartment complex kicked on, and the fire department showed up. All they had to give him was a gray wool blanket." We can't help the cackling that ensues. I'm laughing so hard, tears stream down my face.

We continue chatting and swapping stories for a while longer. It's mostly me giving them dirt on Will from when we were in high school. We're all careful not to bring up the potential of an impending deployment. Bri because I'm sure she knows we are nervous and dreading it, and us because . . . well, she no longer has someone to worry about. Talking with her about it seems cruel, like it would be forcing her to walk back through very painful memories.

Awe-inspiring is the only way to describe Bri. She may very well be the toughest person I've ever met. I've spent the better part of a week dreading being away from Will for a month or two; she has to be away from Thatch forever. How is she so normal? How is she not crying, buried in bed?

"I have to get going soon. I have a volunteer event in the morning, and too much wine gives me a wicked headache," Bri says.

"I get it. It's been so wonderful to meet you. Thank you for coming and for being so nice." I stand to hug her, bidding her farewell.

Bri places a soft hand on my arm, looking me straight in the eyes. "My Thatch and Davenport were close, like brothers. They are more emotional than the others, and yet like to act stronger, unbothered. Here's my number." She hands me her business card. "If you need anything while he's away, you call me first. I know the drill and I will support you every step of the way."

"I don't know what to say. You're being too kind to someone you hardly know." Tears prick the backs of my eyes.

"I know all I need to. You're it, according to him." She nods toward Will, who is trying to not make it obvious that he's totally eavesdropping on this conversation.

"Thank you, really. I mean it. I may just call you even when I don't need anything," I say, clutching her hands in mine.

"I would love that," she responds, hugging me and Lo again, then walking off to say goodbye to all the others.

Lo and I exchange a look. We don't need to say anything, but we both know that she just changed our lives somehow. She is going to be our friend, our confidant, and guide us through this military thing. For the first time in days, I don't have such a heavy weight on my chest. Maybe because I feel less alone, or maybe because deep down, I know I have so much more than Bri, the nicest person in the world, and I'm grateful.

THIRTY-ONE

Cam

"Without Me" - Halsey

Will and I stayed at the party for a bit after Bri left, but not too late. To be honest, I couldn't wait to escape and make the most of what was left of the night, wrapped up in him.

It was epically hot. Safe to say, Will spent a significant amount of time spelunking in every nook and cranny of my lady cave. Frankly, it's a wonder I was even able to stand behind my chair today. Thank God it's Saturday, and I only had to do it for a few hours.

My clientele is building rapidly, which makes me and my bank account happy. I only had to get through two color-and-haircut clients plus one men's cut today. A few more sweeps of the floor at my station and sanitizing the brushes, then I'll be off.

Will is meeting me for a redo lunch at Patty's, and I would be lying if I said I wasn't more than a little excited to experience the ambience,

milkshake, and truffle fries again. My last experience was pure bliss until I thought Will was running a game on me. A redo is exactly what I need to get rid of any bad juju and reestablish the vibes I initially felt.

Making quick work of my close-out tasks, I check out at the desk, pull my tips from the drawer, and head to grab my bag. I'm not trying to sneak out per se, but I'm also not announcing my departure because Daveed will make me stay to chat. I feel bad about giving him the slip, but I know he wants details about last night, and I don't have the time or mental energy.

—

Slipping into the booth that Rhonda directed me to feels a little different than last time. It's not the bar, and I'm not nearly close enough to the jukebox, but it'll do. My preference would have been the bar because it adds to the old-school diner vibe, but it's not conducive to making date conversation.

The view of the clientele from here is also different from last time. I can't see the tables on the other side, but the ones closest to me consist of far more families. There are kids chatting away about new toys they hope to get while running errands, a few fighting with their siblings, and the most adorable little girl practically covered from head to toe in melted ice cream. I feel for her mother, but also can't help smiling at her precious and plump little fingers smearing chocolate in places it shouldn't be.

Seeing these families makes me wonder if Will still wants kids. I do, though not for a while. I'm too focused on building my career right now, but one day. Picturing Will with a chubby little baby squirming and squealing with laughter makes my uterus hurt. I need to stop thinking about it, or my timeline might move up. Seriously, I can almost feel my eggs dropping, ready to rock.

Rhonda, again adorned in her vintage waitress dress, saddles up to the table.

"Can I get you anything while you wait, toots?"

"Coffee would be great. He should be here soon, we said twelve thirty and he's never late for anything."

"Coffee it is, sweetheart, but I hate to break it to you. It's already twelve forty-five," she says, pity written all over her face.

"Wait, really?" I ask, grabbing for my phone, which I'd stuffed in my purse on the way in the door. I guess I spaced out people watching a little longer than I realized.

She nods and walks off to get my coffee, leaving me with my own frantic attempts at opening my lock screen.

No texts, no missed calls from Will, only one unknown number—probably a telemarketer. What if something happened? I sent him a message to tell him I was on my way, but I hadn't checked for a reply.

Hitting send on his number, I listen for the usual ring but instead it goes straight to voicemail. Shit! When I left this morning, I kissed him goodbye as he was half asleep and crept out. I start running through all the possible scenarios in my head. Could he have forgotten? Was he in an accident?

He couldn't have gotten called up for work. I can't imagine after everything we've been working to rebuild that he would have left without saying goodbye. He knew where I was and didn't call, so it can't be that.

I hit send again, just in case his phone was being weird during the first call. Voicemail again!

Okay, breathe, Cam. Everything is going to be fine. We had a perfect night. He isn't standing me up, maybe he took a nap, or his phone died.

No, it was on the charger all night. What is with this diner and bad luck? I need to get out of here. I need to think clearly and not be irrational.

Tossing a ten on the table, I grab my stuff in a hurry and rush to my car. Settling into the seat, I scoot my chair back and make room. I can't leave in case he shows up, but I can lie back and get comfortable. Maybe Lo is with Smith. They could check on him.

Scrolling to Lo's contact, I hit send. It rings three times and she answers. Finally! Someone answered.

"H-hi. Where are you?" She's sobbing.

"What's going on? Why are you crying?" I ask quickly.

"Why aren't you?" she replies, puzzled.

"What? Why would I be crying? What happened?"

"What do you mean what happened? You don't know? Oh Jesus, God, what in the actual fuck?" Pity and pain, thick in her voice.

"Lo! No, I don't know what happened. Can you tell me, please? I'm sitting at Patty's waiting for Will, but he's late for our lunch date."

"He didn't tell you? Oh no . . . no, no, no, no. This is not happening."

"Lorraine, dammit! What is not happening?" She better start talking quickly.

"They're gone. They got the call this morning. Smith ran outta here in a hurry, said some shit was going down and he'd contact me when he could. He gave me a few kisses, a long squeeze, and just left."

"Wait, no. That can't be right. Will wouldn't leave without telling me. Why would he do that when we have been working so hard to rekindle everything? He said I could trust him this time."

"Honey . . . they left. Smith only had an hour to report. He called Butler while putting his pants on and ran like his ass was on fire. Maybe Will didn't have time?" She's trying and failing to rationalize his behavior, and it's making it worse.

"Seriously, Lo? He didn't have time while driving to base to pick up the fucking phone and say goodbye?" There's no world in which that man couldn't have called me for a minute or two.

"I know it looks bad, but maybe there's more to the story. I know he loves you, Cam. Come home and we can figure it out together." Lo's trying to sound reassuring, but the hesitation in her voice is evident.

I've seen this story play out before. "There's only one explanation. I wasn't important enough back in the day, and I'm clearly not now. I gotta go. Don't worry, I'll be home later. Love you."

I hit the end button and stare at my phone in disbelief. This cannot be happening, again. Last time, at least he had the decency to break things off explicitly; this time he just leaves without so much as a peep. Clearly, I'll never be enough for him.

Realistically, I knew this was coming. The deployment part, anyway. I really believed Will would say goodbye, that he would tell me something. It never crossed my mind that he would leave without saying anything. Even if he couldn't come to me in person, he could have called or even texted. I made it clear my phone ringer would always be turned up, and I would answer no matter what.

How dare he make me love him again and then do this. Could he not just let me live my life? He had to waltz back in and disrupt my chance at happiness.

I'm paralyzed. I want to cry but I can't. The tears refuse to fall. My stomach is empty, yet I'm not hungry. I'm so confused, a little lightheaded, driving isn't an option. What am I going to do? How do I pick myself up?

Ugh, my family. Elliott has probably spilled the beans to my parents by this point. Admittedly, I've been dodging Patricia's phone calls for days because I've been afraid of what she'd say about Will. My mom had to pick up the pieces the last time he broke me. She single-handedly stitched me back together when I was little more than scraps of used fabric discarded on the floor. She told me I would love again, that I was beautiful and valuable. She might actually kill Will now for this.

Is it possible for your mind to swirl with thoughts and be completely empty at the same time?

Deciding that fresh air will clear my head and help me regain enough focus to drive home, I slide out of my car. After hitting the lock twice to make sure my bag inside is secure, I start walking.

Wandering the tree-lined streets of Bayshore was one of my favorite things to do no more than a few weeks ago. It's picturesque, to put it mildly. Bungalow houses are mixed in with mansions. Trees sway effortlessly in the breeze, providing the perfect canopy of shade. The cacophony of birds chirping creates the sweetest melodic background music to my hopes and dreams.

Except now it's like being George Bailey in the black-and-white version of *It's a Wonderful Life*. Everything is in shades of gray; my hopes and dreams are dashed. All I hear are the sounds of Saturday trash pickup, moms yelling at kids to get in cars for practice, and my heart breaking. I fucking knew better. That nagging feeling in my mind never went away, I just ignored it.

Without even thinking, I pluck my phone from my pocket and hit send on Will's number one last time. It goes straight to voicemail, as expected, but this time I leave a message.

"Will . . . what in the ever-loving fuck is going on? You made me a promise. You made me believe in us again and then you just up and leave without a word. I-I w-won't do the same. This is your notice. I love you and I always will, but I'm done. Don't die over there, but also don't ever contact me again. I mean it this time, Rambo. Do. Not. Call. Me. Ever. Again."

Pain sears through every ounce of my body. I'm bawling my eyes out, pissed off, and at the same time, gripped with fear. Telling him off was supposed to make me feel better. At least turn the pain into anger. News flash, it didn't. Guilt claws at my insides. I want there to be an explanation, but I know there isn't. Well, there is: He was playing around with me. I didn't mean to him what he does to me—that's the status quo with Will, and I fell for it again.

Gahhh! Why would he do this to me, to us? The tears start to fall faster, big mascara-filled drops stain my face.

Standing in the middle of the crosswalk, I search my phone for the only person I know can help right now. The line rings twice and then cuts on.

"Hey, I've been calling you for three days. What the hell took you so long?" he asks.

"Elliott . . . I need you!" I manage to say on a sob.

A car horn blares, jolting me to get the hell out of the middle of the street that I apparently stopped in.

"Dammit, Cam. Where are you? Is that a car? Are you okay?"

"I'm not okay. I'm walking in Bayshore. Can you come?"

"I'm already here. I've been calling to tell you I was coming. When you didn't respond, I planned to surprise you. Come pick me up, baggage claim three."

"I love you . . . I'm on my way." I take off running toward my car.

Elliott doesn't make spur of the moment trips. Why he's here is a mystery, but relief washes over me. He's the only one who truly knows me. Lo is my best friend, but there's something to be said about having the one person who's been there for it all. My ride or die, my protector, confidant, built-in bestie for life.

My big brother is here, and I'm going to get him, come hell or high water. He will help me fix this, figure it out, or at the very least, get me drunk enough to forget it.

THIRTY-TWO

Will

"Set You Free" - The Black Keys

8:16 AM Saturday

My phone rings loudly, startling me awake. The special ringtone set for our commander lets me know I can't ignore it. Briefly, dread washes over me, sending signals to my gut and brain that this is the call I've been preparing for.

"Davenport," I answer succinctly, trying to mask the grogginess in my voice.

"It's go time. Rally at strip seven. You have one hour."

The line cuts off before I can ask any questions. Not that I would; I know better than to question the commander.

Jumping out of bed, I dial Smith while turning on the shower. I don't have a ton of time, but it could be weeks before I get another

shower and waking up under the cold spray now is paramount.

"Hey, man. Why are you waking me up?" Smith answers, his voice gruff and groggy after a night out.

"Rally at strip seven, one hour. See you there," I say matter-of-factly and hang up.

There's no need to stay on the line. He has to call Butler, and we all have to move quickly. We've never had to report this fast, and I hope like hell all of our phone chain practices will pay off.

Jumping in the shower, I perform the quickest wash and rinse of my life. I dry off, dress, and grab my bag, never glancing at the clock, just moving. I'm ready for this. I've practiced, prepared everything, and can easily make it in time.

Shit! Cam. She's at work. I'll never make it to say goodbye in person, but I have to tell her. I can't leave without telling her she's my life, my everything. Grabbing my stuff, I circle back to my room and snag my phone before heading to tell Amy.

Amy is half asleep, but she wakes up enough to wish me well, tell me she loves me, demand I come home in one piece, and ask to sleep in my bed while I'm gone. God, this girl! I give her a squeeze and kiss her forehead, promising everything she asked.

Sprinting to my Jeep, I sling my bag in the backseat and rev her up. Grabbing my phone from my pocket, my thumb is hovering over Cam's number when the phone starts blaring the commander's ringtone again.

"Yes, sir?"

"Davenport. We have a problem. Ruiz isn't answering. The rest of the team is on their way. I need you to go get his ass and get him here. Now."

Son of a bitch! Where could Ruiz be? He was at the party last night. He didn't seem drunk, and he barely played any pong. Hitting send on his number, it rings once and goes to voicemail.

That asshole better be dying because he's going to get us all in trouble. Now is not the time to be missing. Throwing it in gear, I speed off to his apartment calling his phone on an endless loop.

—

8:46 AM Saturday

It only takes banging on the door four times and kicking it twice for Ruiz to groggily answer. He cracks the door slightly, which I take to my advantage by throwing it open the rest of the way.

"Whoa, dude, where's the fire?" He acts surprised to see me busting up in his apartment with no warning.

"We gotta go. Rally is in thirty, you dickwad. Way to answer your phone," I huff at him.

"My phone never rang. I swear it. Oh shit—" I hear a woman call out from his bedroom to ask what's going on. He looks like he might throw up.

"Seriously, dude?"

He sprints away from me and into the bedroom to tell Miss One Night Stand that it's time to go. There's some arguing about silencing his phone and then an icy breeze as she pushes past me, half-dressed and running out the door.

I shake my head. I am going to give him so much shit for this.

"We gotta burn tracks, bro," I yell when he returns, dressed and ready to go.

—

9:06 AM Saturday

Somehow, we made it with ten minutes to spare. I haven't had time to call Cam, and I'm praying she answers because they will take my phone soon.

We jump out of the Jeep, make sure the top is secured, and head toward the small briefing area to dump our bags and check in for equipment. A team of three airmen are standing behind a rickety table, ready to hand off equipment, give us our weapons, and pass out sleeping pills.

Based on the plane idling on the runway, it looks like we're going grunt style, in the cargo hull on top of aid packages. No first-class tickets available where we're headed.

"Sit down, we're going to do this quick and dirty," shouts Sergeant Montgomery.

As we sit, I glance at my watch. I'm running out of time. My phone will get stored until we get back, meaning they are going to take it any minute now. Montgomery is briefing the mission. We're going into a heavily occupied, terrorist-run area to set up initial communications for a special operations Army unit. The plan is to fly into a base nearby and then travel via underground allied networks to our destination. If executed precisely, the mission should be completed in three weeks' time.

I've been through this before. Three weeks means more like six, if we're lucky. Could be worse, but traveling underground means we are depending on civilians to sneak us in. Shit could get hairy quickly.

Montgomery releases us to grab our equipment and any supplies needed, and to turn over our phones. *Shit!* I'm grabbing my stuff and reaching for my phone to dial Cam when Bri walks up.

"Bri? What are you doing here?"

"Hey! I was volunteering this morning at the spouses' club and overheard that y'all were leaving. I know it doesn't make sense, but I thought I'd feel better to see you all off." She glances around, taking in who's noticed her since she's clearly not supposed to be here.

Reaching out, I pull her into a hug. I don't know why, but I feel better knowing she came. She has seen us off on our other missions, so it just wouldn't feel right without her being here today.

"Davenport, give me your phone. Bri, you're not supposed to be here, but I'm going to turn in his phone and look the other way," Montgomery says in his typical gruff voice, but there's markedly soft lines around his eyes as though he is acknowledging how this must feel for her.

If it was anyone else, he'd be having a complete conniption over them being here. Either he still feels bad for her or he's coming down with something. I'm relieved, regardless.

"Thanks, I'll be quick," she responds with a cautious smile.

"Hey, before you run off, I need a favor. I need your phone. I haven't been able to say goodbye to Cam," I plead.

She hands it over without question.

"Make it quick. I'm going to wish the others well and then you gotta go and I need to scoot before I get in trouble," she whispers to me while looking around inconspicuously.

Thanking her, I dial Cam's number as quickly as possible. It rings five times and then goes to voicemail. Waiting for the recording to come on, I'm about to leave a message when Bri comes back and says it's time to go. Hitting end reluctantly, I hand the phone back to her and pull her in for one more hug.

"Bri, she's going to think I left without saying goodbye. I need to know that you will tell her. Tell her I love her and I never want to live without her. Make her believe I would have done anything to see her or talk to her one more time."

"William, do not worry about it for a second more. I will take care of it. She will be waiting when you get back. She loves you too. Now go and be careful. Remember, level head on a swivel, come home in one piece." She squeezes my arm one last time, repeating the words Thatch and I used to say to each other. It's like I can hear his voice when she does it, and I say it back a knot in my throat: "Level head on a swivel, come home in one piece."

With a final nod, I sprint toward the hull, gear covering me like some sort of goddamn pack mule. Ideally, we would have this shit already on the ground, but that's not a luxury this time.

If you haven't been in a cargo hold of a plane before, there's very little it could be compared to. It's similar to your grandma's basement, if the basement was filled with Humvees, a plethora of guns, and aid rations.

Settling into my jump seat next to Smith, I carefully uncap the first of several bottles of water I plan to drink. We have to strap in for takeoff and landing—not that the hammock seat seemingly made of old seat belts or its measly straps are securing anything.

I toss back a sleeping pill while taking a long pull from the bottle. Pills like this one are standard-issue when boarding a plane like this. Everyone gets a few.

"You good, man?" Smith asks.

"Yeah. I'm fine. I didn't say goodbye to her," I reply, dropping my head into my hands.

"Why? How? What the hell is wrong with you?" Scolding me is his favorite pastime.

"I had to get Ruiz's ass and time slipped away. I tried calling from Bri's phone, but she didn't answer."

"Duuuudddeee! You gonna be able to keep your head in the game?" The engines are roaring now, we have to shout just to hear each other.

"Yeah. I'm straight . . . Bri will handle it." I try my hardest to infuse confidence into my shaky reply.

Smith doesn't say anything else, just grabs my shoulder and

squeezes. There isn't anything to say. We have a job to do, and I have to believe that Bri will make it right for me. The churning in my gut indicates it's not that simple, but mistakes on jobs like this cost lives. I refuse to lose another brother, or myself, to these assholes.

Takeoff is smooth-ish. Riding in style like we are leaves a lot to be desired. Once we hit altitude, everyone unbuckles and finds a place to sprawl out. Twelve hours on an uncomfortable swinging seat is a nonstarter. Looking around, scoping the perfect spot, I grab my pack and shuffle as steadily as I can to a wooden crate that's about a foot tall and long enough for me to sprawl out on. It's placed up against the tire of a Humvee, making it the perfect place to prop my head. There's *nothing* like a hard rubber tire for a pillow.

Sleeping on the floor helps to lessen the frigid air that coats the plane like a wet blanket. It's not without risk; falling off during turbulence is a real possibility, but I can't find it in me to care right now.

Rolling out my sleep mat and bag, I get comfortable enough to feel the sleeping pill take effect. Nodding off, visions of Cam looking devastated dance in my head. There's no room to toss and turn, but tell that to my brain and stomach as they riot against my will to catch some much-needed rest.

—

5:24 AM Sunday

Metal peppers the side of the plane, pinging off the wings and echoing throughout the hold like small bells ringing in your ears. Mixing with the whoosh of the engines, it's an indescribable sound.

The knowledge of what the metal is heightens my awareness. The pounding of my heartbeat quickens, and adrenaline fills my veins. We must be getting close, not that there's a window to look out of and check. It's normal to take on heat as you're entering enemy territory, but it doesn't make it any less intense.

Similar to how dramatic music plays in a suspenseful movie right before the killer appears, these sounds are foreboding. We aren't welcome where we're headed. My instincts are telling me this mission is not going to go well. I'm usually confident, calm, cool under pressure, but this feels off. Something isn't right. Maybe it's Cam and how I left things, or maybe it's whatever we are about to face. Shivers rack my body. This is bad. Really bad.

Smith shoots me a look from across the plane, where he's sprawled out on his bedroll. He's lying under one of two overhead lights, which offers just enough brightness for me to make out what he's trying to convey: He feels it too. I don't need to talk to him to know he's nervous. Subliminally, with one look and a nod, I tell Smith I get it, but also to fix his face so the others don't catch on.

We are leaders on this team. We have a responsibility to keep it together. What I can't figure out is why it all feels different this time. There isn't anything special about this mission compared to the last. If anything, it's too familiar, yet it seems to carry more weight than before. Maybe it's Thatch. Knowing what he went through, being back here without him. Or maybe it's that I have more to lose. Amy is counting on me, but Cam is everything. Not knowing if I'll see her again . . . it's unbearable.

The lights shut off, indicating we're close. Next, it's the engines. The pilots turn them to half power as we start a stealth descent. This is our cue to get back in our seats. We circle our destination slowly as we make our way back to our seats, carefully but quickly, securing our gear along the way.

The engines cut off and a silent darkness overtakes the plane. Now all I can hear are the sounds of small arms bullets clinking and clanking as the enemy fires upon us. The circling continues and suddenly stops.

We are in a free-falling descent; based on the turbulence, it's going to be a rough landing.

Everything is vibrating, shaking from the movement of air carrying us down. The men around me are vibrating too. Some with anticipation and some with angst, like caged animals. It's a charged environment.

Our wheels touch down in a rough and bumpy impact with the makeshift runway. We made it. Now the work begins. I have one goal—survive.

THIRTY-THREE

Cam

"I Can Do It with a Broken Heart" - Taylor Swift

Elliott—the perfect companion to any breakup, the shoulder I've cried on literally my entire life, and also the one single solitary person who gets me, all of me. I don't have to edit myself to present some perfect version; he meets me where I am, figuratively and literally, no matter what.

I won't claim he always reserves judgment, because let's be honest, if your siblings don't offer up some much-needed harsh reality checks at times, then who will. I heard once that your siblings are the most important people in your life because you have them the longest. Your parents eventually die—I know, cold but true—and your significant other comes too late, often missing the first twenty plus years of your life.

For me, Elliott is the one true constant. Sure, he's busy a lot of the time, but when it really counts, he shows up. Like now. He didn't even

know this thing with Will was about to blow up, but he came anyway. Originally, he came for selfish reasons. His idiot ex cheated on him and he needed to nurse his own heartbreak, yet instead of wallowing he chose to spend time with me. He picked me when he could have gone a million other places. He showed up to a place where he anticipated being surrounded by disgustingly happy people, because those people included me.

I'm not an expert on soulmates, but I believe your siblings can be a sort of soulmate. For sure, the one person you're most tightly bonded with, the ride-or-die kind.

Despite his own broken heart, my brother's been the only thing holding me together the past three days. Showering, leaving my house, and eating are things he has thrust upon me against my will. A small, maybe microscopic, part of me is thankful.

Daveed gave me the week off to "get my adorable head on straight," which was mildly offensive and also extremely generous. Being relieved from the salon is lifesaving; dealing with people right now would be the emotional equivalent to nails on a chalkboard.

I still can't believe Will left without saying a word. Trusting in what we had wasn't easy for me and he knew that. Past experience told me not to fall for him a second time around, and yet head over heels I went.

Why is it always like this with love? You go about life minding your own business and then—boom. Out of nowhere, Cupid hits you with his arrow, and all sense of self-preservation flies out the window. *I freaking knew better!* Now I'm left with nothing, no explanation, no air in my lungs, struggling to breathe without him.

It's safe to say I'm equal parts sad and angry. Sad because it felt different this time, more mature. It felt like this could be the forever kind of love I've longed for. Angry because it's just plain rude. Leaving for deployment without a goodbye is the ultimate form of ghosting, I've decided.

Gossip magazines should make a whole section on the best ways to ghost someone. This would top every list because you can't even do the crazy ex thing and drive past their house or haunt their favorite bar. He's just gone—totally and completely off the grid.

On top of all this, part of me feels like a shitty sister. Elliott came for his own escape of sorts. He finally dumps the no-good girlfriend, and he has to come here to deal with my sad-sack ass. Taking him out would make us both feel better, I'm just not sure I can make it more than twenty minutes without a complete breakdown.

To top it off, Bri's been calling me nonstop. I didn't know it was her at first. But a slew of text messages confirmed it since I inevitably lost the business card she gave me. Answering her calls and pouring my pitiful loss out to her seems selfish. What kind of person would I be if I complained to the widow about being dumped? Logically, ignoring her forever isn't an option, since Lo is likely to still see her when Smith returns. But I need more time to lick my wounds.

"Hey, how's my favorite roomie doing?" Lo asks as she plops herself entirely too close for comfort on my bed.

"Ughhh . . . just go away." I shove at her to move.

"No! You need to get your ass up. I know you're heartbroken, and, trust me, I will be the first in line to kick Will's ass when the guys get back, but enough wallowing. I know you're not going to let a man get you down like this. You are beautiful and smart and this is his loss."

Doesn't she know that my heart isn't mine anymore? Will ripped it out of my chest and took it to God knows where, strapped on his freaking back like an afterthought.

"Lo, seriously? How would you feel if you were me?"

"I'd be sad but more furious than anything. I'd get my butt out of bed and hit the bar. You need to drink like a fish and flaunt everything you got until the name Will is just someone you used to know."

"You would not do that, and we both know it." I give her my sternest look; she's being a complete hypocrite right now. "You would cry and wallow for weeks and then one day be miraculously all better and ready to make out with any available stunner on girls' night out."

"Okay, fine . . ." Her hands are in the air in surrender. "You're right! The difference is that in this case, you don't even know if he actually dumped you. For all we know, something came up and he couldn't contact you. Crazy things happen every day, Cameron. Also, there's Elliott . . . he's only here for two more days, and I gotta be honest, I'm tired of being the head of the entertainment committee."

Groaning and rolling over, I give her a very muffled and defiant, "Fiiineee . . . give me an hour and tell him to get ready."

"Will do, princess," she says, slapping me on the backside and hopping off my bed.

Fucking fantastic! Now I have to pull it together, think of something fun to do, and probably get drunk. At least the last part sounds somewhat appealing.

—

"Okkaaay . . . just lemme get this straight. She told you she was going on a trip with a friend from college and instead actually went on a romantic getaway with another dude?" Lo recaps Elliott's miserable breakup loud enough for the entire bar to hear.

"Ugh, yes. Keep your voice down." Hanging his head in his hands, my brother confirms what we both already know to be true.

"What in the actual fuck is wrong with people?" Lo's face is full of disgust as she seeks out our waitress.

We decided to come to Castaway Bay because it felt timely with

Elliott and me so recently being "castaway." Pathetic we may be, but we're also taking this self-pity tour seriously, really leaning into the pain.

Stunned is not the right word for what I feel about all my brother has been through. He's a goddamn walking male model, with the kindest heart. How dare he get cheated on. It's unconscionable.

"Please, tell me what . . . her . . . excuse . . . was. I mean, other than being the biggest idiot on the planet," I chime in between big gulps of icy-cold draft beer. Not my usual go-to, but at this rate anything will do.

"You know, I didn't even give her a chance to give me one. I just told her to get her shit out and not to be at my place when I got home."

"Go you. I wish I coulda told Will to get his shit. Except we didn't even live together, so there was no shit to get," I say pitifully, laying my head down to feel the table's cool rough wood on my cheek. Tears roll silently down my face for what feels like the millionth time since we left the house. It's honestly a bit disturbing how much water I've lost from sheer crying at this point.

"Alright, nope." Lo slides her hand under my head, gently peeling me off the table. "I've seen and heard enough of this. Both of you, God, like two freaking peas in a pitiful pod. Can we get mad now? I'm ordering shots, and for each one we drink, we are going to toast something horrible and mean until you either feel better or get alcohol poisoning. Whichever comes first is fine by me."

Our waiter, Linda, the most adorable little thing, sashays her way to our table at Lo's summoning. "Can I get you anything else? My shift is almost up, so I can cash you out or transfer your ticket to the new girl coming on."

"You can transfer it, beautiful. This is for you." Elliott hands her a hundred-dollar bill and winks. Bleh! Heartbroken and yet still able to turn the waitress into a puddle of emotions with a generous tip and a wink. It's disgusting.

"Okay, Rico Suave, let's not spend all our money in one place," Lo chastises.

"What? You wanted me to feel better, didn't you?" he asks, acting innocent.

"Sure . . . but you're sleeping on the couch. I refuse to sip coffee with some rando in my living room. Keep it in your pants for a couple more days, please," she says with a mixture of stern mom face and pride.

We all bust into a fit of giggles. I'm talking the full belly laughs that hurt your stomach and make your cheeks feel like they are so strained they might pop right off. Excusing myself, I head to the bathroom to wipe my face, do my business, and mentally prepare my insult toasts.

It's actually a nice bathroom for such a small beach bar. I take a couple extra minutes in the stall to deep breathe, desperately attempting to pull myself together enough to be fun for a few more hours. Reaching for the latch, awareness settles in my stomach like a sinking ship. I'm not sure exactly how I know or what instinct is set in motion, but I can feel a confrontation brewing deep in my bones.

Another deep breath in through my nose and out through my mouth, then I pull the stall door open and—bam! Bri is standing at the sink, washing her hands. Shame lurches inside me, clawing at my throat. I've been purposely avoiding her, but there is only one exit and I know she sees me.

"Cam, oh my gosh. Thank God I ran into you." She quickly dries her hands before sweeping me into a hug. I can't stop the sob that bellows out of me or the tears that flow freely down my cheeks. It's official: If I don't die from alcohol poisoning, it'll be from dehydration.

"Oh honey, don't cry. I'm sure he's fine. Why haven't you been answering my calls?"

Does she not know? Wait, how could she know? I haven't answered her, and Lo doesn't have her number. She thinks I'm crying with worry or fear, not heartbreak.

"Uh, um, I'm not, he's not . . . I'm sure he's fine. Not that it's my place to know." I stutter out the response, not knowing what else to say.

Bri pulls back from our hug and grabs my face, placing both hands firmly on my cheeks. "Cam, Will loves you."

"Thanks, but no, he doesn't." I close my eyes and suck in air through my nose, willing my body to keep it together.

"Yes, he really, *really* does. I've been trying to contact you for days. Cam, he tried calling you. There was a whole mess when they left. Ruiz didn't answer the call, and Will had to find him. He ran out of time, but when I heard they were leaving, I went to the air strip to wish them well, for Thatch. Will used my phone because they put his phone in lockup, but you didn't answer. He made me promise to tell you that he loves you, that you are his life. I'm sorry I didn't tell you over text, it just felt like something that needed to be said in person."

All I can do is stare at her. This can't be happening. She is saying the words, but it's like they're bouncing around in my brain, making me more jumbled and confused.

The door bursts open and in rushes Lo, frantic. "Oh, thank fuck. I thought you died in here or ran out the back and ditched us," she belts out. "Wait . . . what . . . what's happening right now?" she asks, finally noticing Bri, who's still holding my face in her hands.

"I'm telling her that Will is in love with her."

"Ohhh so you don't know what he did then. Okay, umm, *sooo* . . ." Lo begins, stuttering out her words.

Bri releases her hand from my face and holds it up to stop Lo from talking.

"I know the real story. What happened and why he was so delayed in calling her." She proceeds to recant the whole ordeal to Lo, hitting me a second time with the details.

Numb, happy, worried, nauseous—all the feelings are coursing through my veins. Could what Bri's telling me be true? If I believe this, will it all come crashing down when Will comes home and tells me he didn't mean any of it?

"I told you something probably came up. I knew it in my bones that he didn't actually dump you." Lo smugly crosses her arms and juts out her hip.

"Yeah, okay, Miss I'm-Going-to-Be-First-in-Line-to-Kick-His-Ass," I say on an eye roll. "Bri, I appreciate you trying to cover for him, but I didn't have any missed calls from you the day he left. He never called, even if he told you he did," I explain. None of what she's saying makes sense.

I'm certain I didn't have any missed calls from her that day. I looked through my call log a dozen times, and there was only that one missed from a telemarketer.

"That can't be right, honey. I saw him call, he was frantic. Check your phone again." She's adamant about this, but it doesn't make any sense.

Yanking my phone out of my pocket, I open the call log and start scrolling through it just to appease her. In place of the telemarketing number is Bri's name. I gasp. *What the hell—ohhh.* I programmed her number later the next day after she texted begging me to call her back.

Can this really be happening? Did he actually call me and I missed it? Are we not broken up? Acid burns my throat. My stomach churns, turning me pale and clammy. Every ounce of my being is in love with this man. It hurts to breathe without him. Believing he dumped me was less painful than knowing he wanted to say goodbye and couldn't.

I feel cheated, robbed, like I worked hard and won the prize, but it was given to someone else on a technicality. How am I supposed to reconcile the fear and love—and my shame from so easily mistrusting him? How will he react when he finds out I didn't have faith in us when it really mattered?

Shaking me from my thoughts, Lo asks, "You ready to get back out there before Elliott falls in love with a server?"

"Yeah, yup . . . let's do it." I plaster on a fake smile trying to sound peppy but convincing no one that my world wasn't just rocked again for the second time in a matter of days.

Lo invites Bri to hang out with us, stating that maybe her beautiful face will cheer up Elliott and that this is the best night of her life since maybe we will get to have a besties double wedding after all. I remain confused and cautious. Aching for Will to love me and him actually doing it are two very different things. All the evidence is there, and I know now that Bri has been trying to contact me, so why do I feel like I'm waiting to wake up and find out it's all a dream? Is being in love really just being on edge forever with fear of what could go wrong?

THIRTY-FOUR

Will

"Thickfreakness" - The Black Keys

Sand, sand, and well . . . more sand. It covers the painstakingly barren land we're stationed on like finely ground flour. It coats everything, including my lungs; I can feel the muck of it in my eyes, up my nose, and in other equally undesirable places.

Aside from the heat and the danger, the sand is the worst part of this whole thing. It's not just a matter of comfort either, it's insidious, slowly working its way into your clothes, gear—hell, even into my brain. Not literally, but it's all I can think about when I'm not solely focused on staying alive.

I stare off into the distance and imagine shapes, people, places being erected from the vast nothingness. I imagine counting the sand and how representative it is of the millions of people populating the earth. Those people that I'm here to protect, to honor, the ones who've sacrificed. Then there's Cam—how did I get her, out of all the people,

when I'm not even deserving.

We've spent the last week in and out of towns, hiding in abandoned buildings demolished by war, and in plain sight while we travel. Our caravan consists of three Humvees, a supply truck, and a couple of MRAPs, which are essentially indestructible Humvees. We brought the essentials needed to set up a forward-operating base, and while one team has worked to fortify our location with makeshift sandbag walls and fencing, my team has established basic communications.

Progress has been steady and mostly in uninhabited places. Too uninhabited. It's eerily quiet, given that it's the local terrorist stronghold; it's not as if they don't know we're here. Their lack of engagement is unsettling at best, downright bone-chilling at worst.

I find myself wishing for some type of response, and yet I'm paralyzed by the thought of not making it home. I sense the same from the rest of the team. It's the old adage: sitting ducks. We are waiting on a team to arrive for the mission that we will accompany them on, just hoping we don't get attacked in the meantime.

Thatch should be here. He always made days like this go by a little bit quicker. He'd crack a joke or do something stupid that would cut the tension, bringing us back from the fear if only for a few minutes.

A thud from a foam ball hits my shoulder. I turn to face Ramos. "Shifts up, hit the hay, man," he says, solemnly.

"Thanks. Head on a swivel . . . it's too quiet. I don't like it." I gesture for him to keep his eyes peeled on the horizon, to watch for threats.

"Yeah." One word and a nod. He doesn't have to say anything else. He gets it.

Traipsing through the sand toward the bunk tent, my legs feel like they weigh a thousand pounds. Lying on my cot is worse than keeping watch. My head hits the bedroll and all thoughts immediately turn to Cam. I wonder if Bri talked to her, if she knows how I feel. Or does she think I just left? Is she moving on because I broke her once and for all?

Replaying that day we left, it's obvious there were so many times I could've called—should've called. There was time while I was driving, waiting on Ruiz, when we first got to the strip. Why did I think I didn't have time? What made me wait?

I didn't have doubts about her then, and I still don't have them now. Am I really that dense and in my own world that I let time go by, allowing her to possibly believe she wasn't important? Even if Bri talked to her, what happened has got to sound like the lamest excuse someone has ever given for leaving without saying a goodbye.

I've thought over every minute of our time together, from the instant I saw her at the country bar to leaving without a word, pondering all the things I should've done better. And yet, I'm unbelievably thankful for those days together. I've spent the last five years of my life operating like a machine. Always knowing what's expected of me and following through on every mission.

I can come up with only one excuse for not making a better effort, and it doesn't even begin to scratch the surface of being a good one: I was protecting myself. It sounds messed up. Telling her how I feel would seemingly have been better for my mental status going into this deployment, and yet the thought of hearing the pain in her voice when I told her I couldn't make it to hug her one last time . . . I guess I couldn't do it. Sure, not knowing where we stand is miserable, but at the time, wondering if this would be the thing to send her running . . . I chickened out.

Tossing and turning, I attempt to get comfortable in what is decidedly the hardest cot on the planet. My pillow is lumpy and filled with sand. My skin crawls with sweat, dirt, and a variety of bugs that somehow maneuver past the mosquito nets. A few guys are playing cards, cheering loudly just a few feet away from where I'm attempting uselessly to sleep. If you long to know what hell is like, come here.

Thankfully, one of the first skills you learn as a soldier is to fall asleep quickly and under any conditions. I feel the ache in my bones start to ease, and I sense that sleep is not far from me. Pulling my sleep sack up over my face to shut out any light, I begin to drift away when—bang! The sound of truck doors slamming and new voices approaching has me groaning to no one but myself. Dammit, they're here. Now the real work begins.

"Rise and shine, give God the glory, boys. We brief in ten. Get your gear and be ready to roll out!" Montgomery shouts to everyone and no one in particular.

Taking a few deep breaths to steady my nerves and revive myself from the sheer lack of sleep, I toss back the cover of my sleep sack and swing my legs over to the floor, forcing myself upright. Smith spots me from his cot a few down from mine, determination shines in his eyes. He is ready and tells me without a word to buck up, it's time to roll.

Grabbing my vest, helmet, and gear, I make my way with the rest of our team to the MWR tent. We usually use this space to blow off some steam, workout, or eat, but since space is limited it's now a makeshift briefing room. We stand silently, waiting to be addressed, when a beast of a man waltzes in and introduces himself as Chief. No one knows where he got the nickname, but based on the sheer size of him and the way he commands the room, it's fitting.

Chief explains the mission: We are going into the nearest town to break up a meeting of the local leaders and heads of a well-known terrorist cell. He tells Montgomery our primary job is to keep comms up in case shit goes sideways and to provide cover if necessary. His team will do the heavy lifting, going in hot under what's presumed to be a heavily guarded meeting.

The situation isn't really a new one, they always seem to be heavily guarded. However, it's tricky because local leaders are not to be harmed. In the hustle and chaos of everything, ensuring half the attendees' safety is not easily guaranteed, but harming them would all but secure their reliance on the terrorist group and instantaneously make us the "bad guys."

Pictures circulate around the room, clearly indicating who the primary targets are. Outside of these few, anyone else who engages first is fair game. I commit the images to memory and pass them along to Butler, standing beside me.

Grabbing my shoulder, Smith asks, "Ready to rock?"

"Ready as I'll ever be. You got everything you need?"

"Yep . . . let's load up and get this shit over with." He turns to move toward our vehicle.

We pile into the Humvee in silence, breathing through the fear and steeling ourselves for what's to come.

—

Driving into what appears to be an abandoned town tells me everything I need to know. This group has the locals living in fear, so much so that not a single person can be seen out on the street. They've taken to hiding in their homes, just hoping to survive.

We stop behind a tall concrete building that looks to have several apartments or homes in it. It's not where we are ultimately going, but it's a good place to hide the vehicles and we're still close enough if we need to make a break for it quickly. Sliding out, I check my vest, weapon, and helmet one more time. Smith is hauling the radio box that transmits our walkies, so our unit slides in around him to keep him secure.

Moving like this is something we've practiced more times than I can count. *We are a well-oiled machine, we've trained for this, we will survive.* At least that's what I continue to tell myself, over and over again, to ease the fear and give myself the ability to breathe rather than panic.

During missions like this, we operate using hand signals so we draw the least amount of attention. The silence is necessary yet deafening. The only sound is the faint shuffling of boots and my own heartbeat thumping rapidly.

Quickly approaching the abandoned building that is serving as the meeting location, we set up on the perimeter while the team in charge moves inside. I scan the space around us on repeat, looking for threats—really, anything out of place—while we wait.

Smith turns the receiver's volume on, setting it to low so we can hear the comms in our ear pieces but not loud enough for anyone else within close range to hear.

More silence mixed with faint sounds of boots inside the building thumping upstairs.

Out of nowhere, the sound of bullets clanking off metal echoes in my ears. Next, the crackle of Chief calling for a medic, shouting, "Man down!" and asking for back up. A quick signal from Montgomery pointing at Butler and me tells us to head into the unknown.

We move quickly, smashing our backs up against the wall and scanning each room we enter for threats. Finding the stairs, we head up. I'm facing forward, weapon raised, as Butler walks up backward to ensure we aren't being followed.

We take three flights at an expeditious pace, halting when we see the medic working on Ray. He motions for us to go forward and meet up with the rest of the team and that he's watching our backs. Side by side, Butler and I take the stairs two at a time. Adrenaline is pumping through my veins and gone is any fear that lingered before coming into the building.

We make eye contact with Chief, and he motions for us to begin clearing rooms. We are drawing blanks at every turn until the sound of gunfire once again rains down around us. Glancing at Butler, I see him nod, and we begin to make our way toward the sound and the remainder of the team we are backing up.

I go first, peering into the small room where all targets appear to be neutralized. I'm lowering my weapon, as Chief and his team have done, when a whirring sound buzzes from behind me, past my ear and toward Scout, one of Chief's men. Turning quickly, my weapon raised, I see Butler fire off a couple of rounds, neutralizing the target across the hall. But not before they get two shots off.

It's like slow motion. I can see the shots buzzing toward me, and yet there isn't enough time to move out of the way. The sound is what I notice first—my flesh being broken and penetrated—followed by the searing pain in my shoulder and left bicep. Stunned, I look at Butler and see his mouth moving, making the word *medic*, but I hear nothing.

My ears are ringing, my wounds are oozing, and the world is turning to shades of gray around me. Butler jams a rag up against my shoulder and arm, pressing with all his might, deepening the ache. My teeth start to chatter as I slowly slink down to the floor.

"Stay with me . . ." The words Butler is shouting at me are faint, but I can hear them. Thank God I can hear something. Helping me to my feet, the team surrounds me as we make our way down and out of the building. I don't know how, but I'm walking. I have to walk, to move, to get the hell out of here before the world fades to black.

Seeing it fading around me, in and out, I know the time is coming and it's close. The rag pressed on my wounds is soaked through, all the life I have is seeping out of me at a rapid clip. We clear the building and Smith is in my face. His words are like whispers as the light fades.

My knees buckle first, plunging me into the powdery dirt. My eyes close as my body is being rolled over, images of Cam flashing in my mind. Her smiling, laughing, the scent of her lingering in my nose. She's the best person I know, selfless and caring. She's the light in all the dark around me. All the things I wish I would have said bounce around in my mind like colorful ribbons dancing around a dark room. Then the world goes black.

THIRTY-FIVE

Cam

"Heartbroken" - Diplo & Jessie Murph

Wind whistles outside my window as rain pelts the side of our building. Tampa has bad storms from time to time, even wrestling with hurricanes occasionally, but this storm seems to be one of epic proportions. Lo barely avoided being blown off the road when she went to pick up pizza, and Elliott's flight was the last to leave prior to all planes being grounded.

I've always been a fan of a good storm. Maybe it's the country girl in me, knowing how great the rain is for the crops and soil quality, or maybe it's just the way a perfect rain can bring peace, lulling me to sleep. This storm feels different, though, almost foreboding of bad things to come. The lights have flickered on and off several times, prompting us to carefully place candles around the apartment, just in case.

I'm curled up in the coziest spot on the couch with a slice of pepperoni and onion, watching and debating with Lo about some "sister wives" on TV.

"I just don't get it . . . How are they okay sharing this dude? He isn't even that nice." Lo's talking around a mouthful of pizza.

"I think it's all about the independence they get and the extra help to raise the kids." I take a big gulp of wine. I can see how it would be nice to have someone to help with the school run, dinners, childcare. It's the sharing-a-man part that I could never do.

"So, you would do this? If Will wanted to marry two women, would you agree?" Lo pins me down with her stare. She knows that would be a hard pass for me.

"Hell, no. I am way too overbearing for that and I don't share well. I'm just saying, I think they do it for reasons outside of the man."

"I don't know. I think they are forced into it, like a cult or something." Lo is open-minded about a lot of things, but this clearly isn't one of them.

"I mean, we don't watch the show to agree with them. We watch it for the drama," I remind her, taking a sip of smooth red and carefully placing my glass back on the end table.

A bolt of lightning flashes across the sky, illuminating the living room and obliterating our power. I look at Lo, my eyes adjusting to the sudden darkness that has descended upon us, and I see that she is suddenly as creeped out as I am.

"Why am I scared of the dark all the sudden?" I ask her hesitantly.

"I don't know, but this is creepy. We need to light these candles. Come on, help me."

We both extricate ourselves from the couch and are moving toward the kitchen to grab lighters when there is a loud *thump, thump, thump* on the door. Glancing at Lo, I make my way to the peephole, hoping it's not an ax murderer waiting on the other side. Slowly looking through, standing tiptoe, I see it's Bri. What the hell is she doing here in this storm?

Quickly unclasping the locks and swinging the door open, I sweep a drenched Bri into the foyer, dripping water everywhere.

"Hey, are you okay? What's going on? Lo get some towels!" I rush out in a huff.

"Hi. Sorry to barge in, I need to talk to you." Misery is etched in her wrinkled brow.

"Okay . . . come in. Let's get you some dry clothes and then you can tell me whatever it is." I try to reassure her, but I can see this effort just deepens her worry.

Lo comes over holding some leggings, a hoodie, and a towel to sop up the water. Bri makes quick work of changing in the bathroom and then settles in next to me on the couch.

"Cam, I don't really know where to start. There's something I need to tell you," Bri chokes out the words as tears bubble at the corners of her eyes.

"You're scaring me, just spit it out," I snap at her. I don't intend to come across so crass, but she is making me nervous. Is she here to tell me she lied about the whole thing with Will? Did she just pretend to call me and say it was him? Are they secretly in love?

Oh God . . . did something happen to him? Is he dead? My mind is spiraling out of control.

"Listen . . . . I can tell by your expression that there are about a million thoughts racing through your head right now. First, let me say that I shouldn't even really know this but I have a friend who keeps me in the loop when the team deploys. Second, Will is alive." Her voice is shaky, like she's trying to be calm and confident but can't quite seem to get her body to fake it at this moment. "Will was injured, Cam. He was transferred to Germany for surgery and now is on his way to Andrews Air Force Base for more treatment. I do not know the extent of the injuries, only that it was bad enough to medevac him to Landstuhl."

I hear Lo berating Bri with questions about the rest of the team, but all I can do is sit in stunned silence. My heart is in my throat, my stomach is churning with pizza grease and worry, and my mind is wondering if he's going to be okay, what this means, and if I can see him. Taking a deep breath in, I close my eyes and say a prayer to all the powers that be.

"Lo, stop. Is he . . . is he going to be okay?" I mutter the words in a whisper.

"I don't know. I wish I could promise you he will be, but I can't. Since I'm not family, they won't give me any information. I know that there were other injuries, but none on their direct team. I know that Butler was the one to get to him first. We can go, Cam. I can get you on base and into the hospital to see him. I have a friend in DC who will escort us since neither of us has a working base ID," Bri explains.

"We can go, I can go." I turn the words over in my mind. I can be there with him, I can see him. "Yeah, okay . . . let's do that," I manage as I stand, turning in circles because I don't know where to start.

Bri gently squeezes my hand, tugging me back down to the couch, saying, "We can't leave until tomorrow. The flights are grounded until this storm passes. I booked three tickets on a flight leaving at eight in the morning. I have my stuff in the car, so I can just stay here tonight, if that's alright with you. We will swing by and get Amy at about six and head out."

"Ohhh, okay. Does Amy know? How much was the ticket? I need to call Daveed . . ." I ramble as the questions continue to breeze through my head, much like the wind blowing outside.

"Amy knows. they notified their mother, and she called me as soon as she heard to ask me to help her tell you. I was already on my way and told her not to rush over given the storm. Don't worry about the ticket right now, we can deal with that later. You should go call Daveed and start packing for at least three days." Her voice is calm and steady now that she's gotten the worst of the news out. She's confident and commanding in a way that I find oddly comforting in this moment.

I all but sprint into my room, stumbling into things along the way due to the lack of light. Instead of packing, though, all I can do is sit on my bed, head in my hands, and cry. Loud sobs slip out of me, despite my attempts to be quiet about it. I cannot lose him. I want to take every ounce of pain he is feeling upon myself, relieve him of the demons and scars he is inevitably going to carry.

Powerless is what I am, though. I can't fix this, can't wish it away no matter how hard I try. I have to face it head on. Will needs me to love him through this and all that comes with it. Determination settles into my bones like hot iron being poured into a mold. Nothing will stand in my way of seeing him, supporting him, or loving him from here to the end of all my days. Every worry I had about him leaving or being hurt again vanishes into thin air. Nothing else matters as long as I have a little more time.

—

Amy, Bri, and I wait patiently outside the airport in the arrivals pickup zone for her friend, Regina. Bri has briefed us on her friend, explaining that she is a nurse at the hospital on base, a spunky woman in her fifties who doesn't take shit from anyone but who also has seen the worst of the worst come through her doors, which fills her with a sense of unparalleled compassion.

A black SUV zooms around cars and comes hurtling up to the curb much faster than it should.

"Hey, ladies, hop in. We need to make tracks before the traffic settles in," Regina bellows.

Glancing at Amy, I shrug and we toss our bags into the open trunk. Bri slides into the passenger seat while Amy and I make our way into the back.

"Okay, girls, I'm going to give you some tough love. I see the looks on your faces and I get that you're worried, but it's all going to be fine. I checked on Will this morning and he is quite banged up. But you all need to fix those faces or I'm not bringing you to see him. Do you understand me?" she reprimands.

"Yes, ma'am. How is he?" I ask, tentatively.

"I've seen worse, sweetheart. At least those assholes didn't mess up that pretty face. Hot damn, I tell you, that man is a model."

We burst into a fit of giggles over her assessment of Will's face. He is adorably handsome, but something about this nurse calling him out about it heals a part of my soul. I shouldn't be laughing at a time like this, but it's cathartic—it feels good to feel something other than heartache.

"In all seriousness, though, you need to know that with a lot of these soldiers, their physical wounds are far less worrisome than their emotional ones." Regina glances at Bri and reaches for her hand to offer a gentle squeeze.

"We will support him no matter what, he just has to be okay," Amy says, still stifling a laugh.

"That's the first I have heard either of them laugh in well over a day, thank you." Bri winks at her and smiles. How is she okay, how is she not breaking down with all she's been through, I wonder.

We ride the rest of the way in silence, listening to the thrumming of the music mixed with the sounds of traffic surrounding us.

Pulling up to the base's gate, we all show our driver's licenses and

Regina signs us in for visitors' badges. The guards are stoic but polite as we pass through. I'm sure they see grieving and worried families on a daily basis, a few young women shifting between laughing and crying are par for the course.

Stopping before we enter the corridor that Will's room is off of, Regina puts her hand up and spins to face us one last time. "Remember, he could look much worse. He is probably asleep from all the sedation they gave him. Talk to him, hold his hand, but be gentle and positive. No boo-hooing in that room or I will personally kick you out. My shift is about to start, so you will be stuck here for the next twelve hours unless you want to walk to the gate and get an Uber. You girls will be just fine, lean on each other to get him through this." She presses a kiss to each of our cheeks and then swipes her badge to open the doors.

Hospitals are all the same. They smell distinctly like bodily fluids mixed with bleach, the beeping from machines creates a cacophony of sounds, and employees race around from room to room, speaking in what I like to call "doctor speech," which makes absolutely zero sense to a normal person.

We walk to Will's room, number 362, and enter slowly. He's lying on the bed, hooked up to machines. There are leads on his chest monitoring his breathing and heart rate, multiple IVs, and his arm is bandaged from his shoulder to his fingertips. He looks peaceful, like he's sleeping and not at all in pain.

Regina wasn't lying about his face. That chiseled jawline, perfectly straight nose, and curly hair flopped over his forehead in the front. Those ridiculously long eyelashes. He is breathtakingly beautiful. I want to lean in and kiss him, but we still haven't talked about everything that happened.

Bri has reassured me close to a thousand times that Will loves me, but I can't help thinking or feeling like there is more to the story of why he didn't call sooner. He had to have had time in between getting the call and chasing down Ruiz. My insecurities prevent me from planting one on him. We need to talk first. I would hate to do something he doesn't want while he's out of it.

I sit in the chair closest to his noninjured arm, grasping for his hand to give it a squeeze. Bri and Amy sit in the chairs opposite me, and we all just stare at him in silence. What are we supposed to do or say? Should we let him sleep, or should we try to talk to him? Bri stands up, moving closer to the edge of the bed. She gently strokes a hand down the side of his face with tears in her eyes and says, "Will . . . I brought Cam and Amy to see you. We're glad you're going to be okay." She cares for him, it's so clear how much he means to her, how much we all mean to her. Guilt eats at my stomach. She shouldn't have to live through this, not after all she's endured.

His eyelids flutter but he doesn't wake up, doesn't say a word. Amy stands and gently runs her hand over his curly hair saying, "Will, it's Aims. You look like shit, big bro, but I'm happy to see you." I swear he smirks, but again, he doesn't wake up.

I should say something, but I don't know what to say, and I don't want to talk to him in front of Bri and Amy. I know it sounds petty, but this thing we have is between us. Glancing at them both, they look at me with sympathy written on their faces.

A doctor comes in, followed by a couple of residents.

"My name is Captain Boswell and this is Jenkins, Reed, and Walters." He points to each resident so we know who is who. "Staff Sergeant Davenport was wounded in two places. He took a shot to the shoulder and one in his bicep. His shoulder was the worst off. We repaired what we could with surgery, but he is going to need a lot of physical therapy to get back on duty." Captain Boswell looks at us to make sure we are following. Amy has pulled out a notepad and is beginning to write things down. "He's on a heavy dose of antibiotics, and we are keeping him comfortable with pain medication. I will need to monitor him for a few more days at a minimum before he can fly home. Once he's home, he will need to be debriefed about what happened and begin therapy right away so his shoulder joint doesn't seize up. Now, which one of you is Cameron?"

"That's me." I raise my hand, standing from my chair.

"Can I speak with you for a moment in the hall?" The residents file out of the room with the captain following behind. He turns briefly to make sure I am, in fact, coming with him. I step into the empty hallway, trailing him as he continues over to the main nurses' station.

"Ma'am, I have some paperwork that I need you to sign." He lays out a couple of papers on the desk and places a pen on top.

"Papers? For what?"

"It seems that while you aren't family or his spouse, Davenport listed you as his medical proxy. I need you to sign consent forms for the continuing treatment."

"Th-that can't be right. When, how . . ." I'm at a loss for words. When did he list me as his proxy? How did he know I would come?

"Listen, I don't have time to explain it all, but he put you down for a reason. Whatever's between you two is your deal. I just need you to sign." The captain points at the papers, indicating where I should put my name down, and I grab the pen, marking everything up even though I'm not sure this is my role to play.

"All set, thank you, ma'am. Oh, one more thing. Based on how scared you look, I can tell this is your first time, so I'm going to give you some advice. Get him in therapy right away, not just for the shoulder but for his mind too." I nod at the captain; doing that was already on my list. I plan to make Will call Tina immediately. "And go see someone yourself. He is going to get better, and he is going to deploy again. I've seen too many people like yourself think they are okay until their loved one leaves again and the fear becomes too much to handle. If you love him, make sure you are okay with what he is going to have to do time and time again." With that, the captain collects his papers and walks away, leaving me standing in the hallway alone with my thoughts.

I don't want Will to do this. I don't want to go through this again. But I will, I know it in the depths of my soul. I will never leave his side, and I will support him no matter what. Even if it breaks my heart each time he leaves.

I walk back into Will's room, taking my seat and grabbing his hand once more. Bri stands abruptly and asks Amy to join her in trying to find the cafeteria for some coffee. Bri must sense that I'm not ready to have this conversation with other people present, even if Will is conked out. They offer to bring me back something and then scurry out of the room.

Sighing, I give Will's hand another squeeze and say, "Hey, you. I don't know if you can hear me or if you're off in la-la land, but I'm glad you're okay." The words drip out of me slowly as I fight back tears. I close my eyes tightly and lay my head down on his hand, needing to feel him here with me.

"I don't know what I would do without you. Even all the years we were apart, I still never really felt like you left. You've always had a piece of my heart—I'm not sure I'm ever getting it back." The tears flow freely down my face now, and a permanent lump in my throat forms.

"No, you aren't, Wright," Will responds with a raspy voice.

Lifting my head to look at him, his bright blue eyes pierce through my soul. He is staring at me so clearly, and yet he looks shocked to see me here.

"Will, thank God. Oh my gosh. Wait, what am I not?" I stutter out, surprised that he's actually awake and here talking to me.

Clearing his throat, Will smirks and says, "Getting that piece of your heart back."

"Ohhh, I, umm . . . yeah, I don't want it back." All I can do is look at him, silent tears streaking down my face.

"Cameron. I'm sorry. I tried to call you, but I should've tried harder. I was caught up in the chaos of leaving and finding Ruiz, but more than that, I was scared if I heard your voice that I would either not leave or you would run. I don't think you know, or even really see, just how special you are to people, to me. I didn't want to leave without saying a proper goodbye. The goodbye you deserved. And I know it sounds lame, but I don't know—my sense of duty won out when faced with risking my heart. You deserve the world, and here I am begging you to let me try again, knowing I don't deserve it." He hangs his head in shame, the hurt inside him evident.

"Stop it right now, Rambo. You deserve all the love in the world. You are my best friend, the one who makes me better. Can you be a big dummy sometimes? Absolutely, no doubt. But you are mine. I love that you are so loyal to your team, but you need to know that I can't breathe without you. I love you." In my heart, I know there are some questions I should ask, but the moment he opened his mouth and looked at me, all my fears melted away. This won't be perfect and it won't be easy, but the fact is, I love him. Whether it's smart to or not.

"I love you too. More than you will ever know or understand. Our hearts were stitched together a long time ago, and even though we have stretched the strength of that bond beyond reason, it never broke. But more than that, I see you, Cameron. You spend all this time worrying about what others think of you, but I've noticed how you're the first to check on your friends, you go out of your way to make others feel comfortable, and you work harder than anyone I know. You don't shy away from things that scare you and you take huge risks. You are my life, and if you take this risk with me, I'm going to spend every day proving that I'm worthy of you."

Tears stream freely down both our faces, and Will tugs my hand, pulling me up out of the chair and closer to him. I gently rub my hand down his cheek and steal a couple sweet but chaste kisses.

We have a long road ahead of us, not just with the physical rehabilitation that needs to happen, but also with the emotional. I believe he wanted to give me a proper goodbye and couldn't. That's a fear we have to deal with. I also know that what happened over there has a story to accompany it. One that he may or may not ever want to share. Either way, I will fight for him, support him, and love him no matter how bumpy the journey may become. As he said, we've been stitched together for years, soul to soul, in an unbreakable bond. His wounds are my wounds, his heart is my heart, his battles are my battles, and his love is my love.

"Hey, Wright. I need to ask you something." He smiles at me, looking deep into my eyes.

"What is it?"

"Still think it wasn't fate?" His eyebrow raises and he shifts a bit to turn toward me, wincing in pain.

"I-I don't know . . . Maybe it was coincidental, I'm definitely here for some reason, I'll give you that, Rambo." I smooth my hands over his cheeks, pressing another kiss to his lips.

"Let's call it coincidentally kismet then." All those weeks ago, he said that it was fate that brought us back together while I argued it was nothing more than a coincidence, and I still do. But I know now that what happened with Will and me was a mixture of both.

"Okay, Rambo. You and me . . . we are coincidentally kismet."

Acknowledgements

What a journey it has been! When I started writing this book in 2023, I never in my wildest dreams thought I would be holding a printed copy in my hand. I wouldn't have made it to this day without the support of so many people I hold near and dear to my heart. I will do my absolute best to thank each and every one of you but please know if you are not on this particular list, you still have my gratitude and my heart.

Cory— thank you for not laughing at me hysterically the first time I mentioned this hair brained idea to you. I know you thought it was a whim or another random hobby that I would probably stop a few months in, but per usual you supported me anyway. There isn't a single other person in this world that I could imagine doing life with. You push me to be better in all the ways that count and I love you more than words could ever explain.

L & G—my sweet boys, I got lucky with you two. I hope in pursuing this dream, I've shown you that the world is your oyster. It's never too late to do something wild, as long as it makes you happy.

Annie (Spare Words Novel Editing)— I was lost in the overwhelming world of publishing before I met you. From being so nervous to submit my writing sample to voice texting you all my random thoughts and dreams; your insight into this story has been the guiding light I needed. Thank you for sprinkling your magic all over this book and truly leading me down the path to creating something beautiful. I'm so excited to continue our journey together (I'm feeling witchy!).

Briana (Ozor Edits)—you have become a forever friend through this process. From fixing all the grammar and teaching me that every sentence does not in fact need an ellipsis, to dealing with deadline extensions and all my menty B's. I am so grateful for your efforts in making this the best book it could be.

Kels and Ada (Be the Archetype), Mary and Julie (Books & Moods), and Ellie (Love Notes PR)—this book would never be what it is today without your expertise. From creating beautiful art work and marketing Kels, Ada, and Mary, to getting this in the hands of so many readers Ellie; I am forever grateful and indebted to you. More than your work though, I am thrilled to call you each my friend.

To the early readers that stuck through terrible first drafts and too many revisions to count; thanks for staying with me. Michelle—your guidance into this entire process has been remarkable. I could not have written this book without you. Kenzie—thank you for making me giggle with your enthusiastic comments. Whit—you're my first fan and greatest confidence booster. Ang—thank you for sharing my love of all things swoony romance. I was afraid you would think I'd lost my mind but you never did. Mom—thanks for crying real tears over this work and always supporting me no matter what. I am brave because of YOU. Dad—thanks for reading this whole book, even if the spicy scenes made it awkward for you. Steve (aka the best bonus dad)—thanks for being my cheerleader and always imparting your wisdom when I need it. Many of the most profound thoughts in this book have come from things you've taught me. My siblings—in many ways Elliott & Cam's relationship is a love letter to you. You might all think I'm completely crazy but you love me anyway and I'll never forget it.

To the beautiful and talented Indies that have lifted me up along the way—I see you, I support you, I love you. I'm looking at you; Kate, Ray, Margaret, Michelle, Mal & Lindsey.

To my best friends—A & M. I know you never expected any of this from me but you also have never left my side. We may be far in distance but never in heart. I wouldn't have the courage to do big things if it wasn't for the safety net you provide.

Finally, to YOU, the readers—thank you for taking a chance on a sorta nutty project manager who decided to write a book with absolutely zero experience. I fell in love with writing while I went through this process and you were cheering me along the whole way on socials. The fact that you would spend your hard-earned dollars to support me is beyond anything I could ever fathom. Your support keeps me going and keeps me sane.

Love Always—KC

About The Author

Corporate Girl turned Author, Kelli Cooke, writes vibrant, funny, and authentic love stories. As a hopeless romantic, Kelli strives to bring a creative twist on what love looks like in real life infused with the kind of comedy that will keep you laughing long after finishing her books. While comedy is the star she also focuses on threading in raw emotion and hopes to impact hearts for years to come.

When she's not writing, she can be found chasing around her two kids or binge watching a show with her husband. Kelli never expected to become an author but has embraced harnessing her creative ability and adores sharing her vibrant tales with her readers.

www.ingramcontent.com/pod-product-compliance
Lightning Source LLC
Chambersburg PA
CBHW011847300726

48970CB00009B/2683